I0744604

HALF MOON WHIM

HALF MOON

Whim

HALF MOON WHIM

Half Moon Bay
Book 5

ERIN BROCKUS

GREEN SAGE
PRESS

Copyright © 2022 Erin Brockus

This is a work of fiction. Names, characters, businesses, places, events, locales, and incidents are either the products of the author's imagination or used in a fictitious manner. Any resemblance to actual persons, living or dead, or actual events is purely coincidental.

All rights reserved. No part of this book may be reproduced or used in any manner without the prior written permission of the copyright owner, except for the use of brief quotations in a book review.

Cover design by GetCovers

Edited by A. Waugh

Ebook ISBN: 978-1-957003-09-2

Paperback ISBN: 978-1-957003-10-8

Hardcover ISBN: 978-1-957003-11-5

Chapter One

OCTOBER...

THE WARM CARIBBEAN SEA washed over Sara Collins's feet as she walked barefoot down the beach, carrying her flip-flops in one hand. Shading her eyes from the late-morning St. Croix sunshine, she squinted at her destination. A white, cottage-style house with a lovely, full-length covered porch faced the ocean a fair distance away from the bungalow where she had spent the previous several nights. Half Moon Bay Resort had been closed for the previous several days, only this morning returning to normal. Since guests would begin arriving in a few hours, she was leaving so her former bungalow could be prepared for them.

As she approached, her sister Hope's house looked the same—everything around her did—but the world was fundamentally different now. A massive shift had occurred, and a new era had started. Sara lifted the skirt of her breezy yellow sundress and climbed the short flight of stairs onto the porch. A quiet *woof* greeted her as a short-coated yellow dog sat up on his padded bed, watching her closely.

"Hello there, Cruz. I'm going to crash here until my flight. You're not going to get all protective and bite me, are you?" Sara used a soft, friendly voice and Cruz responded with a thumping tail, approaching so she could pat his head.

With a relieved sigh, she scratched behind his ears. He'd been mistreated by his former owner, who was euphemistically known as Creepy Guy, and he was wary of people unless he knew them well. Though Sara had never met the man, the aftermath he'd left on Cruz was evident. Apparently, she had been around enough the past few days to pass muster, which made her smile. "Thank you for not running away or attacking me. Creepy Guy sure did a number on you, didn't he? Poor baby." She glanced around, locating her packed suitcase near the sliding glass door. *Well, I won't be needing that for the next few hours. It can just stay there.*

Sara slid open the unlocked door, and Cruz shimmied through the narrow opening as soon as he could, eager for the cool interior. She entered more hesitantly. Shutting the slider behind her, her gaze took in an expansive great room with a kitchen at the far end. The house was silent, and despite the cozy, welcoming decorative touches, Sara was uncomfortable. This wasn't just her big sister's house anymore.

This was Hope and Alex Monroe's house.

Hope had owned Half Moon Bay for a year and a half, and Alex had been the dive operations manager and head guide for over six. But the resort wasn't Hope's anymore—it was officially *theirs*. Their wedding had taken place two evenings ago, an intimate sunset ceremony on the resort beach.

The bride and groom had retired to a guest bungalow and hadn't made another appearance until the previous afternoon, when they had joined the rest of the small wedding party at the infinity pool. Hope and Alex radiated happiness as they embraced their family and close friends. Now Sara was the last of the wedding party to leave. Best man Mike Baker and his wife Emma had left the previous evening, and Alex's sister Kate Fletcher and her family departed earlier that morning.

Still standing near the slider, Sara took in a deep lungful of the cool air, trying to convince herself she wasn't an outsider. Her musings were interrupted by a loud thump from the kitchen corner. Cruz stared at Sara, his water bowl tipping back and forth on the floor before finally settling.

She grinned, glad to have something productive to do. "Thirsty, huh? I can take care of that. It's just you and me for a while yet, Cruz. You're probably glad to have things back to normal around here." She padded over and filled his bowl with water, trying to avoid his wagging tail as she set it down. "Hope and Alex are both working. She's getting the resort ready to accept guests, and Alex is taking out a group of divers staying in a condo. He wanted to give Tommy and Robert some time off, so he's driving." She scowled. "Apparently, that asshole divemaster Jack is working too."

Cruz ignored her, not as interested in Hope and Alex's whereabouts as quenching his thirst. And even less interested in the work schedules of Captain Tommy Williams and Divemaster Robert Davis. And as far as she was concerned, Jack Powell wasn't even worth thinking about.

Sara straightened and caught sight of Hope's bridal bouquet, sitting in a vase on the kitchen table. She shook her head, still not able to fully process the image of the two of them exchanging vows. Or, more specifically, her own reaction to it. As maid of honor, she'd had a full view of Alex during the ceremony.

Sara had never been traditional or domestic, so it was all the more surprising that seeing Alex stare at Hope like she was the only thing in the universe had induced such longing in her. Wanting a man to look at *her* like that. Hope was fond of saying she never thought marriage was in the cards for her. Until she fell in love with Alex.

Sara breathed a deep sigh, then shook herself. *Stop being a sap.*

Cruz finished drinking and curled up in his bed in the corner, closing his eyes with a happy sigh. "Well, I'm not going to get any stimulating conversation from you. Maybe I'll head down to the pier and see if Selena is back at work yet." He cracked an eye open, then closed it again and she smirked. "The only thing worse than talking to the dog is talking to yourself. Get a move on, girl."

Soon Sara was climbing onto the pier, the wooden slats creaking pleasantly under her feet. Though Half Moon Bay was primarily a scuba diving resort, Hope had opened a spa recently. She'd spoken with the new massage therapist, Selena Allen, several times prior to the wedding, and immediately bonded with her enthusiastic personality, especially since the spa was Sara's kind of place.

Halfway down the pier, she passed through a tunnel of buildings and made her way past the dive shop to a long stair-case at the north end. A covered deck with an incredible ocean view dominated the area at the top of the stairs and served as the outdoor massage area. Next to the glass entrance door, a wooden wall formed a privacy screen, and a second, more nondescript door led to a restroom. Sara entered the clean, brightly lit spa, where Selena stood behind the glass check-in counter, refilling a small bottle with massage oil. The warm scent of sandalwood filled the air.

The massage therapist glanced up at the door's opening, her dark face bursting into a wide smile at Sara's entry. She was a trim, small woman in her mid-twenties, wearing a light-blue staff polo shirt. *What I wouldn't give to have her small, petite frame... Lucky girl.*

Sara made an effort to dress well and appear professionally styled and made-up, partly to compensate for her voluptuous and curvy figure. No manner of diet or exercise had ever changed that and now, at age thirty-three, she was resigned to her fate. But that didn't mean she wasn't self-conscious about it

"Sara! You stayin' a few more days?"

"No, I'm flying out this evening. Hope's working, so I thought I'd come up here." Her gaze took in the mani-pedi station along one wall, with a full stylist area in the corner. Like a magnet, she was drawn toward the hair salon. Several windows let in plenty of light. "You have a massage scheduled?"

Selena finished filling the bottle, shaking her head. "Not till tomorrow. I'm just gettin' ready."

Sara ran a hand over the back of the stylist chair where she had cut Hope's hair and given her a deep-conditioning treatment the day prior to the wedding. They had chatted throughout, almost like old times. Immediately afterward, they had met the rest of the wedding party on the resort dive boat, *Surface Interval.*

Heat crept up Sara's neck as she tried to push away the memory of what had happened next. The resort's newest employee, the divemaster Jack, had tripped and dumped an enormous bucket of water over her head, drenching her from head to foot. In front of everyone. She'd been mortified and embarrassed but determined not to show it.

As Sara passed by a window next to the stylist station, movement at the end of the pier caught her eye. A gleaming white boat was tied up and the group of divers was already headed away. "There's good sound insulation in here. I didn't even hear the boat come in."

"They did a great job on the construction. It always stays nice and cool in here, too."

Sara turned toward the front door. "I'd better get going.

Hope said she'd be finished about lunch time." The two women said their goodbyes, then Sara opened the door, turning left to descend the stairs.

And collided right into a warm body, smashing her nose into a shoulder. "Oof!" Wincing, she rubbed it as she staggered back. She was preparing to apologize as she looked up into a pair of huge, gorgeous brown eyes that widened in recognition.

Unfortunately, the eyes belonged to Jack. The horrible divemaster.

Her chagrin instantly erupted into fury, and she dropped her hand from her face. "Goddammit, watch where you're going. Pouring water over me wasn't enough? You have to break my nose too?"

Jack's face flushed crimson as he took a big step back, holding up both hands. "I'm sorry! I need to use the restroom and wasn't watching where I was going."

He was of average height, but at five feet three, she still had to look up at him. He spoke with a very slight twang. Texas? "Yeah. No kidding. You really need to stay the hell away from me, understand?"

His obvious embarrassment was replaced by a flash of anger that he quickly covered, raking a hand through his short, dark-brown hair. He had a strong jaw and sharp cheekbones, and really was rather good looking.

Too bad it's all wasted on him.

"Look, I'm not doing it on purpose. Lighten up, princess."

Clenching her jaw tightly, Sara drew herself as tall as she could. "No. I won't. But fortunately for both of us, I'm leaving later today." She breezed around him toward the staircase. "Have a nice life, Jack."

———

Sara stomped up the pier, but by the time she turned to walk north along the beach, her irritation had dissipated. It was quickly replaced by tranquil peace as a soft breeze blew through her long brown hair, and the line of palm trees waved gently back and forth. They stretched along the back of the long crescent of white sand that gave the bay its name. Half Moon Bay sat on the western side of the island, but she'd be gone before the sun descended to the ocean.

Sara had intended to head toward the lobby office, but changed her mind, strolling north along the beach instead. *Enjoy it while it lasts. I'll be sleeping in Charleston tonight.* She kicked off her flip-flops and let the waves wash over her feet, a small smile on her face as she soaked in the peaceful setting.

"Hey! Wait for me. Where are you going?" Hope called out behind her, and Sara stopped as her big sister hurried toward her, dressed in a dive-themed Half Moon Bay T-shirt and long black shorts. Her hair was much lighter than Sara's, especially since moving to St. Croix. She had it loosely wound in a clip and wore no make-up, yet she was still gorgeous. Totally not fair.

"I thought you'd be waiting in the cool house," Hope said.

"Are you kidding? These are my last few hours in paradise. No way am I wasting them." Sara turned and they continued north. "I've never walked to this end of the beach, and thought I'd check it out. So, how's married life?"

Sara rolled her eyes as Hope broke into a face-cracking grin. "Incredible! We've been living together for over a year, so it shouldn't really make a difference. But it does."

"Who would have thought you'd become the face of wedded bliss?"

Hope arched a brow at her. "Careful. That sounds suspiciously close to sour grapes."

Sara had to laugh. "I'm very happy for you. Both of you."

They were nearing the north end of the beach. The sand competed with iron-shore rocky ground as the crescent swept out to their left. As it narrowed to a point, the rocky ground won. Sara put her flip-flops back on and the two women picked their way carefully onto the thin spit of land.

Sara shaded her eyes with one hand as she took in the expansive view. "This is beautiful. Nothing but ocean ahead and the resort behind us." In the other direction was nothing but wild jungle. She itched to paint it. *Oh, these colors!*

To their left, a large expanse of dark coral reef descended from the rocky edge and disappeared into the depths in a stunning variety of blue shades. Hope pointed at it. "That's the house reef. We're lucky to have it so close. Most resorts don't have something this nice. It gives the guests something to dive or snorkel, even if it's too rough for the boat to go out."

Her sister had gotten off to a rocky start at the resort, but she had turned it into a resounding success—with Alex's help, who was a great deal more than dive manager and instructor. The women picked their way back to the soft sand and continued toward the resort. "No plans to develop this end?" Sara asked.

Hope laughed. "Actually, Alex and I don't own this end." Sara caught her unconscious *Alex and I,* but remained silent. Hope pointed to an orange wooden stake pounded into the edge of the sand just south of the spit. "That's the property marker there. I met the owner once, who comes out here occasionally. As politely as possible, I asked for right of first refusal if he ever wants to sell it. He wasn't interested in selling, but at least he likes it undeveloped. It would be terrible if he built a big restaurant or something here."   –

Sara laughed. "Big sister. Resort mogul."

They continued past four northern bungalows and a central complex of buildings. As they passed by the pier on their right, Alex was strolling toward them, and they paused to wait. He was tall and gorgeous, with bright blue eyes and short, light hair —he and her sister were a stunning couple. Alex broke eye contact with Hope long enough to say hello to Sara before sweeping up to his wife and enveloping her in a long kiss.

Sara propped her hand on her hip. "Hey! I'm standing right here, you know. Don't you two have any decency?"

They both ignored her, but finally pried themselves apart. "Good trip?" Hope asked, a dizzy smile on her face.

He nodded, stroking a finger across her chin. "Perfect day for me to drive the boat and very experienced divers. It was a walk in the park for Jack."

At the divemaster's name, Sara scowled and resumed the trek toward their house. The couple fell in beside her. They entered the house, and Cruz was much happier to see them than he had Sara. After a quick shower, Alex joined them in the kitchen as Hope prepared lunch.

"So Kate and her family got away this morning?" Sara asked, standing behind one of the kitchen chairs.

Hope stopped stirring the salad and a long look passed between her and Alex. Sara could practically see information being passed between them. *Jeez, they've only been married two days and they're doing that already?*

Alex turned to her. "Yeah. They didn't have any problems. Katie and Dave were sad to go, but we talked to them about something that cheered them up a bit."

Hope wrapped one arm around Alex's waist as she gestured at the chair Sara was standing behind. "Please sit down. We have something to share with you."

Chapter Two

THIRTY MINUTES LATER, Sara sat numb in her chair and tried to pick her jaw up off the floor. Hope and Alex sat across the table from her, both wearing identical smiles. She alternated her gaze between them. "Are you serious? You found a *treasure*? As in pirate booty?"

"Well, I wouldn't necessarily classify Barnaby as a pirate," Alex said. "He was more of an opportunist." Hope rose and removed a bottle of red wine from the cooler, placing it on the table before heading toward her office at the front of the house.

"Getting it out of the cave was a bitch, but Hope and I got it done," Alex continued. "Now we have the whole area fenced off and the tunnels are covered with steel gates, above and below water. The whole thing is top secret. Hardly anyone knows about it."

Hope returned and set two golden chalices on the table, placing one in front of Sara. "Go on. Take a look."

Sara gaped at the work of art before her. The goblet was around eight inches tall and inlaid with emeralds and diamonds around the broad cup. It tapered to a long stem with four columns of diamonds running vertically to the flaring base. Sara tentatively stroked a finger down the golden surface, hardly daring to touch it. "Is this real?"

"Pick it up," Hope said. "That will answer your question."

Sara slid her hand to the base of the cup and lifted. She barely got the chalice an inch off the table before the weight nearly made her drop it. With her heart hammering out of her chest, she used both hands to lift the goblet close to her face, slowly spinning it to inspect every angle. Then she deliberately set it back down and clasped her shaking hands together on the table. "Wow."

"Yeah, that was our reaction," Alex said with a small smile as Hope uncorked the wine and poured some into each chalice.

She lifted hers, also using both hands, and held it toward Sara. "How about a toast to interesting possibilities?"

With a laugh that came out only slightly unhinged, Sara touched her goblet to Hope's. The two cups made a solid clunking noise, then Sara raised hers to her mouth, still in shock as she rolled the decadent, dark wine around in her mouth. "And there's more like this?"

"A lot more," Hope said. "We've got it divided into two safe deposit boxes at different banks. Earlier this month we auctioned off a portion of it." Hope passed her goblet to Alex, who took a long sip, his muscular bicep flexing as he lifted it. "That's why we wanted to tell you about it. We came away with a lot of money, Sara. We'd like to share $100,000 with you."

Sara's jaw dropped again. "Huh?"

"Katie and Dave are getting the same amount," Alex said, leaning forward. "It's very important to us to spread some of this around. Please say you'll accept."

Sara turned her gaze back to Hope as goosebumps rippled down her arms. "$100,000? Hope, that's a ridiculous amount of money. I can't accept that much."

"I promise, you can. Sara, we grossed close to four million

dollars. Even after the auction house took their percentage and our CPA took out the portion for taxes, we've still got a *lot* left."

Sara just sat there, staring at the chalice. The diamonds glittered in the light.

"We're leaving it in the bank for now," Alex said. "We still haven't decided what improvements we want to make to the resort. But sharing some with you and Katie is our highest priority." He glanced at his wife. "And I think Hope has something else to discuss too."

I'm not sure I can handle anything more.

Hope glanced at the clock. "We need to head to the airport soon, but I really miss you. Once I installed the hair station in the spa, I could only picture *you* working there. I need someone to do manicures and pedicures too, which is right up your alley. But what I really need is someone to manage the spa. Someone experienced, and you're the perfect fit. The spa isn't very busy yet, but that will change with you in charge. You've always wanted to run a salon, and you mentioned you're not happy anymore where you are. This is a pretty nice setting, isn't it?"

Sara firmly pushed her goblet away. The last thing she needed was her head spinning even more. "I don't know, Hope. Of course it sounds amazing. All of it. But I refuse to be a charity case. I'm not going to just let you pay my way. I have absolutely no idea what I'd do with $100,000, but I'd need to earn enough to support myself."

"We wouldn't expect anything less," Alex said. "No one wants to feel like they aren't pulling their weight." Then a grin split his face. "Besides, I can't see you as the begging type."

"That's for damn sure," she said, some of her usual fire coming back now. "Hope, my head is about to explode. I need to think about this. I can't give you an answer right now."

"No, of course not. We have your money set aside in a separate bank account. We can leave it there, or wire it to your account, whichever you prefer."

"Leave it there for now. Please." Sara picked at her fingernails for a long moment before raising her gaze to look them each in the eye. "Thanks. Both of you. I'm pretty speechless, which doesn't happen very often. Just the fact that you want me to move down here means a lot to me." Then she smirked at Alex. "Well, that Hope wants me to move."

With a laugh, Alex leaned back in his chair and raised both hands. "This was a joint decision, Sara."

Sara's smirk relaxed. "I know. I can't resist elbowing you a little."

"There's always a place for you here." A glint entered Alex's eyes. "Though I'm not sure St. Croix is ready for both Collins sisters."

AN HOUR LATER, Sara was buckled into the passenger seat as Hope drove her to the airport in her Jeep. Sara watched the passing scenery with new attention. *Could I really live here?* The vegetation thinned out, revealing the sparkling Caribbean Sea, with its impossible shades of blue. *There are worse places...*

Between the resort and Frederiksted, the closest town, they passed a new, modern complex of buildings on the ocean side. A stretch of white sand peeked behind them. Hope pointed toward it. "That's a new apartment complex that opened recently. Isn't it gorgeous? That would be a great place for you to live. That way you could have your own home, but still be close to both town and the resort."

Sara turned sharply to her. "You've got this all figured out, don't you? Do you have my Mr. Perfect picked out too?"

"Oh, calm down. I have no intention of playing matchmaker. And how could I not think about you when I saw those apartments? You want to go talk to the manager real quick?"

Sara slumped in her seat. "No, keep going. I'm sure they're gorgeous." She took a deep breath and blew it out. "I'm sorry. I don't mean to sound defensive. I'm still in shock."

"I know. Just think about our offer—that's all I ask."

Before she knew it, Sara had wound her way through the check-in line at the airport, Hope staying with her as she checked her luggage. The sisters ambled over to the security line, and the moment Sara had been dreading appeared at last. Hope's eyes were misty, making her tear up too.

"Thank you for all you did. My wedding was a dream come true, and a lot of it was because of you."

Sara tried to brush off her surging emotion. "I think the groom might have had a little to do with it too." They embraced, holding each other tight. "I'm so happy for you. If anyone deserves a happy-ever-after, it's you."

SARA TRIED to watch a movie on the flight, but thoughts of warm breezes, turquoise water, and a chance to finally make her dream a reality kept distracting her. Once in the Charleston airport parking lot, she threw her luggage into the trunk of her elderly Honda Civic and performed her customary crossing of the fingers before turning the key in the ignition. The car wheezed and coughed a few times, but started eventually, and Sara heaved a relieved sigh as she pulled out.

It was after midnight and she rolled the window down, letting the breeze keep her awake. The air smelled totally different from St. Croix, more industrial. Sara entered her one-bedroom apartment, wincing at the raised voices coming from next door. *Great. Doug and Marcy are at it again. Hopefully they'll shut up soon.*

She left her luggage in the entry and dropped onto her couch with its red tie-died cover, glancing around the apartment. The kitchen was mostly unadorned—she wasn't much of a cook. But the living room was a riot of color. She didn't have any particular favorites, and loved all colors, as long as they were bright. Sara had lived there for six years, and even before the new owner took over the salon where she worked, she'd been itching to move on. But a seismic shift had just occurred mere hours ago. Her world was now off-kilter.

Oh, big sister. What are you getting me into?

Chapter Three

THE DIVERS' lights illuminated the octopus as it slid across the sandy bottom in the darkness. Dive guide Jack Powell grinned around his regulator as the strange creature progressed through a kaleidoscope of color changes. It had started off nearly white to match the sand, then became a brilliant turquoise before finally settling on a mottled brown as it climbed slowly up the side of a coral head. The creature wrapped its eight legs tightly around the outcropping and instantly developed stubby protrusions all over its mantle as it shifted to a reddish-brown, matching the coral. It sat there motionless except for the regular movement of its valve as it breathed, seemingly unperturbed by the divers' lights.

Jack never tired of them, and they were partially why he jumped at any chance to lead a night dive. Octopuses hid in crevices during the day, but night was when they hunted. He glanced around, confirming there were four other lights—his group was all there. The octopus moved one leg beneath it and rhythmically moved its mantle as it found something delicious in the coral and maneuvered the meal into its beak. Then it continued its search, instantly becoming smooth as the nubs disappeared. Within seconds, it disappeared into an impossibly small crack in the reef.

Jack checked his dive computer and led the group toward the boat. Night dives rarely went over forty-five minutes, fifteen minutes shorter than their daytime dives. Although the water temperature was identical, the lack of light caused the divers to feel cooler and eager to don sweatshirts waiting on the boat above.

Hanging from a rope below the boat, a green strobe light flashed in the darkness. Jack stopped the group near it as they hovered for their required safety stop. Watching the light, Jack smiled slightly around his regulator and contrasted his two jobs. The previous day, he had worked three dives at his other position at Ocean Surf Resort. Dive operations came in two flavors —organized and disorganized. And these two exemplified that, though both were understanding of his need to work multiple jobs. Yesterday, the night dive at Ocean Surf had been a confusing, tiring slog. He had struggled to lead the group back to the dark boat despite setting an accurate heading on his compass.

But tonight, Alex had dropped the green strobe so the boat's location would be easily visible to all divers. This also calmed any who might be uneasy at the prospect of being underwater in complete darkness. Alex had given Tommy the evening off and taken over captain duties himself, another thing Jack liked. Even though he was the dive manager of Half Moon Bay, Alex was never afraid to get into the trenches and do the hard work himself.

After surfacing, Jack stayed in the water and helped divers remove their fins. Alex then helped them walk to their spots on the boat so they could remove their tanks. Gravity was a bitch after diving. Everyone got on board without issue, and Jack was the last to tuck his fins under one arm and climb aboard. The group exclaimed about the dive, everyone excited. Sixteen-year-old Annie had just completed her first night dive and was telling Alex all about it.

"An octopus! Really? And you weren't scared?" Alex asked as he slid her fins under the bench.

"No. It was really cool. You don't like octopuses?"

"What if they suck my face off?" He stood, straight faced. "Maybe next time you can take me and keep me safe."

Annie and her parents laughed. "Deal," she said. "Don't worry, I'll protect you."

Jack smiled, enjoying Alex's joking, but the man was hard to read. He didn't talk about himself, except that he was a marine biologist, which made Jack wonder why he was working as a dive guide. Jack had been completely unaware Alex was involved with Hope until he mentioned they were getting married. *I should get to know him better. Especially since I want to work here more.*

After a quick head count, Alex climbed the ladder to the elevated bridge of *Surface Interval* and started the engine as Jack pulled both stern ladders out of the water and secured them. It was a quick trip back to the resort, and the divers were soon off the boat, headed toward showers and dinner. The two men busied themselves dismantling the dive equipment from the tanks so they could wash and store it, all to repeat the process after tomorrow's dives.

They were pulling Buoyancy Compensation Devices off the tanks when the sound of rushing footsteps echoed down the pier. Hope hurried toward them, holding a bag of ice against one cheek. Alex straightened immediately, and Jack followed suit.

"We need a little help at the bar," she said, stopping in front of them. "A couple of locals are getting out of hand, and it's too much for Clark to handle. I'm glad you're back." She readjusted the ice bag on her face as Alex inhaled sharply.

"Did they hit you?" he asked in an even, tight voice, and Jack's blood pressure skyrocketed.

Hope waved her free hand carelessly. "No, nothing like that. I was at the wrong place at the wrong time, trying to break it up and got hit with a flailing arm. But these two aren't the kind of people we want in our bar, especially with the divers coming over soon. Can you guys come help?"

Alex turned to Jack, his eyes blazing even as his face remained expressionless. Jack took an involuntary step back. *Whoa, that's a change.* "Can you handle yourself in a fight if it comes to that?"

Jack snorted, already itching to mix it up. "Please, I'm from Texas. Come on." He jumped out of the boat and strode up the pier, his feet thwacking on the boards. He had to glance behind to verify his boss was following—Alex hardly made any sound. Jack had no idea whether the man could fight. *Is that why you asked me about it? Don't worry, I'll show you how it's done.* No local troublemakers were going to cause a scene in Jack's newly adopted home.

Loud voices could be heard before he reached the edge of the pool bar with its thatch roof and tables nestled in the sand. A man dressed in a muscle shirt that read *Pirates Forever* stood with his legs apart and arms crossed over his chest, inches away from Clark Bailey, the bartender, who held both arms out in a calming gesture. The troublemaker's hair was a muddy brown, truly craptastic mullet. A dark, burly man with a large hoop through his right ear was tugging on his buddy's arm. Pirate Dude was the one with the loud voice. Earring was much quieter as he glanced quickly around the bar before saying in a Caribbean accent, "Come on, screw the orders. Let's get out of here. I think this is that place."

Jack stormed up to Pirate Dude, getting between him and Clark. The guy was a couple of inches taller, but that didn't matter when his blood was up. "What's your problem, man? People are just trying to relax here. It's time to hit the road."

"Maybe I don't want to hit the road." Pirate Dude sneered at Jack and hooked his thumb at the newly installed banner, which read *Half Moon Bay Resort—Home to St. Croix's Best Bartender!* "The *famous* bartender is being an asshole. He needs to apologize and give me a free drink or I'm gonna kick his ass for him."

Hope appeared in Jack's peripheral vision, placing the ice on a red mark on her cheek. Fury roiled Jack's gut as he looked back and forth between the two troublemakers. "You're the ones who are gonna get your asses kicked. Did one of you hit Hope?"

A shadow fell across him as Alex joined his side and spoke in a soft, seething voice. "That's what I'd like to know. And I have absolutely no intention of asking nicely. Which one of you two is responsible for the bruise on my *wife's* cheek?"

A remarkable change overtook the two men. Earring's eyes got huge as he tugged even harder on Pirate Dude's arm, who wasn't looking so tough anymore. Confused, Jack turned to Alex. He mirrored Pirate Dude's position from a few moments before, standing tall and aggressive, and his eyes belonged to someone Jack had never seen before. The temperature could have dropped ten degrees, and a shiver ran down his spine as he watched Alex.

A sheen of sweat dotted Earring's forehead. "Come on, man! I told you this was the place. That's the dude who took down Charles. We need to split!"

Pirate Dude took several steps back and deflated, focusing on Alex. "No one hit her, I swear. I had no idea she was behind me. I don't go around beating on women. And I *really* didn't know she was your wife. We'll leave now."

Alex took a step toward him, a pulse throbbing in his

temple. Hope strode forward and placed a restraining hand on his forearm. "Honey, please. They're leaving. Let them go."

His furious eyes lasered into the two men, who continued backing up.

Earring held out a hand. "Relax, man. We're out of here, ok?" The two men scurried for the exit.

Jack's adrenaline was fading, but his fists were still clenched at his sides. He took several steps down the path just to make sure they were gone before turning back. Alex was still completely motionless, his eyes focused on where the men had disappeared. Hope murmured softly to him. His chest moved back and forth like a bellows, and Jack tried to make sense of what had just happened. Alex had always been friendly and approachable, but right now, he was anything but.

What the hell? Pirate Dude was about to mix it up with me until he saw Alex. Then he couldn't get away fast enough.

Alex took a deep breath and nodded at Hope. Then his face smoothed as he looked around the bar, as if surprised other people were there. A few guests were scattered about, and his menacing demeanor disappeared, now replaced with his usual confident, authoritative countenance. Alex was one of those guys people noticed. "Ok, folks. Looks like the show's over. Sorry. It's rare, but sometimes we get people like that in here. Bars tend to attract troublemakers." The guests went back to their drinks as he turned to Jack. "Can you finish at the pier? I need to take Hope home and make sure everything's ok."

Hope sighed, the ice bag now at her side. She had a small red mark on her cheek, but it wasn't turning into anything more. "I'm fine. I already told you that."

Alex whipped his head to her. "I know you did. But *I* need to know." Their glances held for a long moment before Hope nodded.

Jack spoke up. "I'll finish. Don't worry about it. You two take off."

Alex met his eyes and nodded. "Thanks."

Hope turned to the bartender. "Give everyone a free round, Clark."

He nodded, already behind the bar. Alex wrapped his arm around Hope's shoulders, pulling her tightly against him as they headed out.

Jack approached the bar, waving off the beer Clark held up since he was still on duty. "Does this kind of thing happen often?"

Clark gave him a tight smile. "No, thank God. It's been a long time since we've had to get Alex involved. Thanks for your help. You guys got back just in time."

Jack nodded, then left the bar to finish cleaning up. *Get Alex involved? What does that mean?* There was more to Half Moon Bay than he had guessed.

It didn't take Jack long to get things rinsed and put away. He winced as he carried off a five-gallon bucket of fresh water they kept on board, heat flaming up his face involuntarily. Dumping a full container over Hope's gorgeous sister hadn't been one of his smoother moments. There weren't many moments in his life when he'd wished a trap door would just open and he could disappear, but that was one. When she and Hope had walked down the steps from the spa that day, he hadn't even noticed Hope. Sara had been all long, brown hair and glorious curves.

But his wince turned into an irritated scowl at how she'd treated him before she left the island. *Not one of the nicest people I've ever met. Good thing she's gone and far away from here.*

And beautiful or not, he wasn't sure he was ready to get involved again. He'd been divorced for over two years, but the sting of being left still hadn't abated. But at least the ordeal had provided the push he'd needed to move and start working as a divemaster, pretty much his dream job. Well, except for the pay. *And that's why I have two jobs.* But if he could get more hours at Half Moon Bay, maybe he'd only need one.

An hour later, Jack parked his Ford Ranger in its assigned parking space and entered his apartment. With a deep sigh, he made straight for the fridge, removing a Leatherback beer, and opening it. The apartment was modern and brand new, and he still smelled fresh paint each time he entered. His sketchpad lay on the kitchen table, open to his current work. Jack had started drawing a yellow-tail damsel fish but hadn't quite captured its essence and had continued sketching a living reef around it, hoping to coax the figure to life. It was still a work in progress. But he was beat—no sketching tonight.

Jack opened the sliding-glass door and sat in a chair on his ground-floor patio to enjoy the major reason he had rented the place. It cost more than he should spend, but some things were priceless. Even in the dark, he could easily picture the sweeping ocean view in front of him, and he closed his eyes, taking a long pull as the waves brushed against the beach.

He was doing his best to make a new start in St. Croix. But coming home to a lonely apartment got to him. Staring at the hypnotic push and pull of the waves, he forced himself to look at the bright side. "It beats a miserable marriage."

Chapter Four

NOVEMBER...

A cold Charleston rain drummed against the glass windows of the salon. Eight stations lined the walls, but only Sara was working that morning. She flung a plastic cape around her client's torso and wrapped a length of tissue around her neck. Penny heaved a big sigh and met Sara's eyes in the mirror. "I can't stand it anymore. Chop it all off."

More than ten years of experience made Sara a master at hiding her reactions to clients, even as she thought, *Oh, God. Not this again!* She gave Penny a warm smile. "We've been through this, remember? I refused to cut it off a year ago, and you thanked me for it. You just need something a little different."

"This is beyond redemption."

Sara laughed, running her hands through the woman's mousy brown hair. It hung well past her shoulders, stringy and sulking. "It's not that bad," she lied. "Tell you what—I'll give you a long A-line cut and flat iron it. When you come back next time, if you still want it shorter, we can cut it then."

Forty-five minutes later, she ran her flat iron through the last section of Penny's hair as the woman beamed in the mirror. "Sara, you're a genius! I love it."

"Thank you, madam. Just doing my job." Sara grinned, admitting this one might be a winner, even with Penny's thin hair.

Then a thundercloud walked through the front door in the form of Mathilde, the salon's owner. Her glossy dark-blonde hair was twisted into a chignon, and she wore a dark-gray suit with a pencil skirt. Scowling, she trudged toward the offices in the back without even glancing at Sara.

Say goodbye to my good mood…

As soon as she said farewell to Penny, receiving a generous tip to boot, Mathilde called out behind her. "Sara, I need to see you for a moment."

Suppressing a sigh, she fixed a pleasant smile on her face and approached her boss at the back of the room. "Good morning, Mathilde."

"Hardly. Jenny called in sick."

Again? Oh, Jenny, I'm gonna kill you.

"I'm going to need you to work in her clients who haven't cancelled."

"I've got a pretty full schedule."

The salon owner rifled through the mail, her red manicured fingernails flashing. "We all have our problems, don't we? It's time to be a team player, Sara. I'm sure you can find a way to work some more people in." She turned around, then thew over her shoulder, "And clean up your station. It looks like a pigsty."

That's because you called me back here before I had a chance to clean up, you bitch! But she kept her mouth shut. Mathilde was nearly to her office anyway and had clearly ended the conversation. Sara shot daggers at Jenny's station as she swept her own. This was the third time in two weeks she had called in. And she wasn't faking it—Mathilde made Jenny so nervous and miserable, it literally made her ill.

The bell over the door jingled as two women walked in. One was her own client, and the other was Jenny's. With a bright smile to welcome both, Sara planned how to handle both at the same time, as well as the onslaught to come.

By 4 P.M., Sara was wiped out. She'd managed to accommodate everyone, using two stations at once for most of the day. Her phone buzzed in her pocket as she finished ringing up her most recent client, and she waved off the small crowd waiting in hard plastic chairs, pleading a restroom break. Locking the bathroom door behind her, Sara slumped against it as she pulled out her phone. The text was from her best friend Marissa.

> Marissa: Meet for drinks @ 5:30?

> Sara: Oh, God, yes!!!!

> Marissa: Good day, huh? LOL.

> Sara: I can't even... Meet you at Tendrils?

> Marissa: First round's on me!

SARA POCKETED her phone and closed her eyes, leaning against the door. "Ok, now you've got a light at the end of the tunnel. Just get through the next hour. You can do this." With a groan, she opened the door, holding her head proudly as she marched to work through the last of the crowd.

TENDRILS WAS AN UPSCALE, modern bar located a block's walk from the salon. The rain had ended, but it was pitch dark. When Sara got there at 5:45, Marissa was already seated at a table. She was fresh from work as an office manager and still dressed in a long-sleeved blouse and tailored slacks, her light-brown, curly hair pulled back in a large barrette. She brightened as Sara slumped into her seat. "I already ordered two double mojitos. Help is on the way."

Sara laughed and rested her forehead in her hand. "Thanks. I think I'll order food too. I don't want the booze going straight to my head. I had to eat my lunch in frantic gulps. I didn't even have time to sit down today."

"Mathilde the Wicked Witch?"

"None other. I can't believe how much things have changed in just six months!"

The server brought over their drinks and Sara took a long gulp, smacking her lips at the minty taste. She ordered a chef salad before returning to her mojito.

"It must be even more of a shock after relaxing on a sandy beach," Marissa said, then narrowed her eyes. "On *my* sandy beach. Hope owes me a lot more than two dozen roses."

Sara laughed, her bad day slipping away. "You just discovered the raffle. I was the one who entered her in it. And it was damn nice of her to send you flowers, you know." A week had passed since Sara's return, and today was the fourth day of rain in a row, making her even more miserable. "I'm having a tough time getting back into the groove."

"Still, it sounds like a nice getaway. I love weddings! Do you have pictures?"

"Oh, yeah." Sara swiped through several photos and handed over her phone. She'd brought up a picture of Hope and Alex after the ceremony as they posed against the sunset.

Marissa opened her eyes wide as she zoomed the picture with her fingers. "Gawd! They're gorgeous. Look at that uniform. He's quite hunkalicious, isn't he?"

"Back off, missy. That's my brother-in-law you're talking about." Sara snorted. "They both completely tune me out if the other is in the same room. Trust me. That man is as off the market as a guy can get."

Marissa passed the phone back. "Only window shopping anyway." She paused while Sara's salad came, and she dug in. "Now back to your job conundrum. What are you going to do?"

Sara dropped her fork and told Marissa about her day. "Things just keep going from bad to worse. I pride myself on being dependable, but now *I'm* thinking about calling in sick."

"Sounds like it's time for a new job."

Sara met Marissa's eyes head-on. "That's what I've been thinking. Here's the thing—I've been offered one. In St. Croix, at my sister's spa." She wasn't about to mention the $100,000 that was sitting in a bank.

Marissa sat up straight. "Ooh! So, is your flight booked?"

Sara laughed. "No. I'm worried there won't be enough work to keep me busy."

"Is that all? Are you worried about working for your sister?"

"No, we get along great. That shouldn't be an issue." Yet Sara had been in Hope's shadow her whole life. Maybe there was a way to make Hope's spa her own creation.

Marissa paused for a drink. "To be honest, I'm surprised you're hesitating. I was thrilled when you wanted to move here, but it's been six years now. That's a pretty long time for you to stay in one place. You've always been the feather, blowing where the breeze takes you."

Sara finished eating and pushed her plate away. "I don't know if it's because I'm getting older, but moving seems like a lot more hassle than it used to. Maybe I'm ready to settle down more. But you're right. I need to look for a new job."

"Sounds like a hell of an opportunity to me. I think you should take it."

"We'll see."

Marissa had a gleam in her eye now. "Settle down, huh? You looking for Mr. Right?"

"Hardly... But watching Hope and Alex get married affected me more than I thought it would. You've been married for a while. Any regrets?"

Marissa reared back. "Sara! Of course not. Blake is the best thing that's ever happened to me. And when Olivia came along, she only made things better. Well, and more tiring. You just need to find the right guy, that's all."

"That's all? Ha—easy for you to say. Honestly, all I want is a man who accepts me for who I am." Sara held up her mojito. "Carefree, curvy, and fabulous!"

Marissa gave her a tolerant smile. She was well aware Sara's exuberance tended to cover her self-consciousness. "All I'm saying is that a fresh start seems to have worked out pretty well for your sister, hasn't it?"

THE NEXT DAY, work was a repeat. *I'm living the movie Groundhog Day.* Jenny called in sick again and Mathilde was even bitchier. Sara was currently cutting the hair of one of Jenny's regulars, while one of her longest-standing clients sat in the waiting area long past her appointment time. Sara tried to ignore the woman glancing at her watch, but a tight ball grew in her gut with each passing second.

Fifteen minutes later, her client stood. "Sara, this isn't working. You've already rescheduled me once, and now I'm going to be late for my next appointment. I need to find someone else. I'm sorry." Waving a hand absently, she rushed out the door into the late afternoon. Sara's eyes filled with tears as she tried to keep an even expression.

"Sorry about that." The woman in her chair shot her an awkward smile.

Sara blinked away the tears and set down her shears. "Don't apologize. It's not your fault at all. What do you think?"

The woman studied her reflection. "I've been going to Jenny for a year now. But honestly, you did a much better job. Thanks."

At least someone's happy...

An hour later, Sara locked the front door and turned around to face the carnage. Once again, she had bounced between two stations, trying to keep up. She had cleaned after each client, but there was no denying the two stations were a disaster. *Ok, time to get this straightened up.* She grabbed a broom.

High-heeled footsteps echoed in the silent room as Mathilde strode from her office. "Good God, Sara. This place looks terrible. Can't you even clean up after yourself?"

That's it! Sara threw the broom on the floor and rounded on her. "No, Mathilde, I can't clean up after myself. Not when I have to work two stations for eight hours straight. Trying to do the impossible *and* keep everyone happy. You know what happened today? I lost one of my best clients!"

Mathilde's hair was curled in loose waves that fell forward as she inclined her head. "I know you've been working hard these two days. If Jenny calls in sick again, she's gone."

Sara stood with both hands on her hips, not even trying to

keep her voice down anymore. "It's not just Jenny! I'm the only one still showing up. Maybe if you treated your workers like human beings, they wouldn't call in sick all the time. Did you ever think of that?"

"Stop it. This is one of the most prestigious salons in Charleston. You're lucky to work here."

"Oh, shut up. You're the one who's lucky to have me. But that's ending. Now. I quit, Mathilde. I'll gather my supplies, then I'm out of here. So long." She whirled around and, grabbing her clippers and shears, packing everything into a wooden box.

Mathilde finally recovered her voice, clutching the pearls around her neck. "You can't just quit with no notice!"

"Yeah? Watch me." Sara slammed her box shut and stomped toward the door.

"I can make sure you never work in this town again, Sara. Don't be stupid."

Sara didn't bother to respond, but a wide smile spread across her face as she crossed the parking lot to her car.

I won't need to work in this town again.

As soon as she got home, she slammed her box on the kitchen counter and called Hope. "Are you still looking for a stylist?"

"Hello to you too. You sound a little stressed."

"I just quit my job. That bitch pushed me too far today."

"Well, I happen to know someone *much* nicer who still needs a stylist and manager. But only the best will do."

Sara grinned, already feeling the weight falling from her shoulders. "Well today is your lucky day. Look out St. Croix. Sara Collins is on her way."

Chapter Five

JACK STRODE down the brick walkway toward the gear room at Ocean Surf Resort. Cameron walked next to him, tying his long, bleached-blond hair into a manbun. Jack refrained from rolling his eyes. Though several years younger than Jack, Cameron had been a divemaster at Ocean Surf for several years and therefore outranked him. And he wasn't shy about flaunting that.

Mark Lowry, the instructor and manager, pulled the two men aside. "We've got a full boat today. Due to a scheduling mix up, you'll have to take extra people in your groups. Cameron, you've got ten, and Jack, you've got twelve."

"Twelve?" Jack asked, raking a hand through his hair. He glanced at the ocean and relaxed sightly at its flat-calm appearance. "Good thing it's a nice day."

"Yeah, I know it's a lot. We'll pick easy dive sites today to minimize any problems." Mark nodded and headed toward the office.

Cameron smirked at Jack as they continued. "We can switch if you want. I don't have any problem with that many."

Jack stared him down. "I didn't say it was a problem. It's just not ideal. Someone's bound to kick up sand and ruin things for everyone else." But it was a problem if something went wrong. Twelve was a lot of divers to keep track of.

The two men entered the dark, cluttered gear room. Most of the BCDs hung on hangers, but several were piled up in a corner. Regulators hung crookedly on the wall, several to each hook. Cameron made a beeline for the regulators. "I'll grab the regs. You can load the tanks."

Of course. I'd never expect you to do the heavy lifting. But as the new guy, Jack knew better than to complain.

The dives were Murphy's Law in action. Jack had two brand new divers who could *not* figure out their buoyancy. He finally had to grab a hold of the guy's arm and show him how to inflate or deflate to maintain himself neutrally. Eventually he got the hang of it. Somewhat.

The frustration was clear in the narrowed eyes and wrinkled brows of the other divers as Jack tried to show them the highlights of the dive and the creatures he found. But the succession of people either kicked up the sand so much the animal could hardly be seen, or scared it off altogether.

I better not count on great tips today...

But he completed both dives without any major disasters and spent most of the afternoon cleaning up, since there wasn't a third dive scheduled. Cameron cut out early, of course. Jack was sorting through the mess of BCDs in the gear room corner when Mark walked in. "Sorry about today. We overbooked without realizing it."

Yeah. That's a big surprise. "That's ok. It happens. I had some unhappy divers in my group, though."

"They'll forget about it tomorrow, when we're back to normal."

I doubt that. And it won't do me much good, since I'm not working tomorrow.

"Sorry I can't give you more hours," Mark said. "Except for today's snafu, our business has dropped off lately. Are you getting work up at Half Moon Bay?"

"Yeah. Alex is fitting me into the schedule when he can." He'd only had one shift with the Half Moon Bay instructor since the night dive and near-fight afterward. Alex had hardly said anything about it, except to mention Hope was fine when Jack had asked, and to thank him for his help again. They had been returning dive gear to the storage room at the end of the day when Alex had startled him by breaking into a broad grin. "Oh—I have some good news. You're gonna love it."

Jack tried not to get his hopes up that he was about to get more hours. "Lay it on me, then."

"Guess who's moving to St. Croix next month?"

Jack went blank. That was not what he was expecting. "Uh... someone I should know?"

Alex's grin widened. "You might want to install some hurricane shutters. Sara is coming here to manage the spa."

Oh shit. That's all I need at the place I actually enjoy working. He fought to remain neutral. "Oh. I'm sure Hope is really happy about that."

"Pretty much over the moon. You, on the other hand, might want to step lightly."

Jack hadn't even told Alex about colliding with her. *Oh well, we're both adults. I'm sure we can co-exist for a couple of hours each day.*

He wasn't about to turn down any extra shifts, and loved working at the organized, professional Half Moon Bay, which brought him back to the present and Ocean Surf. He wouldn't be working for Alex if not for Mark's referral. He turned to the older man with a small smile. "Thanks for recommending me."

"Sure. We're a tight-knit group on this island. I've known Alex for years."

"I worked a night dive not long ago that turned out pretty interesting. I'm still trying to figure it out. When we got back, there were two idiots in the bar causing a ruckus. I was about to throw a punch at one of them when Alex appeared next to me. The two guys took one look at him, tucked their tails in between their legs, and ran away."

Mark raised his eyebrows, a smile forming. "Ah, you got a bar-fight initiation, huh? That happens here too once in a while, though our bartender is big enough to handle any troublemakers." Then he burst out laughing. "Yeah, once they saw Alex, I bet those guys couldn't get out of there fast enough."

Ok, he definitely knows something I don't. "And why would that be?"

Mark's smile faded. "He didn't say anything to you about it?"

Jack shrugged, uncomfortable now. "He doesn't talk much about himself."

"That doesn't surprise me—Alex is a pretty private guy. He'll probably open up, eventually. Or if you're that interested, ask him yourself."

Jack was more curious than ever, but knew a brick wall when he saw one. And he respected Mark for honoring Alex's privacy. "Thanks. I'd better get this finished up." As Mark left the stuffy, claustrophobic room, Jack turned back to the BCD pile.

God, this place is a mess.

***

"To Sara!" The voices rang out as Sara clinked her champagne flute to theirs. Zoe, another good friend, had joined her and Marissa for a farewell dinner.

Marissa pouted. "I'm going to miss you terribly."

"Then you'll just have to come visit me, won't you?"

"How did you get everything arranged so quickly, anyway?" Zoe asked, brushing back her long black hair.

"I didn't have much choice, since I quit my job with no notice."

"Oh yeah," Marissa raised her flute again. "We need another toast to that, for sure. You're my hero, Sara."

A giggle escaped as Sara sipped her champagne. "Not very professional, I admit. But it was worth it just to see the look on Mathilde's face."

"Still," Zoe said. "You leave in another week, right?"

"Yeah, just after Thanksgiving. It'll work out fine. It always does. And you, my dear," she held up her flute to Marissa, "get the honor of hosting me for one final Thanksgiving dinner."

They toasted all around, then Sara continued. "My furniture isn't worth the hassle of trying to sell, so I'm having a thrift shop pick up the entire lot the day before I move. Hope is arranging for a one-bedroom furnished apartment for me as we speak."

This was a white lie. The apartment at the complex they had passed on the way to the airport was unfurnished. Since agreeing to move and manage the spa, Hope had called daily, giddy with the details of her decorating adventures. And she insisted on footing the bill. But Sara didn't want Marissa and Zoe getting curious about how she could afford her new furniture.

The treasure windfall was still sitting in the bank, though Hope wanted Sara's name on the account as soon as she moved. But she was still uncomfortable accepting the money. Hope had always looked after her, but Sara had no intention of just accepting the gift, wanting it to go toward something concrete and productive.

Which she was having a hard time figuring out. She liked

the idea of managing the spa, but she liked the idea of owning one even more. Which could prove difficult when Hope already owned the salon. *Guess I don't have to figure this all out right now, do I?*

"My little brother is ecstatic to buy your car," Marissa said, then laughed. "He can't wait until you're gone!"

Sara arched a brow sardonically. "He might feel differently once he owns it. Even a thousand dollars might be too much for that jalopy."

Zoe leaned forward, speculation gleaming in her eyes. "You've been there twice now. Any guy you've noticed? Is the place swarming with lifeguards and pool boys?"

Sara laughed. "No, sorry to disappoint you. It's a small but very tranquil resort. The dive staff doubles as lifeguards when they aren't underwater." She groaned, shaking her head. "The only guy I've had repeated contact with is this total klutz of a divemaster they just hired. The two times I've met him, he's dumped a water bucket over me and almost knocked me flat on my ass."

Marissa tittered. "Ok, not too promising, I'll admit. But is he at least cute?"

"I have no idea. The only times I've met him, my eyes have been closed in self-preservation. I plan to stay far away from him, and I'm sure he feels the same way." If she were being fair, Sara would admit Jack had beautiful eyes, with ridiculously long, thick eyelashes.

But she had no intention of being fair.

Chapter Six

SARA SQUINTED as she left the airplane, digging into her purse for her oversized sunglasses. She slid them on with delight, the bruising tropical sun now diminished to a soft glow. These had been her crowning purchase at the thrift store when she and Marissa had finalized the sale of her furnishings. They had beckoned from a locked glass case and Sara happily forked over her money when the shopkeeper gave her a deal on them, apparently feeling guilty that Sara was practically donating all her belongings.

Imagining paparazzi snapping photos as she descended the airplane steps in the new-to-her Armani shades, Sara entered the terminal. Sparkly earrings that dangled nearly to her shoulders highlighted her long black and green sundress. She had put together the whole outfit this morning to give her a confidence boost after a nervous night of tossing and turning had induced a flurry of second thoughts. Fortunately, her plan worked, and she strolled across the tile floor toward the arrivals hall with her head held high.

Spotting Hope immediately, Sara matched her wide smile and hurried to her sister. Hope clapped her hands as she bounced up and down. After embracing, she pressed Sara back to arm's length, laughing. "Wow. You look like a movie star. All you need is a scowling bodyguard behind you."

"Nope, just me. Speaking of scowling bodyguards, where's yours?"

Hope slid an arm around her shoulders as they headed toward the baggage claim. "Alex is working this morning. He sends his—and I quote—eternal brotherly love and devotion."

Sara snorted. "Yeah, I'll bet."

"How many suitcases do you have?"

"Three. That was the hardest part. Picking what went and what stayed behind. One suitcase is dedicated to my painting supplies."

"I didn't know if you'd just buy new painting stuff once you got here."

"No, I buy quality, so I wasn't about to leave anything behind." While she dabbled in oil and acrylic painting, her true passion was watercolors.

As was typical with airlines, Sara's first bag appeared on the carousel right away and the third appeared just as she was ready to give up. Hope led one wheeled bag by its handle while Sara wrestled the other two, and they headed toward the doors.

"I can't wait to show you your apartment!" Hope said. "They did a wonderful job with the complex. It's got a private beach and a really nice pool, not to mention a clubhouse with a fitness center. A bar and restaurant are opening soon."

Sara raised a brow but remained silent. They hefted the suitcases into the back of Hope's Jeep. As Sara buckled into the passenger seat, she finally shot Hope a skeptical glance. "And you're sure I can afford this?"

"Yes. I made up a monthly budget for you with estimated expenses balanced against your salary. You'll be fine."

"Of course you did." Sara shook her head with a grin. "I'm

still not sure about accepting a full-time salary when I don't know if I'll have enough work to justify it." She was mesmerized by the jagged, brilliant green mountains on her right and the aqua hues to her left.

Hope glanced at her before turning back to the highway. "This is the exact same salary I would offer anyone I hired to be spa manager. I swear. You're not getting special treatment."

"Ok, I believe you." Sara had researched spa manager salaries and confirmed this for herself, though she wasn't going to tell Hope that.

They passed through colorful Frederiksted and continued a short distance until the apartment complex appeared on their left, and Hope turned in. The entry featured two flanking rows of palm trees, then they circled behind the large clubhouse and office. The buildings were painted white with a soft blue trim. Large glass windows showcased both the front and back of the clubhouse. A huge resort-style pool sprawled behind it, and Sara craned her neck as they drove by. There was a rectangular area for lap swimming and a sandy beach entry. The unfinished restaurant sat to one side, yellow caution tape draped across the entrance.

Five two-story apartment buildings were placed around the grounds, featuring different views. Everything Sara glimpsed was modern, fresh, and brand new, and her heart thumped in her chest. Hope pulled into a covered parking spot and turned off the engine. "This is your assigned stall." Then she frowned, turning to her. "We're going to have to get you a car. I was lucky—my Jeep was included."

"You were more than lucky, big sister. But I agree, car shopping will be a priority."

Hope had stuck her tongue out at Sara's first statement, but now she unbuckled and exited the car. "We can leave the suitcases here for now. I'm dying for you to see your new digs!"

"We don't need to check in at the office?"

"You can stop by at some point and introduce yourself, but everything is ready to go. Come on!" Hope grabbed her hand and headed toward the end of the building and a staircase to the second floor, practically dragging Sara up the stairs.

An end unit. Nice!

There was a landing at the top of the stairs with a solid door to their left, painted the same soft blue as the trim. A bright blue and yellow doormat sat out front. Hope held out a key attached to a Half Moon Bay Resort key chain. "Here, you do the honors. It's your place."

Sara slid the key in, and the front door opened silently. She entered a large open-concept area, and Hope shut the door behind her. The great room was immediately in front, with a kitchen to her left. On the other side of the great room were two closed doors, presumably the bedroom and bath.

But Sara hardly noticed the room. A large sliding glass door took up most of the back wall. The vertical blind was open, and all she could see was blue. "Is that the ocean?"

"Go check it out."

Forcing her feet to move, Sara slid open the glass door. *Am I dreaming right now?* She stepped onto a large, covered deck, surrounded by the soft sound of waves splashing onto the shore. A couch and loveseat sat in an L shape on one side, with a matching table and two chairs on the other. The fabric was a gentle gray with royal blue and yellow pillows accenting the furniture.

"The deck is big enough to place your easel here in the middle. With this view, you should have plenty of inspiration to paint."

Tears sprang to Sara's eyes. "Hope, I don't even know what to say. You're *sure* I can afford this?"

"Yes! They're offering a special rate to the first tenants." She pointed to another building to their right that was closer to the water. "And look. That building is the oceanfront unit and the most expensive. I thought this one was a better combination of view and affordability. I wanted you to have the top floor for a better view."

She turned to embrace Hope. "Thank you. It's amazing." The interior enticed and they went back inside. The medium gray couch and loveseat faced her with a brilliant royal blue and yellow area rug underneath the coffee table.

"I decided on neutrals for the furniture so you can accent it however you want. But I picked out some pieces for you so it would look homey from the start. I know you love bright colors."

A large watercolor hung on one white wall, an image of turquoise ocean and the multi-colored buildings of Frederiksted. Sara cocked her head, recognizing the style. "Is that the same artist who did the paintings you have in your house?"

Hope nodded. "He's just a street vendor, but I think he's fantastic. I've bought several paintings from him."

A few minutes later, all three of her suitcases were lined up neatly inside the front door. Hope gave Sara's shoulder a squeeze. "I'll leave you to get unpacked and settled in. A rental service is dropping off a car this afternoon, so you have wheels until you can buy something. Give me a call tomorrow morning and we'll get together."

Then Hope was gone, and Sara stood alone in her new home. She inhaled a deep breath of freshly painted air as excitement rippled down her spine. It had been a while since she'd felt the sense of keen anticipation. Striding to the door, Sara went to work.

First up was the suitcase containing the clothes she couldn't part with. She dragged it into her bedroom and discovered a bright room with a king-size bed. A modern, white-striped comforter and fluffy pillows adorned it, and a multi-hued blue runner draped across the foot. Sara smiled, recognizing the same linens that graced the beds at the resort.

The suitcases were unpacked within an hour, though her clothes looked lonely in the large walk-in closet. Art supplies were scattered across the kitchen table, but she was decidedly tired at this point. Her stomach growled and she checked the time. *No wonder. It's after 2 p.m. Well, food could be a problem.*

Crossing to her new kitchen, Sara examined it. A multitude of white cabinets accented a gray quartz countertop, and the stainless-steel appliances glimmered. "This is nice enough I might actually learn to cook."

She opened the refrigerator, finding it fully stocked with all the necessities she might need. A full-size door opened to a pantry that was also full of staples. Sara smiled as her heart clenched. "Oh, Hope. You never miss a trick, do you?"

As she ate a quick lunch, a knock sounded on her door—the rental agency delivering her car. Then it was time to explore the apartment complex. She followed the path at the foot of the stairs back toward the clubhouse and pool. It was very quiet, and Sara strolled through lush foliage, enjoying the breeze as it stirred the palm trees around her.

A man stood at the pool's edge. He was about her age and dressed in tan linen pants and a white Cuban shirt with the sleeves rolled up. His brown hair was slicked back, and he wore aviator sunglasses. Standing straight with his arms crossed, he swept his gaze around the area, inspecting it thoroughly. He noticed her and broke into a smile, exuding a confident and assertive aura, and his sunglasses couldn't hide his eyes as he scanned up and down her body. "Hello, there."

Intrigued, Sara tilted her head and matched his gaze, stopping next to him. "Hello to you too. You look like a man surveying his domain."

That made him laugh. "Actually, you could say that. I'm the

developer of this complex. I came by to make sure everything is operational. Do you live here?"

"As of a couple of hours ago, yes."

"Well, then. Let me be one of the first to welcome you." He held his hand out. "Wayne Timmons."

"Pleased to meet you, Wayne. I'm Sara." She shook his hand.

"How did you come to be at Serenity? Are you new to the island?"

She flipped a long lock of hair over her shoulder, and he followed the movement with his eyes. *Ok, St. Croix just got interesting...* "I moved here today. I'm a stylist and took a position here managing a spa." She had no intention of telling him it was her sister's property.

He raised his sunglasses, revealing a pair of greenish-brown eyes. He was very good looking, in a dashing, sophisticated way. "Really? Spas are a thriving business. I'm sure you'll be successful." He had been making strong eye contact with her, but dropped his gaze to withdraw a wallet from his back pocket. "In fact, I'm surveying land parcels right now, looking for a location to build my own spa." He dug a business card out of his pocket and handed it to her with a suggestive smile. "If you're ever interested in a change, give me a call."

Sara glanced at the card, which read *Cornerstone Development* with a prominent logo, and as promised, his phone number was listed, along with his email. "Well, I haven't even started my new position yet, but I'll keep it in mind." She couldn't resist a flirty smile.

He returned it with his own smile, then checked his Rolex with a sigh. "I've got to head to an appointment. But since this complex is just opening, I'm here frequently. Maybe we'll run into each other again. It was nice to meet you, Sara."

"Same to you, Wayne."

He nodded to her, then strode toward the clubhouse, and she watched his retreating form. He was close to six feet tall, with decent shoulders. *Ok, that was promising. I definitely wouldn't mind meeting him again. Things are looking up...*

THAT EVENING, Jack sat at his kitchen table. His sketchbook had called to him as soon as he got home. After eating at the table, it was easy enough to pull his pad and charcoal pencil toward him. A soft thump came from above, causing him to pause as he shaded in a sunbeam in the water above the reef, and he glanced up.

Did someone move in today?

The noise wasn't repeated, so he continued. The yellow-tail damsel fish was now fully complete, and he was pleased he had managed to capture some of the brilliance of the fish, even in black and white. A faint sliding noise drifted from above, hardly noticeable, but Jack sat back with a sigh. "Looks like I've officially got a neighbor. As long as he's quiet, that's fine by me."

Though a little sad to have his peaceful life upset, it was bound to happen sooner or later. Jack returned to his sketch.

HE WORKED the next morning at Half Moon Bay. Tommy and Alex worked together with ease, but both made an effort to include Jack. As he rinsed gear, his gaze drifted to the north end of Half Moon Bay, behind the house reef. It was a scrubby, secluded area, and had to boast an incredible view. He'd been thinking about bringing his sketch book and heading out there after work, but had forgotten it. He made a mental note to remember next time.

Jack turned his mind back to work and the thoughts occupying his mind lately—how he could get more hours at Half Moon Bay. He carried the dripping BCDs to the gear room, where Alex was hanging regulators.

He's a pretty straight-forward guy. How about the direct approach? "Hey, Alex. If you need any help, feel free to call me. I'm happy to fill in, or teach DSD, or whatever." Discover Scuba Diving was a class divemasters were authorized to teach, since it didn't go into the specifics or length of a full scuba certification. Most divemasters, not to mention instructors, hated teaching it because the students consisted mostly of hungover vacationers who weren't really interested in more than trying something different.

But Jack wasn't picky. He was willing to pay his dues.

Alex hung an arm over the row of regulators. "I might be able to give you more shifts. April has been busy whenever I've called her lately."

The problem with being the new guy was that everyone outranked you and got called first. "Perfect. Just let me know."

Alex drifted to an open corner of the room, next to the air compressor. "And I'm looking at getting a membrane system installed so we can dive Nitrox. That'll lead to more business too." An enriched-air system, Nitrox decreased the risk of decompression sickness, or the bends, and was increasingly popular. "And I'll definitely let you know the next time someone wants a DSD." Alex grinned, pointing at a thin dark-skinned boy walking by. "You have no idea how lucky you are. Now that we've got Zach filling tanks, DSDs might be the only difficult task you'll get."

Zach Turner, a local high school senior, was their part-time helper. He glanced at Alex as he passed by the two men toward the dive shop, walking backward as he hooked both thumbs toward himself. "That's right. Indispensable, right here."

"Yeah, don't get cocky, Zach," Alex said. "You're starting

your open water class next week. I'm expecting great things from you."

Zach laughed. "Well, that's up to the teacher, huh?" With that, he spun around and entered the room to fill tanks.

A smile lingered on Jack's face. Zach was a small, yet determined kid. He'd probably do great in his scuba class. He turned his attention back to Alex, curious. Jack had never asked him about his background, and Alex hadn't brought it up himself, either. The two men worked well together, so Jack figured he'd get to know him eventually. "Give me a call. I'll help however I can."

Alex sobered. "I know it can be tough to make ends meet as a divemaster. You do a great job. I'll give you work anytime I can."

Jack went back to dunking the BCDs into the fresh-water trough, rinsing the salt out of them. Then the sound of laughter filled the area, and he glanced up as Hope and Sara stepped off the stairs to the spa, headed his way. They didn't pause their conversation except for a friendly nod from Hope. Sara just glared as they passed by, and he gave her a hard stare in return.

He was hoping Sara would be less attractive upon her return. Nope—still stunning. Jack sighed, turning back to his work as he reminded himself of her personality.

Great, she's arrived, and still as pleasant as ever. She's got trouble written all over her, and she's Hope's sister. As long as we stay out of each other's way, everything will be fine.

Chapter Seven

WALKING JUST BEHIND ROBERT, Jack entered Breakers Bar & Grill. The two men made their way down a brick path to the large bar and sat on two stools. The bartender, whose black curls were neatly cropped, nodded. "Hey, Robert. Usual?" Robert nodded and introduced Jack, who ordered a Leatherback.

Maurice, the bartender, was built like a linebacker. He brought over two beers and the two men toasted. Jack regarded the bar as he took a drink. There was a mixture of locals and tourists, and there was no music blaring, making conversation easy. Tables were spread over the brick floor, and several were nestled in the sand outside, close to the waves as they swept ashore.

"Cool place," Jack said.

The overhead lights shone on Robert's dark, shaved head. "Yeah, it's been one of my favorites for a long time. Despite Maurice's presence."

Maurice snorted as he shook a martini, then nodded his head at Jack. "You a divemaster too?"

"Yeah. I work at Half Moon Bay and Ocean Surf."

"Not too many divemasters are as lazy as Robert, only workin' at one place."

Robert took a drink before grinning. He had extremely white teeth, which made his smile dazzling. "Only because my photography business is doin' well enough. I hustled plenty before that."

Maurice cupped a hand to the side of his mouth and said in a loud stage whisper to Jack, "He's lazy." Then he went to the other side of the bar to serve the martini.

Robert threw a peanut at his head before turning to Jack. "You gettin' settled in?"

Jack nodded. "Apartment's all set up, and between the two jobs, I'm making ends meet." He'd recently moved to St. Croix and hadn't made many friends yet. When Robert had asked Jack if he wanted to stop for a beer, he'd jumped at the chance.

"Where are you from?"

"Texas, near Galveston," Jack replied. "I was in construction for a long time. My ex-wife and I got certified to dive about ten years ago and I just fell in love with it. Like I had finally found what I was meant to do." He took a pull on his beer. "My wife, not so much."

"Yeah, that's pretty common."

"I kept taking advanced certifications and got my divemaster license three years ago, but I never really used it. Then my marriage ended. It took me a while to get my footing back, and I moved to St. Thomas about a year ago. Decided it was time to work as a divemaster full time."

Robert grinned. "St. Thomas, huh? How was that?"

Jack closed his eyes and swallowed as Robert laughed. "A nightmare. I worked for a cattle-boat operation that took out divers from the big cruise ships. I got really good at handling train wrecks and emergencies, though." He laughed and shook his head. "I moved here a couple of months ago. I like St. Croix much more. It's a lot more laid back, and neither outfit I work for caters to the cruise-ship crowd, which is an extra plus."

"They're both good operations, especially Half Moon Bay. I've known Alex for a while now."

"You're from here?"

Robert nodded. "Born and raised. My dad is a fisherman, so I've been around the water since I could walk. And I'm a fellow member of the divorced club. My ex had expensive tastes, and even working two jobs plus my photography gig, I couldn't make ends meet. When I told her we needed to cut back, she did. Me." He laughed and took another long pull.

"Ouch. Sorry. To be honest, I'm still not sure why my wife left. I did everything I could to make her happy. She changed her hair color and appearance every other month. She was never happy."

Robert looked at him steadily. "Maybe it didn't have anythin' to do with you. Hard to be happy with someone else if you're not happy with yourself first."

"You might be right about that. I kept trying to tell her she was fine just the way she was—I didn't want to change anything about her. Then I came home from the construction site one day to find her side of the closet all cleaned out and a note saying she was gone."

"I'm sorry, man."

Then Jack gave an exuberant laugh and tilted his head toward Robert. "Enough time has passed that I can focus on the funny part. My given name is John. She literally left me a Dear John letter."

A broad grin crossed Robert's face. "Life goes on, right? Alex just married the love of his life. And that guy used to be shut down *tight*. Keep lookin', man. You'll find her."

Jack stared absently at the Breakers coaster on the counter. *But do I? Am I even interested in a relationship? I didn't fight very hard to keep the last one.* He broke his reverie to take a long pull. He had plenty else to worry about just paying his bills.

———

With a cheery wave, Sara said goodbye to the guest and shut the spa door. Then she twisted the lock and slumped against it, closing her eyes.

Selena laughed from behind the counter. "Oh, wow. You need a drink, girl. I'm meeting April at a nice place we go to occasionally. You want to come?"

Sara snapped her eyes open. She had no idea who April was, but couldn't care less at the moment. "You had me at drink. When and where?"

Selena gave her directions as she picked up her purse. It was nearly 5 p.m. "I'm headed straight there."

"Wait a second. Can I invite Hope too?"

Selena brightened. "Sure! We can do a girls' night. Make it a regular occurrence." Then she laughed. "I really didn't think you were going to talk that lady out of the bright purple."

"Thank God I don't actually have the color she wanted. And she finally listened to me—that what sounds great on vacation might not be so fantastic once she gets home and back in her normal life."

"The dark blonde looked really good on her."

"All's well that ends well. I need to clean up and I'll meet you there. I'll text Hope now."

Sara pulled into the dirt parking lot of Charlie's, a nondescript bar Selena had told her was strictly a local hangout, and she could see why. Being in central St. Croix, the emerald mountains rose all around it, offering a view of nothing, which didn't make it very attractive to tourists. And therefore, even more alluring to locals.

She patted the steering wheel of her two-year-old Toyota RAV4. Hope had provided the name of her banker and Sara was quickly approved for a loan, and she had bought the car two days ago. Her new wheels had been shockingly expensive, as was the case with everything on the island. "Thank you. You're practical *and* reliable. Definite upgrade from my last car."

The bar had a covered wood-floor deck with several tables. Sara opened the solid wooden door and entered a surprisingly bright large room. Several windows let in plenty of light and party lights blinked from the exposed ductwork.

Selena was waving from a corner table, sitting next to a woman with long, honey-blonde hair. As Sara made her way over, she automatically compared the beautiful shade to the woman's eyebrow color and skin tone, deducing the color was natural.

"Sara, this is April," Selena said. "We've been neighbors for a few years, and she works as a divemaster once in a while at Half Moon Bay."

She and April exchanged hellos as Sara's text tone went off. She dug out her phone and frowned at it. "Bummer. It's Hope. Something just came up at the resort and she's not going to make it."

"Maybe next time, then," Selena said.

"How are you liking St. Croix so far?" April asked.

"What's not to like? I'm getting unpacked, and I've officially been here a week. Now that I've got a car, hopefully I can get around a little more. Though I haven't even met any of my neighbors yet, so I guess I can't use the car as an excuse."

Selena turned to April and raised a brow. "Sara lives at Serenity."

"Ooh! I'm jealous. But that place is out of my price range."

"Hope got me an early-tenant special rate, or I couldn't either. I've never seen you at Half Moon Bay."

The server brought a bucket of Leatherbacks and April opened hers. "I'm only part-time. I work there and at a dive shop on the south shore. I also work as a server some evenings."

"Wow," Sara said. "That's a lot. I'm surprised Alex didn't give you more hours instead of hiring Jack."

April shrugged and a slight shadow crossed her face. "I'm not always available when he needs help. And Jack is a good fit —I was impressed when I worked with him. There's plenty of work to go around."

Sara snorted. "Then you saw a different side of Jack than I did. We didn't exactly hit it off."

Selena giggled and told April about Jack's baptism of Sara.

April turned to her with a grin. "Well, that doesn't sound fun."

"And our next meetings didn't go much better. If I'm going to get lucky in love here, it certainly won't be with him." A vision of the real-estate developer flashed through her head. *Wayne, on the other hand...* She focused on April. "Are you single?"

April's smile faded. "Yes."

Sara's ears perked up at the change. "Hmm. Sounds like a story there. If we're going to start a regular girls' night, we need gossip!"

"Oh, it's nothing dramatic." April dropped her gaze to her beer, hesitating. "There was a guy, but we never even got together before he fell in love with someone else. It wasn't meant to be."

Sara held up her beer in a toast. "Here we are, three gorgeous and fully employed women. Any man is lucky to have us. So, let's make sure at least one of us gets hooked up before too long!"

The next afternoon, Sara regarded the dim room before her. Located under the staircase leading to the spa, the small storage room was filled with miscellaneous dive equipment. The closet in the spa was quickly overflowing, which she had mentioned to Hope, and her sister had presented her with the key. "See if this room will work for you. I don't think Alex uses it for much, so I'm sure you can take it over."

A bare bulb illuminated storage shelves lining both walls. It would be perfect for storing the excess linens and supplies a growing spa was sure to need. She turned off the light and relocked the door. *But I'm not about to encroach on Alex's domain without talking to him first.*

Her relationship with her brother-in-law was somewhat delicate. The first time they met, Sara had more or less steamrolled right over him in the guise of protecting Hope. But after learning more about him, she had come to regret her behavior somewhat.

Not that I'd ever admit that to him, she thought with a smile.

Still, finding out that the man you had concluded was a suspiciously middle-aged beach bum was actually a highly decorated former Navy SEAL trying to heal from grievous mental and physical wounds was knowledge Sara was still adjusting to. She liked to think she wasn't intimidated by any man, but Alex made her pause.

And I'll set myself on fire before letting him know that.

Animated laughter distracted her as Alex and Zach walked down the pier, both wearing scuba tanks with fins tucked under their arms. She moved to the gear room and leaned against the doorframe as they divested themselves of their tanks and BCDs. "So are you officially a diver now, Zach?"

He looked up, and she had to laugh at his face-splitting grin.

"Nah, not yet. This was just my first pool session. I've got one more, plus my second classroom lecture before I can hit the ocean for my checkouts."

Sara straightened. "I didn't realize there was that much to it."

"Diving isn't exactly a natural activity," Alex added with a smile. "It takes a while to learn it all. But Zach is doing great—he won't have any trouble."

"I can't wait to see the new corals, and the nursery!"

Before the wedding, Alex had told her about his coral nursery and transplanted fragments now growing on the house reef. She had to admit it was fascinating. "Sounds like it won't be long."

Alex turned back to the boy. "You want to finish rinsing the gear? I need to talk to Sara." After Zach's nod, Alex joined her in the dim tunnel. "Hope told me you needed more storage for the spa. Does that storeroom work ok?"

She confirmed it was perfect and Alex promised to have it cleaned out by the end of the week. Pleased with her progress, Sara strolled to the end of the pier, standing near the edge as she enjoyed the shady palapa. The sound of bubbles breaking the surface came from her right as a diver headed toward the pier.

She swept her gaze over the calm ocean, her imagination working overtime. *It's hard to believe a whole roof is under there somewhere. I wonder what it looks like.* A hurricane had torn the entire roof off the long building that now housed the spa, and deposited it several hundred yards away, fully intact under forty feet of water.

The diver surfaced and climbed the ladder next to her. It was Jack, and he nodded to her coolly as he climbed onto the dock. Curiosity about the coral project warred with her desire to avoid him, but curiosity won. "Were you diving the coral nursery?"

He had been walking away but turned back. Water dripped down his face, beads sliding over his sharp cheekbones.

He's really not that bad looking. Maybe talking about diving will help us find some common ground.

"Yes. I've taken over a lot of the maintenance, making sure the fragments stay strong."

"How can you tell?"

He stretched his back and frowned, as if the answer was obvious. "If they lose all their color, turn white and die, it means they're not real healthy."

Sara reared back as a hot flush crept up her face. *Why do I even bother talking to this asshole?* "Well, excuse me for asking. Piss off, then." She swept past him as she stormed back to the spa.

Chapter Eight

JACK GRABBED his sketchbook from the passenger seat, then slammed the door of his truck. He was irritated, mostly with himself. Hunching his shoulders, he had no trouble imagining his mother's stern frown at how he had just treated Sara. He skirted the lobby building and headed north on the beach. For once, Sara had asked him a legitimate, interested question, and he had blown her off.

No. Worse than blown off.

He'd been every bit as rude as she had been previously. And he *loved* the coral restoration project, fascinated with the prospect of keeping reefs regenerating and healthy. But Sara never failed to put him on the defensive. *You try and figure that woman out, Mama.* But this time he'd been firmly in the wrong.

Putting the perplexing Sara out of his mind, Jack studied the area as he reached the narrow spit of land at the north end of the bay. His artist's eye had zeroed in on this piece of land almost from his first day at Half Moon Bay Resort, and now he finally had time to check it out.

After picking his way carefully over the sharp rocks, he stopped halfway out. The breeze ruffled his hair as a smile spread across his face. *I knew it!* The spit had an incredible view, both out to sea and toward the resort back to his left. He found a flat rock and settled onto it, sitting cross-legged as he opened his sketchbook.

Charcoal pencil in hand, he let his gaze relax and the scene came to him. He immediately focused on the pier, with the complex of buildings halfway down and *Surface Interval* tied at the end. He began sketching before he was even aware of it, and soon lost himself in the soothing activity.

After the skeleton of the scene was drawn, he began drawing a form between the palapa and dive shop. He let his hand move freely, without conscious thought. At first, it was a mystery, but a small smile formed on Jack's face as the figure revealed itself as a mermaid. He continued, drawing full breasts and long, flowing hair that a man couldn't help running his hands through.

Then he opened his eyes wide. The figure was unquestionably Sara—even though he'd never seen her breasts. But that hadn't stopped him from noticing them. Not by a long shot.

The sound of footsteps came from behind him. "A mermaid at Half Moon Bay, huh?" asked a gravelly voice.

Startled, Jack whipped around. An elderly man stood in a yellow-and-brown plaid shirt and wrinkled brown trousers that were only slightly less dark than the skin of his face. He had snowy white hair and his face was deeply lined, but he had a kind expression. "Sorry. Didn't mean to scare you."

"I didn't even hear you come up." Jack flushed as he glanced at Sara the Mermaid, and he closed his book. "I was just messing around."

The man raised his brows. "Just messin', huh? Looked like a good drawin' to me. Haven't seen you out here before."

Why shouldn't I be? I work for the resort. But he wasn't about to be rude to the old man—his mother's frown was still prominent in his mind. "I haven't been on the island that long. I work for Half Moon Bay, so I figured I'd come out to this point and look around. It's got a great view."

"That it does. And a fellow artist is always welcome out here. But just so you know, this isn't part of Half Moon Bay Resort. I own this little bit of land."

Jack rocketed to his feet. Being interrupted while sketching was one thing, but finding out he was trespassing was quite another. He was from Texas, after all. Wars had been started over less. "Oh, I didn't realize! I'm sorry."

The old man laughed and held out a hand. "Hold on there, son. It's quite all right. I'm Dexter Ridgeway. Pleased to meet you." Jack shook his gnarled hand, the palm rough and calloused.

"Jack Powell."

"What do you do over at Half Moon Bay?"

Jack told him about being a divemaster and splitting his time between the two shops.

"It's hard to make ends meet. I understand just fine. My family has owned this land for generations. But it's been whittled away over the years, and this sliver is all that's left. I like to come out here with my oils and paint sometimes."

Jack noted Dexter's empty hands. "But not today?"

"No. Just out here reminiscing, you might say. Just know you're welcome out here any time, as long as you clean up after yourself."

"Thanks, and you don't have to worry about that."

Dexter looked him straight in the eye. "I know I don't—I'm a fair judge of character. Maybe I'll see you out here soon, Jack. You take care now." With a nod, the man carefully made his way over the iron shore spit and disappeared into the jungle just behind.

He came out here just to leave again? Jack rubbed the back of his neck, sure he had interrupted whatever Dexter had intended. Shaking off the encounter, he opened his sketchbook again, a flush rising at the mermaid front and center in the drawing. But none of his pencils had erasers. He was stuck with the image unless he wanted to throw away the whole page. And he believed strongly that all art came from a place of truth. There was a reason he had drawn Sara. He just didn't know what it was.

Maybe because she's a pain in the ass and drives me to distraction?

He bent his head to the task, and nearly two hours passed before he was done. He'd moved to different rocks a few times to change positions, making a mental note to pack a chair of some sort next time. But as the sun drifted toward the horizon, he closed the cover on his completed sketch and headed home with the vision of his drawing prominent in his mind. The pier was sharply defined, as was the boat tied at the end of it. And in the middle, a mermaid named Sara was unquestionably the focal point of the sketch.

As soon as Sara got home from work, she headed straight for the shower. After washing away her irritation with Jack, she circled her long, wet hair into a messy bun and pulled on a pair of comfy yoga pants. She rifled through her T-shirts until she found the perfect one. Marissa had presented this treasure to her last Christmas, shortly after Sara's breakup with her boyfriend. They hadn't been together long and weren't terribly serious, but Sara had assumed they had an exclusive relationship. Until she glanced at his phone and saw all the sexts with his other girlfriend.

He hadn't kept many belongings at her place, but the paltry

amount hadn't stopped Sara from flinging open her front window and throwing every one of them into the wintry Charleston rain. And that had been that. A week later, on Christmas Eve, Marissa had presented her with an oversized pink T-shirt that read in a gold glittery font, *Don't You Wish Your Girlfriend Was Hot Like Me!* There was no question it was accompanying her to St. Croix.

Now in a much better mood, she grabbed her tablet and padded to the immaculate and intimidating kitchen, determined to conquer it. A faint thump sounded from downstairs, letting her know her neighbor was home. She hadn't yet been around to make an introduction, but it was on her list.

Prior investigations of the refrigerator had revealed two large hunks of cheese. Cheddar, which she recognized, and something mysterious named Gruyere, which she didn't. But an idea had begun to germinate, and after verifying she had a bag of elbow pasta in her pantry, all that was needed was a recipe.

She picked up her tablet to google a recipe with the cryptic Gruyere. Multiple pages resulted. "Ok, now I'm in business. Even I should be able to make macaroni and cheese."

Half an hour later, she had two large piles of grated cheese and one extremely sore arm. After glancing through the ingredients, she started pulling together the remaining items, thoroughly pleased with herself now. "Two cups of milk." She pulled open the refrigerator and scanned the door. Many items were neatly arranged, but no milk. The interior shelves didn't contain any, either. Her shoulders slumped at the memory of her drinking the last of the container the previous day.

There was a small market a mile away, but another thump from below gave her a different idea. "It might be cliché, but what better reason to meet my new neighbor?" She gave a momentary pause to consider her decidedly casual appearance, then shrugged. *Who cares? It's not like it's anyone I know.*

After grabbing a large measuring cup, she slipped into flip-flops, trotted down the steps, and knocked on the door. There was a doorbell, but knocking was friendlier. The sound of shuffling feet approached from the other side, and Sara fixed an expectant smile on her face as the door opened. The smile crashed to the floor when Jack stood facing her.

Oh shit! Are you kidding me?

His face went slack, and his jaw dropped as he stared at her. The two of them were silent for a long moment.

"Uh, hi, Sara."

She blinked rapidly, trying to recover her composure. "I came downstairs to borrow a cup of milk. You live here?"

"Yeah. For a couple of months now. So, you're my upstairs neighbor?" He just stood there, as if he were in shock.

A hot flush inflamed her face. "Yes. Sorry, I didn't mean to bother you. I'll head to the store." She was turning away when he called out.

"Sara, of course you can have some milk. There's no reason to go all the way to the market. Come on in."

With her face still mimicking the surface of the sun, she stepped over the threshold and stood in the doorway. Before her was a duplicate of her own apartment. Jack's furniture was a very dark gray, and the entire area was neat and clean. Several charcoal drawings were scattered over the coffee table, and a closed sketchpad lay on the kitchen table. She schooled her face as she studied them, shocked that he had a creative bent.

He's an artist? And a pretty good one, from the looks of these.

Jack returned to her with an open gallon of milk, walking with a soft, confident stride. A small smile lit his face. "What are you making?"

Sara stared at him. She'd noticed his large brown eyes before, but his thick hair and handsome features hadn't fully registered until now. But those incredibly thick eyelashes!

"Huh?" *God, what is wrong with me? I can't stand this guy. Why am I all tongue-tied?*

"The milk. What are you making?"

"Oh. Macaroni and cheese."

He grinned. "Kraft or Velveeta?"

Damn. Nice smile too.

Despite her best intentions, a smile escaped in return. "Neither, I'll have you know. I'm making it from scratch."

"Ah. A gourmet, then." He took her measuring cup and walked back to the kitchen, placing it on the counter before pouring.

She followed, folding her arms on the cool quartz surface, and trying not to be charmed by his soft Texas twang. "Not really. My kitchen scares me to death, so I'm trying to show it who's boss."

Jack laughed, warm and carefree, and Sara wanted to hear it again. He met her gaze, breathing a low sigh. "I'm glad you're here. I owe you an apology. Again. I was out of line this afternoon, and I've been feeling bad about it. I guess I've apologized for dumping water on you and almost breaking your nose, so what's one more?"

Sara arched a brow. "Well, technically, you haven't apologized for almost breaking my nose."

"Can one apology cover two idiotic moves?"

She tilted her head back and forth. "Hmm, debatable. But I'll let it slide. Maybe you should stay on that side of the counter, just to be safe."

His eyes grew warm and the heat in her face started heading south. She dug her thumbnail into her thigh. *Stop it! He'll probably trip you next!*

He dropped his gaze to her breasts, and his smile widened as he quickly raised his eyes back to hers. The warm flush fled, and Sara was getting ready to rip his head off when he said,

"Nice shirt."

And just like that, the heat of anger turned to embarrassment. She was standing there in a messy bun, leggings, and that ridiculous T-shirt. And no make-up. She did her best to recover the situation. "It was a Christmas present from my best friend. She was trying to cheer me up after a breakup, but it's ancient history now." She fixated on his brown eyes, and he stared back confidently, with a kind expression. Finally, Sara wrenched her gaze to the measuring cup and pulled it toward her.

"Gourmet mac and cheese, huh?"

She shrugged. "It seemed like a sensible first choice. Not sure I'd go so far as gourmet, though."

"You know, I've got a reputation as a great mac and cheese taste tester." Then he opened his eyes wide, as if he couldn't believe he had just said that. He straightened, and the spell was broken.

Sara lifted the full measuring cup. "Let's not get ahead of ourselves. We've managed to have one conversation without a disaster. I think we should leave it at that."

He nodded, and she was pleased to see a blush rise over his face. "Probably a good idea. Otherwise, I might spill it all over you."

Sara turned back just before leaving. "Tell you what. If it turns out to be edible, I'll leave a container for you at work tomorrow."

Chapter Nine

THE NEXT MORNING, Sara's first stop was the lobby, giving front-desk clerk Martine a friendly hello as she passed by. Her pleasant expression fell as soon as she eyed the office. Hope was already at work, but general manager Patti Thomas's desk was empty. Sara closed the door and sat down in the chair in front of her sister's desk, crossing her arms.

Hope glanced up. "Good morning. We're having a shut-door meeting?"

"You set me up, didn't you?"

Hope's face registered nothing but blank surprise, and she was the worst liar in the world. Sara had almost called her as soon as she returned from Jack's apartment, but a cooling-off period wasn't a bad idea, so she finished dinner instead. A container of the mac and cheese was buried in her purse, to be left in the restaurant kitchen for Jack's lunch, as promised. She was trying not to think about the ramifications of that.

"Sara, what are you talking about?"

"You know nothing about my downstairs neighbor? Really?"

Hope's face was blank. "No, why should I?"

Sara narrowed her eyes, inspecting her sister carefully. She reluctantly concluded Hope was telling the truth and relaxed her shoulders. "I had to borrow some milk last night. I went downstairs to meet my neighbor and kill two birds with one stone."

"Eminently practical. But I still don't see why you're accusing me of a set-up."

"My downstairs neighbor is Jack."

At first, Hope just stared at her. Then she sucked her bottom lip in between her teeth, trying to keep a neutral expression. Sara scowled and Hope finally lost it, raising both hands to her face as she burst into laughter. "Oh my God! That's hilarious. Did he have any water buckets handy?"

"Well, I'm glad I can provide your comic entertainment for the day. I didn't find it funny."

"What did you do?"

"We stared at each other for a long time. I'm pretty sure he was as shocked as I was. But we managed to have a reasonably civil conversation, and I got my milk. And escaped bodily harm too."

"That sounds like progress."

"You really had no idea he lived there?"

Hope held up both hands, biting her cheek. "None, I swear! Alex processed his paperwork, and I doubt he even asked where Jack lived."

Mollified now, Sara stood. "Ok, you're forgiven."

"I didn't do anything!"

"That's why I'm letting you off so easily. I'd better get to work."

Turning her mind back to her job, Sara headed to the spa. Selena stood in the massage room, changing the sheets. Sara leaned against the open doorframe. "It's a crying shame we only have one massage table in here. I need to talk to Hope about that. At a romantic tropical resort, we need to offer couples massages."

"I've had plenty of requests for it."

"But we need another massage therapist for it, and there's not enough work to put someone else on the payroll. Do you know anyone who freelances and would be interested in extra work?"

Selena tucked a blanket around the table then turned to Sara. "I can think of several. And everyone's interested in extra cash."

With a nod, Sara moved to her station. She had a client arriving soon who wanted an updo and make-up for a tropical photo shoot. Sara frowned at the small area around her. *That's the biggest problem with this spa. It's not scalable.* The space might have been more than adequate as Alex's former one-bedroom apartment, but as a spa it was *small.* But Hope made do with what she had available, and Sara didn't know how to tell her it wasn't adequate.

Sara's final client, who was there for a mani-pedi, finished in the late afternoon. Selena had already left, so Sara locked up and strolled down the stairs, relishing the breeze drifting through her hair. A pair of divers were just climbing the ladder onto the pier, chattering together as Sara approached. "Good dive?"

"Fantastic!" said the woman, whose short brown hair dripped saltwater. "We dove the house reef. I've never seen an active restoration project before. You can see the new corals, and how the fish and other critters are incorporating them." The two headed toward the dive shop to rinse their dive gear.

Sara sat on a wooden bench that faced the house reef and northern crescent of Half Moon Bay. The prospect of diving was intriguing—especially seeing the coral project up close and personal. But that meant learning how to dive, which presented some complications.

Her musings were interrupted by her phone ringing with Marissa's ring tone, and a wide smile crossed her face. "Hello there. Do you miss me yet?"

"I do. Not least because my first haircut since you left didn't go so well. The woman you referred me to was booked solid, so I took a chance. It didn't pay off. How's life in the tropics?"

"It's going well. My apartment is beautiful, and there's even a pretty, white-sand beach. I'm going to paint the view soon. I'm at the resort right now, staring at the house reef."

"What's that?"

"Oh, just a coral reef that's close enough to dive right from the resort. I haven't actually snorkeled it, but it sounds pretty cool."

"Why snorkel? You can learn to dive now."

Sara hesitated. "Diving is sounding pretty appealing, actually. It's the getting certified part that might present some difficulties."

"Why? Didn't you say your hunkalicious brother-in-law was a dive instructor?"

"Yes, but Alex and I are still getting to know each other. I wasn't real easy on him to start, and I'm afraid he might drown me."

Marissa laughed. "Knowing you, he might feel the impulse, but I doubt he'd act on it. I don't think Hope would be very happy with him. What's the real reason, Sara?"

A small smile crossed her face. She never could get anything by Marissa. They'd been friends since high school, though Marissa didn't know any of the details of Alex's past. "Alex was a diver in the military. A very skilled diver. And Hope... you've met her. She's gorgeous and athletic and successful in everything. What if I'm terrible at it, and he has to flunk me?" She didn't want to say out loud that the prospect of being taught diving by a former SEAL intimidated the hell out of her.

"Is he an asshole or something?"

"No, it's not that. Though this would provide a perfect opportunity for a little payback for how I treated him last summer."

"I'm sure you could find another instructor. There's got to be more than one on St. Croix."

"Ah, the passive-aggressive approach. Just thumb my nose at him and learn from someone else."

"You could just tell them you felt it was a conflict of interest, or something."

Sara sighed, stretching her legs out. "We'll see. I don't have to decide today."

AFTER ENDING THE CALL, Sara strolled up the pier as she panned her gaze across the resort. The faint sounds of calypso music emanated from the thatch-roofed pool bar. Clark kept the volume low, so the music provided ambiance without being distracting. The infinity pool was in front of her, where Jack stood in waist deep water with a middle-aged woman who was nearly panting, her eyes enormous. Jack spoke to her in soothing tones, and the woman visibly relaxed. He patted her shoulder, and she nodded several times. Sara couldn't hear the conversation, but the woman immediately responded to his calming manner. She replaced the regulator in her mouth and the pair kneeled below the surface.

Sara continued, passing the lobby toward the small parking lot and her RAV4. Her mind returned to the prospect of learning to dive. *Jeez, are these my two choices for instruction? A*

Navy SEAL who will probably make my class hell, and a guy who can't stop causing me problems?

She got in her car and headed home, still thinking about Jack and the woman he was teaching. *I might have to choose between the lesser of two evils. I wonder if he liked the macaroni and cheese.*

"I don't disagree with you," Hope said as she leaned against the glass counter in the dive shop. "But the resort doesn't have a bunch of empty buildings just sitting around, so I had to use Alex's old apartment."

It was the next morning and Sara was waiting for her client. She had popped in to talk with Hope, who worked in the dive shop while the boat was out on dive trips. "I get it," Sara said. "I just wanted you to know. I think getting this spa to be profitable could be a problem with its current footprint."

"Well, we can certainly install another massage table in the room and on deck, especially if Selena can find someone to work when we get couples' massages scheduled."

Movement caught Sara's eye, and she glanced out the glass door at the boat approaching the pier. "They're back, and my client should be along any time. I'll get out of the way."

Moving to the edge of the wooden dock near the stairs, she enjoyed watching the hive of activity surrounding the boat. That day Alex was captain, with Jack and April as divemasters. Sara had spent a couple of lunches with April in the restaurant kitchen.

After the guests headed toward their bungalows, Jack and April each took an armful of wetsuits to dunk in the freshwater tanks, chatting amiably back and forth. Sara's attention sharpened when April straightened and looked back toward *Surface*

Interval, and a small smile crossed her face. Then it fell, replaced by a wide-eyed expression of pure, unadulterated longing.

O-ho! Is April crushing on one of the guests?

With gleeful anticipation, Sara turned, already working out how she could set April up with the guest. Alex strode confidently down the pier and a wide smile crossed his face as he looked toward the dive shop. Sara's heart dropped to her feet as she glanced back at April. There was no mistaking it. She was looking straight at Alex. Hope stepped out of the dive shop and headed straight for her husband, and it was clear Alex didn't even see April. The two embraced as he boosted Hope to eye level for a kiss. Sara glanced back at April, who now had a neutral, guarded look on her face. She bent to the open trough, swirling the wetsuits in the soapy water with Jack.

Oh my God! There's no way I misconstrued that.

The memory flashed of their girls' night out, when April had mentioned the man she was interested in who had chosen someone else. Sara straightened, focusing on April with laser-beam intensity. *Oh, no. This won't do at all. Time to get her fixed up with someone, pronto. Does Hope know?*

Then her gaze zeroed in on Jack, standing next to April. *He's never mentioned a girlfriend, and they have a lot in common. Opportunity is knocking!* Sara approached the pair, leaning casually against the side of the building. "Good morning, you two?"

"Really good," April said with a big smile. "We saw a pod of dolphins on our surface interval."

Alex and Hope joined them. "They played in the wake of the boat for a long time," he said. "I had a great time driving today."

Hope patted his chest. "I need to get back in the dive shop. I'll see you later." With a wave, she disappeared inside the door.

April was watching Alex again, and Sara pounced. "Well, Jack, you're lucky to have someone as nice as April to show you the ins and outs of the operation here. You two look like you work really well together."

He and April gave her polite nods but didn't say anything.

"I'm just saying a good working relationship is hard to find. You two are lucky." Then Sara's client walked around the corner. "Time for me to run. Alex, you treat these two right. They make a great team." With a regal nod, she turned and led her client to the stairs.

One final glance revealed Alex staring straight at her, his brow furrowed. She gave him a jaunty wave before heading up the stairs.

April and Jack are perfect for each other. Operation Sara to the Rescue is officially commencing.

Chapter Ten

JACK UNSLUNG A BCD from his shoulder and hung it up as April replaced the coiled regulators on their pegs. She glanced at her watch. "I think that's about it. Now I get to move on to my next job."

He smiled at her. "Yeah, I've got two gigs too. See you next time."

As April moved out the door, Jack's thoughts returned to Sara, and he shook his head. Was she pushing him toward April for some reason? He liked April but didn't have any romantic feelings toward her. *Why would Sara even care?*

He still couldn't get over her being his neighbor. She was the last person he'd expected when he'd opened his front door the other night. *At least you managed to keep from causing her bodily harm.* Then he winced. *Though it wasn't exactly smooth to invite yourself over for dinner. What got into me?* That was the mystery. The words had tumbled out of his mouth before the thought had fully formed. At least they were on more cordial footing now.

He made his way to the dive shop, where Alex and Hope stood behind the counter. Alex nodded, and Jack stopped across from him. "I was just looking at the dive schedule for the next week," Alex said. "We've got two full-day trips scheduled. Robert told me he's got a photo shoot, so do you want the hours?"

"That would be great."

"I'll put you down, then."

The bell above the door jingled and Robert walked in with Patti hot on his heels. He carried a large, flat cardboard box, and shot Alex and Hope a brilliant smile. "How 'bout that? Just the two I wanted to see!" He placed the cardboard box on the counter and nodded to Jack.

Patti peered over his shoulder. "He's bein' very mysterious. Just said he had a present for you two and wanted my opinion."

Hope wrapped an arm around Alex's waist and pulled him close, saying, "Well, don't keep us all in suspense."

Still smiling, Robert carefully opened the package with a box knife, revealing something flat covered in bubble wrap. "Everyone ready?" Eyebrows arched, he glanced around the assemblage.

Jack grinned as Patti poked Robert in the side with one ebony index finger and said, "Get on with it already."

With a flourish, Robert broke apart the taped bubble wrap and held up a large glass photograph. The room went silent as everyone studied the photo of Hope and Alex on their wedding day. Robert had taken the picture as Alex boosted Hope into the air before him, but Jack's attention was drawn to the dress-white Navy uniform Alex wore.

He's ex-military?

In the photo, Hope was in the process of putting Alex's peaked cap on her head, but all Jack could see were the rows of medals on Alex's chest. He also wore two large pins above and below them. Jack turned his gaze to the couple, and both wore identical stunned smiles.

Patti raised a hand to her ample breast. "Just look at you two. Oh, Robert. That is amazin'!"

Hope finally found her voice. "It really is. Thank you so much."

In the picture, Hope and Alex gazed at each other like nothing else existed in the universe. Jack had to admit it was an incredible portrait.

"You like it, then?" Robert beamed at their bewildered nods. "I knew I got a great photo when you two did this. I just needed to sort through them to find the perfect one."

"Great job, Robert," Jack said.

Patti drew herself upright, her natural confidence obvious to all. "This is goin' in the lobby. Front and center, next to the staff photos." Alex and Hope opened their mouths, but Patti pointed at them. "Don't you two argue with me! If you want one for your house, we'll have another made. I'm claimin' this one."

Alex grinned. "Ok, it's yours. I learned recently that arguing with women is not a good idea." Hope dug her elbow into his side, and he laughed.

Jack had already learned Patti was a force to be reckoned with. The gears turning in her head were almost visible, and Jack couldn't resist a smile as she pointed at Hope. "Underneath this, let's hang a framed copy of your magazine cover. It's perfect."

Hope turned to Alex with a faint smile. "And maybe we can hang another article too?"

Alex's smile faded, but he met her gaze.

"We're a team, remember?" Hope asked.

He hesitated for a long moment before saying, "Ok." He turned to Patti. "Boss Lady wants to frame my article and hang it too."

Jack had no idea what was going on, but he didn't interrupt as tears filled Patti's eyes. "I'm very happy to hear you say that,

Alex." Then she blinked several times, pulling herself together before patting Robert's shoulder. "Come on, then. Pack all this up and let's head to the lobby. We can decide where it goes, and I'll have Tommy hang it tomorrow."

Robert soon had the photo packaged up and Patti herded him out of the dive shop. Jack turned to Alex. "I didn't know you were in the Navy."

"Yeah. For over eighteen years."

"Pretty impressive medal collection, man."

A long look passed between him and Hope, and she gave him a tiny nod. He turned back to Jack, his expression serious. "I was a SEAL. It's not something I talk much about. I didn't keep it from you on purpose—it's not something that comes up in normal conversation. But a newspaper article came out earlier this year that talked all about it, so it's kind of common knowledge now. Though I wish otherwise."

Jack tried to keep his face neutrally interested. *Holy shit! A SEAL? No wonder those two guys in the bar split when he showed up.* And Mark's cryptic comment after the near fight made sense now too.

Some of his expression must have escaped, because Hope explained. "We had some trouble with an employee last fall. Charles pulled a gun and Alex had to disarm him, but got shot in the process. There was a trial, and he was sentenced to twenty years in prison. It was quite a news item on the island."

"I bet."

Alex still had his arm around Hope, but now he stood stiffly, his discomfort evident. Clearly there was more to the story, but Alex didn't want to talk about it.

"Well, I'm done for the day, so I'll head out," Jack said. "See you in a couple of days."

As Jack passed the bar on the way to his Ranger, he had to laugh at himself as the memory of the almost-bar fight came back to him. "Good thing I didn't ask Alex if he knew how to fight." Driving home, Jack concluded that maybe Half Moon Bay Resort wasn't always the peaceful oasis he had assumed it was.

ONCE HOME, Jack headed for his patio. The sun was nearing the horizon, and the palette of pink and lavender sky called to him. He ambled toward the small private beach behind the complex. The colors arced above him, nature's beauty on full display as he walked barefoot on the sand.

A woman stood facing away from him, applying a brush to a white canvas propped on an easel. He crossed to her, surprise growing when he recognized Sara. She was painting the sunset and ocean before them in vivid watercolors, and she clearly had talent. "I can see why you were inspired to paint. This is a pretty spectacular sunset."

She squeaked and whirled around, her long hair flying. "You scared the hell out of me, Jack!"

Heat spread across his cheeks. *Jeez, I can't do anything right, can I?* "Sorry. I should have made some noise."

For once, she didn't look pissed off as she turned back to her canvas. "It's ok."

Emboldened, he stood by her side, studying the painting. "That's really good. I didn't know you could paint."

"There's a lot you don't know about me." But there was no venom in her voice. It was more of a teasing tone. "I saw several sketches when I was in your apartment the other night. Those yours?"

"Yeah. I've always loved to draw, especially underwater scenes. I like the challenge of bringing such a colorful world to life using only black and white."

Sara set her brush on the easel, darting a quick glance at him before looking down again in a quick flash of uncertainty. Jack was intrigued. So far, she had lived up to Alex's nickname of Hurricane Sara, and this was the first hint of anything but confidence or anger. She took a breath. "Speaking of the underwater world, I've been thinking about getting certified to dive. I'd really like to see that coral project for myself."

He smiled, determined to be encouraging this time. "You live in the right place for it. Shouldn't be too hard."

"I hope not, but we'll see." She paused again, picking up her brush, only to set it back down again. Then she met his gaze head-on. "Could you certify me?"

That was the last thing he'd been expecting. "Me?" He rubbed between his nose and upper lip, trying not to smile. "Uh, you realize your brother-in-law is a rather well-qualified instructor, don't you?"

The light was fading, but there was enough to see the pink on her cheeks as she narrowed her eyes. "What makes you think that?"

His smile broadened. He was impressed that she wanted to verify what he knew before saying more. "Alex told me about his background. That he was a SEAL. He's probably the most overqualified dive instructor in the Caribbean, you know."

She turned toward the sunset. "I know. That's the problem. I've never been very athletic, and Alex and I have a somewhat complicated history. I just thought it might be easier for both of us if I learned from someone else. I saw you with a student in the pool the other day—that's why I thought I'd ask you."

Jack was drawn toward this quiet, almost self-conscious Sara. She wore a pastel sundress that left her shoulders bare, and he had a strong urge to stroke his fingers across her supple skin. He blinked, firmly turning his mind back to the conversation. "I was teaching an intro scuba class. I'm a divemaster, not an instructor, so I can't do an open water certification. The coral nursery and transplants on the house reef would be within the depth limits of what I can teach, but that would be a waste, Sara. If you got fully certified, you could dive with anyone. Like Hope." *Maybe even me.*

Her shoulders fell. "Oh. I didn't realize you couldn't teach too."

A small ball of warmth spread through his chest. "I've seen Alex with students and new divers. I'm sure you'd do fine. Tell you what—if you decide to go ahead, I'll help you with any skills you have trouble with. How's that sound?"

She studied him, and butterflies tickled his stomach when a small smile appeared on her face. The orange sunset reflected in her warm brown eyes, and he couldn't look away. *Please say yes.*

"Ok, you've got a deal. But I want you to remember this conversation for posterity. In case Alex decides to fit me with a nice pair of concrete shoes."

Chapter Eleven

DECEMBER...

Sara walked into the resort restaurant. A cheery blinking Christmas tree stood in one corner, wrapped boxes tucked around its base, but the festive atmosphere didn't calm the anxious ball in her stomach. Hope and Alex were already seated at their corner table. She sat with a thump and took a sip of the iced tea Hope had already ordered for her.

"We should have lunch more often." Hope beamed, gazing between Alex and Sara.

Alex shot her a rueful smile. "We have a hard enough time coordinating our schedules. It's a minor miracle all three of us managed to get together in the middle of the day."

"Especially me," Sara added. "It just depends on when I have clients scheduled."

Hope's broad smile plummeted off her face. "Well, aren't you two the wet blankets?"

"You're right. This is everything I've ever dreamed of," Sara said. "Better?"

"Now you're just being sarcastic. And it's the holidays too," Hope said, then conversation paused as they ate their lunches.

Hope caught Sara's eye and raised a brow, but she replied with a tiny head shake. *Nope, I'll bring it up.* Sara had enlisted her sister earlier for moral support, which was why Hope was nearly vibrating in her chair.

Alex tossed his napkin on the table, finished. "Ok, I saw that look and can tell when two Collinses are in cahoots about something. What's up?"

Ok, here we go. Sara set her fork down, meeting his gaze. "I think your coral-restoration project is really interesting, and I've been thinking about learning to dive."

He broke into a small smile. "And did you have any instructors in mind?"

"Well, you're the only one I know, so that puts you at the head of the line."

Alex laughed. "There's an ego boost!"

Hope touched his forearm. "She's a little nervous about it."

His eyes softened. "Most people are. That's normal."

"Not nervous exactly, more concerned," Sara said. "But if Zach can learn to dive, I certainly should be able to."

"He did great," Alex said. "The kid's stronger than he looks."

Sara paused, spinning her glass on the table, reluctant to look up. "I'm a little worried about the physical aspects of it. I'm not the most athletic person in the world."

"You'll be fine, though you might want to start swimming regularly. There's a swim test and you have to tread water for ten minutes."

"There's a pool at my apartment complex. I started doing laps this morning." Taking a deep breath, Sara raised her head, narrowing her eyes at him. "Do you promise you won't make the class impossible or miserable? You won't try to turn me into some knockoff SEAL or something?"

Alex leaned back in his chair with a grin. "Take it easy, Sara. It'll be completely conventional. No drown-proofing classes, I promise."

Hope gaped at him. "*Drown-proofing?* What on earth does that entail?" Then she held out a hand. "Never mind. I don't even want to know."

"More to the point, neither do I," Sara added. "Especially in regard to me."

"You'll do great. I haven't lost a student in a long time."

Hope smacked him. "Stop that. It doesn't help."

"Ok, ok. All kidding aside, we'll take it as slowly as you need to. I don't certify anyone unless they're confident in their skills. I'll get you the course materials and we can get started next week. Can you adjust your schedule to have a few hours free in the afternoons?"

"Yes. Don't make me regret this, Alex."

He sighed. "Would you relax? Sara, I'm pretty good at this. Plus, I like being married to your sister. If something bad happened to you, she'd strangle me."

THE NEXT DAY, Sara stood behind the counter in the spa, working on an idea. The resort was too small to fill their schedule with only guests. They needed outside people too, and the answer was to advertise more to locals. She drummed her fingers on the glass counter.

We're not busy enough right now, yet we don't have the capacity to expand if things take off. But we'll just have to cross that bridge when we get there.

A separate name for the facility had been Sara's first priority

—Hibiscus Spa—and Hope's public relations firm had made new advertising brochures and a beautiful sign. To appeal to outside clients, the spa had to differentiate itself from the resort. She had also set up a dedicated Facebook page and was making regular posts. Now, with a satisfied smile, she posted a 50% off flash sale for mani-pedis. "Let's see if that brings anyone in."

She moved her gaze to the window, revealing April as she carried an armful of regulators from the boat. It was lunchtime, and Sara had a one-hour break until her next client. She frowned at April. Operation Sara to the Rescue wasn't proceeding very effectively. April appeared to have a solid working relationship with Jack. But Sara couldn't detect any sparks flying despite several conversations spent trying to interest April in the new divemaster.

Which was ridiculous. Jack was handsome, reliable, and even pleasant to April. *I just need to keep at it.*

After her stomach gave an angry growl, she rose and descended the stairs from the spa as Alex and April walked toward the dive shop. He saw her and called out, "Hang on. I'll be right back with your course packet."

She chatted with April until he returned and handed her a long, blue zipper pouch. Sara accepted it with a small thrill, and a smile rose on her face.

"Learning to dive, huh? You'll love it." April grinned at her, then turned her smile to the man next to her. "And rumor has it, Alex is a decent instructor too."

Sara's heart lurched as Hope's face flashed into her mind. April's comment had been innocent, but Sara wasn't going to pass up an opportunity, and thought quickly. "I'm looking forward to it. Though I'm sorry you had to put up with him today, instead of Jack."

"It's good to have female divemasters," Alex said. "Too much testosterone makes the boat smell."

April laughed a little too loudly. "Ah, I'm used to it. Occupational hazard. There's a lot more men than women in this business."

Sara met April's gaze. "Jack's doing a really good job. You think so?"

"Yeah, he's fine." April shrugged, then cast a glance at the gear room. "I'm going to hang the regs and head to lunch."

When Sara turned back, Alex was staring straight at her with a decidedly speculative look in his eye. "I'm not the most perceptive guy in the world, but I have to ask. Are you trying to hook up Jack and April?"

Sara grabbed his upper arm and steered him toward the other side of the pier. "Maybe I am."

Alex rolled his eyes. "Why would you do that? Just stay out of it—things are finally settling down around here."

"Why?" she hissed. "I'm trying to distract her. Because the man April *really* wants just happens to be recently married."

Alex stilled and his eyes became cool. "Are you accusing me of something?"

Sara sighed and waved a hand at him. "Of course not. You might not have feelings for her, but I can assure you it's *not* mutual. I simply thought it would be better all-around if April found someone else."

"Look, I can't help how she feels, but she has never once made any inappropriate advance toward me. Even when I was single. And she's very aware I'm in love with Hope." He raked a hand through his short hair, his wedding ring flashing in the sun. "Why am I defending myself to you, anyway?"

"Calm down. I'm just trying to solve the problem in a way that makes everyone happy. Is that so awful?"

"Yes. You just can't resist stirring things up, can you? If this causes any issues and one of them quits, you can find me a new divemaster." Glaring, he stalked off.

"I only have your best interests at heart, you know," she said sweetly to his back.

Putting the Alex-April-Jack triangle from her mind, Sara's stomach reminded her it was time to eat, and she headed to the kitchen. The resort provided lunch for all employees and sous chef Pauline whipped up Sara a grilled chicken breast. April sat at the employee table, already eating.

"How many dive shops do you work for?" Sara asked, sitting down.

"Two. I've been trying to get on full-time, but it's not easy. I work as a server too. To be honest, I might move on at some point. The long-time employees on this island tend to stick around. My other dive shop needs more help for the next few months, so that will help for now."

Sara saw her opening. "Then I imagine Jack will be working more here. Especially with Robert doing more photography."

April nodded. "He wants more hours, so he should be happy."

Sara gave her a sly smile. "But you won't be working with him as much, which is too bad. I think you two look cute together. He is pretty good looking... those huge brown eyes! Though those eyelashes are completely wasted on a man."

April sat back and met her gaze with a hard stare. "Jeez, Sara. If you think he's so gorgeous, why don't you date him? I'm not interested."

"Me? Don't be ridiculous."

"What's ridiculous about it?"

"He damn near kills me every time we're around each other!" *Though that isn't exactly true, is it?*

April grinned. "Yet here you are, alive and kicking. I don't know, Sara. Maybe the lady doth protest too much."

"Oh, stop quoting Shakespeare at me."

"Then why are you blushing?"

Sara straightened, lifting her chin and ignoring the heat in her face. And her fluttering heartbeat. "Because it's hot in here. Why else?"

But as she strolled down the pier, Sara couldn't deny that the idea of dating Jack wasn't quite so horrendous anymore. Maybe even slightly attractive.

Maybe.

A FEW EVENINGS LATER, Sara stood on the small beach at her apartment, lost in the soothing motions of painting the scene before her. It was the same landscape as before, but a different focus this time. The colors were more muted tonight, so she focused on the hues of the ocean instead of the sky.

Behind her, quiet footsteps were followed by a soft cough. "Mind if I join you?"

She turned and Jack stood with his sketch book. He wore a dark green polo shirt and gray cargo shorts. It didn't escape her notice that he had coughed so he wouldn't startle her, and a tiny smile escaped. "Be my guest."

He sat cross-legged on the sand and began sketching. She glanced at his progress and saw he focused his drawing on the ocean too. She added a wide swath of indigo to the horizon of her painting. "April told me she's going to work more at one of her other jobs, so you might get more hours at Half Moon Bay."

"That's good news. I like the way Alex runs things, so I'll take whatever I can get. Serenity is a little spendy, but I couldn't resist living so close to the ocean."

"I like it too. I've never lived on the sea like this before." She watched his hand as he drew. His movements were confident and gentle, as if he was trying to coax the sunset onto his page, rather than force the image. Experience had taught her forcing art never worked.

"Is Hope your only sibling?"

"Yes. Our father left when we were kids and she practically raised me."

He stopped drawing to look at her. "Wow. I'm sorry."

She shrugged a little. "It's fine. Water under the bridge at this point."

"How do you like working for her?"

Sara paused, twirling her brush as she gazed at the horizon. "It's been a good change for me. I've never been one to put down roots, so I didn't need much convincing when Hope offered me a job here. We'll see how it works out in the long run."

He went back to his drawing, but Sara noticed his mouth had tightened a little. "Maybe it will grow on you—I love it here. Being a divemaster is great. Well, most of the time. Speaking of diving, you start your certification soon, don't you?"

"In a few days. I've been swimming every morning. I'm kind of surprised how much I like it."

"The swim tests for open water certification aren't too bad. Remember, you can come to me if you have any problems with your class."

She turned to find him staring straight at her. He had a full, generous mouth. Why had she never noticed that? A delicious flutter ran through her as their gazes held. The idea of dating him was definitely getting more attractive. "I'll do that. Thanks."

Chapter Twelve

JACK DRAGGED a hand over his sweaty forehead before removing his BCD and regulator from the tank. *Surface Interval* was now quiet after the afternoon trip. It had been humid and still all day, as if the clouds above were holding their collective breaths, waiting to explode. But the threatened rain held off. Family man Tommy was hosing down the boat, eager to get home. He'd been attending a local boxing gym, and his rash guard was a little looser than it used to be.

"You want me to finish washing things down?" Jack asked.

Tommy smiled at him. "Nah. I'm almost done. Thanks for workin' this afternoon."

"Sure. I'm filling in so Alex can give Sara her first classroom session." Jack shook his head, then laughed. "I'm still not sure whether being taught by a former SEAL is a really good thing or a really bad thing."

"She'll be fine. Alex knows what he's doin'."

"I don't doubt that. I still find it hard to believe—that he was a SEAL. He's so calm and easygoing, though that night up at the bar I sure saw a different side of him. Hope mentioned something about trouble with a former employee. Sounds like you guys had some excitement."

Tommy's smile faded as he regarded Jack. "And what did Alex say?"

"Not much. He doesn't talk a whole lot about himself."

"No, you're right about that." Tommy cocked his head. "Have you been up to the lobby since I hung their weddin' photo?"

"No, why?"

"You might want to check it out. I'm not goin' to say anythin' if Alex didn't, but there's an article on the wall that might interest you."

Man, this is a tight-knit bunch... Jack was impressed, and Alex had mentioned something about an article when he saw the wedding portrait. "It's no big deal, but thanks."

THIRTY MINUTES LATER, Jack was carrying his equipment toward his truck. He worked the next day at Ocean Surf, so he had to carry his gear back and forth, which was a pain in the ass. As he tossed the duffel bag in the truck bed, his gaze was drawn toward the lobby.

Why not?

He climbed the stairs and entered the bright, welcoming building. Front-desk clerk Martine gave him a warm smile, her even white teeth contrasting with her light-brown skin.

"I'm here to check out the new addition to the staff wall."

Martine's smile widened. "You can't miss it. You wouldn't believe how many guests head straight for that picture. It's like a tractor beam."

Jack crossed the lobby and experienced that for himself. Even though there were individual photos of all the staff hanging, including him, the large glass print of Alex and Hope dominated. A faint smile came to Jack's face, unable to resist its power. And he was happy for them, though maybe just a little sad that he hadn't found the same fulfillment in his own marriage.

Don't go down that rabbit hole...

Instead, he moved his gaze below the large photo where two smaller frames hung. On the left was a copy of *Entrepreneur Today* magazine, and he startled at the figure of Hope on the cover, standing on the pier. Then he looked to the right and understood immediately what Tommy had meant. It was the article he had referenced, including a photo of Alex in dress blues. Jack began to read.

He had managed to close his gaping mouth three-quarters of the way through it, and read the final sentence three times. *Monroe was contacted repeatedly for this article. His only reply was, "no comment."*

"Didn't stop you from printing it, though, did it? Bastard reporter..." Jack murmured the words softly to himself, now understanding why everyone was so protective of Alex.

Not just a SEAL, he's a goddamn war hero.

After waving goodbye to Martine, he headed toward his truck. He glanced at his duffel, but his yellow and black fins weren't there. "Shit. I left them on the boat." Spinning on his heel, he turned toward the pier. As he trotted up the stairs, Sara and Alex were waving goodbye. She headed toward the palapa as Alex walked up the pier, and the two men nodded to each other.

"Forgot my fins. I need them at Ocean Surf tomorrow."

Alex stopped. "You want to use our equipment when you're here? That would save you from having to move everything back and forth. I can set some aside for you."

"That would be great! Thanks." He thought about mentioning the article but didn't want to sound like a fanboy.

And it was pretty clear Alex didn't welcome the notoriety, even if he had allowed the article to be displayed. If he wasn't going to call attention to it, neither would Jack. Alex continued on his way and Jack headed toward the boat.

Sara sat under the palapa on the swing, using one foot to propel herself back and forth, and his stomach did a flip-flop. He'd had a dream about her the previous night. A very naughty dream. But during their conversation on the beach the other evening, she had said she wasn't too serious about her new home, which gave him pause. Still, he was drawn to her. "Hey, Sara," he said as he stepped on board and scooped his fins under one arm.

"You're still here? I thought you would have knocked off a while ago."

He returned to the swing and sat next to her, setting his fins on the dock. She was still dressed for work in slacks and a colorful blouse. Her long hair was curled, and a dark red lipstick adorned her full mouth. "Yeah, I stopped by the lobby to check out the Alex and Hope show," he said with a smile to let her know he wasn't being disparaging. "They're an impressive pair."

Sara sighed. "Yes, they are."

"How was your first classroom session?"

She was subdued tonight. "Ok. There's more theory than I thought. Physics—seriously?"

He laughed. "You'd be amazed at what water pressure can do. And how much it increases the deeper you dive."

"Yeah, we went over that. I just have to keep reminding myself that plenty of people have succeeded in this. Including Hope, of course."

"You seem plenty smart to me. Is there any part you need help with?"

Please say yes...

"No, it's just that, once again, I'm following in Hope's footsteps. And trying to measure up."

She hesitated, watching the horizon, and he had to resist the urge to wrap an arm around her. This vulnerable side tugged at him hard. *Jack, she's Hope's sister and Alex's sister-in-law. This has trouble written all over it.* But his body didn't seem to mind at all. In fact, he found her damn near irresistible.

"It's worse because Alex is the one teaching me," she continued. "And there's no way I'll measure up in his eyes."

"Don't say that. I'm sure he's not comparing the two of you at all."

Sara turned to him, a flash of irritation igniting in her eyes. "Oh, give me a break. How could he not? Jack, have you seen my sister?"

He had no idea what that meant. "Um, yes."

"Then you know she's gorgeous. And successful. She could be a swimsuit model if she wanted to. And I'm... none of that."

Unable to resist, he reached out and lifted a lock of silky hair over her shoulder. She didn't pull away. "You're right about one thing. You're not Hope. You're Sara, and I happen to think you're not so terrible." *There's an understatement.*

She smiled and slid her eyes to his. Jack's heart pounded. "So you appreciate me now that you're not trying to kill me?"

He twitched the corner of his mouth. "Something like that. And stop comparing yourself to Hope. She doesn't have your spark, you know."

She leaned toward him, and he forced himself not to look at her mouth.

"Is that right?" she asked. "Better be careful. Sparks can light fires."

"Good thing we're surrounded by water, then. And how is it you're single?" Jack held his breath. *Is she going to bite my head off for asking that?* He didn't know her history, but he was pretty sure there wasn't a man in her life.

She kept the same soft, introspective tone. "I never wanted to be tied down. And I have yet to meet a man who changed my mind about that."

That fit with what she'd said previously. There was a connection between them now, but he wanted a woman he could depend on. The last time he'd tried to stay with a woman who didn't want to be there, it hadn't ended so well. *Getting a little ahead of myself here, aren't I?* "That's smarter than committing to someone you've got doubts about."

She raised a brow. "Something you have personal experience with?"

"You could say that. I was married for eight years and got divorced the year before last."

"I'm sorry. That's common enough these days. How old are you, anyway?"

"Thirty-two. You?"

"Thirty-three." She grinned. "I should be giving you advice, since I'm the wiser one here."

Jack could have pointed out that older didn't necessarily mean wiser, but he wasn't stupid enough to say it out loud. "If it's about diving, maybe I'm the wiser one." With a regretful sigh, he glanced at his fins. "I'd better get going. I've got an early morning tomorrow at Ocean Surf. And remember, I'm just downstairs if you have any issues with your class."

As he stood, their eyes held for a long moment before she nodded to him. Jack walked back toward his truck and a smile rose on his face.

Chapter Thirteen

THE SUN WAS LESS than an hour from setting when Sara dumped her purse on the kitchen counter, heading straight to her bedroom to change into a swimsuit. After tugging on a blue one-piece, she quickly braided her hair into a long tail, looking at her body in the mirror as she plaited it. It was a modest suit— the only kind she was comfortable in. But it did show off her breasts and a smirk rose. "Eat your heart out, Hope. You might have a nice rack, but that's the one department I handily have you beat."

She'd had a conversation with April over lunch that day, getting tips on her certification, which had mostly consisted of the divemaster saying, "Would you relax? You'll do fine."

Of course you'd say that, you think Alex walks on water. And Sara couldn't deny that April wasn't the divemaster she wanted help from.

Throwing on a cover-up and grabbing a towel, she trotted down the stairs, her mind returning to Jack. They had certainly gotten off to a rocky start, but she was big enough to admit she had misjudged him. The other night when she'd been sitting on the swing, there had been a strong current between them. A current that had brought home to her how incredibly kissable his mouth was. In addition to those giant brown eyes, he was sweet and funny, and always calm. She snorted. *That might balance my assertiveness rather well.*

The last thought brought her to a standstill. *Am I really thinking about getting together with him?*

Yeah, maybe I am...

She stood outside the landing, staring at the ocean. It was flat and welcoming this evening, and it was hard to believe it was mid-December from the weather. *Should I swim in the ocean instead of the pool? That would give me some confidence for sure.* Sara frowned. It might not be safe alone, and she wasn't the strongest swimmer in the world. Still undecided, she worried her lip between her teeth.

The sound of footsteps came from her left, where Jack slowly approached with his head down and both hands in his pockets.

"You don't exactly look on top of the world."

He whipped his head up, and a smile replaced the tiredness. She couldn't help returning it as he said, "Things just started looking up. I had a long day at Ocean Surf. One of the other divemasters is an asshole, and the manager doesn't like to *micromanage.* I have a feeling Cameron and I have a reckoning coming. It feels like high school sometimes." His gaze took in her cover-up and towel. "Going for a swim, I take it?"

"Yeah. My swim test is tomorrow, so I was thinking about practicing in the ocean."

Jack reared back, his eyes enormous. "Alex is making you do an *ocean swim?*"

Sara laughed. "No, just the normal lap swim in the pool. But I'm kind of nervous about it. I thought swimming in the ocean would make tomorrow look easy and boost my confidence. Except I'm scared to do it by myself." She pulled her long braid over one shoulder and ran her hand down it. Jack followed every movement, and a satisfied ripple traveled through her abdomen. *Oh yeah. There are sparks flying now.* "Is your offer to help still available?"

"You want me to swim with you?"

Her heart lurched. "Only if you want to. You don't have—"

He grinned crookedly at her. "Sara, I'd love to. Just let me grab a towel. I'm already wearing swim trunks."

Sara rubbed the back of her neck as she and Jack stopped next to one of the chaise lounges on the beach and deposited their towels on it. She brushed at her cover-up, delaying the inevitable. But Jack didn't have the same hesitation and lifted his shirt off with ease, tossing it on top of his towel. He shaded his eyes with his hand, evaluating the water. "There might be a little current out there, so we'll start off swimming into it. That way, the water will be pushing us the last half of the swim."

She listened, but much of her attention was spent checking him out without being obvious about it. He had a trim body but wasn't overly muscular. In short, he was very attractive without being intimidating. "Sounds like a plan."

Unable to delay any longer, she pulled off her cover-up and headed straight for the ocean, imagining every flaw in her body as she refused to meet Jack's eyes. When she stepped in, the water was so close to the air's temperature she hardly noticed any difference. Her self-consciousness slipped away as she dove into the shallows, the water enveloping her. When she rose and began her freestyle stroke, Jack was already swimming at her side.

They continued straight out from the beach, and he drew ahead, but quickly slowed, allowing her to catch up. They swam shoulder to shoulder, and Sara watched small white fish swimming below them. Soon, he pulled up and looked to shore, and she did likewise. Their chaise lounge was further up the beach than she had been expecting. She had thought they were swimming straight away, but the current was carrying them parallel to shore.

"This is far enough out," Jack said. "And like I thought, there's some current. Let's start swimming against it. Just go slow and steady—I'm right here if you need me."

She nodded and resumed swimming, immediately noticing the force of the water against her. When she sighted to the right, the beach chair was now closer. They'd made up a little distance, but less than she'd hoped for. Sara put it out of her mind and continued following Jack's instructions. She kept a moderate pace that kept her breathing from getting out of hand, but fatigue was already setting into her arms. The next time she sighted, the chair was just passing out of her sight.

She paused for a moment. "How long have we been going?"

Jack checked his watch. "A little over five minutes."

"What? We've hardly moved at all!"

"Because we're swimming into the current. You're doing great. Don't pay attention to the distance. How long do you want to swim?"

"I was thinking thirty minutes."

"Sounds good. We'll continue for another fifteen, then reevaluate. Just concentrate on swimming. I've got everything else."

"Ok. Thanks." She started again, grateful for the help, and secure that she was with an expert. She had learned in her class that dive professionals had extensive rescue and emergency skills.

Soon Sara found her rhythm, each stroke becoming easier, and her confidence grew. She occasionally brushed Jack's arm, just to reassure herself of his presence. But now she was strong enough to continue for longer than thirty minutes and smiled to herself.

Jack stopped to tread water. "Sara, stop."

"Wow, it's been fifteen minutes already? I felt like I was flying through the water!"

"No, I'm stopping us early. The current has changed. It's the opposite direction now—that's why it feels easier."

"Oh, shit! Should we go back to shore?"

"No, we're fine." He laughed. "You wanted your swim test to be a breeze. This should accomplish that."

The shore crept by as they drifted with the current. "I see what you're talking about. Let's head back."

He put a hand on her shoulder, meeting her gaze. "We're fine, Sara. This current isn't too strong. Slow and steady, remember?"

She was acutely aware of the warmth of his hand, and placed hers over it and squeezed. "I remember. Stay with me, all right?"

"Count on it. Let's go."

They started and, once again, Sara felt the push of the water against her. She was already tired, and her heart pounded. Worse, the negative chatter in her head rose in magnitudes.

What am I doing out here? I'm not an athlete! I'm going to drown. Head back to shore before it's too late!

She growled and told her inner voice to shut up, but a peek at the shore revealed they hadn't moved much, though the beach was closer now—Jack was angling them in. Her stomach plummeted but she was determined to forge on, placing her head in the water and forcing her fatigued arms to turn over. Several strokes later, she couldn't resist another peek at the shore.

The landmarks were nearly identical. The small sphere of dread that had been building in her stomach became a beach ball and tears threatened. Sara pulled up, breathing hard. "Jack! We've hardly moved. I can't do this."

"Sara, it's fine."

"What was I thinking? This was a stupid idea."

He put both arms on her shoulders. "Sara—"

Her breath was coming faster and faster. "At this rate I won't even be able to finish my swim test tomorrow."

"Sara!"

His shout finally got through to her and she snapped at him. "What?"

"Put your feet down."

"And drown? You're supposed to be helping me, goddammit!"

He arched a brow. "Put. Your. Feet. Down."

She did, and they landed in silky sand. The water was waist deep. "Oh. Ok, then."

His face immediately softened, and a small grin cracked it. "See? You're perfectly safe. But we've still got a way to go yet, so we need to get back to it. Just remember, if you get too tired or get nervous, you can always stand up. There's no danger."

"You'll stay with me?"

"Of course. You got this."

"I got this."

They started swimming again, and Sara continued chanting, *I got this.* Now she stroked more confidently. It could have been due to the current slowing or the fact that she could stand whenever she wanted to, but she didn't care. Jack stayed by her shoulder, and her self-confidence grew with each passing minute. His encouraging presence further reassured her, and they stroked their arms in unison, occasionally brushing fingers. A tingle of electricity rocketed through her every time they touched. The next time she sighted, their beach chair was closing in, and she increased her pace, a grin spreading across her face.

When the chair was directly across from their position, Sara stood and raised her arms toward the darkening sky. "Ha! I did it."

The light was fading around them as Jack matched her smile. He reached up and gave her an enthusiastic high ten. "Of course you did!"

They smiled at each other as he entwined his fingers with hers, standing in the warm water with their hands clasped above their heads. Breathing hard, Sara stared into his beautiful, warm brown eyes. Their gazes locked and their smiles faded. She could feel every inch of where their hands touched, and she brushed her thumb over the back of his hand. Now her deep breathing wasn't because of the swimming, and her desire to kiss him was overpowering. From the way he dropped his gaze to her mouth and held on, she wasn't the only one.

Without a word, they moved toward each other. She met his lips, letting go of his hands to encircle his waist. His mouth was soft and warm, and the only sound around them was the ocean softly washing up on the shore. Jack cupped her head with one hand and wrapped the other around her shoulders, pulling her tightly to him. His gentle, searching kiss became passionate and a soft moan escaped him.

Sara swiped her tongue over his, desire rolling through her now as he opened his mouth to probe hers. She could taste the salt on his tongue. He moved his hand to her ass, pushing her hard against him, and it was her turn to moan as the length of him pressed between them.

"God, I want you," he whispered against her mouth, then smashed his teeth against hers. He slipped his hand under her suit to her breast, his thumb slowly stroking.

Sara pressed her hips hard against him, moaning softly as she murmured, "Me too." His touch went straight through her, and it was more than physical desire. It was the sense that he wanted *her*—the unsure Sara she normally kept hidden. Pulling back, she broke the kiss as they stared at each other, both breathing hard. "Do you have a condom?"

He jerked a nod. "Back at my apartment."

"Let's go, then."

Instead, he pulled her tight again, attacking her mouth as he squeezed her breast with one hand and her ass with the other. She looped a leg around the back of his knees, leaning into his touch as she reached down to squeeze him. His breath caught at that, then he pulled away and grabbed her hand.

"Come on," he said, hurrying them to shore.

THEY STUMBLED THROUGH THE DOOR, and Jack kicked it shut, pushing Sara against the wall as he raked his mouth over hers. She was on fire now—this side of him was completely unexpected. He had always been reserved and quiet, and his ardor made her own self-consciousness flee.

He broke their kiss and stared at her. "You've seen the rest of my apartment. Care for a tour of the bedroom?"

"Oh, yes." Her voice was deeper, throatier.

Grasping her hand more gently this time, Jack led her into his darkened bedroom. As soon as they entered, he turned around and moved in again, opening his mouth to encircle her tongue with his. He slipped his hands down her back and tugged off her elastic hair tie, slowly unplaiting the wet strands, then running his fingers through them. "You have no idea how much I've wanted to touch your hair."

"Well, I hope you don't plan to stop there."

He smiled but didn't answer, instead hooking both index fingers around her suit straps and pulling them off her shoulders and down. His eyes fixated as her breasts were revealed, and his breath became louder in the silent room.

Sara stood tall, her confidence rising as he pulled the suit over her full hips, and it fell to the floor. He returned his gaze to hers, breathing, "Wow." Then he rushed forward, holding her face with both hands as he crushed his mouth to hers. Sara ran her hands over the broad planes of his back, grinding into him as he devoured her mouth.

Jack moved both hands to her breasts, circling with his thumbs, and a loud groan escaped him. All remaining traces of her insecurity fled. She was only conscious of Jack kissing her like she was the oasis at the end of his desert journey. And that only fueled her response more, desire throbbing up and down her body now.

Sara quickly untied his swim trunks and they fell to the ground. Grasping him firmly, she moved her hand up and down as he pushed against her.

"Oh my God. Don't stop that, please." Almost panting, he stroked one hand over her side and to her hip, tracing two fingers over her skin. He moved his fingers along the front of her thigh and slowly up the inside. He barely touched her, and her entire body shivered.

Then at last, Jack slipped his hand between her legs and her shiver became a weak-kneed shudder. She gasped, and withdrawing his tongue from her mouth, he gave her a smile that didn't diminish the shudder at all. He led her to his king-size bed. As she slid across the mattress, he removed a box of condoms from his nightstand and tossed it on top of it before crawling in next to her. The box was unopened, and Sara smiled slightly. Jack didn't strike her as the promiscuous type, but the evidence was still reassuring.

They melted together again. His naked body was warm, and water beaded over his back from their swim. She hardly noticed.

She pulled him back to her mouth for a long, very wet kiss, and ran her hands firmly across his shoulders. The muscle was firm underneath his heated skin.

"What do you like, Sara? This?" He moved his hand back between her legs and she arched, crying out. "I'll take that as a yes." He kissed along her cheek, finally breathing in her ear. "Would you like it more if I used my mouth?" Her eyes flew open, but he pressed his tongue in her ear, making her groan. This was an awkward issue for her—something she definitely enjoyed but was self-conscious about.

He wouldn't ask if he didn't want to, would he? Sara took the plunge. "Yes, I would like that."

He moved down her neck and pressed both her breasts together, moving his mouth back and forth between them. "God, Sara. You're incredible. I want you so bad." Then he slowly kissed his way down her abdomen.

She parted her legs, and for once let herself go, completely comfortable with him. He began rhythmically moving his tongue, and she grasped his head with both hands. Her sensitivity was so intense it didn't take long for her climax to roll over her, then through her. Eventually, her cries slowly diminished, and she let go of his hair. He was watching her with a smile, and she smiled back, still twitching at the strength of it.

Jack climbed to the nightstand, opening the box of condoms. Sara grabbed his arm. "Wait. What about you?"

He held up the foil-wrapped packet. "We're not done yet."

"That's not what I mean."

"I know." His eyes softened, then he tore open the packet, rolling the condom on. He stretched out next to her, pressing his body against hers. "Right now, I want to be inside you. More than anything else in the world."

She grabbed the back of his head and kissed him. Their tongues danced together as she rolled onto her back, and he went with her. He entered her slowly, moaning softly as he pushed his full length into her.

As she wrapped her arms around his waist, they began moving together. She ran both hands over his back and cupped his ass, eager to learn every inch of him. Every inch. Leaning on one elbow, he fanned her hair over her breast. It was wet and cold, raising goosebumps on her inflamed skin. But his heat quickly replaced the coolness as he lowered, chest to chest with her.

Their movements escalated, and he began calling out, pounding into her. Sara held him tightly, urging him ever closer, ever deeper, until finally he stiffened. This time he whispered her name, his mouth pressed to her ear.

Eyes closed tightly, she held him even tighter.

Chapter Fourteen

DIM MORNING LIGHT filtered through the blinds as Jack lay in bed, watching Sara sleep. She faced him, relaxed, and her long hair was now completely dry, though very tousled. The sheet had slipped, revealing one spectacular breast. She took his breath away, all soft curves, though tempered with a sharp tongue. A smile rose on his face. *I wasn't complaining about her tongue last night, was I? Especially the second time.*

But the smile fell as the implications of their night hit him. *That was completely unexpected. Where do we go from here?* There was something about this woman that stopped all logical thought in him. He couldn't resist her searing flame but was acutely aware she could scorch him to the bone.

Jack slowly rolled over and slid out of bed, quickly dressing before heading to the kitchen to make coffee. He stared at the carafe as it brewed, not really seeing it. Last night was the first time he'd made love since his wife. He wasn't good at casual relationships and had gotten completely caught up in the moment.

So, what do I want?

He poured a cup of coffee and glanced at the closed

bedroom door, raising a corner of his lips. That was easy. He wanted to go back in there and screw her brains out. But he pushed that thought firmly away. First, he needed to know how Sara felt about this. The flashes of vulnerability she sometimes displayed shot straight to his heart. The more he got to know her, the more he wanted to know. Right now, whether she regretted last night was what he wanted to know most.

He was standing at the sliding glass door, watching the dawn break, when Sara's voice called out, "Jack!"

He moved to the door and swung it open to reveal Sara sitting against his headboard, the sheet loosely draped over her. One breast was *almost* revealed, and he tried not to stare.

"Jack…"

He lifted his gaze to hers, swallowing down an enormous ball of anxiety. *She's going to say this was a huge mistake. It should never have happened, and she can't stand me.* He searched for a clever remark, but that had never been his strong suit. "Good morning… is something wrong?"

A mischievous grin lit her face, and the ball in his stomach deflated—much better than regret. Or anger. "Um, yes. I don't have anything to wear, and I really don't want to put on a wet swimsuit. Do you have a shirt I could borrow?"

Jack couldn't resist a grin, and she matched it. And with that, his anxiety faded away. He was average height at 5'9", but she was pretty short, and he had something that would do the trick. In short order, he handed her a dark-red Texas Longhorns T-shirt. "You want a cup of coffee?"

She lifted the shirt over her head and the sheet fell, giving him another glimpse of her amazing breasts. *Keep it together, Jack.*

"That sounds great. I'll be out in a second." His shirt fell to mid-thigh as she headed toward the bathroom. He tore his eyes away and left the bedroom to remove a second mug from the cabinet.

Soon she joined him in the kitchen and by then he'd screwed up his courage. Jack poured her cup three-quarters full and pulled her into his arms, kissing her soundly. He tried not to think about the fact that she was naked under the shirt, but couldn't resist rubbing his thumbs over her breasts. She kissed him back thoroughly, then pulled back with a smirk. "Good thing I had a drink of water in the bathroom, or you'd regret that kiss."

"Not a chance." He pushed the mug toward her. "I don't know how you like it."

"Oh, I beg to differ." Her cheeks turned a wonderful shade of pink. "Cream and sugar."

He took out a bag of sugar, then turned to the fridge. "Milk ok?"

"Of course. We've already established you keep a ready supply of milk around." After mixing the coffee to her liking, she took a long sip, then glanced at the clock and frowned. "I need to get going. Do you work today?"

Jack shook his head. "Day off. I've got some errands to run, and I'd like to get some sketching done." She stood relaxed, resting with one hip cocked, but his nerves were back, trying to claw through the lining of his stomach. "I'd like to see you again. You want to have dinner?"

She giggled. "I guess we did kind of get things mixed up, didn't we?"

"Do you regret that?"

She became serious and tipped her head. "No, not at all. Do you?"

His heart pounded as he stared at her, unable to look away even as he imagined a *Danger* sign flashing over her head. "I'm really glad we did."

Breaking the trance, she set her mug on the counter. "I have a really full day. I've got several clients this morning and my first pool session is this afternoon. How about I make you dinner tomorrow night?"

"Mac and cheese?"

"I'll try something even more exotic. Maybe add bacon this time. Really knock your socks off."

"You already did that, Sara."

SEVERAL HOURS LATER, Jack bumped down a dirt track north of Half Moon Bay Resort. He shifted his Ranger into four-wheel-drive just on principle. The heavy vegetation on both sides of the road slowly thinned until clear, blue sky appeared in front of him. He frowned, pulling off the track to park behind a beat-up old gray Ford Taurus. *Great. Company? In the middle of nowhere?*

Retrieving his sketchbook and pencil from the passenger seat, Jack exited, deep in thought as he walked toward the ocean. He passed the old sedan, its engine still ticking. *Maybe the car belongs to a beach walker, and I'll have the place to myself.*

Sara had been happy and upbeat, giving him a kiss on the cheek when she'd left. Though certainly glad she wanted to see him again, he couldn't help being more cautious about their night together. He'd had several buddies who had managed the 'friends with benefits' situation, but Jack wasn't like that.

He was interested in Sara. Hell, he couldn't wait to see her again. But this situation could go very badly for him if things didn't work out. Her sister and brother-in-law owned the resort he worked at, after all. A job he wanted to turn into a full-time gig. He was trying to make a life in St. Croix. Whereas Sara had moved down quickly—almost on a whim.

As he climbed a gentle rise onto the beach, a man sat on a stool on the rocky ground ahead. An easel was set up before him, and he had a wooden palette of paints in one hand. Recognizing Dexter, Jack's reluctance about meeting someone disappeared.

The divemaster didn't make much noise as he crept over the sharp rocks of the spit, but Dexter turned around. "Well, there, if it isn't Jack. How you doin' today?"

"I'm good. You must have incredible hearing."

He laughed. "Not accordin' to my late wife."

Jack wasn't sure how to respond to that, so he didn't. "Mind if I join you?"

"Sure, as long as you don't mind listenin' to an old man talk now and again."

Jack smiled, settling on a large flat rock nearby. "Not at all. Talk all you want." He enjoyed being around older people, and their stories were usually worth hearing. He started sketching the ocean before him, trying to capture the different hues. "So, this land has been in your family a long time?"

"It has. Since the emancipation. Once they finally told my ancestors about Lincoln's decree, that is. The local governor gave away some land plots to a few of the newly freed slaves. Most of it was hard rock or marsh. Useless land. But he included a few prime pieces—only to appease his superiors, of course. They drew a bunch of names, and my great-great-great-grandfather won these sixty acres at Half Moon Bay. Pure luck of the draw."

"Wow. At least some good came from such an awful experience." Jack almost flinched at the triteness of his words, but Dexter didn't react.

"And that's a fact. Since this land was too thick to farm, my family made their livin' from the sea." He paused, looking back toward the resort before holding out a gnarled index finger. "See that bungalow down there? The one closest to us?"

Jack nodded.

"My family had a proper house in the jungle, but we used to have a beach hut there. Real primitive. All handmade with a thatch roof. But I practically grew up in that thing. Loved it there."

Jack studied the resort, trying to picture it as a pure stretch of beach with no improvements except the rickety shack. It was a beautiful image. "How did the resort get there?"

Dexter sighed and returned to his painting of a frigate bird. "Damn government, that's how. The property taxes were killin' us. My daddy finally sold off most of the land in the 1990s to the couple who built the resort. But they did a good job of it. Kept it family-run and friendly. From what I heard, the woman who got it from them has the same philosophy."

"And it's still family run. She just married the dive manager."

Dexter laughed, a dry, raspy sound, and slapped his leg. "Well, that's all right, then. I'm tryin' to hang on to this little parcel, but I'm gettin' on in years. Every once in a while, somebody offers me a princely sum for it. That nice lady who owns Half Moon Bay Resort was one of them." He sighed and dabbed a line of black over the bird's back. "Someday, I probably should take one of them up on it. But not quite yet, I don't think."

The two men returned to their projects in companionable silence, and Jack's newly complicated love life faded to the back of his mind. God knew he could have worse problems.

Chapter Fifteen

SARA HUNG up the spa phone. Her final client of the morning had a headache and had rescheduled for the following day. *Probably a hangover...*

Smiling to herself, she danced down the stairs. *I certainly don't have a headache this morning.* In fact, she was on cloud nine. Her night with Jack had been a very pleasant surprise—one she wanted to repeat soon. Both of them had been caught up after the drama of her swim, and his cautious questioning of her that morning had been beyond sweet. Making love had been amazing. Especially how comfortable she'd been with him. He was just what she needed—a breath of fresh air.

She opened the dive shop door where Hope was speaking with a guest. "We can probably set up an Intro class tomorrow afternoon for you," she said to the man. "But the pool is already booked this afternoon."

Sara strolled around the bright, clean shop, inspecting masks and resort T-shirts as she hummed a song. Hope scheduled the guest and he left, the bell above the door softly jingling. Holding the shirt up to the light, Sara tried to catch different angles of the pattern, a smile playing at the corners of her mouth.

Hope laughed from behind the counter. "What has gotten into you? You're practically floating on air."

She froze. *Oops. It's that obvious?* "Nothing in particular. Just the effects of living in paradise." Breezing over to a row of fins, she peered closely. Who knew there were so many different styles?

"Oh please. You don't fool me for a second. Dish, Sara. What's up?"

She sent Hope a sidelong glance, then fully turned toward her and strolled up to the counter. "Fine. If you must know, Jack and I got to know each other a little better last night. Well, a lot better."

"What?"

Sara giggled. "He was helping me with my swimming, and we got a little carried away."

"I thought you hated him."

"Mmm, not so much anymore." Then Sara sighed, dropping the coy act. "We've been getting along for a while now. He's not the jerk I thought he was at first."

Hope rested her elbow on the counter, propping her chin on her open palm. "No, he's not, and I'm glad you finally figured that out. But now I get to grill you! How was it? Hopefully not a D!" She laughed.

"Oh, no." Sara cocked her head, a flush coming over her. When she and Marissa had been younger, they had talked for hours about their love lives. Until Marissa met her husband. Then she had clammed up, much to Sara's disappointment. So she was surprised at her own reluctance to answer Hope's question. "It was great. Can we retire the letter-grade system? It seems a little immature now." Then she parked a hand on one hip. "And why are you so interested, Mrs. Deliriously Happy?"

The dive boat could be heard returning as Hope waved a careless hand at her. She straightened and came around the counter. "Consider it retired. But Alex and I are an old married couple now. I have to live vicariously through you." Her ears were bright pink.

Hope was a terrible liar, and Sara couldn't hold back a laugh. "Uh-huh. Sure."

Hope leaned back against the counter as Sara resumed her window shopping, checking out wetsuits. She'd never worn one.

"Are you ready for your first pool session?"

An uneasy flutter ran through Sara's stomach. "As I'll ever be, I guess."

"Chill out. Alex is very good at what he does, you know."

Sara shot her another sidelong glance. "Of course you would say that." She ran a hand over the neoprene fabric. It was fairly thick and looked constricting. *That thing can't be comfortable...*

The door opened and Alex walked in, raising his brows at the two women. "Time for a sister-to-sister chat?"

"You could say that," Sara said.

He gave Hope a quick kiss and moved behind the counter, opening a thick file folder. "Leaving the dirty work to Robert and Tommy?" Hope asked.

"I need to prepare for Sara's class," he replied, then glanced at Sara, a glint in his eyes. "I don't have much time to prepare all the obstacles."

Sara mock-glared at him. Then something occurred to her. *It has been entirely too long since I've poked the bear. And Hope just gave me a golden opportunity.* "Be careful, Alex. If you make things too difficult, I'll complain to your old lady here. Now that you're married, it doesn't sound like she's putting up with your antics anymore. In fact, she just got through telling me that the honeymoon's over and you just don't affect her the same anymore."

She kept her most innocent expression, clasping her hands

in front of her as Hope whipped her head around with a furious glower. "Sara!"

Alex ignored Sara, completely focused on Hope as he straightened to his full height. He slowly sauntered around the counter, pinning his wife with his eyes. "Is that right?" he asked in a soft, sensual voice.

Sara considered herself Alex-proof, but even she could almost *see* the waves of pure male pheromones he was giving off as he approached Hope. She stood frozen, completely helpless against him, like an antelope staring at a tiger. Except this antelope wanted to be eaten whole. Badly. "I didn't say that," she squeaked.

He stopped before her and slowly drew an index finger down the side of her face. Hope inhaled sharply, parting her lips.

"Oh?" he breathed. "You shouldn't be telling tall tales, Mrs. Monroe. That could have dangerous consequences."

"Dangerous?" Hope's chest moved with the force of her breathing.

"Very."

Sara rolled her eyes. "For God's sake. Stop it, you two. Of course she didn't say that, Alex."

They still ignored her.

"We'll just have to continue this conversation later," Alex said.

Hope stepped closer, pressing her hand against his chest. Their faces were an inch apart. "Promise?"

"I think you already know the answer to that." Then he threw her a ten-thousand-megawatt smile and her knees actually *buckled.* He spun on his heel, and Sara snickered. Heading toward the door, he glanced her way. "You have more important things to think about than stirring the pot, you know. Like your swim test. I'll see you at the pool in a couple of hours."

"Wouldn't miss it, Alex." But his reminder brought back the uneasy slithering in her gut. *Why did I pick today to do that? Not smart, Sara!*

Alex closed the door behind him, and she turned back, needing a distraction from her pre-class anxiety. Hope was still leaning against the counter. She pressed both palms against it for support, as if she were made of putty, and just blinked at the closed door.

Sara shook her head, laughing. "You know, Mom and Dad got your name all wrong. It should be Hopeless."

Sara stood in the shallow end of the pool, trying to keep from shaking. She had passed the water skills with high marks, the swim test presenting no difficulties. Treading water for ten minutes had been more challenging, but Alex kept up a steady conversation about marine life as he performed it with her, which distracted her and made the time go by quickly. Then they had moved on to the next phase of the class, which involved wetsuits and actual scuba gear—breathing underwater. Which was the most exciting part.

At least that's what she kept telling herself.

They stood side by side in waist-deep water, and her anxiety ratcheted up steadily. She'd been right about the wetsuit she had examined in the dive shop. It was constricting. And after she added the BCD with its attached tank and regulator, she could hardly breathe.

"All we're going to do is put our face in the water," Alex said. "Then we'll do the same with a mask on. Finally, we'll add the regulator and breathe off it. We'll take it slow and get used to it, ok?"

"Sounds good." She was hell-bent on not admitting her fear

to him, and with any luck, he couldn't see it, though her hands were trembling a little. Despite his teasing that morning, he had been reassuring and calm during their session. It was a different side of him, one that made Sara slightly less convinced he was out to drown her.

Alex moved them slightly deeper into the pool and the weight of her tank nearly disappeared. *Ok, that's better. I can do this. I can put my face in the water, for God's sake.* In unison, they bent at the waist, holding their breath as they submerged their faces. The water clung to her closed eyes and tried to enter her nostrils. Sara's heart leapt out of her chest, and she bolted upright, trying not to gasp.

Shit! I'm learning scuba from a goddamn Navy SEAL, and I can't even put my face in the water! He's going to make me do fifty pushups, then flunk me for sure.

She was breathing hard, and tears began pricking her eyes as Alex lifted up beside her. He gave her a small smile, and his eyes were soft. "Relax, Sara. It's normal to be nervous about this."

"I'm not nervous!" she practically yelled, her voice shrill.

"You're doing fine. Let's try it with your mask on, and that way you'll be able to see. We'll just keep our faces on the surface."

Her face was on fire. He talked to her gently and encouragingly, like she was a skittish horse that needed to be calmed. Gritting her teeth, she soldiered on and replaced the mask.

"Now, lower your face again. All you have to do is get used to the water on it, so close your eyes if you want. It'll be fine."

"Ok. Let's go."

With a deep breath, Sara screwed her eyes shut and put her face in the water. With the mask over her eyes, she could no longer feel the water against them, which immediately settled her. She was able to leave her face in longer this time. Lifting out, she gave Alex a shaky smile. "That was better."

"Good. Let's do it again."

"Did Hope have problems with this?"

"Hope had her own issues. Stop comparing yourself. I'm serious here—you're doing great."

Keeping her eyes closed, she put her face back in.

After a moment, Alex spoke next to her. "Sara, open your eyes."

Shaking her head, she lifted and took a deep breath, then replaced her face. It was a little easier this time, but she kept her eyes clenched shut.

"It's ok. Relax and open your eyes."

Finally, she hesitantly opened them. In front of her feet, a small, yellow rubber duck lay on the bottom of the pool. It was wearing sunglasses. Sara immediately started giggling, lifting her head out as she stared at it. "Alex, did you toss a rubber ducky in the pool?"

He was grinning at her. "That's Donald. He makes an appearance anytime someone is nervous. Just to remind them the cool kids hang out underwater."

She straightened, laughing hard now. Still smiling, Alex softened his expression. "You're doing fine, Sara. A lot of people get nervous about this. We'll take things as slow as we need to."

"Thanks."

She returned her face to the water and watched the small duck roll back and forth on the bottom. Then, closing her eyes, she removed the mask and was able to keep her face submerged. After several rounds of that, she put the regulator in her mouth and took her first breath underwater, discovering that it was actually easier because she didn't worry about her air supply.

Before she knew it, Sara was kneeling on the bottom of the pool facing Alex. Breathing with the regulator in her mouth, she observed the pool around her from a totally new point of view. By the end of the class, she was able to flood her mask with water, then exhale air through her nose to clear it, as well as remove and replace her regulator underwater.

Back on the pool deck, pride in her accomplishment rolled through her. She glanced at Alex as she unhooked her scuba gear. "Thank you. I know I sometimes give you a hard time—I can't help it. But I really felt like I got the hang of it by the end."

"You're welcome, and you did great. What you went through is very common. You just needed to believe you could do it, then you were fine." He grinned, his white teeth flashing. "Besides, Boss Lady would tear my ass off if you didn't have a good time. She's dying to dive with you."

Chapter Sixteen

"BOTTOMS UP," Jack said as he touched his beer to Robert's. The two men sat at Breakers, once again at the bar. Soft reggae filled the night air, and a breeze kept the thatch-covered restaurant cool. "How was work today?"

"Same old, same old. How about you?"

Jack had spent the day at Ocean Surf, and guided the less experienced group, of course. "I had a bunch of newbies. They were ok, though there was one guy I had to keep hold of. He kept adding too much air to his BCD and shooting up."

Robert grinned. "Never a dull moment with new divers."

"I don't mind. I enjoy teaching them and it's fun when the lightbulb finally goes off."

"How come you're not an instructor, then?"

"Money and time. I'd like to someday." A smile escaped. "But I need to figure out how to make a living with this first."

Robert nodded. "That's the rub. It takes a lot of dough to become an instructor. But then you can make more money. But you can't save any money for the instructor course because you're broke all the time."

"But it beats working in a cubicle, doesn't it?"

Robert held his bottle out in a toast. "Amen to that." After a long pull, he gave Jack a sly look, trying to keep in a grin. "Seems like your love life has picked up since we were out last."

"It's only been a week! No keeping secrets on this island, that's for sure."

Robert burst into laughter. "You're right about that. You should have seen Alex and Hope. They thought they were so on the down low. Everyone could see they were interested in each other, except the two of them. Tommy and I were considerin' a bet." Both men stopped to laugh, then Robert shook his head. "After they finally got together, it was pretty obvious, even though they still tried to play it cool. Don't try to hide it, dude."

Jack's smile faded as he picked at the label on his beer. "Be honest with me. Am I making a big mistake by getting involved with Sara?"

Robert raised his brows. "Why would you say that? You're both adults. It's no one else's business."

"Come on. You know better than that. Her sister and brother-in-law own the resort. Alex is my direct boss. If things go up in flames, whose side do you think they'll take?"

Robert shrugged. "Yeah, you've got a point, there. But they're both pretty fair people, and you get along with both of them."

"Yeah. But what do you think Alex would do if his favorite sister-in-law's heart got broken by me?"

Robert grinned, then tried to hide it by rubbing a finger over his upper lip. "Uh, he'd probably break you in half."

"Exactly. I'm not afraid to mix it up with anyone, but Alex isn't exactly anyone, is he?"

"No, he isn't." Then he turned to look fully at Jack. "Why are you so worried about this? Are you guys that serious already?"

"No." But over the previous week, they had spent more

nights together than apart. He was doing his best to keep his distance emotionally, but that was getting harder.

"Seems like you're lookin' to cross a bridge you can't even see yet. Relax, man, and enjoy yourself."

Jack finished his beer. "You're probably right, but I'm still gun shy. I got left once, and Sara doesn't seem like the serious type. I just don't want it to happen again. This is the first time I've gotten involved since my divorce, so maybe I'm over-thinking it."

"Getting left does leave a mark, doesn't it?"

Jack stared at the bar, eyes unfocused. "When my wife was going through her fads, she never even tried to include me. I always felt like an outsider, like I wasn't important. In my own marriage! I can't go through that again." He sighed, shaking his head rapidly to snap out of the unhappy memories. "But that's no reason to look for problems with Sara that aren't even there." He tossed a five-dollar bill on the bar counter and bartender Maurice nodded at him. "I better go. See you later."

After returning to Serenity, Jack sat in his pickup, staring at Sara's apartment. It was after eight, and her lights were obvious against the black sky. *I should go straight to my apartment and get ready for bed.*

Instead, he exited the Ranger and climbed the stairs, almost without conscious thought. Sara answered his knock, dressed in a T-shirt—plain this time—and black leggings. Her hair fell in a flat sheet halfway down her back and he just drank her in, his heart thumping. She gave him a crooked grin, leaning one hand on the open door. "If you'd let me know you were coming, I could make myself presentable. You always catch me at my worst."

He smiled back, and all thoughts of his failed marriage fled. "If this is your worst, you worry way too much."

After giving him a welcome kiss, she headed toward the kitchen, beckoning him. "Suit yourself. Want a glass of red wine?" A half-full glass sat on the counter, next to an open bottle.

"Sure. Pour away."

They settled on her couch, and she nestled into the hollow of his shoulder, like she belonged there. He planted a kiss on top of her head. "Is tomorrow the big day?"

"The first of two, yes. Alex is splitting the final check-out over two days."

Jack nodded. "That's usually how it's done. How are you feeling about it now?" Her second pool session had gone well, but being in open water often brought out the jitters in students.

"I'm looking forward to it. I'm a lot more confident than I was at first." She paused and an adorable pink flush spread across her neck. "Remember when I told you I was nervous during the first pool session?"

"Yeah."

"I didn't go into the specifics with you. It was too embarrassing." She sat up and faced him. "Jack, I couldn't even put my face in the water. All I could think of was that Alex was a SEAL and God knows what he had to go through. It only made me more nervous."

"But you got over it. You told me by the end of the class, you were doing great."

"Yeah. He did a good job calming me down."

"Why are you so worried about what Hope and Alex think about you?"

"I can't help it." She narrowed her eyes at him. "Did he tell you what a wreck I was?"

"Of course not. He just said you did great. And you did."

"I had the hang of it by the end of the second pool session. I can't wait to see the house reef and the new corals. That's what made me want to get certified from the start."

He brushed a long lock of hair away from her face. As he'd gotten to know Sara better, one of her greatest surprises was that she wasn't as confident and brash as she acted. He was touched she felt comfortable enough to share her insecurities with him. "Most people get nervous at some point learning to dive. Even when I've taught DSD classes, which don't go that deep, some people are petrified. Then they see it's all the same stuff they learned in the pool, and they get over their fear." *Well, most of them.* He'd had a few who took one look at the open ocean and changed their minds.

"That's what Alex said too." She glanced at him, her head cocked. "How did you end up being a dive guide in St. Croix, anyway?"

"I used to divemaster for a shop in Galveston, mostly helping with classes. But I really wanted to lead dives. So, after I got divorced, I didn't have any reason to stay there, and decided to make a new start. I moved to St. Thomas and worked for a shop there."

"Did you get to lead dives there?"

He laughed and shuddered. "Yes, lots of them. It was a case of be careful what you ask for because you might get it. Really high stress. Plus, St. Thomas is really busy and crowded with tourists. Within six months, I'd had enough and moved here. It was a good choice."

"Why did you get divorced?"

Nervous laughter rolled out of him. "Boy, you don't beat around the bush, do you?"

She arched an eyebrow, and a small smile grew. "I'm known for being rather direct."

Jack shifted positions, crossing an ankle over his knee. "My wife wasn't the happiest person. She was always searching for something, never satisfied with what she had... what *we* had. What I could give her. She was in a book club, and even tried diving for a while, but lost interest to get consumed by yoga. She said it was to please me. I tried to tell her that wasn't necessary. Any of it. I didn't want to change anything about her." *I just wanted her to love me back.*

He sighed, resting his head on the back of the couch. "But Diane couldn't see that. And we'd start arguing, and things just got worse."

Sara straightened. "Wait. Your ex-wife's name is Diane?" She covered her mouth with her hand, trying not to laugh, then gave up, giggling. "I'm sorry. I'm not trying to be rude. But seriously—Jack and Diane?"

He joined in her laughter, glad he was able to find the humor in it now. "Yeah. Maybe we were doomed from the start. We got all kinds of grief over that."

She squeezed his hand. "Go on. I didn't mean to interrupt you."

"There's not much more to tell. The final straw was when she got into golf. She bought this incredibly expensive set of clubs without consulting me. There was no way we could afford it, and we got into a huge fight about it. When I came home from work the next day, she was gone. Diane hooked up with a guy soon afterwards, but I licked my wounds for a long time." He hesitated. *Should I say it? Why not?* "Until now. You're the first woman I've been with since the divorce."

She tightened her hand on his. "That makes me feel pretty special."

"Because you are. Even wearing five gallons of water."

Sara smacked him in the ribs as he burst out laughing. "Jerk. Stop bringing that up."

He leaned closer, stroking a finger across her collarbone. He felt lighter now that they had that conversation out of the way. "Well, there are things we can do besides talk, you know."

Her eyes became smoky. "Mmm. Much better things."

The sultry cast to her eyes sent his pulse into the stratosphere, then she pressed her full, lush lips to his. He ran both hands through the silky strands of her hair, still not believing how soft it was. How it just slid through his fingers. He couldn't get enough, and opened his mouth, tasting the red wine on her tongue, and all the blood in his body went south.

She broke the kiss to set her wineglass on the coffee table before taking his and doing the same. "Come on. We've got all night to figure it out."

Chapter Seventeen

SARA HUGGED herself as she darted her eyes all over the multicolored reef. A small brown and white fish swam right up to her mask, flitting back and forth before rushing back to its coral home to chase away a much bigger fish. She grinned around her regulator and glanced at Alex, who was writing on his slate. He turned it around.

Damsel fish—very protective!

She nodded, and they continued.

She was officially a certified diver, and Alex was leading her over the house reef to end her second open-water session. Though nervous before the first, once surrounded by the underwater environment, her tension had been replaced by fascination. Sara had enjoyed their previous snorkeling tours, but now she understood why Hope was so enthusiastic about diving.

There was no comparison.

The rubber ducky incident had broken through her fear and the rest of her class had gone very well. She even admitted that her concern about Alex making things difficult had proven completely unfounded. He had been calm and encouraging throughout.

Now I need to find a new way to tease him.

She turned to watch him peering into coral crevices, trying to find animals to show her. Further down the reef, Alex pointed to several stubby pieces of brown coral anchored by a large white area at their base where they attached to the rock. They looked kind of ugly. She raised her gaze to Alex writing on his slate, then he flipped it around:

Coral transplants. Doing really well!

With a sharp inhale, Sara looked again, now noticing the areas where the corals were growing over glue at their base, becoming one with the reef.

After he pointed them out, she recognized many scattered about the reef, making her even more excited. It made her want to see the nursery even more, but before the dive, Alex had explained they didn't have time to go over there.

Jack can show me.

Most fish, used to people, simply ignored the two divers. Occasionally, one would dart out at her, usually damsel fishes like the one earlier. Alex slowly led, and she did her best not to bump into him or the reef. Then he stilled and held up his hand to her, pinching his thumb to his fingers and away like a hand-puppet. She shrugged at him, not understanding, and he pointed back at a coral head.

As Sara examined the reef more closely, a large yellow and green eel stared at her, tucked back into its hole with just its head exposed. It rhythmically opened and closed its mouth as it breathed. Alex showed her his slate. Yellow margin moray. She gave the eel a respectful distance, glad it was content to stay in its lair. After checking his dive computer, Alex motioned them into shore, where they performed their safety stop, breathing off the excess nitrogen their bodies had accumulated over the dive.

Finally surfacing, Sara inflated her BCD and thought about shouting. *Nah, that's a little over the top.*

But her grin must have given away her thoughts because Alex gave her a wide smile and high five. "Congrats. See, that wasn't so hard, was it?"

"It's still awkward, but I was more relaxed by the end."

"Give it time. Every dive you'll get more comfortable."

As they waded to shore, Hope stood in the shallows, nearly bouncing up and down. "How did it go?"

Alex gave her a kiss. "Another certified diver in the family."

Hope squealed and gave Sara a clumsy hug. "Great job!"

Sara's smile could have broken her face. "I must admit, I'm pretty proud of myself."

"You should be—we certainly are." Hope removed the arm she'd been holding behind her back, revealing a bottle of champagne. "Let's go back to the house and celebrate. I already talked to Zach, and he'll take care of your gear."

Sara glanced down the pier as they walked by. Jack was wheeling a cart filled with tanks toward the compressor room, intent on his task, and didn't see her. *Too bad he can't join us. But I guess he's still on the clock.* She felt a regretful pang, then hurried after Hope and Alex.

Sara headed straight for their guest bath to shower. Afterward, she wrapped her hair into a bun and entered the kitchen. A freshly showered Alex was already there, popping the cork on the bubbly. He poured into the three flutes Hope had set out and they sat around the table. A Christmas tree stood in the corner of the great room, but that was the only embellishment. Hope decorated the resort fully, but kept their house simple.

"I can't wait to dive with you!" Hope said. "We'll try to get on the boat as soon as possible."

"Don't get your expectations too high," Sara said. "I was all over the place down there."

Alex finished his glass and set his flute on the table. "You just need some practice. And you've got plenty of people to dive with."

"No offense, Hope, but I feel better having Alex or Jack in the water for my first few dives."

Hope smiled at her. "Of course. Believe it or not, the first time I dove without Alex was just a few months ago. He's like my big security blanket." The two shared a smile.

"And I'll try not to collide with anyone's fins, either."

"Definitely learn from my mistakes." Hope's smile faded. "God knows there's been a lot to choose from."

"What? My perfect sister, making mistakes?"

"I've done some remarkably stupid, impulsive things since I've been here."

"I've thought about tying a giant bungee cord to her," Alex teased. "Then I could just yank her back when needed." Then he sobered, brushing back a lock of Hope's hair. "Don't regret being who you are. I don't."

Sara leaned forward. "I agree. It makes me happy to hear you talk like that."

Hope's face went blank. "That I'm stupid and impulsive?"

Sara and Alex both laughed, and he poured out the rest of the bottle.

"Yes, actually," Sara said. "The fire is back in your eyes. Hope, you just drifted through life for so many years. You're finally living again." She turned to Alex. "When we were kids, her neighborhood nickname was Headstrong Hope. She was the ringleader of all the shenanigans we could dream up."

"I can believe that."

"It changed overnight after Dad left. And after Caleb... your spark went out completely." The aftermath Caleb, Hope's first boyfriend, left behind had scarred Hope deeply. In response, Sara had preferred not to get too serious with the men she dated. Now she leaned forward and squeezed Hope's hand. "You've found who you were always meant to be."

Hope's eyes glittered as she gave Sara a smile and squeezed back. "Thank you. I do feel that way sometimes. But I also wouldn't mind doing less of the stupid things, like silting things up in dark caves."

"Something tells me you won't do that again," Alex said.

"Am I ever going to see this mythical pool and cave?" Sara asked.

"Sure," Hope said. "We could go over there now, if you'd like."

"Why not? I'd love to see it."

Hope turned to Alex, and he shook his head. "I'll let you two go without me. I need to finish the paperwork for Sara's class."

She stared at him, and something passed between them. "I've never been there without you, except for that first time."

"You'll be fine. It's safe, and you can take Cruz. Remember, I promised to stand aside when needed?" The two moved toward each other, and Hope reached a hand to his face as they kissed.

Sara scraped her seat back and stood. "It's probably a good thing you're not coming, Alex. Otherwise, I bet you two would ditch me in the middle of the jungle so you could be alone."

THIRTY MINUTES LATER, the two sisters hiked down a faint path in the jungle. Cruz bounded ahead, weaving over and around obstacles. Sara had changed back into her swimsuit and cover-up prior to leaving, and was grateful she'd worn sports sandals. "How far away is this thing?"

"It's just ahead." Hope had kept up a steady stream of

conversation, telling Sara how she had discovered the pool, and how Alex had dived into it and found the underwater passage. They came to a tall chain-link fence with a padlocked gate, and Hope produced the key.

Sara craned her neck left and right, but the fence went on and on. "Wow, you guys went all out here."

Once through, they continued down the path, and Hope continued, "We're still trying to figure out what to do with it. It's so beautiful that it's a shame to keep it to ourselves. And we have all the passages gated off, so it's safe. We just don't want word to get out that we found treasure here."

The trees thinned and they entered a large clearing. Sara continued forward, stopping at a small sandy beach, gaping at what was before her. The large pool was surrounded by boulders, which rose to a sheer rock hillside. In the middle of the wall was a black, yawning mouth. The only sound was birdsong and Cruz's lapping at the shore. It was remarkably peaceful. "Holy shit, Hope. You weren't kidding. This is amazing."

Nodding, Hope set her backpack down on a flat rock near the water and pulled out two headlamps. "You want to go for a swim? The water's cold, but it's great after the sweaty hike."

"Absolutely."

They stripped to their swimsuits and entered the water. It was cool, but not uncomfortably so, and Sara laughed at Hope's pinched expression. "You really don't like the cold anymore, do you?"

"Not particularly."

"It's pretty comfortable to me. Of course, I have more insulation than you do."

"Oh, stop it. You have a beautiful figure, and you know it. Let's head toward the cave first."

They swam across the pool and entered the dim cave, turning on their headlamps. Sara's beam danced around the huge interior as she followed her sister to a rocky shelf that extended back on one side.

As they treaded water, Hope pointed toward the back wall of the plateau. "Barnaby lived in a room back there for months. We know he left here to try to find rescue, but he was never heard from again. He must have died somewhere on the island."

"How sad. Poor guy."

Hope led Sara to the back of the cave, and they treaded water where a sheer wall soared to the ceiling. "The underwater passage is just below us, about fifteen feet down."

Sara got chills just imagining it. "And you dove that? In complete darkness?"

"Yes, but I learned some valuable lessons. Number one is when you're with an expert, it's a good idea to listen to his advice."

Sara snorted. "Headstrong Hope rears her head again."

Hope laughed. "Something like that. Let's get out—I'm getting cold."

After they toweled off, Hope spread out a blanket and they settled on it, taking a long drink from their water bottles. Cruz curled up next to Hope and closed his eyes with a happy sigh, resting his muzzle on her thigh. The sun warmed Sara quickly, and she smiled at the dog. "You sure have won him over. And no more trouble from Creepy Guy?"

Hope laughed and patted the dog's head. "No. We all hope Creepy Guy is in the past, but we'll see. He was a real piece of work."

Sara rested on an elbow, looking around the area. "There's no way in hell you'd get me to dive that cave, but this place is great. I can see why you'd want to advertise it."

"Not really advertise it, per se. But I've thought about calling it Half Moon Grotto and making it available only to our guests."

"That's a great idea. The resort's small, so it could be a private oasis."

"I'm starting to think about expanding and building some more bungalows. Alex and I have talked about what to do with all this money, but we haven't made any decisions yet. Which reminds me, missy. You still need to go to the bank to get your name added to the account."

"I know. I've had plenty to keep me busy."

Hope smiled and wrapped her arms around her knees. "Things are going well with Jack?"

"Yeah, they are. We're not too serious, but we have a good time together."

Hope's smile faded. "Be careful here. You might not be serious, but he had his heart broken by his ex-wife. At least that's what I'm guessing. He doesn't strike me as a footloose and fancy-free kind of guy."

Sara raised a brow. "Well, aren't you the expert? At this point, I think I know more about him than you."

Hope held up a hand. "Take it easy. I'm well aware of that. Just remember that not everyone is as carefree about relationships as you, ok?"

"I'm not sure where this will go. Or if I want a long-term relationship. But Jack's different from anyone else I've been with. He's quiet, very sweet and dedicated. I'm incredibly comfortable around him—not self-conscious."

Hope smiled at her. "Sounds like the baseline for something wonderful to me."

Chapter Eighteen

JACK EYED A DRAB, dark alley as Alex parked his classic Land Cruiser at the back door of Emerald Isle Scuba in Frederiksted. Earlier, Alex had mentioned needing to pick up a dozen Nitrox tanks after the afternoon trip. Jack had volunteered to help, and now here they were.

Alex pointed down the narrow lane. "There's a watering hole down that way. You want to stop for a drink afterwards?"

"Sounds good," Jack said, pleased at the chance to get to know his boss a little more.

Alex had parked at the shop's rear entrance, so they didn't have to haul the heavy tanks a long distance. As they entered the store, Alex knocked loudly on the back wall. "Yo, Gordon! You around?"

A middle-aged man wearing a bright-pink, ukulele-covered shirt entered from the front of the shop. "Your tanks are right there." He spoke with a deep Southern accent.

Jack followed his pointing finger to the twelve shiny aluminum tanks. A green and yellow band encircled them, with NITROX written in yellow letters. Gordon handed a receipt to

Alex, who frowned as he looked it over. "This isn't enough. You only charged me for eight tanks."

"I know. Consider it a special discount for friends."

Alex stared steadily at him. "I'm already getting a wholesale rate, so I want to pay for all of them. You don't have to treat me different than anyone else. What happened that night was just bad luck."

Gordon had a gray ponytail and florid face, which was getting redder with each passing second. Jack tried to follow the conversation, completely confused.

Gordon continued, "Alex, I'm not charging you full price ever again, so stop asking. I can barely look you in the eye as it is."

The lightbulb went off in Jack's head, but he stayed quiet.

Alex sighed. "Yes, you can. The whole thing is in the past now, and it wasn't your fault, ok? Charge me for all twelve. I mean it." With an even stare, he passed over a credit card and Gordon walked heavily to the front of the shop.

"This is where you and Hope were when you were shot?" Jack asked quietly.

Alex nodded. "We were picking up new regulators, and an employee Hope was trying to help decided to rob us instead. Or he tried to until I knocked him out." He glanced at Jack. "You read the article in the lobby?"

Jack nodded.

Alex gave an uncomfortable roll of his left shoulder. "Gordon almost had to close up shop because of it. People shunned this place for a long time. The whole situation was just a case of being in the wrong place at the wrong time, so I try to throw him some business."

Jack wasn't sure he'd be as forgiving, but he just nodded.

Gordon came back with Alex's card, and he signed the slip

before handing it back to the shop owner. "Thanks, man," Gordon said. "You need a hand loading them?"

Alex grinned and hooked a thumb at Jack. "Nah. This time, I actually did bring extra muscle with me." Then his smile faded. "And I'm a lot more prepared these days too."

The two men quickly loaded the tanks into the back of Alex's car, and he drove to a bar a few blocks away. Jack had never been there before. Housed in a red brick building, most guests sat on an outdoor patio to enjoy the evening. The sky was still holding onto daylight as they sat on two stools at an elevated table, a nearby tiki torch flickering.

After their Leatherbacks arrived, Jack held his up. "Here's to making it out of Emerald Isle Scuba in one piece."

Alex laughed, shaking his head. "I'm not too worried about lightning striking twice, so let's change the subject. The new membrane system is being installed next week. Once it's inspected and ready to go, I plan to expand the dive operation."

"Nitrox will be good. I certainly prefer it."

"We're planning an afternoon trip just about every day, and three-tank full-day trips once or twice a week. You want more hours?"

That was music to Jack's ears. "Definitely."

"I'm glad to hear you say that. April told me the other day that she's working more at her other job and to call you first when I need someone."

Thank you, April! He couldn't imagine why she would prefer her other gig, but to each her own. "I'd prefer it if Half Moon Bay was my primary job, and I just filled in for Mark once in a while."

Alex grinned before taking a drink. "Don't tell me that! Mark's the one who referred you to me, and now I'm poaching you. How long have you been a divemaster?"

"I've been doing it full time for about a year, but I got my license in Galveston three years ago. After I got divorced, it seemed like a good time to make it my full-time occupation, so I moved to the sunny Caribbean."

Jack was smiling, but Alex watched him steadily. "No kids, I take it?"

"No. I wouldn't have minded, but my wife... wasn't interested." Jack had the distinct impression he was being evaluated.

"I can imagine Sara keeps you on your toes."

"She's not dull, that's for sure." He stared back at Alex. "I think she's pretty terrific, boss."

"Good. Because she's family. She and I don't always see eye to eye, but the last thing I want is for her to get hurt. I'm glad you're not the kind of man who would do that."

And that's about as clear a warning as you could ask for, Jack.

He held Alex's gaze. Backing down now would be a mistake, and this wasn't a man to show weakness to. "No. I'm not."

Alex nodded and tipped his beer up. He froze with it halfway to his mouth, tracking something with his eyes. Curious, Jack turned on his stool. The two men who had caused the trouble at the Half Moon Bay bar were talking to each other as they moved across the patio. Pirate Guy was wearing a Tampa Bay Buccaneers jersey, keeping with the pirate theme, and his mullet was as craptastic as before. His large friend still sported the big hoop earring. They walked past the hostess station and continued out of sight.

Jack turned back. "Weren't they the two assholes we almost mixed it up with?"

Alex's mouth was set in a grim line as he swept his gaze around the restaurant. His eyes turned to ice as he stilled, staring into the far corner of the restaurant behind Jack. "Yes. And I just noticed what table they left."

Jack craned over his shoulder. A tanned man with brown,

slicked-back hair was tucked into the far corner table. Aviator sunglasses were hinged over the breast pocket of an expensive button-down shirt. He sipped a glass of white wine, swinging one crossed leg casually back and forth.

Jack turned back. "Friend of yours?"

Alex snorted, his eyes burning as he stared at the man. "More like asshole-of-the-year candidate. I wouldn't be surprised if those two are his local muscle." He dug a twenty out of his pocket, laid it on the table, and stood, a grim smile forming. "I think I'm in the mood to say hello."

Jack wasn't about to miss this, so he followed as Alex made his way across the patio. The seated man had been looking the other way when the former SEAL stopped in front of the table, Jack at his side. Turning back and seeing Alex, he widened his eyes for a moment, but recovered quickly, a smooth smile crossing his face as he lifted his wine glass. "Well, if it's not Alex Monroe. Such a tiny island, isn't it?"

"You were in such a hurry when you left, I hoped you were sailing away for good, Wayne."

The man remained seated, relaxing in his chair. "Yes, I'm sure you were. But St. Croix is such an up-and-coming place. So many opportunities to explore."

Alex clenched both hands into fists, but kept his voice quiet. "As long as you explore them far from us. I mean it, Timmons. If you set foot on Half Moon Bay, I'll flatten you."

Jack kept his face expressionless, presenting a unified front. He had no doubt Alex could pound this guy into the pavement if he wanted to.

Timmons took a sip, a bored look on his face. "Last time I checked, it was still a free country and a free island, Monroe. But you'll be happy to know I can't think of any reason to visit your little resort. I'm not in the market for a dog any time soon."

Dog? What the hell?

"Good. Stay away, Wayne." With a final glower, Alex spun and headed toward the exit.

Jack had to hurry to catch up. "That was interesting. I'm gonna go out on a limb and answer my own question. Definitely not a friend."

Alex hissed through his teeth as they climbed into his car. He started the engine and they headed toward the resort. "Hardly. He showed up at the resort in his sailboat a few months ago and caused all sorts of trouble—in just a couple of days. You've seen Cruz, right? Hope's dog?"

Jack nodded.

"About a year and a half ago, Cruz just showed up out of the blue. Scared of everyone and everything. But Hope eventually won him over. Hell, he even likes me now. Then Timmons ties up at our dock and it turns out Cruz used to be his dog."

Alex barked laughter that wasn't amused. "He went apeshit when he saw Cruz with Hope, yelling at her and demanding his dog back. He even grabbed her arm and threatened her. Cruz attacked him, and then I got involved. Wayne ended up going on his merry way—without Cruz—and I hoped we'd seen the last of him. Apparently not."

Jack stared at him, scenarios running through his head over what "*I got involved*" meant. "He went apeshit over a lost dog?"

Alex darted a glance at him, then laughed before turning back to the road. "You had to be there."

"Well, it doesn't sound like he's planning on visiting Half Moon Bay any time soon."

"He better not, for his sake."

Chapter Nineteen

AS SARA TOSSED several throw pillows onto her bed, her gaze caught on the nightstand. She opened the drawer, revealing a half-empty box of condoms. More importantly, the thin cardboard container behind them was revealed. Her contraceptive patches. Jack had left her apartment a short time before, off to work at Ocean Surf. They had been together for several weeks now, and it was time for the *exclusive* talk.

Sara still had several boxes of patches from her prior relationship, and had applied one the previous week. Now they were fully operational, and the time had come to ditch the condoms. Not something men were generally opposed to. Plus it would make a nice Christmas present, which was only days away. Jack was working at Ocean Surf on the big day, so they had decided on a low-key holiday without presents. *When we meet up tonight, I can make Jack a happy man.* The thought brought a smile to her face, and she headed out to work.

The day was heavy with threatening rain, and Sara's blouse became stuck to her skin during the short trip from her car to Hibiscus. When she walked in, Selena was preparing the beds inside the inside massage room. Hope had followed through and ordered two more tables, and couples were scheduled several times a week now, both inside and out. The spa was appropriately festive, with a small, decorated tree and garland hanging from the check-in counter.

"Going to be an indoor massage day, huh?" Sara asked, fanning her shirt.

"I sure hope so. Though some people want their massage outdoors, no matter what the weather." Selena came into the reception area and squinted at a distant squall line on the ocean. "Looks like the divers are goin' to have some rain today."

"I don't suppose it matters if they get wet, does it?"

Selena laughed. "No, I guess not. I saw Alex and Robert workin' this mornin'. You miss bein' separated from your sweetie durin' the day?"

Sara frowned at Selena's broad grin. "We can manage to be apart for a few hours."

Selena guffawed, bending at the waist. "I still can't believe you two are together! At first, you practically hissed every time he came near."

"I might have possibly misjudged the man."

Selena had stopped laughing, but her smile remained. "I think you two make a great couple. And who knows? Maybe Half Moon Bay will have another weddin' soon."

Sara reared back. "Jeez. Hold up there, Selena. We've been together less than a *month*. I admit he's very cute, but I like being a single girl. I'm not in any rush to get tied down."

"Really? I can't wait to get married and have a family."

Sara leaned against the counter. "I will admit watching Hope and Alex together has warmed me to the subject a little. But Jack and I are pretty casual. And I plan to keep it that way."

Late that afternoon, Sara sat in a lounge chair on the beach behind their apartment building. A short shower had passed, leaving the air fresh and new. It astonished her how few people used their beach. It wasn't large, but the sand was powdery and pure white, with a gentle entry into the welcoming ocean. She had thought about retrieving her easel but was enjoying just sitting there as she waited for Jack, who was taking a shower.

Behind her, the slider opened, and Jack leaned over to brush his lips over hers, lingering with a deep hum in his chest. "Now that is what I like to come home to." He settled onto the lounger next to hers.

"How was work?"

He sighed. "Typical. Cameron was a dick as usual. Most dive people are hard workers, but not that guy. I've kept my cool so far, but I have a feeling a confrontation's coming."

"Maybe that's what he's waiting for. To see how far he can push you."

"That's what I'm starting to think. He might not like the answer, though."

Sara smiled at the thought of soft-spoken, easy-going Jack getting in someone's face. She liked that he had a long fuse, but didn't let himself get pushed around. After they had discussed her day, which had passed much more serenely, she took a deep breath, preparing to broach the subject that had been on her mind. "I have something to show you. That I think you'll like."

He turned sideways, leaning closer with a smile. "Better than the present view? Not sure that's possible, but you can show me anything."

"Consider it your Christmas present." She lifted her shirt and pulled the front of her shorts down slightly to expose the patch on her lower stomach, near her hip. She tapped it twice. "Voila."

His face went blank. "What is it?"

"It's a birth control patch. I've had it on for a week. You haven't noticed it?"

"No..."

"It is pretty inconspicuous. That's the idea, after all." She rearranged her clothing and sat up. *Stop chit-chatting, for God's sake!* "What I'm trying to say, Mr. Jack Powell, is that if you're prepared to make this an exclusive arrangement, we can stop using the condoms."

He stared at her, then narrowed his eyes. "I kind of assumed we *were* exclusive, Sara. Have you been seeing someone else?"

Wayne's face momentarily flashed into her mind. She hadn't seen him after their meeting on her first day on the island, or even thought about him recently. "No! Of course not."

A deep red flush was spreading across Jack's face and her heart hammered. *Uh-oh. This is not going how I envisioned.*

"I don't do anything *but* exclusive," he said tightly. "I didn't realize you felt differently."

"I don't! That's what I'm trying to say. I thought you'd be happy about this."

A veil had come over his face. "I haven't been single in a long time. I'm pretty rusty with the dating rules. You're much more up to speed than me."

Sara bolted upright, inhaling sharply. "What the hell is that supposed to mean?"

"You told me yourself. That you avoid serious relationships."

She itched to slap him, but held back. "Are you calling me a slut?"

"No," he said, speaking more calmly now, even as a pulse raced in his neck. "You and I just seem to have different ideas about what a relationship is."

"Good God. We haven't even been together that long.

Aren't you being slightly melodramatic?" She stood before she could boil over. "Just forget it. I'm going upstairs."

———

JACK SAT numb on the lounger, stunned. *What the hell just happened?* He sat back, lacing both hands on top of his head as he stared mindlessly at the waves tumbling onto the shore. When she'd mentioned exclusivity, he'd blurted out the first thing that came to his mind. But it had honestly never even occurred to him to think otherwise. He'd known a lot of guys over the years who thought differently, but not him.

Maybe I came across a little too cold. But this was a perfect example of what had bothered him since the beginning. Sara was free-thinking and spirited. It was one of his favorite things about her.

Except the thought of her being free-thinking where he was concerned.

Alex's quiet warning popped into his head, and he rubbed his eyes, groaning. "Jack, you have a lot to lose here. This could screw up everything you're trying to accomplish."

But Sara knocked him senseless. She had almost from the beginning, despite their rocky start. He wanted to be with her. Badly.

But does she feel the same way about me?

AFTER MAKING HIMSELF DINNER, he sat down in front of the TV to watch football, but he couldn't concentrate. Quiet thumps indicated Sara occasionally moving around upstairs, and his gaze drifted up again and again. As their earlier discussion ran through his head, Jack's face warmed, and he swiped a hand over his chin. "Shit, I really overreacted there."

Communication wasn't one of his strengths, and Sara obviously hadn't been pleased with his reaction. His first instinct had been to focus on her announcement as a reason to stay away from her. But was that fair? He leaned forward, resting his face in his hands. "I need to apologize. I was an asshole."

Another sound came from upstairs, and he stood with a sigh and left his apartment, climbing the stairs. He raised his hand before her door to knock, then hesitated. *What if she's still really pissed? She'll probably yell at me.* He scowled at himself. "Stop being such a wimp. You deserve to get yelled at." With that, he rapped three times and held his breath, expecting the worst.

When Sara opened the door, her eyes were big and red-rimmed, and the breath he'd been holding exploded out.

Oh, shit. This is worse.

He hated it when women cried, even more when he was the cause. She sniffed and stared at him, but didn't say anything.

"Do you think we could try that conversation again?" he asked. "I'm not really sure what happened there, except that I reacted like a complete asshole. I'm sorry."

Her bottom lip trembled, and his heart flopped over, raising all four of its proverbial legs in the air. "I was trying to make you happy," she whispered.

He still stood on her threshold. "Can I come in?" He spoke softly, but his gut was twisting.

She jerked a nod. "Please?"

With that he rushed forward, holding his arms out. She tumbled into them and cried against his shoulder. He led her to the couch, then cradled her against his chest, feeling like dog shit.

No, worse.

"I'm sorry. Please stop crying." He stroked her head softly, repeating the words every now and again for good measure, and eventually she quieted.

Sara sat up, snuffling, and reached behind the couch. She grabbed a box of tissues off the table, dabbing her eyes. "I didn't mean to make you mad. I thought you'd be happy."

"Oh, darlin', I'm not mad. I'm so sorry. Like I told you this afternoon, I'm pretty rusty at all this. I didn't put it well. At all."

"You don't think I'm a slut?"

"Of course not." *God, Powell. What is wrong with you?* Then something occurred to him, and he cupped her face. "I never said you were a slut. It never even entered my mind."

"You kind of insinuated I was easy."

"I'm sorry. You said you had never gotten seriously involved before. I took that to mean you keep your relationships... casual." He held his breath, hoping she wouldn't blow up at that.

She didn't. Instead, she sat back on the couch, leaning her head back. "I have kept them casual. I lived with a guy when I was twenty-one—I was head over heels. Until he left me for a hot chick with a killer body. He was pretty clear about the reasons." She rolled her head to meet his gaze. "You're not the only one who's afraid of getting hurt, ok?"

He turned sideways to face her as he stroked a finger down her arm. "He was an idiot. You are a hot chick with a killer body."

She stared tiredly at the wall. "You don't have to humor me. It's ok."

"What do you mean? Sara, I think you're incredible. All of you. I wouldn't change a thing."

Her eyes misted up again. *Shit, did I say the wrong thing again?*

"Thanks. That means a lot to me." She turned to look him full in the face. "Jack, I like being with you, and I've never been promiscuous—ever. But I'm not looking for a deep, serious relationship. Is that ok with you?"

And that's the million-dollar question. But maybe one that doesn't need to be answered just yet. "Yes. We moved pretty quickly into this. Let's just take things as they come, all right?"

She smiled. "That sounds great. I feel really comfortable around you, and that's important to me."

"Good. It's important to me too." He relaxed again, slowly drawing a finger across her shoulder. "I think your curves are glorious. You're exactly what a woman should look like." He moved to the center of her low-cut top, drawing his index finger down that deep, delicious valley. "And don't get me started on your breasts." When he met her gaze again, she was smiling. He locked his eyes on her mouth. "I could go on for days about your lips."

He gently kissed her, wanting to be soft and seductive. But she grabbed the back of his head and smashed into his mouth, her tongue demanding.

Oh my God, this woman.

He forced himself to pull back. They were both breathing hard, their faces inches apart. "So that patch of yours is fully operational?"

She smiled. "It is."

"Then what are we waiting for?" He took her hand and led her to the bedroom.

Soft moonlight filtered into the room as he pulled Sara's shirt over her head. He stroked her face, kissing her softly. She needed to be loved right now, not devoured.

Loved? Where did that come from?

Jack pushed the thought from his mind, and they quickly undressed each other before sliding between the sheets of her bed. He stretched out next to her, propping his head in his hand as he rested on one elbow. He slowly drew one hand down the side of her neck, over her collarbone, and finally cupped one full breast. Unable to resist, he bent over and drew it into his mouth. Her skin was like warm cream, and she moaned, arching her back closer.

Sara possessed the most incredible breasts he'd ever seen. He had literally had dreams about them. He moved back to her ear, hard as a rock as he pressed himself against her thigh. "Don't ever doubt how sexy you are. Can't you tell what you do to me?" he whispered against her ear. Moving his mouth back to hers one fluttery kiss at a time, Jack slid his tongue in, wrapping it around hers as he fanned his fingers over her stomach. Then he moved his way lower. She opened one leg and gasped as he slipped his fingers home. Pressing harder against his mouth, she murmured, "I really want you."

I noticed.

He smiled but didn't say the words out loud, not wanting to disturb the chemistry that was building. She opened wide and urged him on top of her. He eased his way inside, *fully* naked for the first time. The intense sensation—the sheer intimacy of it— rocketed through him. "Oh God. You feel amazing."

She laughed, a deep, soft sound that was different from her usual laugh, and a shudder wracked him. They moved faster, and he completely gave in to his own need, drowning in the all-encompassing sensation. He growled deep in his chest, and Sara cupped his ass with both hands, urging him on. He continued driving into her as his climax rose and surrounded him. He froze in place, crying out at the force of it.

Slowly, he regained the use of his muscles, languidly kissing across Sara's neck. He shifted half-off her, tracing his hand down her side then up her thigh, wanting to give her a small sense of what he'd just experienced. She grasped his wrist, stopping the motion. "You don't need to."

He faced her. "I might be clueless, but I'm not that clueless."

She gave him a warm, almost shy smile. "Jack, you already gave me everything I needed." She lifted his hand to her mouth and kissed it softly.

He enfolded her, their arms wrapping tightly around each other. *Oh, my Sara. I'm not sure we want the same things in life, but, my God, we are good together.*

Chapter Twenty

JANUARY...

Sara stood in the stuffy gear room, fanning herself with one hand to ward off the afternoon heat. There was an air conditioner high on one wall, but it only got turned on when Alex worked on equipment. Electricity was *expensive* on the island, and not something to be wasted. She and Jack were back on solid ground since their tiff and the make-up session afterward. It had been a long time since she'd been with a man who saw her. The real her.

The Sara she tried to keep hidden.

But that night, Jack had looked deep inside and hadn't blinked. Sara just had to decide whether that thrilled or terrified her. She wasn't cut out to be Betty Crocker and he seemed ok with that. For now, at least. She had discovered that the future generally worked out as it was meant to, so she didn't worry about things too much.

To her relief, Christmas had been a low-key affair. Sara and Jack had held true to their agreement and skipped presents for each other. Jack worked the morning at Ocean Surf, and it was also Hope's turn to work the holiday. She and Alex had set aside a long table in the restaurant for employees who didn't have dinner plans. Sara and Jack joined them, along with two house-keepers and several landscapers. Hope helped with the dinner service, so Alex acted as their host. It had been a very touching dinner, with the leaders of Half Moon Bay making sure no one felt left out on the important holiday.

Hope and Alex had presented each employee with a generous Christmas bonus, Hope explaining it was because they wanted to share a windfall they had received. As part of the management team, Sara received $5000, and even part-time employees received $1000.

A smile still graced Sara's face as she approached the neatly arranged gear area, excited about starting the new year, as well as the prospect immediately ahead. She picked up a rental regu-lator and slung a BCD over her shoulder as the door opened. Expecting Jack, Sara still smiled as Zach entered. "Closing up shop?"

"Yeah," the boy said. "Just makin' sure I cleaned everythin' up. You goin' divin'?"

She nodded. "Just waiting for Jack, who's teaching an intro class. He's going to show me the coral nursery!"

Finally...

Zach opened his eyes wide, and enthusiasm poured out of every cell in his body. "Oh! You'll love it. I've dived it twice with Alex. He actually let me start some new fragments! It was so cool."

Sara laughed. Zach was infectious—everyone loved him. "I've been eager to see it too, but couldn't work out a time with Jack until now. You want to join us?"

"I'd love to!"

She had tagged along in Jack's group twice now, but had

never dived alone with him. Her heart slid a little as that prospect disappeared, but it wasn't like they'd never have another opportunity. "Excellent. I'll have two experts to show me."

"I'll head to the pool and see if Jack needs any help. Maybe speed him up some." Zach whirled and rushed through the door, but stopped just outside. "Here he comes now. Must be done. I'll go get the rest of the stuff."

Jack entered the room, sending an amused glance up the pier. "Something's sure got him excited." Then his smile took on a decidedly suggestive look as he slid his gaze to her. "Something's sure got me excited. Hi there, darlin'." He swept up to her and kissed her hard, moving her backward several steps.

Giggling, she smacked him on both shoulders. She loved his drawled *darlin'*. Only a Texan could pull that off. "Take it easy there. But yes. I invited Zach to join us, and he's pretty stoked about it."

Jack's shoulders fell. "I was kind of looking forward to it being just us."

"Me too. But I couldn't resist inviting him."

A reluctant smile rose on his face. "Yeah, I probably would have too."

She ran a finger over his raspy jawline. "Maybe you'll get me alone later."

"That sounds promising—"

Whatever else Jack might have said was interrupted when Zach re-entered, wearing two BCDs and carrying a reg in each hand. Jack was similarly dressed but had set his reg on the workbench, where he now went to pick it up. "Ok, gang. Let's get the rest of our stuff and set up."

Zach's wide smile disappeared as he looked between them. "Wait a minute. I'm not buttin' in on a date here, am I?"

Jack grinned. "No, don't worry. Diving is hardly a date."

Zach snorted. "You obviously haven't seen Alex and Hope when they come back from divin' together."

Sara laughed. "Well, we're not nearly as disgusting as those two."

The trio jumped off the pier, descending through the clear water, and Jack set a heading on his compass. Sara didn't have one, but relaxed, knowing she was with an expert. As they progressed across the white sand, Zach kept pulling ahead. Jack finally grabbed his fin, moving his arms up and down in a *slow down* gesture. Zach just shrugged and grinned around his regulator.

They swam much farther than Sara had been expecting before the large structure appeared out of the hazy blue water.

I can't believe it got blown that far!

The structure, which had been a roof in its previous life, looked like a gigantic tent, and Jack led them in a slow circle around it. He was an effortless diver, completely at ease in the water. Even Zach moved comfortably, adjusting his buoyancy with skill. There was no doubt who the newbie in this group was. But even that knowledge couldn't dampen Sara's excitement. The first things that caught her attention were the white plastic tree-like structures spaced at even intervals along the roof. Alex had described them to her, but seeing them with her own eyes brought the scene to life. Small pieces of coral hung from each branch by a loop of fishing line, with each tree housing corals in different stages of development.

Near the far edge, Jack hovered before a cluster of growths directly attached to the roof. He wrote on his slate and turned it around.

Brain coral. These are mine :)

Each of the small pieces comprised of raised ridges, folded into patterns like its namesake. Sara inspected them closely, fascinated by the intricacy.

Shifting her gaze back to the plastic trees, she was eager to investigate them further, and finned along the line. A plastic tag hung from each tree, listing the type of coral it contained—staghorn, elkhorn, lettuce, star. Each species was different colors and sizes, and it was a more impressive project than she had expected. Her heart soared as she moved closer, thrilled at finally experiencing it firsthand.

While studying the forking, flat pieces of elkhorn coral, movement on a branch caught her eye. A brown crab, the size of her palm and with long, hairy legs, delicately moved down the coral. Sara's first reaction was horror, but curiosity soon overtook the fear as she watched the strange creature picking at the coral fragments, maneuvering delicious morsels into its mouth.

Jack has to see this! He'll love it. He and Zach were two trees down, and Jack was pointing to a piece of light-green coral. Sara took off with an enthusiastic sweep of her legs. Eager to get Jack's attention, she was swimming hard when her fin smacked against an obstruction.

The *crack* behind her was loud in the silent water.

Oh no! Please tell me that wasn't what I think it was...

With her heart plummeting, Sara whirled around. The water was already cloudy as the coral fragments scattered in slow motion. The white plastic frame slowly drifted toward the roof's surface. Desperate to rescue it, Sara rushed forward, kicking as hard as she could. A matching *crack* sounded from behind her.

Oh, please no. This can't be happening!

Forgetting the first tree, she spun around, and her eyes confirmed what her heart already knew. A second tree gracefully eased to the roof's surface as coral fragments were flung far and wide.

Sara lifted her eyes from the disaster to focus on Jack and Zach. They were frozen, hovering motionless at the next tree.

Both were wide-eyed, wearing matching expressions of horror. Quickly swimming away from the roof, Sara turned to take stock of the damage.

Maybe it's not that bad. Think positive!

Both trees lay flat on the roof. Broken corals lay everywhere, and a cloud of sediment was spreading through the clear water. More starts had tumbled down the sloped surface and were buried in the sand below. Her breath hitched at the destruction before her.

Stop it! Think—how can we fix this?

Jack surged over, and rapid bursts of bubbles exploded from his regulator. Zach held both hands to the top of his head, like he was trying to keep his head from exploding. *Really, Zach? Isn't that a little over the top?*

But getting irritated at Zach was hardly productive. It was her fault. Sara frantically jabbed at Jack in a thumb's up gesture. He nodded, and the trio ascended to the surface.

Jack ripped his mask around his neck. "Oh my God, Sara! What the hell happened?"

"Oh, man," Zach added. "This is so not good."

Sara whipped her eyes between them. "I forgot where my fins were! I kicked the tree and when I went to see what happened, I kicked the other one!"

Jack closed his eyes and rubbed them with both hands. "Oh, shit."

Sara groaned. "Alex is going to kill me."

Jack snapped his eyes wide open. "Oh, bullshit! He's not going to kill you. He's going to kill *me!*"

Zach nodded sagely. "He's got a point there."

Sara held a hand out, trying to placate the crowd. "Alex isn't going to kill anyone, ok? I'm sure he'll understand it was an accident. You're both getting upset over nothing."

Both of them stared slack-jawed at her.

"You've never seen him pissed off, have you?" Zach said, then gave a terrified bark of laughter.

She took a deep breath, inhaling as much confidence—or maybe delusion—as possible. "Please. I can handle Alex in my sleep. We'll simply ask him how to repair the damage and proceed accordingly." She sent a beseeching look to Jack, rushing the next words out. "Please don't make me do this alone."

He scowled. "You can't dive alone! Of course I'll help. Assuming I'm still alive."

Another nervous titter escaped Zach, and Sara's heart twisted as she stared at the wide-eyed boy. "You're completely blameless, so just relax."

"Uh-huh. Pretty sure I'm what's called collateral damage."

Jack turned to him. "She's right—you don't have to be involved in this. Alex told me he was going to the shooting range this afternoon." He pressed both palms against his forehead. "Oh God. I'm so dead." Pulling his hands down, Jack schooled his expression. "What I'm trying to say is that he's not even around right now. Zach, just go home and go to school tomorrow. Sara and I will figure out a plan." He met her eyes. "I'm working with Alex in the morning, and I can tell him about it then. I'll see him before you will."

Sara's heart tried to pound out of her chest. "I can come with you. We'll face him together."

Jack shook his head. "No, I need to do this alone. Really."

Sara glanced down. Forty feet below the surface, a dense cloud surrounded the coral nursery. Stomach sinking, she nodded at Jack.

Chapter Twenty-One

JACK ARRIVED at Half Moon Bay early the next morning, hoping for a chance to talk to Alex alone. But Tommy was already there, and the two men were both hard at work getting the boat ready. With a sigh, Jack jumped in too, resigned to wait until after the trip to speak with Alex about the coral-nursery debacle.

There was a slight tension on the boat. At first, Jack thought it was coming from him and his anxiety. As they traveled to the first dive site, Alex was noticeably quieter and more serious. Tommy worked double-time to improve the mood on the boat and did a great job of keeping things fun with the guests. But Alex's mood made Jack even more nervous.

Great, I have to tell him his favorite project got clobbered, and he's already in a bad mood.

Fortunately, they had fantastic dives and the time underwater improved Alex's temper. He was more like his usual self and laughing with the divers by the time they returned to the dock. As soon as the guests were off the boat, he slung two BCDs over his shoulders and headed for the gear room.

Never one to shirk an unpleasant task, Jack lifted two more

and followed. He entered the gear room and shut the door. "Can I talk to you for a second?"

Alex hung his BCD and turned, moving his eyes to the shut door, then back to Jack. "Sure. What's up?"

"I need to tell you something, and you're not going to like it." He straightened his spine, meeting Alex's gaze. "I took Sara and Zach on a dive yesterday to the nursery. I wasn't watching closely enough, and two PVC trees got knocked over. They're obliterated. All three of us feel terrible."

Alex had stood expressionless during his explanation. Now he lifted a brow. "So that's what happened, huh?"

"You knew already?"

He leaned against his workbench. "Yeah. I went for a swim this morning, right over the roof. I could see from the surface that something was wrong, so I free dived down to verify it."

"Forty feet?"

Alex eyed him steadily. "I'm trained in a lot of things, Jack."

He swallowed. *Don't remind me.*

"Who knocked them over?"

"Doesn't matter who did it. It was my fault. Sara and Zach were my responsibility, and I wasn't paying enough attention."

A tiny smile crossed Alex's face, as if he couldn't help it. "So, it was Sara."

Jack stared at him but didn't reply. He wasn't about to blame her when he was the divemaster.

Alex's smile widened, but something else flickered through his eyes. Jack was pretty sure it was respect. "I knew things wouldn't be dull with her around. And I'm sure she didn't do it on purpose."

"As soon as we're done cleaning up, I'll go down and repair it as best I can."

"I'll go with you."

Jack pressed his lips together, wanting to say that he didn't have to, but Alex wasn't the type to let someone else repair his project. And it didn't escape him that Alex's reply had been a statement, not a question.

Jack nodded. "I'm really sorry. We all are. Sara and Zach love that coral project." The previous night, Sara had been in tears, wanting to call Alex and confess. Jack had finally convinced her to let him handle it. He did *not* want Alex thinking he was afraid to stand up to the former SEAL, even if he was. A little.

Finally, Alex relaxed his posture. "It's all right. We can repair it and start some new fragments to replace the ones that got killed."

Jack winced.

Alex stared at him. "Can I give you a little advice? It's maybe not the best idea to take two brand new divers to a delicate area and let them get close. I was pretty careful when I showed them the transplants on the house reef."

Jack laced his fingers together on top of his head. "Yeah. This was one of the stupider things I've done as a divemaster. And both Sara and Zach wanted to tell you themselves, by the way. But I told them it was my fault, not theirs."

"I'm glad you told me." Alex turned and removed his rebreather from its hanger. He opened the backpack-like canister and removed a small cylinder, walking over to the compressor with it. "I need to fill this while we finish cleaning up."

Jack had seen the rebreather hanging with Alex's gear, but had never seen him dive with the specialized air system. "I know a guy who has a rebreather, but I've never used one."

"It's what we used most often during ops. And this repair is going to take a while—probably more than one session. The rebreather allows me to stay down longer. You can take off when you run low on air. We'll get the trees fixed in a few days."

It was after 7 p.m. when Jack entered his apartment, exhausted and still cold, even after blasting the heater in his truck all the way home. When Alex had told him he could leave after running low on air, Jack never even considered it. Instead, after working for an hour, he had returned to the pier and swapped out tanks before returning to the nursery. Alex's eyes had clearly showed surprise when he'd returned. Jack had swapped out tanks a third time, and fortunately, Alex called it a night before the third one ran dry.

By then, Jack had been nearly shivering and his hands were clumsy. He had no idea how Alex stayed down so long, and without the warming exercise of swimming back and forth from the pier. Then again, maybe he did know.

Damn rebreather. Damn SEAL.

He'd just tossed his keys on the counter when his exterior wall vibrated with the sound of footsteps trotting down the stairs. This was quickly followed by a knock on his door. He'd texted Sara prior to starting the repair work, but had been too tired to think about it after they had finished. He opened the door. "Sorry. I forgot to text you when we were done."

She darted her eyes all over his body, studying his face. "You're ok? He didn't punch you out or anything?"

Jack snorted and led her to the couch. "Nope. He was actually fairly mellow about it. But he already knew. That might have helped."

She furrowed her brow. "I didn't tell him. Or Hope—I swear."

"I know. He discovered the damage when he was swimming this morning. We spent several hours on it, and I think we can finish tomorrow. We'll need to look out for some damaged coral to use as a source for new fragments, though." He rubbed his face with both hands.

She eyed the sweatshirt he wore with the hood tightened around his face. "You want a back rub?"

Lowering his hands, he smiled at her. "That sounds great. But what I really need is a long, hot shower and dinner."

"I haven't eaten either. You shower and I'll order us dinner. The restaurant here just opened, and I grabbed a menu. You'll feel better in no time." She headed toward the door, then turned back. "Thanks, Jack. I really screwed up."

He gave her a tired smile. "No, you didn't. It was an accident. Besides, I learned all kinds of new stuff about the nursery today. Now I'm an expert."

She flashed him a brilliant smile that almost made the whole ordeal worth it, then walked out the door. With an exhausted groan, Jack trudged toward the shower.

THE NEXT DAY passed in a flurry of activity for Sara. Her advertising efforts were paying off. The spa was booked solid most days now, and they had recently hired Evie, one of Selena's recruits, who was also trained to perform manicures and pedicures. Sara's packed schedule prevented her from ruminating over the conversation with Alex that had started the day. He had accepted her apology with grace, showing no signs of anger, but she still felt terrible. She'd had lunch with Hope, who confirmed that Alex didn't hate her.

"Any more than usual, at least," Sara had said with a smirk.

"Do you hate him?"

"Of course not!"

Hope shrugged. "That's how he feels. I don't begin to understand why you two enjoy circling around each other, swiping with a front paw once in a while. You both enjoy picking at each other, yet you'd be mortified if the other actually did think less of you."

Sara sighed. "Before this disaster, I would have said it was because I had the upper hand. I only want the best for you, and he knows that. But I think I just leveled the playing field."

"As the wholly impartial person caught in the middle, I think that's a good thing."

Now, as Sara scanned the appointment book, she sighed heavily, her mind back on work.

"What's got you down in the dumps?" Selena asked. "The schedule is full!"

Sara smiled at her. "I know. It's a good thing. I just wish we had more room to expand."

Selena panned around the area. "Don't know how we could do that. Unless we move the reception somewhere else. But how would that work?"

"It wouldn't. We'll just have to be happy with what we've got."

That was the problem, and shame twisted her gut. She wasn't happy with what they had. *Hope has been so good to me! How can I tell her managing a tiny spa isn't what I want? She wants to spend her money expanding the resort and the bungalows, not the spa. Stop being ungrateful, Sara!*

But she couldn't help imagining the possibilities of a larger facility, with more staff and more offerings. Her dream...

Chapter Twenty-Two

LAUGHTER RANG out around the table and Sara couldn't help joining in, even though she was the subject. This time, Hope and her friend Cindy had joined Selena, April, and herself for drinks at Charlie's.

April sat back in her chair with a grin. "When I told you to date Jack if you thought he was so hot, I didn't think you'd actually take me up on it."

"I'm never one to give advice I'm not willing to follow myself."

"You're luckier than me, that's for sure," Selena said.

Hope leaned forward. "You two didn't exactly hit it off, but I think you make a great couple."

Sara grinned back. "Oh, be quiet. You don't get a vote. You're married to a Greek god who cracks walnuts with his pecs."

The laughter increased as Hope sat back, pressing her lips together primly. "Be nice, Sara. I do too get a vote. And I'll have you know I've never seen him crack anything bigger than pecans."

"It must be genetic," Cindy said. Since the wedding, she'd

had several of her thin black braids dyed bright blue, and they looked spectacular against her ebony skin. "You two move here and find great men right away. I've been lookin' for years."

"Does Jack have any brothers?" Selena asked.

"Yes. He has two sisters and three brothers, but they live in Texas. Sorry, ladies."

"Wow," Hope said. "That's a whole lotta siblings."

Sara shrugged. "You know what they say about things being bigger in Texas."

April rested her chin on her palm, grinning. "I guess you're in a position to know, huh?"

The heat washed over Sara's cheeks as the table erupted into laughter. "No comment, except that I'm a happy woman." It was time to change the subject, so she turned her attention to April. "No one interesting at the other dive shop where you work?"

She had been watching Hope and April carefully, but couldn't detect any tension between them. Sara would still be more comfortable if April were involved with someone, but if Hope wasn't concerned, then she couldn't interfere too much, despite itching to do so. She'd never asked Hope about April, a rare flash of reluctance in not wanting to upset her sister's happiness.

April shook her head. "There's just one other divemaster. He's in his fifties and married."

Hope glanced at her watch. "Speaking of married, I'd better get going. I'm meeting Alex for dinner. We're having a date night." She turned to Sara. "We're diving the house reef tomorrow afternoon, right?"

"Even if I have to drag you away from the office or your oven. I'm not taking no for an answer this time." Hope had canceled on her twice.

She laughed and stood. "Don't worry, I cleared the decks. I

don't want to be late—I haven't even seen Alex today. See you guys later."

After Hope left, Cindy turned back to her daiquiri. "That's what I want. What they have."

Selena smiled. "What? A tall, gorgeous man head over heels in love with you? Who wouldn't?"

Sara set her beer on the table with a frown. "Me, actually." They all turned to stare at her. "I'm not just saying that because he's my brother-in-law. I'd much rather have an everyday kind of man. Someone like Alex would be just... too much."

"I'm not sure that's a compliment to Jack," April said.

"Yes, it is. He's sensitive and artistic. And dependable. I like him a lot." A big smile had come over her face. She'd never consciously thought about what she found so attractive about Jack, but was happy with her answer. "And those huge brown eyes. I'm kind of a sucker for those. Ok, he is pretty good looking."

Cindy raised her glass. "To finding our fish in the sea. And throwing back the bad ones."

THE NEXT AFTERNOON, Sara put her scuba kit together alongside Hope. They kneeled under the shady palapa, preparing to dive the house reef. Hope pulled off her T-shirt, revealing an orange bikini top. Sara stared, sure she had to be imagining it. *Must be a shadow.* Then Hope moved into the sunlight and there was no mistaking it. Sara giggled, which quickly turned into guffaws.

Hope stared. "What's so funny?"

"God, Hope! You've got a huge bite mark on your boob!" It was at the top of her breast, just above the material.

She frowned and pressed a hand to it. "Dammit. I thought it

would have faded by now. Good thing we decided not to go on the afternoon boat trip."

Sara couldn't stop laughing. "He *bites* you?"

Hope sighed absently and screwed her regulator onto the tank. "No, biting is usually my thing. Alex decided on a little payback last night."

Sara's laughter died away as she studied her sister. "Wow. I didn't realize you two were so... vigorous."

Hope grinned and her ears turned pink. "What can I say? We're a happy couple."

Sara let the subject go, still surprised how much Hope had changed.

But apparently Hope wasn't finished yet. She sat up, looking thoughtful. "I've always felt so safe with Alex that even sex that's a little rough has never... triggered me. And he's incredibly sensitive about all of it."

Sara gave her a small smile, acknowledging that Hope and Alex shared facets of themselves that others never saw. "I'm very happy for you. I can't tell you how much."

Hope stared evenly at her. "There's a lot of benefits to a committed relationship, you know. Maybe now *you're* the one who needs to be reminded that not all men run off."

"I know. And I admit some of my fear to commit is because of Dad. But don't try to sell me a ball and chain just yet."

They both laughed and returned to their equipment, but Sara was brought back to that awful time. Caleb's attack had resulted in Hope being hospitalized, and Sara, only fifteen, had been terribly worried about her. Her older sister had changed drastically afterwards. Eventually, the physical wounds had healed, and testifying against Caleb had helped provide some closure for her. But Sara had begun to despair of Hope ever overcoming the emotional wounds. It had taken Half Moon Bay —and especially Alex—for that.

Sara fumbled with her regulator, bringing herself back to the present, and Hope arched a brow. "Everything ok? Need help with that?"

Exhaling the entire memory to the past, where it firmly belonged, Sara shook her head and screwed the reg onto its tank. "No help needed. Everything is going great. St. Croix has been good for both of us."

THE SISTERS JUMPED off the side of the pier and into the warm water. Hope led, since she had dived the house reef many times and was much more experienced. She moved gracefully and effortlessly underwater. Sara was still trying to get the hang of diving, but a couple of dives since the coral nursery disaster had gotten her back on the horse. Her confidence—and skill—had grown accordingly. With enough experience, diving was something Sara thought she could actually match Hope at.

The house reef was thriving. Hope pointed out several coral transplants, including some Alex hadn't shown Sara on her check-out dive. Her heart stilled when a sea turtle swam by, not believing how close it approached. Or its size—its shell was three feet long. The turtle calmly glanced at her, but studied Hope closely before swimming away. Before she knew it, Sara was low on air, and they returned across the sandy shallows of the bay, climbing the ladder onto the pier.

As they walked toward the gear room, bartender Clark exited the dive shop and hurried up the pier, carrying an empty box. Hope frowned. "Poor Clark. Kamila had a rough pregnancy and delivered their son, but he's had one stomach problem after another. I've been mixing drinks so Clark can have some time off. He's been stressed."

Sara smiled at her. "He's lucky to work here. You'll bend over backwards to help him out."

Hope shrugged. "It's the least I can do." She craned her neck up at the spa as they passed by. "You're doing a great job. Seems like we're fully booked most of the time now."

"Thanks, we are. It's working well now that we have Evie doing nails and massages. I just wish we had more room. I wonder if we can fit another hair station and a couple of mani-pedi spots."

"Why don't you and Selena go visit some other spas on the island? Get an idea of how they run things? That might give you some ideas."

Sara stopped. "That's a great idea. Especially if I can get you to foot the bill for a massage."

"That's only fair." Hope grinned. "My hair has never looked this good."

SOFT, ambient music emanated from hidden speakers as Sara stood with Selena in the large reception room of Orchid, one of the most successful spas on St. Croix. This room alone was nearly as large as all of Hibiscus. They had each received a massage, using two of the ten rooms, and the owner had just given them a tour of the facility.

The experience had left Sara more frustrated than inspired. Orchid was a beautiful, serene facility, with tropical hardwood furnishings accented with green plants. Exotic potted orchids were displayed throughout, and a living wall of exotic green plants stood behind the check-in area. But the tour only highlighted that their own Hibiscus Spa couldn't accommodate any expansion.

Sara and Selena said goodbye to the owner and continued into the warm afternoon. They walked down a pebble path fringed with more orchids, and the soft music continued. A man walked toward them and as he got closer, Sara recognized Wayne Timmons, who owned Serenity. *He probably won't even remember me.*

He wore tailored slacks and a dark-red Cuban shirt and gave them both a polite smile, then his gaze lingered on Sara. He tipped his head to one side and stopped before her. "We've met before. Don't tell me! At Serenity... Sara, wasn't it?"

She schooled her face, not wanting to show her surprise. "Yes. Nice to see you again, Wayne."

"Likewise. I'm here to meet with the manager. I'm doing some research for my spa. Are you enjoying your new role?"

She nodded. "You have an excellent memory, and I'm very fortunate with my job. We were here doing a bit of research ourselves."

He took a step closer, holding her with his eyes. "I've got quite a facility planned, and my offer still stands. I'd be happy to discuss any opportunities you might be interested in."

He had a magnetic pull, but she resisted, no longer interested now that she was with Jack. "Thank you. I'll keep it in mind. Have a good afternoon." With a nod, she stepped around him.

Selena scurried around his other side, but waited until he was out of earshot before grabbing Sara's arm. "Who was *that?*"

"He built Serenity, and he's working on a new spa facility. I met him right after I moved here. He wanted to talk about a position in his spa."

Selena snorted and took one final glance behind them. "I don't think that was the position he's interested in, Sara. Girl, you have all the luck."

"My life is going just fine. But after experiencing Serenity, I'm sure his spa will be something else."

The two women entered Sara's car, and she couldn't deny that if Hibiscus wasn't owned by her sister, she'd be interested in Wayne's business opportunity. Jack's earnest face flashed into her mind, and she sighed.

I'm perfectly capable of keeping my business and love lives separate. Family, on the other hand...

A running film of what Wayne's facility might look like occupied her the entire drive home.

Chapter Twenty-Three

A WEEK LATER, Sara changed into shorts and a T-shirt at the end of the day. She and Jack had fallen into a happy routine of meeting up as soon as they got home, something they both greatly looked forward to. A private smile or passing touch was all they had time for at work, and neither was interested in broadcasting their interest in each other. Which wasn't necessary anyway, since everyone at the resort knew about them.

There was a knock on her door, and a smile rose as she hurried to answer it. Jack stood there with a crooked smile, a backpack slung casually over one shoulder. He wore cargo shorts and a Houston Astros T-shirt. "One of the benefits of living below you is I can tell when you get home. Let's go for a walk."

"A walk? I've been on my feet all day."

His smile widened. "It's not too far, I promise. You'll be glad you did, darlin'." Without waiting for an answer, he turned and trotted down the stairs. *Ok, now I'm curious.*

Sara put on a pair of sports sandals and followed, quickly catching up. "What can I say? I'm a sucker for that Texas twang."

He grinned, clasped her hand, and led her south along the powdery beach. There was a large swath of undeveloped land between the complex and the outer reaches of Frederiksted. The jungle framed the white sandy beach for a hundred yards, then iron shore took over, forming a rocky surface that ended in a tall ledge above the water line. The waves crashed below, occasional spray misting around them.

Jack picked his way across the rock, still leading Sara by the hand. "Be careful here. Don't want to twist an ankle."

"I wouldn't have to worry about twisting my ankle if we were relaxing in my apartment, Jack."

"Come on. Where's your sense of adventure?"

"Reserved for my days off."

He laughed and edged toward the vegetation, continuing into the jungle, where they weaved between the trees. Sara scoured the ground nervously. "If I get bitten by a snake, you're in big trouble."

"There are no snakes on St. Croix, so relax."

"Really? That's much better."

"Well, not many."

She frowned at his back, but continued walking. Ocean waves pounded the cliff to their right. What they followed could hardly be called a path. It was more just bent grass and trampled brush, and Sara was thinking about telling him to turn around when he angled toward the ocean again.

"Just about there..." He turned back and gave her a grin before continuing.

"If you say so. This better be worth it, Jack."

But, true to his word, the jungle ended suddenly, and they emerged into a small cove. The rocky shore rose on both ends out to sea, but a lovely crescent of salt-and-pepper beach lay before them. The ocean was rough here, with rollers crashing onto the beach.

Jack held an arm out, sweeping it before him. "What do you think?"

The turquoise water was even more colorful as it collided against the black, rocky edges of the cove. Her breath caught just looking at it. "It's beautiful! How did you find this?"

He continued, leading her by the hand to the center of the small area. The grains of sand were coarser than their apartment beach. "I like to explore. I went hiking soon after I moved here and discovered this cove. I come out here sometimes to draw. I like to imagine what's underneath the waves. And there's no easy entrance, so it's nice and private." He leaned in and whisked his lips over hers.

"Private, huh?"

"Oh, yeah." With another grin, he unslung his backpack and removed a rolled-up blanket, spreading it on the sand. "Come on. Rest those tired dogs."

Needing no further encouragement, Sara settled onto the blanket, folding her legs next to her. Jack pulled a bottle of wine out of his backpack, along with two stemless glasses. The top inch of the cork stuck out and he pulled it out with a pop, pouring them each a glass.

Sara arched a brow as she accepted hers. "You already opened the wine. A little presumptuous, aren't you?"

Touching her glass, he winked at her. "Didn't want to mess with the corkscrew out here. This way you have no idea how awful I am with those things. And if you had turned me down flat, I was already prepared to drown my misery."

She laughed and watched the water crashing onto the shore before them. Her workday slipped away as she sipped her wine, wonderfully relaxed. "I take it you're more of a beer o'clock guy, rather than wine."

He shrugged. "I guess so. Don't know too much about wine. Beer's easier. My older brother taught me all I needed to know about it. Which was basically which end is up, and that you'll regret it if you get to the point where you can't remember that."

A smile crossed Sara's face as she watched him. "What's it like, being part of such a big family? I can't even imagine."

Jack thought for a minute. "Loud. You get good at knowing when to fight and when to make peace. I'm right in the middle of the birth order, so I was usually the peacemaker."

"Any of your siblings also have an artistic leaning?"

"Not particularly. They seem to think I'm the sensitive one. My older sister is a neurologist, and she's the family over-achiever My brother is a minister—he's the deep thinker in the family. Though he hasn't thought out what to do with his life yet," he added with a laugh.

"Hope was always the driven one and me the lighthearted one. Partially to try to help her take things less seriously."

He swiveled his head to her. She'd told him about their dad, but Caleb was a subject she never brought up. "You two balance each other really well. Does being down here make you want to be more serious about life?"

Her heart sped up at that, but it was an honest question. It deserved an honest answer. "I'm still deciding. I think Hibiscus Spa could be so much more than it is, and it's frustrating sometimes."

"Maybe Hope will expand it."

She rolled a shoulder. "Maybe. She's got so much to manage. I hate to bring it up."

"You two get along well. I'm sure you'll figure it out."

A particularly large wave crashed against the black cliff, then rolled onto the beach in a long curl. "Do you swim here?"

"I did once, when the water was a little calmer. But I'm a pretty strong swimmer. This isn't really a swimming beach."

Sara was enjoying the privacy of the cove as she leaned on an elbow, the motion pulling the V-neck of her shirt down. His eyes were glued to her chest, which brought certain ideas to mind. "Oh? And what kind of beach is it, then? My eyes are up here, in case you forgot."

He met her gaze with a smoldering stare. "I told you. A *private* one. I was hoping it could become our special place."

Jack took her glass and set them both on the sand before stretching out alongside her. He slid his hand behind her head, slowly drawing the long strands of her hair through his fingers. Then he leaned close, pressing a deep kiss against her mouth. The ocean crashed around them as they came together.

SARA SAT ON THE BLANKET, watching the sun slip closer to the horizon. She poured more wine as the waves tumbled ashore. Jack lay naked on the blanket, sleeping on his side and facing her with his knees drawn up. He was breathing deeply, but not quite snoring. She studied his face, with those long, thick eyelashes she'd give anything to have. He had a small scar on his neck, just below the jawline that she liked to kiss, and she wanted to know what had caused it.

Am I falling in love here?

The thought caused tendrils of unease to creep through her abdomen. She enjoyed being in a relationship, but love was something else. That involved trusting on a whole different level, which was why she had tried to keep her relationships casual. The few times she had fallen hard hadn't ended well. But her feelings for Jack couldn't be classified as exactly casual anymore.

He trusted deeply once too. And it didn't end happily for him either. She flashed back to his reaction when they'd had the spat about being exclusive.

"I don't do anything else," he'd said.

Sara didn't either, but she had a strong feeling he had meant his words on a deeper level—that he didn't do casual relationships. Sighing, she turned back to the ocean.

Are you going to break my heart, Jack? Or am I going to break yours?

JACK PULLED ONTO THE HIGHWAY, done at Ocean Surf. Several days had passed since the idyll with Sara at the private cove, and he was meeting Robert at Breakers. And for once, his mind wasn't completely full of her.

Though I wish it was.

The previous evening, he'd thoroughly gone over his finances and confirmed his fears. He was barely making ends meet. He'd been floored when Alex and Hope had given him the $1000 bonus, but that had been quickly spent on his credit card bills. Yesterday was only his third shift in the last week. When he'd lived in Galveston, his primary occupation had been in construction, mostly carpentry work, but he'd dabbled in just about everything. As he neared Breakers, he drove by a house and flinched at the garage being built. *Guess I can see what the construction business is like here, or maybe day labor. Or just look into a third divemaster job.*

At least he was set for the next couple of weeks, thanks to Alex. He pulled into the parking lot, looking forward to some friendly conversation to distract him. It was early on a Tuesday evening, and the bar was mostly empty as he sat on a bar stool. "Hey, Maurice."

"Leatherback?" the big man asked.

"Bring it on."

Robert entered from the opposite side and took the seat next to him. Maurice brought over two beers.

"How's the photo business?" Jack asked.

"Busy. Thanks for workin' for me. Both these shoots came up last minute, and they both want it done tomorrow."

"You don't have to thank me. I need all the work I can get. Tommy is going to St. Thomas to visit family for a couple of weeks, so Half Moon Bay should have plenty of work for both of us, since Alex will be driving. Maybe April too."

"Yeah. I just hope I can fit it all in."

"Wish I had that problem. I might look into construction jobs or another dive operation soon."

Robert tapped the side of his bottle, staring into space for a long moment. Then he turned to face Jack. "I might have an answer for both of us. You like Half Moon Bay, right?"

"Yeah. It's my number one choice."

"I'd like to concentrate more on my photography and do less divin'. What if you and I change positions? You take the primary job, and I'll be on call?"

Jack could hardly believe his ears. "You sure you want to do that?"

"I am. I've been tryin' to figure out how to tell Alex I want to cut back. This would be perfect. I've never been full-time there, but the membrane system is almost done. Business will pick up after that—mark my words. I'll bet in a couple of months you'll have more work at Half Moon Bay than you know what to do with. This could work out great for both of us."

Jack clapped him on the shoulder. "Thanks. This is a huge load off my shoulders. I really didn't want to go back to construction."

Robert grinned. "Don't thank me yet. I should probably warn you about two divers you'll have tomorrow. Two women. One's very experienced, but her friend is brand new. And nervous. The experienced one doesn't pay any attention to her."

"Typical. I don't understand that. People want someone to dive with, then ignore them the whole time."

"Just be prepared to babysit and encourage. She clung to me both dives today."

Jack finished his beer. "That's no problem. I like working with new divers. It's fun to see them gain confidence—one of the best parts of the job." He brightened. "And Sara's joining me tomorrow. Maybe she can buddy up with the nervous nellie and give some reassurance as a fellow new diver."

Robert laughed. "As long as there aren't any coral trees in sight."

"She felt awful about that. I finally got her back to the nursery last week and it went great. She's a good diver. I think she'll enjoy tomorrow."

As HE WALKED toward his apartment, Jack was a strange mix of elation and trepidation. He glanced at Sara's lights but went to his own home, needing to think and wanting to be alone for that.

Everything could be falling into place for me.

But becoming financially dependent upon Half Moon Bay had one unavoidable complication—Sara. And he was falling hard for her.

If things don't work out between us, who do you think Alex and Hope are going to side with? Sara is family. And why would I even want to be with someone who isn't as committed to the relationship as me?

Chapter Twenty-Four

THE FOLLOWING MORNING, sunshine warmed Sara's back as she strolled down the pier, excited to dive on her day off. Jack, Alex, and April were readying *Surface Interval*. Hope couldn't join her for the dive, so she was hoping to buddy up with Jack. He saw her coming and headed her way, a smile lighting his face. "It's a beautiful morning. You looking forward to it?"

"Very much. Especially being with you."

A frown line appeared between his brows, and he pulled her toward the side of the pier. "About that—I need to talk to you. There's another new diver on board. Her buddy is very experienced, but she needs a little reassurance. Since you need to pair up anyway, would you mind diving with them? It might help Ashley feel more comfortable to be with someone else who's also new."

Sara's heart sank, but his idea was logical. "Sure. We can flail together." She laughed when he narrowed his eyes. It hadn't taken her long to figure out that arm flailing was highly discouraged by dive professionals.

Jack led her toward the boat. "They're already here. I'll introduce you."

She climbed aboard as Alex walked around the spacious main deck, pointing a pencil at people as he did a head count. He brightened when he saw her. "And you're twelve. That's everyone."

"Hello to you too, Alex."

"How's my favorite sister-in-law?"

"Fabulous, as usual."

Alex got the attention of the divers who had never been on board before and gave the boat briefing, describing emergency procedures. Jack introduced her to the two women. Ashley was mid-twenties, with a button nose and her brown hair cut in a pixie. She was adorable. Feeling like an ogre by comparison, Sara sat on the side bench next to her, and nodded to Ashley's friend Liz, who was older. She had a somewhat vampirish look, with pale skin and long black hair, which she was circling into a bun. Sara smiled at Ashley. "This is your first dive trip?"

"Yes. Liz has been diving for years and bugging me to join her. So here I am, on day two."

"I'm new too. We'll figure it out together."

April threw the lines, and they proceeded to the dive site. Sara kept up a steady stream of conversation as she tried to keep Ashley's attention. As Alex slowed the boat, the young woman blew out a big breath. "I don't know why I get so nervous."

Liz laughed. "Neither do I. Eighty-two-degree clear water and flat seas. Conditions don't get any easier than this, Ashley."

Well, aren't you the helpful one? But Sara kept a pleasant expression. "I know firsthand that Jack is an excellent divemaster. We're in good hands."

Ashley frowned, eyeing Jack. "I hope so. I really liked Robert. It makes me nervous to switch."

Liz rolled her eyes. "God, Ashley. Enough, already."

"We'll be fine," Sara said. "Jack gave me a fish to identify. We can try to find it together." She described a sergeant major, a common yellow-white fish with black bars. Ashley just nodded absently, watching Jack closely as he gave the dive briefing about the site and likely animal life. Sara tried to ignore Ashley's close attention toward Jack, surprised at the twisting in her stomach.

His group was first in the water, and Sara deflated her BCD and sank below the surface. Liz descended quickly, never sparing a glance for Ashley or Sara. Ashley was having difficulty, but Jack helped deflate her BCD and she began to sink.

After getting an ok signal from her, Jack turned to lead the group over the reef top. Sara added several puffs of air as they leveled off at fifty feet, staying well above the coral. She had learned her lesson about fins and coral. Colorful sergeant majors flitted all around the group, swooping to eat tiny creatures in the water column. Excited, Sara turned to point them out, but Ashley was staring straight at Jack's fins, keeping an even distance away. Sara poked her in the arm and pointed at the fish. Ashley shot her an annoyed glance and focused on Jack again. *Ok. I guess she needs a few minutes to settle down.*

Jack found an enormous green moray stretched out in a crevice, and beckoned the divers over one at a time. Sara leaned against him as she looked at the fearsome creature, welcoming his comforting touch. The eel made her uneasy, even though Alex had told her they weren't aggressive unless provoked.

Sara moved away so Ashley could have her turn. As Jack beckoned, she shook her head. He smiled and held out a hand. Ashley reached for it and swam forward, then transferred her hand to his arm. She maintained a death grip on him, taking a quick glance at the eel before looking away.

Jack took the lead again with Ashley at his side, her hand still gripping his upper arm. Sara narrowed her eyes, the twisting in her stomach turning into a hard, spiky ball.

Are you really nervous, Ashley, or are you going after Jack?

The rest of the dive progressed uneventfully, except Jack had to vent Ashley's BCD several times to keep her from becoming too buoyant. Liz appeared to be having a great time, peeking into crevices and under ledges, while totally ignoring her friend. Meanwhile, Ashley kept a laser focus on Jack, who practically ignored Sara. She ground her teeth against her mouthpiece.

After returning to the boat, Alex helped Sara to her spot, and she shrugged out of her tank. Ashley slumped next to her, staring at the fiberglass deck. "I'm not sure I'll ever get this."

Sara gave her a guilty pat on the shoulder, regretting her earlier thoughts. "Sure you will. Alex certified me not long ago and said it just takes a while."

Ashley gave Alex a quick glance before turning her attention back to Jack, focusing intently. Sara took a deep breath, trying to push down the resentful thoughts that kept rising. Sitting there stewing wouldn't do any good, so she got up to refill her water bottle as April handed out Hope's pineapple tartlets. Sara took one and moved under the covered deck, watching as Jack sat next to Ashley. Her head was still down, and he talked softly to her. Several minutes passed, and she finally looked up, giving Jack a shy smile. A stab of alarm knifed through Sara. He smiled back and nodded, squeezing Ashley's shoulder before rising to switch over equipment for the second dive. Sara's guilt fled, replaced by a hot cauldron as she forced herself to relax. Needing a distraction, she climbed the ladder to stand next to Alex.

"Good dive?"

"Ok." She shot an irritated glance at the deck below. "There's a new diver that's all over Jack."

Alex grinned. "You never struck me as the jealous type."

"I'm not, but that doesn't mean she has to hang all over him."

He turned the wheel, angling them closer to shore. "It's part of the job. She was nervous yesterday too. Some people just need a little extra attention until they get the hang of it. Don't worry about it."

"I'm not sure she even noticed there were fish on that last dive. But don't worry, I'll be a good buddy."

"I'd never expect anything less." He throttled back, inspecting the water. "Looks like we've got a little current here, but not much." He called up Jack and April, and Sara stood off to the side, listening as they discussed the plan for the second dive. They discussed going to a different site, but all three concluded the current was mild enough.

April studied the water. "We'll just start against the current, then drift back. Piece of cake."

Alex stared at Jack, and something passed between them. Jack nodded. "I'll moor us. We'll be fine." With a wink at Sara, he moved off and dove into the water to attach the boat to the submerged mooring ball.

"What was that about?" Sara asked Alex.

"I wanted to make sure Jack was ok with Ashley being in a current, which can make divers a little jittery. But this is mild enough to swim against without much trouble."

As the group descended and began swimming, Sara immediately felt the water's resistance as they finned into the mild current. It was a little more work, but Jack set an easy pace. She smiled as memories of their swim in the current returned to her. *Time to check on my buddy.* Ashley's eyes were wide inside her mask, and she swam right past Sara, catching up with Jack. He gave her a reassuring smile and patted her shoulder.

He found several things of interest on the dive, including a huge conch that left a trail as it traveled slowly across the sand,

and a mottled gray grouper over four feet long. It hung motionless, watching with black eyes as they finned past it. But Ashley was oblivious, looking only at Jack. After twenty minutes, she kept a constant grasp on his upper arm.

Sara was not pleased.

This current is hardly noticeable. And Jack's not doing anything to discourage her! Right in front of me, no less. She stopped to consider Alex's comment about jealousy. *Am I jealous? I can't be! I never am, but this situation is becoming ridiculous.* Liz continued to enjoy her own dive, unconcerned with Ashley. And it was clear that Ashley wasn't interested in being reassured by Sara, either. She wanted Jack.

Halfway through the dive, he turned them around, and the water gently pushed Sara forward. In the weightless environment, it was like flying, nearly effortless. With an encouraging nod, Jack removed Ashley's hand from his arm, but she shook her head, immediately reattaching herself like a limpet. Sara scowled as he patted her hand and led on.

By the time they returned to the boat fifteen minutes later, Ashley had detached herself, though she still stayed near Jack. But her eyes weren't enlarged any longer, and she even peeked into a few crevices as they did their safety stop. After they returned to the boat, Ashley gave Jack another shy smile as he slid into his spot at the stern. As soon as she got her tank off, she walked over and clutched his bicep. Their heads leaned toward each other as they talked.

Fury roiled Sara's gut and she stalked forward to stand in the shade. Alex motored back to the resort, and once again, Jack sat next to Ashley. Now she was smiling and laughing, leaning toward him. After several minutes of conversation, he gave her shoulder a squeeze and started breaking down the gear.

They were ten minutes away from the resort, but the time

did nothing to decrease Sara's anger. She was ready to throw Jack overboard. *I am not jealous. That was completely uncalled-for.* As soon as Alex shut off the boat, she approached Jack. "Can I see you for a minute?"

"Sure," he said with a smile.

"Follow me." Without looking back, she stomped toward the gear room, waiting for him to enter before slamming and locking the door.

Now his brows were drawn. "Is everything ok, darlin'?"

She stormed up to him. "Ok? Darlin'? What the hell is wrong with you?"

His face went blank as he staggered back two steps. "Why are you upset?"

"Because you were practically making out with Ashley all morning! She was all over you, and you ate it up."

"Take it easy. That wasn't it at all."

"Bullshit! God, are all your dives like this?"

His mouth tightened. "Don't you think you're being just a little melodramatic? 'Practically making out'? Give me a break— she was scared. I was doing my job, Sara."

"That's not what it looked like to me. At all."

"What would you have me do? Ignore her until she had a complete panic attack and drowned or bolted for the surface?"

Sara stood still, both arms crossed. "No! But you could have encouraged her to stay with me, couldn't you?"

"A lot of new divers want to stay next to the dive leader. It's common. I don't understand why you're so upset."

"No shit, sherlock."

He raked a hand through his hair, but Sara had to admire his composure. "Can we talk about this later? April needs to get in here to store the gear. And I *am* working, whether you believe it or not."

"All I want is an apology!"

"What for? I didn't do anything wrong! I'm responsible for the whole group, especially people who need help."

"Oh, stop being so damn reasonable! Go back to work. I'm going home." She brushed past him and opened the door. Her footsteps echoed loudly as she stormed up the pier.

Chapter Twenty-Five

JACK TOSSED SEVERAL DIVERS' fins under the bench, trying not to use more force than necessary. Two hours had passed since Sara's blowup, but he was still ticked off. *Hurricane Sara strikes again, I guess.* Next to him, Alex slid two tanks into their holders and frowned at his watch. "Where the hell is he?" Robert was coming directly from his photo shoot since April couldn't work that afternoon. The divers chattered around them, and the boat was due to leave in less than five minutes.

"I'm sure he'll be here." Jack glanced around, verifying that Ashley and Liz were nowhere to be seen, and breathed a relieved sigh. Robert was the least of his problems. After attacking him, Sara had stomped home, but he still had several hours of work left. He grabbed two tanks from the cart and hauled them on board, slamming them in their slots. *At least Ashley's not around to make things worse.*

"Afternoon everyone!" Robert stepped on board with his trademark smile and came up to the two men.

Alex relaxed. "I was starting to wonder if you were standing us up."

"Nah. I got here a while ago. Blame your wife, man. She's the one who held me up. She wants more landscapes from me."

Alex snorted. "Figures. Let's get this show on the road." He climbed to the wheelhouse, and they were soon underway.

Robert leaned close to Jack. "You say anything to him about us switching positions?"

He shook his head. "No, there hasn't been time." *And I've been too damn preoccupied. Time to focus, Jack.*

Robert clapped him on the back. "Perfect. We'll talk to him after the dive today." He scowled up at the wheelhouse. "Assumin' he's not as cranky. That guy hates it when you're late."

I can just imagine how pissed he'd be if he knew Sara had just accused me of flirting with Ashley. Dammit, Sara!

FORTUNATELY, Alex was back to his amiable self by the time they returned to the resort, and the day was over. He was writing in the captain's log when Robert called out, "Hey, boss. Come down here. Jack and I have somethin' to discuss with you."

The three men moved under the shaded canopy to get out of the blistering sun. "What's up?"

"Jack and I have a proposition for you. I'm havin' a hell of a time fitting my photography gigs in with divin', and Jack's lookin' for more work. How would you feel if he took my permanent position, and you made me the on-call guy?"

Alex raised his brows to the sky. "It's fine by me. You're both great, so I'm happy with whatever works for you. That what you want, Jack?"

"Yes. I'll still fill in at Ocean Surf when needed, but I'd love a steady job here."

"I'm glad to hear it," Alex said. "Consider it done. I'll need to change your statuses on the payroll, but that should be pretty painless." He frowned. "If Hope helps me with it, anyway."

"Thanks," Jack said.

Alex turned to Robert. "You're sure about this? I've been trying to split days evenly between the two of you, but I won't be able to do that now that we're expanding the schedule. This will be a lot more hours for Jack."

Robert gave him a warm smile. "I'm ready to start callin' myself a photographer. I've got enough business now to make a real go of it. But that doesn't mean I don't want to help out here. This wouldn't even be happenin' without you and Hope. You better call me, man."

"Don't worry. I'm not that easy to get rid of."

Jack glanced between Alex and Robert. "You guys want to get a beer after we're done?"

"Sure," Robert said.

Alex slumped. "I can't. I'm teaching a Nitrox class in an hour. Have one for me, though."

As he drove to Breakers, thoughts of Sara returned to Jack's mind and his good mood evaporated. He walked down the brick pathway and sat next to Robert at the bar, putting on a happy face.

Robert held up his beer. "Here's to bright futures."

Jack flinched slightly but toasted anyway. "I really appreciate what you did, Robert. Thanks."

"Don't mention it. This works better for both of us."

Jack stared at the ocean, a jumble of mixed emotions inside.

Robert straightened and crossed his arms. "Ok, man. What's up? I thought you'd be way more excited."

Jack darted his eyes back to Robert. "Sorry. I am. Sort of."

He sighed and rolled his head around on his neck. "After the dive this morning, Sara and I got into a fight. You were right about Ashley. She was a nervous wreck, clinging to me the whole morning. Sara wasn't happy."

"A little jealous, was she?"

"I tried to explain I was just reassuring her, but Sara wasn't interested and stormed out. She can be a handful."

Robert flashed his smile. "Those are the best kind."

Jack snorted and took a long pull. "Easy for you to say. It really hit me this afternoon. I'm going to be working there full time, so I'm financially dependent on Alex and Hope. Dating Sara is a big risk."

Robert leaned forward, concerned now. "Was your fight that serious?"

"I have no idea. I couldn't believe it when she laid into me, and haven't had a chance to see her since. She definitely says what's on her mind. But I'm not the best at saying what's on mine. And to tell you the truth, I'm pretty pissed off at her."

"At least you know where you stand with her."

That made him flinch. "Yeah, no doubt about that. The doghouse."

"Give her a day or two to cool off. Let the dust settle a little, then talk it over." He laughed and scraped a hand over the stubble on his head. "Though. I guess that would be easier if you didn't live right below her."

"No kidding. But you're right. I'll just lie low for a day or two and try to keep out of her way."

Back at Serenity, Jack crept into his apartment, then tiptoed as he got ready for bed. He cast a dark glance at the ceiling, angry at having to be quiet in his own home.

THE MORNING DAWNED crystal clear with a hint of breeze, and Jack woke inspired. He grabbed his sketchbook. Jumping into his truck, he headed to the peaceful spit of land at the north end of Half Moon Bay.

After cresting the sandy hillock, he came to an abrupt stop on the rocky ground. The sun behind him cast a pale golden glitter over the ocean, and he was mesmerized, frozen in place. A car came up the bumpy dirt road and when the engine turned off, the morning air became silent once more. Jack smiled as Dexter carefully picked his way toward him, using a carved wooden walking stick for support.

"Well, good mornin' there, Jack. You're out here bright and early."

"I felt like drawing before work. What's your excuse?" he asked with a smile.

Dexter smiled back, his lined face creasing. "This is a special place. I just wanted to watch the mornin' rise again. Who knows how many more I'll get to see—better take advantage."

Jack had brought a folding stool and shook it out, offering it to Dexter. "Have a seat, then. We can watch it together."

"Don't mind if I do. Thank you kindly." The older man thumped into the seat with a grunt.

"What's all this talk about not seeing any more mornings? You look pretty spry to me."

Dexter shook his head. "Not as much as I used to be, and there's no denyin' it. This mornin' I'm feelin' every one of my seventy-five years."

Jack straightened. "Is everything ok?"

Dexter inspected his fingernails, pale pink and white against his dark fingers. "I fell last night. On my way to use the restroom. Got all turned around in the dark."

Heart thumping, Jack bent down and placed a hand on his bony shoulder. "Are you hurt? Do you need to see a doctor?"

"Nah, nothin' like that. But it was a good reminder I'm not thirty anymore. Hell, not even sixty." He sighed, panning his watery brown eyes around the area. "My son has been tryin' for years to get me to move closer—South Carolina. But a man has his pride, and I never even considered it. But that fall last night has me chewin' on the thought a little more, I have to admit."

"Do you have an emergency contact nearby?"

Dexter waved him off. "Don't need that. There's always 911 if it comes to that."

"Do you have a cell phone?"

"Oh yeah. My son got me one of these fancy ones. I only know how to use it to make phone calls, though." He fished the phone out of his pocket, holding it up with a toothy smile.

Jack took the phone from him and brought up Dexter's contacts. He entered his own information, then quickly entered Dexter's number into his own phone. "I put my name and number in here. If you ever need help, you call me, Dexter. See, my name is right here on your recent calls, right under George." He handed back the phone.

Dexter smiled and pocketed his phone again. "George is my son. Don't suppose havin' your number could hurt. You're all right, Jack. Thank you kindly." He turned his gaze back to the ocean. "Now let's watch a new day begin."

Chapter Twenty-Six

SARA CURLED a new section of Jamie's lovely light-brown hair, letting the motions of a familiar activity relax her tense shoulders. A lousy night's sleep hadn't improved her bad mood, but the perspective it provided made her aware she might have been a *little* harsh toward Jack.

Again.

A guest at Half Moon Bay, Jamie had enjoyed a luxurious mani-pedi from their new employee Evie before moving over to Sara, who had given the woman blonde highlights and a soft, layered cut. Finishing the final curl, Sara brushed it all out and stood back, pleased with the results. "Well?"

Jamie's face lit up as she tilted her head this way and that. "Doug won't even recognize me when he gets back from diving. I love it!"

"As far as I'm concerned, that's the only acceptable response."

Jamie flashed a warm smile. "A server in the restaurant told us about all the family connections in this resort. I think that's so cool. You're together with Jack, huh?"

I hope so...

Insecure jealousy was a new emotion for Sara, and she didn't like it. Neither had Jack. She met Jamie's eyes. "Yes."

"My husband has had a great time diving with him. It must be great to work where everyone's got such close bonds."

Sara nodded as they moved to the glass counter. "It is. We're very lucky here."

After Jamie left, Sara checked the schedule, confirming a break for lunch. She wasn't quite ready to talk to Jack about yesterday, but she needed to discuss it with someone. With a long sigh, she sent a text to Hope.

> Sara: You want to meet at noon in the restaurant for lunch? I need my big sister.

> Hope: Sure. Everything ok?

> Sara: So-so. I need a sounding board.

> Hope: Meet you at noon. And you're still working, so no booze! Boss's orders.

Smiling, Sara texted back.

> Sara: Hardass. See you soon.

THE BELL above the glass door jingled, and Ashley tentatively poked her head in. *Well, if it isn't the cause of my problems.* But Sara kept her face friendly.

"Hi," Ashley said quietly. "I was headed for the dive shop, but it's closed. Do you have the key?"

"No. Usually Hope works there in the mornings, but she

had a meeting today. You want me to call and see if she can let you in?"

Ashley shook her head and entered, moving timidly to stand across the counter from Sara. "I wanted to leave a message thanking Jack for his help. We leave this afternoon, so I won't see him. And I'd like to thank you for diving with me yesterday. I didn't see you after the dive to say that."

That's because I was too busy ripping Jack's head off, Sara thought as heat warmed her neck. "You're welcome. You were doing much better by the end of the second dive."

Ashley gave her a shy smile. "I was." She hesitated, a flush creeping over her cheeks. "I heard you're Jack's girlfriend."

"That's true."

"Could you tell him thank you for me? Yesterday, I was shaken up about changing divemasters, but he *really* helped me. I'm kind of embarrassed by how I clung to him, and I'm sure he couldn't wait to get rid of me. But now I'm actually looking forward to our next dive trip. I really needed to get some confidence, since Liz kind of blew me off, and I did. You helped too. Thank you."

Sara smiled at Ashley, her heart twisting at how she'd treated Jack. "You're welcome. He'll love knowing he helped you."

Ashley's smile widened. "Thanks. And hold on to him, Sara. He's a good one." She turned and walked out the door.

Sara closed her eyes and sighed. *Well, now I feel like an idiot.*

HOPE'S CORNER table was empty when Sara sat and ordered two iced teas. Her sister, wearing a crisp navy-blue suit, entered the restaurant and strode confidently toward Sara. Her light-brown hair was flat ironed, and she wore make-up for once.

"Don't you look like the successful resort owner," Sara said as Hope sat down.

"Occasionally I like to look the part."

"How was your meeting?"

Hope took a sip of iced tea. "Productive. It was about some of our new ideas for the resort. I'm more curious about what's going on with you. And why do I think it's about Jack?"

Sara wilted in her seat. "Yesterday's dive was a disaster." She told Hope about the interaction between Jack and Ashley, as well as the argument later, and finished with Ashley's words to her just now. "I'm regretfully coming to the conclusion that maybe I was a little bit of an asshole."

Hope gave her a fond smile. "I have to say, jealous rages have never been your style."

"That's what's weird about it. Why now?"

"Sounds like things are getting serious between you two. Is little sister falling in love?"

Sara glanced at her before lowering her eyes to the table. "I might be."

"He was doing his job, Sara. I've been on enough dives to see the same thing myself. Some divers, especially new ones, just want the security of being next to the expert. And when it's a woman, sometimes they like to hang on. I've seen how he looks at you—that man is hooked."

A smile crossed Sara's face, but it faded as she met Hope's eyes. It was time to ask the question. "How do you deal with it?"

"What?"

"Alex. And admirers." *One admirer in particular...* Hope wasn't clueless—she had to know.

Hope sighed and crossed her arms on the edge of the table. "Sara, if I pulled my hair out every time a woman sent an appreciative glance Alex's way, I'd be bald by now. He's a good-looking man, though he's completely indifferent to that fact. And I know this man to the depths of his soul. I'm not worried."

Sara held her gaze. "Even about April?"

"Nothing has ever happened between her and Alex, and she has never set a toe out of line. I like her." She took a drink, then smirked. "Is that why you were so hell-bent on setting her up with Jack at the beginning?"

Sara laughed and lifted both hands to her face. "Yeah. Did Alex tell you about that?"

"About you trying to play matchmaker, yes. But not why. I figured that out on my own."

Sara's smile fell. "I was worried."

"Uh-huh. And couldn't resist the chance to meddle a little."

"Maybe. But my matchmaking skills leave something to be desired. Look how it turned out."

"It turned out the way it was meant to."

Staring at the table, Sara swiped a hand over her forehead. "I need to apologize to him."

"Probably a good idea. Unless you're trying to push him away?"

"No. I just got really insecure and blew up. It wasn't my best moment."

Hope took her hand. "You don't need to be insecure. You turn heads wherever you go. Maybe it's time to let yourself get close to someone."

That suggestion still caused wriggling snakes to break out in her gut. "The last time we discussed it, he was ok with just taking things as they come. But you're right that I owe him an apology. Wonder what I can do to make it up to him? Something fun, to take the pressure off."

Hope leaned forward, her eyes becoming round. "Why

don't we double date? The four of us could go out to dinner, completely casual."

"I love it! That's perfect."

"I can't believe I'm saying this to you, of all people, but relax a little where Jack is concerned. It's ok to fall in love, little sister."

"I'm not sure I want to."

Hope laughed, a light lilting sound. "Oh, dear. Where love is concerned, what you *want* has nothing to do with it. Both Alex and I could tell you all about that."

As she was leaving for the day, Sara pushed through the double doors into the blindingly bright resort kitchen. Just after lunch with Hope, she had made a special request. Gerold Harrigan stood with his back to her, his white chef's coat clean and crisp against his ebony skin. Sara rested her hands on a stainless-steel island. "Do you have something for me, Gerold?"

He spun around, grinning as he wiped his hands on a towel. "I was just packin' it up. Really knocked myself out this time, if I do say so myself. I'm gonna put this on the menu."

She moved next to him and gave his arm a squeeze before picking up the paper bag. "I'm sure we'll both love it. Thanks."

"I put the wine in a cooler bag. I chose a German Riesling. The dish is so rich you need somethin' dry to complement it."

"You're the best, Gerold."

"Yeah, everybody tells me that. Get outta here." He winked at her, then moved to his stock pot.

As soon as Sara got in her car, she pulled her phone out and thought about what to say. Finally, she typed.

Sara: I have a statement and a question for you:

1. I'm sorry.

2. Will you come over for dinner tonight?

She waited for several minutes, but Jack didn't answer. With anxiety gnawing a hole in her stomach, Sara left the parking lot and pulled onto the highway. She was nearly halfway home when her text tone went off, and she quickly pulled over to the side of the road. Her hands shook slightly as she picked up her phone.

Jack:

1. Thanks

2. Yes

As she was reading, another text came in.

Jack: Anything I can bring?

Sara: All I want is you.

Jack: You're going to serenade me with U2 songs?

She laughed and texted back.

Sara: You wish. I have an amazing singing voice.

Jack: That's not the only thing that's amazing. What time?

Sara: Six

Jack: See you then.

WHEN SHE GOT HOME, Sara changed into one of her favorite dresses, a shimmering blue tie-dyed sundress with spaghetti straps that showed more cleavage than it hid. Wanting to make an impression, she had re-curled her hair and applied make-up. At 5:45, she put the container into the oven, just like Gerold had said.

Promptly at six, her doorbell rang. When she opened the door, Jack stood on her doormat, wearing gray pants and a light-yellow plaid button-down shirt. It only accented his big, brown eyes even more. The same brown eyes that were fixated on her breasts. He slowly moved them down to her feet and back up, then his breath exploded in a rush. "Wow. You look terrific."

"Thank you. You look great, sweetie." She gestured with her arm, and he entered. Sweeping past him, she pulled the bottle of wine out of the refrigerator and poured two glasses.

Jack inhaled deeply. "It smells great in here. What's for dinner?"

"Macaroni and cheese."

He laughed and took a sip of wine. "Stick with the crowd pleaser. Can't go wrong there."

"Oh, but I have an ace in the hole—this one isn't mine. Tonight, we're having Gerold's lobster mac and cheese. He said he's putting it on the menu."

"I look forward to it. But I'll take yours anytime."

Her smile faded and Sara walked around the island. She cupped his face in both hands, pressing a tender kiss to his lips. "I'm sorry I blew up. It was uncalled for."

His smile faded as he eyed her steadily. "I'm glad you're feeling better about it now, but Sara, you need to understand.

I'm responsible for people's lives down there. Panic is the most dangerous thing in the world. My number one job is to keep people safe. And that means reassuring them—and yes—letting them clutch my arm or hold my hand if they need to."

She looked down. "I know. Ashley came to me this morning, wanting to thank you. She wanted you to know you made a big difference." Sara returned her eyes to his. "Hearing that made me really proud. I was being stupid over nothing."

"You didn't feel it was nothing at the time."

"No." She sighed and returned to her glass, taking a sip of Dutch courage. "I started feeling self-conscious as soon as you introduced us. How could you resist her? She was this petite, pretty, adorable little thing. Everything that I'm not."

He brushed a lock of hair behind her ear. "You're right about that."

Sara stepped back. "What?"

"You're everything she's not. Full of fire. You hum like a live wire, and you don't even know it. You're gorgeous when you're all made up like this. But I hope you understand you're every bit as beautiful with no make-up and your hair in a ponytail."

"You're telling me all this was wasted, huh?"

A slow smile rose on his face that made her heart beat out of her chest. "I don't plan on wasting anything."

Chapter Twenty-Seven

JACK CIRCLED his arm around Sara's hip as they strolled down the brick walkway of Breakers. He tried to swallow down his nerves, unable to keep himself from comparing dinner tonight with that of a few nights ago, when they'd made up. Over Gerold's incredible meal, she'd asked if he'd like to have dinner with Alex and Hope, her eyes bright and hopeful. Of course he'd said yes, but he wasn't exactly looking forward to this double date.

He and Sara had made up, but there was still a slight strain between them. Mostly on his side. The other night, he'd been caught up in the euphoria of making up, but it wasn't just that. He had fallen hard for her. She was like a drug for him, one he wasn't sure he could quit if they kept on. But Sara had said more than once she didn't want a serious relationship, which made his turmoil even greater. And now he had to face Alex and Hope on top of it.

Maybe we'll be in a quiet corner of the bar. Robert said the good tables are hard to get here.

Sara stopped in front of the hostess's stand. "We're meeting another couple. The reservation is under Monroe."

The hostess smiled. "Sure. Hope and Alex are already here. Follow me."

She led them toward the beach, where the Monroes were seated at a front-row table in the sand. Jack and Sara sat across from them as the hostess gave them menus. "Nice table," Jack said, watching the soft waves rustle onto the beach mere feet away. "I heard you needed to make reservations weeks in advance to get a table like this."

Hope waved casually at him. "We come here often, so they take care of us."

Jack's stomach flopped over. *I'm sure they do. You two are minor celebrities on this island. Reason four hundred and twenty I need to think about what I'm doing here.*

Hope continued, "I ordered a bottle of cabernet. Is that all right?"

"Fantastic," Sara said. "You know your wines, so I'm sure it will be great."

Just then, their server brought the bottle and four large wine glasses, pouring a taste for Hope. She took her time evaluating it, then nodded at him. After the bottle was poured out and their server left, the two couples clinked their glasses together.

"I'm glad you picked the wine," Jack said. "It's not exactly my strong suit."

"Mine either," Alex said. "I let Hope or Gerold do it whenever possible."

Sara moved the wine around in her mouth before swallowing. "This is really good. I could drink the whole bottle."

Hope snorted. "If you just want to get drunk, there are a lot cheaper ways to do it. This is the red wine we served at our wedding. We wanted to celebrate tonight." Alex ran an arm across her shoulders, and they shared a private smile.

"It's a tradition, then!" Sara said. "I'll try not to give any sappy speeches tonight. Bottoms up."

Jack was uncomfortably aware he was the only person who hadn't been at the wedding, and the sense of being an outsider amplified. *Just pretend they're an ordinary couple you're having dinner with.*

Alex looked at Jack and Sara. "I saw you two in scuba gear this afternoon. Did you dive the house reef?"

Jack shook his head, but was grateful for an easy subject. "The coral nursery. I started some new fragments and wanted to know how they were doing."

Alex grinned. "Uh-oh, and you had Sara with you? Are they still there?"

Jack smiled back. "Your sister-in-law is becoming an excellent diver. She swam all the way under the roof without kicking up a thing."

Sara stuck her tongue out at Alex. "So there."

"That's a relief." Alex lifted his glass and settled back in his chair. "I expect my sister-in-law to be an excellent diver. I'm sure it was Hope's sister who kicked over the frames. Impulsive rampages run in the family."

Hope and Sara both laughed, and Hope dug her elbow into his side. "Watch it, sailor. Trust me, you do not want the two of us ganging up on you."

"Pretty sure I've already been there."

Sara leaned forward, a wide smile spreading across her face. "Oh, you have no idea. I keep trying to tell you I went easy on you."

Jack inspected his wineglass and stared at the sand, trying to tamp down his unease—the sensation of being on the outside, looking in. Hope ordered another bottle of wine, but he refused a refill, needing to keep a clear head. An easy back and forth went on among the other three.

Sara shifted in her seat. "I really am sorry about the coral trees, Alex. I wanted to tell you, but Jack insisted on taking the blame."

Alex lifted a corner of his mouth. "It's ok, Sara. Really."

"Zach wouldn't speak to me for a week."

His smile widened. "He's a smart kid." Then he flinched suddenly with an *oof* as Hope glowered at him. He held up both hands. "Ok, ok. Sara, what do you think would have happened during a bad storm? Or, God forbid, another hurricane?"

Sara's face went blank. "I never thought of that."

"That's why I built it out of PVC, so it's easily reparable. Jack and I got it all fixed, good as new. Well, almost." He raised his glass and Jack touched his to it, but heat rose up his neck at the reminder of the disaster.

Hope changed the subject and asked Jack several questions, trying to draw him in. But as the dinner progressed, he felt more and more like a fifth wheel. On one of his final dinners with Diane, they'd joined a couple she'd met golfing. She'd practically ignored him all night, and he'd felt like a complete outsider. The comparison to tonight was unavoidable.

Do I really belong here?

Sara was completely at ease and drained her second glass quickly. Hope did likewise, ordering another bottle. Jack and Alex still had mostly full glasses and waved off the waiter. "Looks like we're driving home," Alex said, and Hope shrugged at him unapologetically. He smiled and gave her a quick peck.

Jack kept up a good front, laughing appropriately and trying to join the conversation, but by the time the key lime pie arrived, he couldn't wait to leave. All he could do was look across the table, face to face with the couple who held his future in their hands. His dream job. Alex's subtle warning about not hurting Sara kept running through his mind. He only worked occasionally at Ocean Surf now. Mark was disappointed he was working more at Half Moon Bay, but Cameron couldn't care less, of course.

"Is the new membrane system operational yet?" Jack asked, trying to reorient himself.

"Final inspection is in two days." Alex pointed his fork at the two women. "And I expect you two to take a Nitrox class."

"I'm still figuring out how to dive!" Sara said too loudly, setting her glass down with a thump and nearly spilling her wine.

Jack frowned. "Keep it down. Aren't you working tomorrow?"

Sara turned her head. "Yes. What's that got to do with anything?"

All three pairs of eyes were on him, and he fidgeted in his chair. "I just didn't think you'd want to work with a hangover."

"This is true," Hope said. "I have high expectations of my spa manager."

Sara scowled, weaving slightly in her chair. "It's not much to manage, Hope. One hair station, one mani-pedi station, and two massage areas. Maybe we can add on!" Her eyes took on a dreamy cast as she stared at the dark ocean.

Alex watched steadily, alternating his gaze between Jack and Sara as if he had picked up on the tension. Then he turned back to Sara, his expression softening. "Do I get a say in this? I was there first, and I'd like to think if we add on to that building, it will be for the dive operation. The spa isn't the only thing busting at the seams, you know."

Sara gasped and leaned forward. "I know! We can expand both floors of the building. You can have the bottom floor and I'll take the top for the spa. Come on—you guys have tons of money for the expansion. It's time you started spending it."

A notable change came over Hope and Alex. Hope glared at her sister, while a curtain descended over Alex's face and he became expressionless, completely still. *What is going on here?*

Once again, Jack was the only person at the table who had no idea what was happening. He quickly glanced at Sara, and her expression had changed too. Her eyes were wide, and she swallowed hard, reaching for her water glass.

Alex spoke softly, his face still unreadable. "I don't think this is the place for that conversation." He signaled their server, asking for the check. "Let's call it a night. All four of us are working tomorrow." He insisted on paying the bill, even over both Jack's and Sara's protests. Jack tried to hide his relief. The wine alone was probably two hundred dollars.

Both Alex and Hope had tried to include him, but Jack felt like an outsider. Maybe his insecurity was running amuck, but he couldn't ignore the fact that this wasn't just a friendly dinner between two couples. Another unpleasant ripple went down Jack's spine as he watched Alex sign the bill.

He isn't just a concerned brother-in-law.

When he was on the boat, Alex was so friendly and easy-going it was easy to forget his past. But it was like the man could flip a switch and become someone completely different. Someone Jack did not want to get on the wrong side of. Of course Sara was comfortable around them—she was family.

Tonight, Jack couldn't help feeling he wasn't.

Sara regained her light-hearted, happy mood as they drove back to Serenity. "That was fun. We should make it a regular thing." Jack remained silent, one hand gripping the wheel. As he turned off the engine, she leaned over with a smile. "You want to come upstairs? We don't have to end the evening yet."

"I'm pretty beat. Tommy, Alex, and I have a full-day trip

tomorrow. I need to get a good night's sleep." He could hardly resist her soft, effervescent glow, but he needed to. Her face was inches away, and he pressed his hand against her cheek. His heart was trying to jump in five directions at once. "You're so beautiful, Sara. How about tomorrow night?"

She tilted her head. "Are you all right?"

No. I'm in love with you, and I don't know what to do.

"Of course," he said instead. "Let's meet up after I get back from the dive."

"I'll miss you, you know."

He kissed her, then opened his mouth. She tasted like red wine and danger. He wanted nothing more than to take her to his apartment and make love all night long. "I'll miss you too. More than you know."

Chapter Twenty-Eight

JACK WAS in a decidedly grumpy mood when he pulled into the parking lot at Ocean Surf, and absently ran a hand over the stubble on his chin. After a restless night, he hadn't felt like shaving and had several days of growth. *Maybe I'll just grow it out into a beard.*

Even a week after the dinner with Alex and Hope, he was still stressed about his relationship with Sara. When he wasn't with her, she was all he could think about. But her presence was a reminder of the ice he was skating on, and he hated feeling insecure. The situation was too much like his marriage. *Do I need to pick one? Sara or my job?* With a scowl, he left his truck and headed toward the dive shop. Mark stood in the boat, which was tied up on the other side of the boardwalk. Surprised, Jack headed his way.

Mark glanced up from his clipboard and lifted his Ocean Surf Resort cap to swipe a forearm over his brow. "Morning. Martin called in sick, so I'm driving today. It's been a while, but I'm sure I can remember. You mind loading tanks? I need to go over the boat, and Cameron is checking in the divers."

Of course he is. And no doubt checking out *the divers.* The last time Jack had worked, Martin, their usual captain, complained that Mark was letting too much slide. So, Jack wasn't entirely surprised he wasn't there.

The dive shop door opened, and two bikini-clad twenty-something women stepped out, laughing as Cameron trailed just behind. Jack tried not to glare. Cameron tightened his manbun and led the women on board, turning to Jack with a gleeful smile. "Nothing's set up yet? I need to show Stacy and Allie their equipment, man. Chop chop." Cameron sat on the side bench, patting the spots on either side as he beckoned the two women to sit.

Jack quickly schooled his face and hurried toward the gear room, doing his best to remain professional. At least there were plenty of filled tanks. Jack tossed them in the cart with more force than was strictly necessary, trying to burn off his irritation. And his indecision about Sara.

"Great. These are my two options," he muttered to himself. "Half Moon Bay, where work is an emotional minefield because I'm dating Sara. Or here, where everything's a mess and I have to work with an asshole." The third option was what had kept him awake the previous night. He could continue at Half Moon Bay but not date Sara any longer. Break it off now before things got any more serious. Before he got in any deeper.

He glared at the pile of BCDs that had regrown in the corner despite his efforts to keep the area clean, then pushed the cart through the door. "Get on with it. You've got a job to do."

THE MORNING DIDN'T IMPROVE Jack's mood, but he kept his seething irritation hidden. Cameron was even more of a dick than usual. He asked Stacy and Allie out to lunch, and Jack was stunned when Mark looked the other way.

As they motored back to the resort, the boss beckoned Jack

over to the console. "I've missed having you here, but I under-stand you wanting a full-time job. I hope you'll still fill in here."

Jack hesitated, his path forward becoming clearer with every passing moment. Ocean Surf was a disaster. "Feel free to call me when you need help, but I'm not sure how available I'll be. Alex said Half Moon Bay is about to get pretty busy."

When they pulled up to the dock, Cameron was talking to the two women, leaning close. Jack grabbed an armful of wetsuits and headed for the gear room, miserable. *Am I really ready to break up with Sara? Maybe I could work more here and stay with her?*

He was just entering the room when Cameron called out behind him. "Hey, Jack. Wait up." He dumped the wetsuits in the rinse tank as Cameron approached, a giant smile on his face. He knew exactly what Mr. Manbun was going to say. "I'm going to break for lunch. Those two chicks can't get enough of me. If you clean up today, I'll make it up to you."

That's it.

Jack whirled around, his fury erupting. "Oh, like you usually do? You're the laziest son of a bitch I've ever worked with, Cameron. How do you even keep a job? I have no idea why Mark doesn't fire you."

Cameron, his grin now a snarl, stepped nose-to-nose with him. "Oh, shut up, you sanctimonious asshole. We're divemas-ters on a tropical island, for God's sake. Lighten up and have a little fun for once in your life."

A red curtain fell in front of Jack's eyes, and his decision was made for him. "Fun? How's this for fun?"

Cameron's nose made an incredibly satisfying *crack* as he slammed his fist into it.

. . .

Jack shut off his Ranger and checked his reflection in the rear-view mirror. His nose had stopped bleeding, but he was going to have a shiner for sure. He grinned, ignoring the pain. "It's a hell of a lot better than Cameron looks, and that's what counts. At least I quit in style."

But the grin fell off his face as he entered his apartment and bagged up some ice to hold against his eye. Now came the hard part.

The really hard part.

Jack took his ice bag and exited the slider, easing into a lounger on the beach. His ribs were a little sore and would be worse tomorrow. His text tone went off, and he sighed.

Sara: You home? I missed you today.

Jack: I'm out back. Come join me.

Sara froze when she saw the ice bag against his eye. "Bad day at work?"

"Remember me telling you Cameron and I were going to mix it up eventually?"

"Uh-oh. Today was the day?"

"Yep. I'm officially no longer working at Ocean Surf."

"Oh my God! Mark fired you?"

"No. I quit."

"Did you at least win the fight?"

A satisfied smirk rose. "Oh, yeah. Cameron can't fight worth shit."

She snorted and sat down on the lounger beside his, and his smirk fell as acid tried to eat through his stomach. There was no point in delaying. He dropped the ice bag onto the sand, his heart dropping. "Sara, I need to tell you something."

She cocked her head and stared at him.

"I know you don't like deep relationships, but I have a hard time with casual. I've been trying, and I can't do it. When we were out with Alex and Hope, all I could think about was how much I have to lose if things didn't work out between us. I really *need* this job, especially now." He had been inspecting his hands, but now he met her gaze. "I think we should break this off."

Sara's face went slack, and a pulse hammered in her throat. "What? You want to end this? Us?"

"Yes. I need my job at Half Moon Bay. I love my job there." *I love you.* "We can still be friends. If we end this now. But if we keep going, I'm not sure that will be an option for me. I'm sorry."

Her stunned expression was changing before his eyes. She lowered her brows and clenched both hands in her lap. "*Friends?* Have you forgotten how we started out?"

"No. And I don't ever want to go back to that. That's why I want to end this now." *Before I fall any harder for you. Before I end up with a note saying you'd found something better.*

A scarlet flush filled her face. "Oh, come on! Are you scared or something? Are you afraid Alex might throw you off the pier?"

"Sara, he and Hope are your *family*. If someone ends up having to leave, it sure won't be you."

She straightened, lifting her chin as her eyes flashed. "You don't know that. I might not even hang around. Maybe I'll open my own spa somewhere else on the island. Maybe I'll leave all together."

He hissed an exasperated sigh. "That's exactly what I'm talking about! I'm trying to make a life here. St. Croix is my *home*—I'm not just some feather drifting on the tropical breeze. I didn't just move here on some Half Moon whim." He paused, breathing hard. "Look, I care about you. A lot. But this is too much to risk when we don't want the same things." He grabbed the ice bag and stood. "I'm sorry, but this is for the best."

"Jack! Dammit, come back here."

He lifted a hand in a wave without looking back. "Goodnight, Sara."

"We're not even going to discuss this? We're just done?"

Without answering, Jack left the beach and entered his apartment, feeling more alone and miserable than ever.

THE NEXT MORNING, Jack limped down the pier at Half Moon Bay. Hopefully, his sore body would loosen up after diving. A glance in the mirror had confirmed his impressive black eye, but at least it hadn't closed shut. And he had no regrets about that aspect of his situation, happy to wave Ocean Surf goodbye. He sipped the coffee he had bought on the way. It was just past seven, and he was early. By intention. Alex swam most mornings, then started work shortly after. Jack wanted to talk to him before Sara did.

This could be dicey...

As he neared the palapa, Alex was climbing up the ladder onto the pier, dressed only in board shorts. Jack swallowed at the sight of him. The dude was ripped. Sara had absently mentioned once that his near-fatal injury involved his hip, but Jack had never seen any sign of it. His only visible scar was the gunshot wound on his shoulder. Alex picked up a towel and started ruffling his hair. *A fistfight with him is gonna end a lot worse than with Cameron... So make sure you avoid it.*

Alex looked up, peeking through a fold in the towel, then lifted his face out of it. "What happened to you?"

"I had a little disagreement with the other divemaster at Ocean Surf yesterday."

"Must have been some disagreement."

Jack grinned, forcing himself not to flinch as his lip cracked. "You should see the other guy."

Alex laughed and went back to rubbing his hair. "You're here early."

"Yeah. I wanted to talk to you."

He tossed the towel on a wooden bench, inspecting Jack's bruised face. "Am I going to need my rebreather for this? Or my gun?"

Jack laughed, hoping it didn't sound nervous. "No, scouts honor. I didn't sleep well and wanted to get this out of the way early." He sat down on the bench and met Alex's gaze. "Sara and I called it quits last night. We decided we're better off as friends."

Alex raised a brow. "You're sure that black eye is from a divemaster?"

Jack couldn't help a smile as he shook his head. "Yesterday wasn't my best day."

"Sounds like it." Alex sat next to him. "Was this a mutual decision?"

And there's the loaded question...

Jack stared at him steadily, refusing to back down. "It was my idea. Sara and I are pretty different. Maybe too different to be a couple." *God, I wish it was otherwise...*

"Sara's casual, and you're not?"

Jack gazed at the mountains as the sun rose above them. Now that Alex wasn't exploding in defense of his sister-in-law, he dropped his shoulders. "Something like that."

"She ok?"

"I doubt I'm her favorite person right now, but Sara always lands on her feet."

"You ok?"

Jack swiveled his head back, staring into those cool blue

eyes. "I will be. This job is important to me. That's why I'm here —I wanted you to hear this from me."

Alex stared back, expressionless, his face completely unreadable. "Thanks for that... I guess. Just remember. Jobs are pretty easy to replace. Good relationships aren't. But you're a grown man. I'm sure you know what you're doing." He stood and walked up the pier as Jack stared miserably at the rippling ocean.

That's the problem. Right now, I feel like I don't have a clue...

Chapter Twenty-Nine

THE FRONT DOOR closed as Sara's client left, leaving her alone in the large room. Soft music floated from the massage area where Selena worked, but the presence of nearby people didn't ease Sara's loneliness. In the days since they had ended their relationship, Sara had seen Jack several times and made a point of being polite. Anything to keep from acknowledging how shocked and hurt she was. And how embarrassed.

She hadn't told a soul about the breakup, not even Hope, and had no idea if Jack had said anything. But it had to be obvious that their behavior toward each other had changed. As much as she'd tried avoiding Alex, she had caught him staring at her several times, like he was evaluating her. He knew. This wasn't the first time she and a boyfriend had called it quits, but it was usually a mutual decision that involved relief on her part. This time she got dumped—there was no other word for it.

Her musings were interrupted when the front door opened and Hope walked in, wearing the same light-blue polo shirt as Sara. As usual, Cruz trotted at her side. "Hello. I'm working in the dive shop this morning, but there's not much going on, so I thought I'd pop up here for a second."

"We're staying steady."

Hope nodded and met Sara's eyes. "When do you have a break? I want to eat lunch with you."

Sara hesitated, warmth heating her cheeks. "I'm not sure. It's pretty busy today..."

With a frown, Hope marched behind the counter and brought up the schedule on the computer. "There's only a mani-pedi at 12:30. Evie can take it. You're having lunch with me, and that's not a request."

Sara cocked her hip. "Ok, fine. How does Alex put up with you? You're the bossiest person on earth."

"Second bossiest. Alex is worse." Hope met her eyes, a firm cast to her face. "Ok, Sara. I've been giving you your space for the past few days, but enough is enough. I know you and Jack broke up. And it's not like you to be all quiet about it."

Sara massaged small circles around her temples. "We can talk about it over lunch. I don't feel like getting into it right now."

When Sara sat across from Hope, a quiet hum filled the mostly empty restaurant. The boat was just tying up, so they had about half an hour before the lunch crowd hit. Sara didn't beat around the bush. "We decided we were better off as friends instead of lovers."

Hope's eyes softened. "*We* decided?"

Sara slumped in her chair. "It was pretty much his idea. He's scared of letting things get too serious, since we both work here. And he's convinced you and Alex would side with me if things ended badly between us."

"He's not wrong there."

"He basically decided that his job is more important than I am."

"How are you doing?"

"I'm getting used to it. It's better than being enemies, like we were at first. But I have to admit he really grew on me."

"He's a good man. Dependable as hell. He texts Alex to let him know if he's going to be even a few minutes late."

"You're not helping, Hope."

She laughed and held up a hand. "You're right, sorry. This is a weird place to be. Alex and I need to have a relationship with both of you, regardless of how you feel about each other. It is a little complicated, especially if you're not that serious."

Sara rested her elbow on the table and dropped her chin into her palm. "I don't know what I want. I've never had any desire to be tied down, so maybe it is for the best. I sure don't want to latch onto him if he doesn't want to be with me."

"Maybe some distance will give you the perspective you need."

THE AFTERNOON WAS BUSY. Sara, Selena, and Evie all had a steady stream of clients. After talking to Hope, Sara didn't see the point in staying quiet about the breakup any longer and told them. Both were full of sincere regret, but neither said a bad word about Jack, which made Sara feel worse.

A small defiant spark started to kindle inside her.

Stop the pity party. Life goes on. Maybe it's time to find someone who thinks I'm *important.*

Selena had been texting on her phone during spare moments. "What are you so busy texting about?"

With a satisfied smile, Selena hit send and glanced at Sara. "Makin' plans with Hope. For tonight. We're havin' a girls' night out, honey. Time to cheer you up. No one wants to drive all the way to Charlie's, so we're meetin' at a hole-in-the-wall north of here at 5:30."

Sara gave a ghost of a smile as she glanced at the clock. It was nearly five. "Thanks, Selena."

"No problem. Let's close this place up and you can follow me there."

Marimba was an oceanside thatch-covered bar. On the highway, a small hand-painted sign was hammered into the ground next to an almost-invisible dirt road. With Marimba painted in several colors, the sign pointed toward the ocean. If Selena hadn't been in front of her, Sara would have never seen it. Hope followed in her Jeep, and they lined up in the parking lot. The bar exuded a casual vibe with a weathered but sturdy palapa overhead, and the sound of reggae filled the air as they claimed a wooden table for six in the sand. Sara's mood started to lighten right away.

"I had no idea this was here," Hope said. "But Cindy knew all about it. She'll be here any moment." The bar sat on a small beach, and several picnic tables were placed in the sand. But dark, pendulous late-afternoon clouds were building, making their table under the thatch roof a safer bet.

April walked in, her wet hair tucked into a bun, and sat across from Selena. "I haven't been here in ages. Good choice."

They ordered a bucket of Leatherbacks and toasted the end of another day.

"So, you're all here to cheer me up?" Sara asked, scooting over to make room for Cindy.

"Absolutely," April said. "Work relationships are hard. I'm sorry it didn't work out."

"Thanks. I'm sorry too."

"But you guys are still friendly?" Cindy asked, giving Sara a sympathetic hug. "Maybe you can work it out."

Sara sighed. "I don't know. I liked being with Jack, but we want different things in life."

Hope squeezed her hand. "You'll have plenty of opportunities to see each other. If the flame is still there, you'll know."

"We see each other just about every day, so I'll get regular reminders of how he dumped me. And living right above him is a bit awkward." Sara shook her head rapidly. "Enough! Time to move on. Let's drink up, girls!"

A cheer went around the table as they clinked bottles and took a long drink. Then the conversation moved to other subjects, such as Cindy's pending college graduation and a recent dive rescue April had managed.

Selena checked her watch. "I better head out. I'm keepin' an eye on my uncle's place. He rents it and is between tenants right now."

"Where is it?" Cindy asked.

"Just up the highway a bit. It's a super cute beach cottage. You guys want to come with me?"

"Hell yes," April said. "You had me at beach cottage."

"I'd like to see it too," Cindy said. "My lease is up soon, and I'm tryin' to decide whether to stay in my house."

They soon formed a small caravan with Selena in the lead. After turning north onto the highway, she took a left turn a short distance later. The track was gravel and rutted, making the road to Marimba seem like a paved highway. They bounced through the jungle until the path dead-ended in a clearing before a small one-story house. Its siding was the noncolor of weathered gray wood, complemented by a faded green-shingle roof. Selena led the way up to a covered landing and unlocked the front door.

"It's so quiet here." Cindy craned her neck, looking around.

"It's cute, but I wonder if I'd get freaked out livin' all the way out here alone."

Selena smirked as they entered the open great room. "Don't worry about that—you haven't asked the price yet. With what this place rents for, you'd probably need a roommate." April gave a low whistle when Selena divulged the monthly rent.

The cottage was showing its age, but the furniture was modern, if somewhat generic. A tan couch and loveseat anchored the living room, and colorful plants were placed all around. Selena picked up a watering can and leaned over a large potted palm. "All the furnishings are staged. Uncle says it helps to rent the place."

Hope cast a professional eye around and headed toward one side. Sara followed to find two bedrooms and two baths. They returned, and Hope glanced at the unmatched appliances in the cozy kitchen. The whole cottage was rustic and warm. It practically screamed shabby chic. "Why so expensive?" she asked. "Looks like it needs some serious updating."

Sara loved it. "Bite your tongue. Not everything has to be state-of-the-art, you know."

Selena moved to the next plant, pointing with her chin to the back door. "The price is due to the location, not the décor."

Sara's attention was drawn to a glass-paneled door between the kitchen cabinets. She crossed and exited onto a covered patio, where the sound of ocean waves immediately surrounded her. In front, porch stairs descended to a tiny white sand beach cradled within a serene cove. There wasn't another house in sight. "Oh, wow. Now I get the price."

"Told you it was cool," Selena said from behind her.

Hope stood by Sara's side. "Maybe you can room with Cindy. That would solve the awkward living situation."

Sara shot Cindy a wry grin. "No offense, Cin, but no way. I haven't had a roommate since I was twenty-five, and I'm not about to start now. Serenity suits me just fine, even with a certain neighbor."

Cindy gazed longingly over the beach as the sun peeked from behind the clouds. "I love it, but this is too rich for my blood. I'll probably just renew my lease."

The other women went back inside as Hope leaned close to Sara and murmured, "You haven't touched your money. You could afford this if you wanted."

"That's just it. I don't want to. I want to invest that money in something. I just don't know what yet."

"I know the feeling. Alex and I have been mulling it over for months now. We just got the plans to build six new bungalows behind the current ones, so that's exciting. I'd like to build a bigger spa, but I can't find the right location on the property. If I do, you'll be the first to know."

Sara smiled and wrapped an arm around her, giving her a hug. "Thanks. I know Hibiscus could be so much more, but I'm not sure how to make that happen, either."

"It sounds like you've got some soul searching to do, little sister. Maybe a step back from Jack isn't such a bad idea."

"Yeah. That's what I keep trying to tell myself."

Chapter Thirty

MARCH...

SARA EASED down the spa steps to the wooden dock, enjoying the happy chaos of a dive trip returning. The divers headed toward her as Jack followed, BCDs layered over his shoulders. In the passing weeks since their breakup, Sara and Jack had formed a polite, if slightly strained, working relationship. She was determined not to let him see her pain, though that still warred with anger at how he'd ended things. But her bruised ego had received some bolstering recently, and she was regaining her usual attitude.

A guest diverted and came her way, bringing a smile to her face.

"Hello, Sara." Daniel was around her age and there on a solo holiday. He'd made no effort to hide that he was open to a vacation fling. Nothing had ever been said, but Sara knew Hope and Alex well enough to understand sleeping with guests would be highly frowned upon. But a little harmless flirting never hurt anyone...

"Good dives?" she asked, tilting her jaw up. Jack passed by them, watching the whole way. Sara gave Daniel a flirty smile and tried not to feel smug as Jack clenched his teeth, pressing his lips tightly together.

"Fabulous. Are you headed to lunch, by any chance?"

"Yes, with my sister. We're headed to Christiansted."

Daniel sighed theatrically before giving her a rakish grin. His light brown eyes danced over her face, though she couldn't help noticing they didn't hold a candle to Jack's. "I've only got a couple days left, you know. You're missing out."

"Who knew working in paradise would have its downside? Sorry, but we try to keep things strictly professional."

He stepped closer as Jack walked back to the boat, shoulders hunched. "Have a business dinner with me, then."

Sara stepped back with a laugh. "You're persistent, aren't you?"

"I'd like to get to know you better."

She made a show of glancing at her watch. "Sorry, but I really need to run. I'm sure we'll talk again, though."

"I certainly hope so."

Sara had a little more bounce in her stride as she moved toward the lobby to meet her sister.

SARA AND HOPE ate fish and chips as they leaned against the sea wall of the Christiansted marina. The area was bustling with activity. Street performers, tourists, restaurants, and souvenir shops all competed for attention. "Why do fish and chips taste so much better on a tropical island?" Sara asked. The batter covering was crisp and light, with just a touch of local spice.

"Everything tastes better on a tropical island."

"Can't argue with that."

The breeze blew Hope's hair across her face, and she brushed it away. "So, how's it been living above Jack?"

"Not as bad as I feared. We just kind of ignore each other when we're at home."

"Doesn't sound like you guys are getting back together."

Sara hesitated. "It wasn't my idea to break up, and I miss him. But I've adjusted."

"I'm sorry. I really wanted it to work out for you two."

She turned to Hope with a smile, determined not to show how she really felt. That she still thought about him. Hell, that she still dreamed about him. *Maybe I do need to distract myself with someone else.* "There are other fish in the sea. I remember telling you that once, and look at you now."

Wayne's handsome face flashed into Sara's mind. The restaurant and bar at Serenity were fully open now, and the previous week she had run into him as she'd been enjoying a glass of wine. Some lighthearted, flirty banter had gone back and forth. "I even have a couple of prospects."

Hope burst out with her throaty laugh. "I swear. It's like you're catnip for men."

"It does my sore heart some good. And one of the men is a guest, so don't get too excited. I know the rules, even if you've never stated them."

Her smile warmed. "It might send the wrong message. Better put the catnip back in the drawer. Who's the other prospect?"

Sara lifted her chin. "Wouldn't you like to know? Nothing's happening there either. But there's definitely a glimmer. And you'd like him—he's a businessman. But that's all I'm saying."

"Fine. As if you ever let me keep any secrets."

"You're not as nosy as me."

Hope glanced at her watch. "It's almost time for our spa appointment. You ready to head over?"

"More than ready. Lead on."

The spa Hope took her to wasn't as impressive as Orchid, but it was still much bigger than their facility. Instead of soothing greenery, Tranquil Touch had a subtle tropical theme, with abstract paintings on the walls and tapestries in bright, yet relaxing colors. Purple and white potted frangipani trees were spaced throughout.

The two sisters sat at mani-pedi stations and slid out of their sandals as two local women got busy with their pedicures. Across from them, a walk-in stood at the counter and enquired about a haircut and style. With a smile, the hostess led her back, and Sara shook her head, poking Hope on the arm. "That's what I mean about a bigger facility. Last night I had to stay late to style a woman's hair because I couldn't get her in sooner."

Hope sighed. "I know—there's so many possibilities. Now I'm thinking about upgrading the bathrooms in the beach bungalows. The other night, I watched a show that took place in a resort in Bali. The showers were incredible. Outdoors, with a privacy wall all around. My head is spinning. And I don't want a spa being too close to them or it will ruin the quiet ambience."

"You need to do what's right for the resort. And luxurious bungalows will bring in more revenue, no doubt about it." Sara stopped there, keeping the rest of her thoughts to herself.

I don't want to just manage a spa. I want to have a stake in one, some skin in the game. Experience both the risks and the rewards.

Sara hadn't quite found her place at the resort. She felt like a pawn when she wanted to be the queen. Looking at Hope, she wondered if there was room for two queens at Half Moon Bay. Maybe that was why the $100,000 was still sitting in the bank. She didn't want to ride Hope's coattails.

The image of Wayne's business card flashed into her mind.

As Sara opened her front door, the sunset bathed her great room in crimson-tinged light and she froze, her breath catching. *I need to paint this!* Dumping her purse on the couch, she hurriedly grabbed a fresh easel and paints and moved to her deck. A low cloudbank obscured the horizon, blocking the sun but creating stunning hues of red, orange, and lavender, with sunbeams gliding across the ocean.

She caught movement below and didn't need a close look to recognize Jack heading down the beach. His shape and stride were so familiar. He hunched his shoulders as he trudged with his head down, sketchbook tucked under one arm. A sad smile crossed her face. *We both had the same idea... why does he look so unhappy?*

She turned back to the canvas, working quickly in broad strokes to capture the colors. It quickly became an abstract work, and she was able to finish within half an hour. Stepping back, she studied the painting, pleased that she'd captured the vibrant colors. Sara swept her gaze over the empty beach. But Jack had disappeared. To their private cove, perhaps? Though it wasn't theirs anymore.

"He doesn't want you, so put that out of your mind. Put him out of your mind." But the last thing she wanted was to sit around her apartment all evening. Inspiration struck, and she headed out the front door.

It was dark now, and soft landscape lighting accented the path to the pool and restaurant. Sara headed into the bar, her sandals clicking against white marble floors. The tables and bar top were composed of gray slate with orange glass accents. She sat on a stool at one end and ordered a Chardonnay from the same woman who had worked the other times she'd been in.

The bartender's long dark-copper hair hung in a lustrous

sheet down her back. This was complemented by moss-green eyes that crinkled as she smiled. She set a generous glass of wine down on a cocktail napkin. "Sara, right?"

"Oh boy." Sara laughed and rested her forehead in her hand. "I'm already a regular?"

Smiling, the woman wiped the counter with a rag. Her crisp, white button-down shirt was spotless. "You're a resident, so I make it a point to remember. I'm Heather, by the way."

"Nice to meet you." Sara took a deep sip, rolling the thick, buttery wine in her mouth before swallowing. "Nice wine."

"We stock the good stuff here. Even for the house wines."

"Yes, we do," said a voice from behind Sara. Wayne appeared at her side. "We're creating an elegant, tropical destination and the wine selection is part of that." He held a hand out to the seat next to her. "May I join you?"

"Please do."

"What can I get you, Wayne?" Heather asked.

He's on a first-name basis with the staff. That's good.

"Gin and tonic, Hannah."

Well, maybe not. "Heather, you mean," Sara said.

"That's what I meant, simple slip of the tongue." He eased onto the seat next to her, dressed in a navy-blue-and-white-striped Lacoste polo shirt and khaki pants. Heather set the drink in front of him and moved to the opposite corner of the bar. "You look lovely. Then again, I don't believe I've ever seen you look less than lovely."

Sara couldn't help laughing. "Trust me, it happens all the time. You'd probably run away screaming."

He held her gaze, a slight smile playing about his lips. "I seriously doubt that."

His mouth was very kissable, and she wanted to know more about him. "Do you have some fancy penthouse apartment here at Serenity?"

"No, I live on my boat. I usually spend most of my time at sea, but have been on St. Croix for a while now."

"Well, that's different. Are you from a nautical family?"

He laughed, his brown eyes sparkling. "Hardly. I grew up outside Pittsburg. My father was a steel worker, and I vowed to do whatever it took to escape. I worked my ass off, took some risks, and here I am."

"King of your own empire."

"Not quite, but I'm working on it." He eased slightly closer. "Do you realize we've met several times and I hardly know anything about you? Like what spa you work at? You're the mysterious Sara, No Last Name."

"Maybe I like being mysterious." She swirled her wine, relaxing. "It's Collins. I work at Half Moon Bay Resort."

Something unreadable washed across his face, but it was covered so quickly by his usual confident, flirtatious manner she could have imagined it. "Ah. Lovely little resort. Very quaint. Do I recall that last name being similar to the owner's?"

Sara tilted her head, exposing the side of her neck. "You're well informed."

He took a long look before returning his eyes to hers. "That's my job."

"Hope is my sister. But her last name isn't Collins anymore. She got married a few months ago. Do you know Hope and Alex?"

"Not really. We only met in passing." He took a quick sip of his gin and tonic. "I've seen their spa, though. It's rather small. Are you sure I can't interest you in an opportunity to get in on the ground floor of a truly impressive facility?"

She stared at him, and their gazes held. "As a manager?" The words escaped her mouth without conscious thought. "Or would an ownership share be available?"

A slow smile crept across Wayne's face. "An ownership

stake could definitely be available, depending on the amount of capital invested."

Could I really do this? To Hope? Stalling, she took another sip of wine. "That's intriguing, I must admit."

"I'm in the process of narrowing my selections for the property. I'd love to show you the top candidate."

Sara signed the room charge for her wine. "I'll think about it."

He whisked away the bill and tore it in half. "Don't think too long. She who hesitates, loses, you know."

Chapter Thirty-One

WHEN JACK GOT HOME that evening, all he could think about was getting to the cove. The sunset was spectacular, and as he hurried down the narrow jungle path, he was desperate for something to distract him from his misery. The cove opened before him and he sank onto the sand, quickly opening his sketch book. His hand froze mid-air at the sight before him. The sky exploded in a show of crimson, bright orange, and lavender, and the ocean roared onto the strand before him.

He began to draw, and it didn't take long before the familiar activity allowed his mind to wander. Memories of when he and Sara had been there came flooding back. They had been to the cove three times, and they'd made love on the deserted beach each time. A hollow, gaping ache filled him and he closed his eyes, gripping his charcoal pencil tightly.

Was breaking up the right thing to do? Am I any happier now?

He and Sara had formed a new normal. Not exactly friendly, but at least not hostile. For the first week, Alex had watched quietly. But Sara couldn't have mentioned anything too derogatory, or Alex would've had plenty to say to him. That was one thing that had gone right, at least. But the sight of Sara flirting with that diver today had hit him hard.

Right in the gut.

Opening his eyes, he focused on the pad. The beach and cove were finished, and once again, a mermaid had taken shape, stretched out on the sand this time. A mermaid with Sara's features. Jack squinted, but he was having trouble seeing the figure. Then he realized why and whipped his head up, shocked.

It was dark out.

A three-quarter-full moon provided ghostly illumination to the scene. His sketch was nearly finished except for Sara, who was the final missing piece. According to his subconscious, anyway. With a deep sigh, he closed the cover of the pad and slid his pencil into the spiral binding, tossing the sketch book carelessly on the sand. Jack drew his knees up and looped his arms over them, staring at the white stripe of moonlight on the ocean.

"Did I think she was going to waste away without me?" He shook his head, swallowing over the tightness in his throat. "Damned if I do, and damned if I don't." He was in love with her, and a month apart hadn't changed that. But he couldn't stay in a relationship if she didn't feel the same.

I'm just not wired that way. I need a gesture that she's serious. And there wasn't any hint of one...

But another voice had been niggling at the back of his mind, growing louder.

Did you even give her a chance, Jack?

Or was he so terrified of being left again that he never even tried with Sara? The situation was complicated, but so what? He groaned and pressed the heels of his hands against his eyes. "Maybe I'm just not ready to be involved again."

Or maybe you're just giving up without a fight, same as last time.

Jack glanced over his shoulder at the tree line, but the path wasn't even visible. It wasn't going to get any lighter while he sat on the beach feeling sorry for himself, so he grabbed the sketch pad and rose to his feet. Nearing the end of the beach, he reached into a back pocket to pull out his phone. It was empty. "Super. Good time to forget your phone, Powell."

As he started back, he could picture it sitting on his table. *The flashlight would come in handy right about now.* Grimacing, he carefully picked his way through the thick, black vegetation. The jungle was still around him, and he tripped over a tree root but managed to stay on his feet, swearing loudly.

It took much longer than normal, but eventually Jack emerged from the black jungle onto the rocky iron shore. After picking his way over the uneven surface, he breathed a sigh after his feet sank onto the white sand beach of Serenity. He couldn't help glancing at Sara's apartment, noting the lights were off. Burying the thought of her, Jack entered his apartment and glanced at the table. His phone sat right where he thought it would be. Picking it up, he discovered a missed call from Dexter less than five minutes previously. With concern creasing his brow, he dialed the older man.

It rang five times before Dexter answered in a wavering, confused voice. "H-h-hello?"

"It's Jack, Dexter. I saw you called. Is everything all right?"

"Oh. Well, I'm not sure. I cut my finger slicin' an apple."

"How bad?"

"I got it all wrapped up, but I can see blood. I've changed the tissue a couple of times. I don't know. I'm sorry to bother you, Jack. It'll be fine by morning, I'm sure. You have a good night, now."

Alarm stabbed through Jack's stomach. "Wait! Don't hang up. When did you cut it?"

"Oh, about half an hour ago, I guess."

"And it's still bleeding?"

There was a pause and a rustling. "Yeah, it is."

"Stay there, Dexter. I'm on my way." Jack grabbed his keys and headed out the door, phone pressed to his ear.

"You don't have to do that. I'm just a foolish old man."

Jack started his truck. "What's your address, Dexter?" He gave the street and house number to Jack, who programmed it into the truck's GPS. "I'll be there in fifteen minutes. Keep pressure on it, ok? I'll take a look at it, and we'll go to the hospital if you need stitches."

AN HOUR LATER, Jack sat on a hard plastic chair in a curtained bay of the emergency room. Next to him, Dexter lay on a gurney. A doctor finished placing half a dozen stitches on Dexter's left index finger, then straightened. "That should do it. You'll be good as new in a couple of weeks. You feeling ok?"

"Yes, I'm fine," Dexter replied. "Just feelin' a bit embarrassed, is all."

The doctor gave him a kind smile. "Don't. Accidents happen. Otherwise, I wouldn't have a job." He leaned back and ripped off his surgical gloves, tossing them in a round aluminum can. "Ok, you're all set. Your labs came back fine, so I'll get your walking papers and we'll get you out of here soon."

Dexter glanced at Jack before returning his gaze to the tile floor. "Thanks for helpin' me out."

Jack gave his bony shoulder a pat. "Of course. I'm glad you called—that's why I gave you my phone number. You did the right thing."

"I don't get around as well as I used to. I'm startin' to think South Carolina might not be such a bad place to live."

"Your son has somewhere for you?"

Dexter inspected the white gauze wrapped around his finger, blinding white against his dark skin. "He's got a separate little cottage all ready for me. Been callin' just about every week. I got someone offerin' me a lot of money for that land out at Half Moon Bay, and my house in Frederiksted wouldn't take long to sell."

Jack leaned forward, clasping his hands between his knees. "Sounds like your son really wants you there. That must feel good."

"Oh yeah. And with the three grandkids runnin' around, there'd be plenty to keep me busy." He ran a gnarled finger over the white gauze. "Maybe livin' alone isn't the best idea anymore. But I've never lived anywhere except St. Croix."

"It's hard to start over. I've done it myself. But it sounds like you've got a lot to look forward to also."

Jack drove Dexter home, the older man's head bobbing on his shoulders as he dozed. While he changed into pajamas and got ready for the night, Jack cleaned up the blood in the kitchen. There was plenty on the counter, now mostly dry several hours after the event. *No, you definitely shouldn't be living alone anymore, Old Timer.*

By the time Dexter shuffled into the small kitchen, the air was filled with pine scent from the bottle of cleaner the divemaster had found under the sink. "Ah—you didn't have to do that!"

Jack laughed. "I wasn't going to leave it like this. And you need to rest. Can I get you anything else?"

"No! Go on. I'm sure you have to work tomorrow."

"It's not even eleven o'clock. I'll get plenty of sleep." He headed toward the door, weaving through the cluttered living room. "I'll check on you tomorrow morning, ok?"

Dexter nodded. "Thanks again, Jack."

WHEN JACK PARKED HIS TRUCK, the lights were still off in Sara's apartment. *Is she asleep, or is she out with someone?* He stared at it for several minutes before trudging into his home and retrieving a Leatherback from the fridge. He took a seat on his back patio, too keyed up to go to bed right away. Replaying the evening, he shook his head. Dexter was smart enough to ask for help when needed and strong enough to face up to uncomfortable truths. Jack raised his bottle in an imaginary toast. "Good for you, Dexter. Maybe some of your common sense will rub off on me."

Chapter Thirty-Two

"I REALLY HAD HIGHER expectations from a resort spa." Lucille frowned at Sara in the mirror. The sixty-five-year-old woman had arrived with shaggy dark-brown hair, complete with three-inch steel-gray roots. She wanted Sara to dye the whole thing *chic gray*. She had given Lucille a blunt bob and deep conditioning treatment, followed by a new color in a stunning soft silver. But the woman hadn't stopped complaining the entire time. Now finished, she turned her head this way and that, inspecting her new hair. "Well, this looks reasonable, so at least that's a consolation."

"I'm glad you like it. We're looking at ways to expand the spa right now."

Lucille narrowed her eyes. "Good, but it's too late for me. I really wanted my massage on the beach. I can't understand how that isn't an option here. The woman who owns this place assured me it was a high priority. At least she has some idea of minimum standards, even if she's not meeting them."

"Yes, Hope mentioned that she'd had a very encouraging discussion with a guest who gave her lots of ideas. That must have been you! She was very excited when she told me about it." Sara said all this with a straight face, ever the professional.

Hope had actually plodded into the spa first thing that morning, declaring to Sara and Selena, "Brace yourselves. Queen Bitch of the Universe is coming in here today. Do I need to hide the scissors, Sara?"

Sara had laughed and assured Hope she could refrain from stabbing anyone. But after an entire afternoon with Lucille, she wasn't sure anymore. The woman had booked their full package, a massage followed by a mani-pedi and finished off with a complete makeover. It was a four-hour package that had felt like four years.

"You really have a lot of work ahead of you if you want to position this place as an elegant boutique getaway, especially this sorry excuse for a spa. The resort might be sufficient for *divers*," Lucille sniffed the word with a wrinkled nose, "but some of us have higher tastes."

The worst thing was, Sara couldn't disagree with her. *Though she doesn't have to be such a bitch about it.* Sara whisked off the plastic cape as Lucille shifted herself from the chair. "Maybe you'll come back next year," Sara said, trying to stay positive. "We might have a beautiful new facility then." *Yeah, right.*

Lucille signed the room charge receipt with a heavy sigh. "I sincerely doubt that. I know how slowly things happen in these places." She raised her head sharply, inspecting herself in the mirror before turning her attention to Sara. "But I admit you're excellent. You really should reevaluate your employment here. You can do better." Raising a bony index finger tipped with a lavender acrylic nail, she pointed at Sara. "Think about it." With a regal nod, she turned and walked out the door.

. . .

As Sara drove home, her frustration threatened to boil over and she banged her fist on the steering wheel. "Do I really want to see Jack every day at work? It's *over*. Hope wants the best for me, and if that means striking out on my own, she'll support me. I know that." She marched into her apartment and grabbed a Leatherback out of the refrigerator. As she took a long pull, Lucille's words played like a movie in her head. She slammed the bottle on the kitchen counter. "Maybe the horrible old hag is right. It's time to think about my future, and finally step out of Hope's shadow. And Wayne's more than a little interesting—I know what I'm doing."

She hurried to a drawer in the kitchen island and lifted Wayne's business card. She stared at it, drumming her fingers on the quartz counter. *This could be one hell of an opportunity, in more than one respect.* "If I want a quick answer, I'd better call." Quickly tapping out his number, it went to Wayne's voice mail, so she left a message. *Maybe I'll email too.* She had just opened her laptop when her phone rang. She picked it up with a smile. "Hello? This is Sara."

"Sara Collins," Wayne drawled, and a small thrill rippled through her stomach. "My evening just got better. What can I do for you?"

"I was wondering if your tour guide offer was still available."

"It is, but I'm afraid the price has gone up." The smile was clear in his voice. "You might have to join me for a drink again."

A grin rose to her lips as well. "Is that right? I guess that depends on how impressed I am by what you show me." She held her breath, but he didn't strike her as a man who was intimidated by a bold woman. He laughed, a long, confident sound, and it did wonders for her ego. Confidence flooded through her.

"I'll be at Serenity the day after tomorrow. Can you make some time during the afternoon?"

She leaned her elbows on the counter, letting her voice

become smoky. "That's my day off. I can make all the time in the world."

"Excellent. Why don't you meet me in the lobby at 1 p.m. and I'll drive you to the site? We can investigate it together. I'm pretty sure you'll be impressed."

"Don't go getting my hopes up too much, Wayne. I'd hate to be let down."

"I can assure you, that is the last thing on my mind."

WITH HER HAIR FULLY STYLED, Sara strolled along the tranquil path, dressed in a flowing yellow sundress. She had taken extra care getting ready and was pleased with the results. When she entered the Serenity lobby, Wayne was already there, dressed in white linen pants and a dark-gray silk shirt. Her breath deepened as he slowly ran his eyes down her body and back up. He had a generous mouth that was eminently kissable.

Light flirting kept them occupied as he drove them north in his white Tesla Model S. They continued past the turnoff for Half Moon Bay Resort, and turned left onto a dirt track a short distance beyond. Wayne drove slowly, both hands clutching the wheel. "This road is terrible, so I need to be careful. My car isn't made for off-roading."

No kidding. She ran a finger over the buttery black leather seat. Eventually they came to a stop where the jungle opened before them. As soon as Sara opened the door, the sound of ocean waves could be heard. They climbed a small rise and Wayne placed his hand on the small of her back, supporting her as they crested the hillock. Before them was a white sandy beach, and they continued onto a rocky spit of land.

Sara stopped, trying to quell the uneasy sensation in her gut. She glanced to her left and confirmed her fears. Half Moon Bay

Resort lay in the distance. This was the same spit of land she and Hope had explored right after the wedding. "You're building the spa right next to my sister's resort?"

Wayne gave her a slight smile. "The location can't be beat. And I would think it would be a benefit for you. You could be a partner in a spa of your own, yet still remain close to your sister."

"Hope told me she was trying to get the right of first refusal from the owner."

"Well, he didn't say anything about that. And this is one of two front-runners for the location. I just thought you might prefer this one."

Sara frowned, once again drawn toward the resort. "I'm not sure about that. It would directly compete with their spa."

Wayne put his hands in his pockets and rocked back and forth. "That's true, and there's no getting around it. But I'm sure Hope would understand that you had a much better opportunity. And the spa isn't the only draw for her resort."

"Where would your facility be, exactly?"

"Right where we're standing. I'd build it as close to the water's edge as possible, and my plan is to have treatment rooms right on the beach with several more over the water."

Sara glanced down at the house reef. Many small fish scuttled about, busily going about their lives. "Won't that damage the house reef?"

He shrugged. "Some destruction is unavoidable. But you can't make an omelet without cracking some eggs. It will come back in time."

"I don't know, Wayne. We're doing all kinds of things to keep this reef healthy. I've even worked on them. I don't think I could be involved in something that would just ruin it all."

"You don't have to worry about that." He smiled and approached, standing close. She could smell his spicy cologne.

Her mind reminded her to be careful, but her body was having completely different thoughts. "You can't get permits without showing solid environmental plans. I have no intention of bringing a wrecking ball to the site."

Their gazes held for a long moment before Sara tore hers away. "I need to think about this, Wayne."

"Tell you what. Let me show you the other site. I have a meeting soon, so we need to head back. The other parcel I'm considering is just south of Frederiksted, and there's a restaurant nearby. Why don't we tour it tomorrow and I'll take you to dinner afterwards?"

She smiled at him as the hard ball in her stomach dissolved. "I'd love that. I'd really like to see the other site. I don't think Hope would be very happy if I got involved in a spa here."

Wayne tilted his head, his eyes serious as they drew her in. "And do you always try to make Hope happy? What about you?"

As they headed back toward town, his last two questions ricocheted inside Sara's head.

Chapter Thirty-Three

"NICE VIEW, HUH?" Selena asked with a laugh. Sara had accompanied her on her plant-watering chore at her uncle's cottage. But Sara was mesmerized by the view outside the window—this was an incredible spot. Soft, fractal sunbeams sparkled on the ocean as the sun drifted toward the horizon. Finally wrenching herself away, she turned to find Selena had moved on to the next plant. "Why do you have so many plants in here, anyway? Nobody lives here yet."

Selena shrugged. "Uncle insists on it. He says it makes it look homier and more tropical. Then when it gets rented, we pull them all out, along with the furnishings." She leaned over to water a bird of paradise, its spiky red and yellow flowers bursting into the room. Philodendrons and potted palms were also placed throughout the cottage.

"I can't argue with that."

Selena glanced up from her watering can. "So, tell me about your mystery date tomorrow. I'm all ears."

Sara had mentioned a dinner, but said nothing about a new prospective spa, and now guilt tried to gnaw its way out of her stomach. But if Wayne was willing to go with the second site, that could solve all her problems. "He's a new guy I've met. We've run into each other several times and flirted a bit."

Selena grinned slyly, clutching the can with both hands. "It's not that man we saw when we toured Orchid, is it?"

Shit, I forgot she's already met him. There was no point in denying it. "As a matter of fact, yes."

"Oh, he was quite the looker. And definitely interested in you!"

"Tomorrow will tell."

Selena tilted her head quizzically. "You don't look too excited. You were just about glowin' when you and Jack first started goin' out."

"I'm being more cautious this time." Jack's face entered her mind, and she tried to push it away. His thick hair and those big, brown eyes. *Stop it. Move on with your life.* "He's a lot of things Jack isn't. Sophisticated, dashing." *Hell, he has his own empire.* And she respected that he had worked hard for his accomplishments. No silver spoon for Wayne. "At least I'm not making the same mistake twice."

WHEN SARA GOT HOME, Jack's lights were on and she determinedly ignored them, climbing the stairs to her apartment. Her phone rang as soon as she entered, and the ringtone brought a wide smile to her face as she rushed to answer. "Marissa!"

"Well, you're happy to hear from me."

"Of course I am! I miss you."

"Is that right? The phone works both ways, you know."

Sara flopped onto the couch. "I'm sorry. I haven't done a great job keeping in touch."

"It's not your style. You're an out of sight, out of mind kind of girl, so I forgive you. How is life without your enemy to lover, back to enemy?"

"We're hardly enemies. Just not lovers anymore." Sara rubbed her eyes. Wayne was confident and alluring, but Jack was... Jack. And every bit as good looking in other ways. *God, I miss him.*

"I hear regret in your voice, Sara."

"Doesn't matter. He broke up with me."

The sound of a long held breath came over the phone, then Marissa rushed it back out. "You gave me the impression you were very casual with Jack, but it doesn't sound that way now. Are you in love with him?"

Sara stared with unfocused eyes out the dark window. Marissa was always a good sounding board, but it still felt strange to admit it out loud. "Yeah, I am. I didn't realize it until we broke up, and now it's too late."

"Sounds like you two should talk about this."

Sara frowned, her gaze sharpening again. "Hell, no. I'm moving on. I've got a date tomorrow."

"Really? Are you moving on, or moving away?"

"Does it matter? Jack never said he loved me. He broke up with me because he was afraid his job would be threatened."

"Because he didn't want to get involved any deeper. I think both of you were more serious than you'd admit."

Sara sighed. "Maybe. I'm having a tough time deciding what I want. In my job and in a relationship."

"This is the first time I've ever heard you so contemplative. Maybe you *are* ready to settle down in St. Croix."

"Hold your horses. I'm going out with Wayne tomorrow night. He's the successful real estate developer I told you about."

"Since when have you cared what a man did?"

"I don't really. But it's a good feeling that someone like him is interested in me. He's actually been pretty persistent."

"Sara, any man with half a brain would be interested in you." She sighed. "Well, have fun with your tycoon tomorrow. But I want to go on the record here that I think you and Jack have some unresolved issues. Talk to you soon."

———

LATE THE NEXT AFTERNOON, Sara stood beside Wayne on a stretch of gravel just behind a salt-and-pepper beach. In the distance to their north was the restaurant where they were going to have dinner. To the south was scrub brush, but most of the land had been cleared and leveled. The sand sloped sharply to the waterline, where the waves crashed onto the shore. The sound was loud and powerful.

"What do you think?" Wayne asked.

"It's not nearly as peaceful as the other site. The vibe of this place isn't nearly as tranquil."

He was dressed in black dress slacks and a powder blue long-sleeve dress shirt with a red tie. "That site at Half Moon Bay is one of the best parcels available on the whole island. That's why I showed it to you first."

She gave him a crooked smile. "I can see your point."

He reached out and took her hand, stroking it with his thumb as he led her back to his Tesla. "Let's head to dinner. We can talk more about it then."

He pulled onto the highway and headed north, passing by the restaurant. Sara frowned as it drifted by the window. "I thought we were eating there."

"Changed my mind and made a reservation for Breakers. It's quieter and we have a lot to discuss."

The hostess seated them at a table for two in the sand. After she seated Sara, Wayne shook her hand, and Sara had an uncomfortable feeling he had just palmed a large tip. She recalled Hope and Alex getting one of these tables with no problem, which also reminded her of the only other time she had eaten there. "This is a lovely restaurant. I ate here with Hope and Alex not too long ago."

"Ah, the dynamic duo. Are they well?"

There was the slightest edge to his voice, and Sara shifted in her seat. "Very well, and thinking about expanding the resort. Maybe we could bring them in as investors."

Wayne stared steadily at her. "No, I don't think so. I don't like to get too many people involved. Decisions by committee rarely work well. I'd much rather partner with just you."

A small shiver tickled down her back, but she couldn't say whether it was excitement or alarm. "I'm still not sure I'd want to get involved at the northern site. I agree it's much better, but I have to give this some serious thought."

He inclined his head and took a sip of red wine. As dinner progressed, he was more focused on business than her, asking almost no personal questions. Mostly he concentrated on how good of an opportunity his spa would be for Sara. "Siblings get involved in separate business ventures all the time. I think it could work very well, and Half Moon Bay Resort is primarily a dive resort, anyway."

Sara pushed her mostly uneaten dessert away. "It's not just that. I don't want to wreck the environment there. We've worked so hard on that house reef. All of us."

He signaled the server for their check. "And that is why you would make such a good partner, Sara. I'm not looking for someone to just throw money at the problem. You could be personally involved in every aspect of planning and construction."

"I can see why you're successful. You're very persuasive." She had to admit Wayne had a solution for every hesitation she brought up. Except the big one—that she would be in direct competition with Half Moon Bay. His confidence now seemed slightly condescending, as if he didn't care about how their venture might affect Hope and Alex. Still, the fact that he was interested in partnering with her was incredibly flattering.

He continued the conversation as they left the restaurant, ushering her out while pressing his hand to her back. She tried to ignore the sensation that she was being herded. They passed through an arched trellis of frangipani trees, their honey-scent filling the air. "I'm offering you one hell of an opportunity, Sara. You don't strike me as the timid type." He clasped her hand and led her to his car, stopping next to the passenger door.

"I'm not. But I'm also loyal. I'm not going to get involved in something that's going to screw over my sister."

He stepped close and tilted her head up. "Loyalty is always commendable. But there are times you have to risk stepping out too."

The heat in his eyes was unmistakable, and her body responded. He bent his head and their lips met. He kissed her with confidence, softly pressing on the back of her head as he opened his mouth and swiped his tongue across hers. Then he slid both hands to her ass, tightening them as he thrust his tongue into her mouth. But instead of desire, distaste rippled through her. He was too aggressive, bordering on domineering. He broke the kiss to whisper, "Come home with me tonight."

Sara reared away, moving back several steps. "What? No! We've gone out on *one* date."

He cooled immediately. "I'm sorry—I got carried away. I'll take you home now."

The ride back to Serenity was quiet. Sara sat in the passenger seat with her arms crossed, eager for the evening to be over.

Wayne sighed. "Please don't be upset. I came on too strong.

I really want to make this work, so let's meet again soon. We'll just talk business, ok?"

She turned toward him, narrowing her eyes. "Why is it so important that I be involved in this? Surely you can build this on your own and hire a manager."

He gave her a quick glance, a small smile rising. "Two reasons. One—It's good business to hire someone with a personal stake in the success of the venture. And two—I want to spend more time with you. You intrigue the hell out of me, Sara. I'm going to do my best to talk you into that northern site."

She couldn't resist smiling back, though there was something off-putting about Wayne. His confidence became arrogance at times. She wasn't optimistic about their romantic prospects anymore, but having him as a business partner was another story. There had to be a way to build this facility without hurting Hope and Alex—she just needed time to come up with it.

He pulled to a stop in front of her building, and she automatically looked for Jack's pickup, but it wasn't there. She turned back to Wayne. "All right. Let's get together next week. I'll think on this some more and we can talk about it."

He smiled, even as his eyes smoldered. "Don't think too long. I'm not known for my patience."

<hr>

"Another beer?" Maurice asked.

Jack tore his gaze from the secluded table and shook his head. "No thanks, I'm good."

Robert had forgotten his zoom lens at Half Moon Bay and offered to buy Jack dinner at Breakers if he'd bring it. Happy to accept, Jack had brought the lens but left it in his truck. He'd get it after they ate. As he and Robert sat at their usual spot in the bar, Jack was continually distracted by a couple at a private table in the sand. He couldn't stop watching the woman, whose back was toward him. It *had* to be Sara. Naturally his focus narrowed on the man she was with. It sure looked like a date to him, and he lost his appetite, a gnawing ache filling his stomach instead. The man looked familiar, but Jack couldn't place him. He just had a negative feeling about the guy, but then, how else would he feel about someone dating Sara? "Do you know that guy over there behind you? Don't be obvious."

After a surreptitious glance over his shoulder, Robert shook his head. "Never seen the dude. Why?"

"I know I've seen him somewhere, and he didn't make a good impression. But I can't place him." He scraped his bar stool back. "I'm headed to the restroom. I'll grab your lens on the way back."

When he came out of the men's room, he was drawn to the couple again, but the table was now empty. With a sigh, he walked to his pickup and retrieved Robert's lens. As he shut the door, movement caught his eye, and he froze.

Sara and the man stood in front of a white Tesla. They came together in a kiss, and a blade stabbed through Jack's chest. The man moved his hands to Sara's ass, pulling her against him, and Jack couldn't watch anymore. Blood roared in his ears as he stumbled across the dark asphalt parking lot, finally grabbing the frangipani trellis for support. He clutched the camera lens tighter in his hand, his lungs needing more and more air. There was no mistaking what he had just seen, and it hit him like a freight train.

I blew it—she's with someone else now. I was too chickenshit to tell her how I feel and now I've lost her. But I can't shake the feeling that guy is bad news.

Finally, he straightened, scraping a hand over his new beard, and continued into the restaurant, refusing to look back. He schooled his expression and placed the long lens on the table. "Here you go."

Robert brightened. "Ah, thanks. I'm lost without this thing, and I've got a shoot first—" he glanced at Jack and his smile fell. "You ok? You look like you've seen a ghost."

Shit. I'm a terrible actor. "I just saw that couple again in the parking lot. Kissing. It was Sara."

"Oh, damn. That stings."

Jack jerked his head up and down, still stunned. "I wish I could place that guy. We might not be together anymore, but I don't want to see her with some asshole."

Robert's expression turned shrewd. "You sure that's not just your heart talkin'? If she's ready to move on, maybe you should too."

I don't want to move on. I want her!

His head was spinning so much he could hardly focus on Robert. "Yeah, maybe. I don't know up from down anymore. I'd better get going."

When he got home, Sara's SUV was in its usual spot, but that didn't mean anything. It had been her. *Goddammit, who is that guy?!* Jack trudged into his apartment and got ready for bed. As he tried to sleep, he consciously cleared his mind, refusing to dwell on Sara, and soon his body relaxed, edging toward sleep.

Then his eyes flew open.

Alex's furious words reverberated like a lightning bolt, bouncing around the inside of his skull. *"I mean it, Timmons. If you set foot on Half Moon Bay, I'll flatten you."*

Chapter Thirty-Four

THE MORNING SUN was bright and welcome on Sara's face as she stepped onto the wooden planks of the pier. She glanced at the end of the palapa where Jack was placing Nitrox tanks in the boat, and they made eye contact. She stopped short, riveted to his face. He straightened, holding her gaze as he started moving toward the side exit of *Surface Interval*. But Tommy shouted out, "Throw the lines, Jack. Let's go divin'!"

Jack tossed a final, frustrated glance at her before untying a rope on the dock and jumping aboard. *Did he want to talk to me?* Her heart raced as she watched him, now engrossed in his job. He had been looking a bit scruffy lately, but he now sported a full, neatly trimmed beard.

Releasing a breath she'd been unaware of holding, Sara itched to run her fingers across it.

The boat was soon out of the bay and the loudest sound in the deserted, still air was water gently lapping against the pilings below. After rubbing her tired eyes, Sara moved toward the dive shop. *Why am I thinking about Jack?* Because her date with Wayne had only pointed out the differences between the two men. And how she had always been so comfortable

—*accepted*—by Jack. More than any other man she'd ever met. Wayne had made her feel like she was an item in a buffet, to be chosen or not, and without much thought.

It was obvious to her now that she loved Jack, but she wasn't about to be with a man who wouldn't even try to work things out. She needed to *know* how he felt about her. Sara entered the dive shop, where Hope stood at the large display wall, rearranging scuba fins. "Good morning," Sara said. "I'm surprised you're working. I didn't see Alex on the boat."

Hope turned to her with a smile. "He's off today, but I've got a lot going on right now with expansion plans. So here I am, toiling away in the dive shop between phone calls and emails. I'm hoping to work from home later, though. You have a break in the action?"

"Yeah," Sara said. "I've got a client coming soon, but my makeover this afternoon cancelled, leaving me totally open. I might take off early."

A slow smile rose on Hope's face. "Ooh. Maybe spend the afternoon with your mystery man? Word on the street is you had a date last night."

Sara parked a hand on her hip. "Seriously? Is there no privacy around here?"

"None. Trust me. Well, there is, but only if you can keep from being seen. I showed Patti the rock pool, so the days of our private oasis are officially numbered. Half Moon Grotto is in the works." She put the final aqua and black fin on the shelf, then turned fully toward Sara. "So, tell me! How was it? And who is this guy, anyway?"

Sara rifled absently through rash guards hanging on a circular rack. "No one at this point. The date wasn't a resounding success. He was a little aggressive for my taste." She paused, not really focusing on the shirt as uneasiness sent a tickle down her spine. She was still considering Wayne's business proposition and didn't want to discuss it with Hope yet. There was no doubt the site at Half Moon Bay was the better prospect, but she needed to make up her own mind before talking about it with her sister.

Hope's face fell. "Really? I'm sorry. He didn't go too far, did he?"

"No. In fact, once he realized I wasn't happy, he backed way off." *Like he was backpedaling, trying to appease me.* She had her moments of self-doubt now and again, but something about Wayne made her suspicious. How he was single-mindedly pursuing her and pushing her to invest in his spa. *Why me?* "He's very good looking, but I'm not completely comfortable around him."

"Trust your instincts, sis. They're usually spot-on. He sounds like the opposite of Jack."

That made her smile. "Yeah. He kind of is. Jack never made me uncomfortable, even when he was trying to kill me."

They both laughed, then Hope became serious again. "Are you intentionally running in the opposite direction? Or maybe... trying to make Jack jealous?"

Sara scowled. "No! I've never played mind games. Besides, Jack's not interested anymore."

Hope's smile was back. "I wouldn't be too sure about that. He looks at you a lot, you know. And first thing this morning, he came up to me and asked if you were working today."

A soft, fuzzy ball formed in Sara's abdomen, sending warm light through her body, but she was still smarting. "Good. Maybe he's realizing what he gave up. If he's still interested in me, he needs to damn well say so."

"Keep an open mind. That's all I'm saying. Just because love isn't easy doesn't mean it's not worth it."

Sara snorted. "You should start an advice column. The old married lady who knows it all."

Hope didn't smile back. "I went through hell most of my adult life. It wasn't until I finally let myself *believe* Alex was meant for me, that he wouldn't try to destroy me, that it all fell into place. Sometimes you have to take a leap into the unknown, whether you're ready or not."

Hope's words echoed in her head as Sara climbed up to the spa. *Oh, big sister. You have no idea how apt your words could possibly be. Do I stay here, maybe try to work things out with Jack? Or break completely away, and ally myself with Wayne? $100,000 isn't enough to start a spa on my own. I'm much better off with a partner. But do I want Wayne to be that partner?*

Then another thought leaped into her head. To start a spa by herself. She glanced at the white sand beach with its row of bungalows. *Like I could do better than this? Here on St. Croix? Take it easy—it will all work out how it's meant to.*

<hr>

It was just after noon when Sara finished at Hibiscus. *Surface Interval* was back, but the dock was quiet as she headed up the pier.

"Sara! Wait a minute."

She turned to see Jack trotting toward her. The beard looked fantastic on him. She'd always had a weakness for neat facial hair, and Jack was the embodiment of tall, dark, and handsome. Well, tall to her. But the heat that had been forming inside her melted away. *Stop it, Sara.*

He breathed hard as he stared at her, laser focused. "I really need to talk to you. Can we walk for a while? Please?"

Confirming her earlier thoughts, she shrugged. "Suit yourself. I don't have any afternoon clients, so I was leaving early."

"Robert's taking my afternoon group, so I've got some free time too. Thanks." Stepping off the pier, they turned left, heading north along the powdery sand. There was a gap between them, and Jack remained quiet, staring at his feet as he walked.

Sara tried to keep her irritation in check. "You said you wanted to talk to me. So, talk."

He rubbed the back of his neck and took a quick glance at her. "I was at Breakers last night, and I saw you with that guy. Sara, this isn't a good idea."

She stumbled to a stop, whirling in the sand as furious heat rushed up her neck and inflamed her face. "*What?* You want to tell me not to date other men? Are you kidding me? Go to hell, Jack!" She stormed off, hurrying toward the north end of the beach.

So much for talking things out...

Jack ran to catch up. "That's not what I meant. I'm sorry, it came out wrong."

She continued her rapid pace, anger stoking a furnace in her gut. "Jack, you of all people don't get to tell me what to do, or who to see. My God, you've got some nerve. Hell, you don't even care about me!"

He stopped cold, and she turned. His face was slack, completely stunned. "Don't care about you? What are you talking about?"

She rushed up and jabbed him in the chest. "Are you serious? You broke up with me, remember? That's a pretty clear indication."

His chest moved up and down in deep breaths as he stared at her, wide eyed. "Nothing could be further from the truth."

She hissed and turned around again, resuming her march. They were near the rocky spit now. "Oh? And what would you call it?"

"Do I really have to say it?"

She spun around. He hadn't moved, and they stood ten feet

apart. "Say what, Jack? You're not making any sense." Turning around again, she started picking her way across the rocks.

"I love you, goddammit!"

She froze, her heart pounding.

"Sara, I've been in love with you almost from the start."

She slowly turned around, staring at his tormented face.

"The air shimmers when you walk into a room, and I felt incredible when we got together. Hell, we're both artists! But I was so scared. I knew you didn't feel the same way, and it could cost me everything I'm trying to build here. I was afraid you'd leave me." He stopped, his chest heaving, and Sara stared at him. Finally, he continued, "I didn't break up with you because I didn't care. It was because I cared too much."

The angry red furnace had died, and was replaced by soft, pink hope that spread to fill the empty hole in her heart. Sara moved toward him, as if her feet weren't under her control. Her voice was soft now and a small smile played at the corners of her lips. *I can work with this.* "That's terribly presumptuous of you, you know."

He still hadn't moved. "What?"

"That you knew how I felt. You never even asked."

He squeezed his eyes tight before opening them again. "I couldn't hear it. That you wanted to keep it casual, then move on if it suited you."

She stepped closer, searching his brown eyes. They were wide, frightened, and a pulse hammered in his temple. Her heart squeezed, spreading the warmth through her. "I did want to keep it casual. Until we broke up and I realized how miserable I was without you. I wasn't lying when I said I'd never wanted to get serious. It just wasn't true until now—what I feel is anything but casual. I love you, too."

Without warning, Jack rushed toward her, wrapping her in his arms as he kissed her. His mouth felt different, softer with his beard. As their kiss deepened, she ran both hands through his thick hair, then finally brushed her fingers down the silkiness of his beard. Their tongues melded together, and both moaned in unison, pressing tighter against each other.

"I've missed you so much. You have no idea," he said against her mouth.

"I'd lie awake half the night, knowing you were right below me." She kissed him again, just because she could. She stepped hard against him, running her hands across his shoulders. *Why was I in such denial about this? About him?*

When they finally broke apart, he stroked a finger down her cheek, then met her gaze again, his eyes strengthening. "You're ok? That asshole you were with last night didn't hurt you, did he?"

She stepped back, frowning. "I'm fine. Why would you ask that?"

Jack laced his hands on top of his head. "I really screwed that up. Communication isn't my strong suit, but let me try this again. He'd bad news, Sara. I knew I'd seen that man somewhere, but I couldn't place it. It came to me last night as I was trying to sleep."

"What do you mean?"

"He's some real estate developer that Alex and Hope had a run-in with, and Alex *hates* the guy. A few months ago, Alex and I went out for a beer, and he was there. Alex actually threatened him."

Sara took a step back, her mouth going dry as pieces started to come together inside her mind. "Do you know what happened between them?"

"Alex's explanation was kind of weird. Believe it or not, it had to do with Hope's dog. The guy you had dinner with is such a dick that Cruz was desperate to run away from him. He wanted the dog back and threatened Hope. Alex *got involved*—whatever that means—and chased him off."

Sara's head had become fuzzy during his account, and her heart pounded as she pressed a hand against Jack's chest to steady herself. "Wait a minute. Are you telling me Wayne is Creepy Guy?"

Chapter Thirty-Five

JACK STARED AT HER, holding her gaze. "I don't know anything about Creepy Guy, but from what I've gathered, Wayne Timmons isn't a real stellar individual."

Sara wrenched her eyes away, staring at the beautiful, deserted strip of land and seeing it with different eyes now. A gaping hollowness formed inside her as the truth sunk in, and her stomach plummeted. "He's been using me this whole time." Her gaze settled on the resort in the distance. "No wonder he was so set on this location. He wants to get back at Hope and Alex."

"Sara, what are you talking about?" Jack's voice was soft, but his lowered brows made his confusion obvious.

She wrapped both arms around herself as tears threatened. "Wayne is building a luxury spa and has been after me to manage it. Once he found out who I was, he started pushing hard for me to work for him. He even dangled an ownership share in front of me."

"It looked like more than business to me."

She wrenched her head back to Jack, her heart twisting. "It

was. To start with. But I kept comparing him to you. Last night, he kissed me in the parking lot, and I couldn't stand how it made me feel. I made him take me home."

Jack's eyes clouded as his face took on a wounded look. "I was there. I saw you next to his car."

"Did you see me break away from him?"

"No, I had to turn away. I was jealous, even though we weren't together. But I never want to see you with someone like him."

"I don't want to be with someone like him. I want to be with you."

His eyes brimmed with tears. "I miss you so much, it hurts."

How could I have been so stupid to think he didn't care?

"You're not the only one who made a mistake. I've been blind and selfish." She clenched her eyes shut. "God, I've been so selfish. All I've ever wanted was a man who accepted me as I am. I've said that my whole life. And I *knew* that was you. I was just too proud to admit it to myself. I'm so sorry, Jack."

Then they were kissing again. Jack held her so tightly she could hardly breathe. "I'm sorry too," he whispered. "You can't imagine how much. I can't believe you're in my arms right now."

He yanked her head back to his mouth, kissing her fiercely, and Sara met him with equal passion. She ran her hands all over him, still in shock at everything. Goosebumps rose on his arms where she stroked her hand. Then Jack pulled away, cradling her face in both hands. "Why do you say he was using a spa to get back at Alex and Hope?"

She glanced at the water. "He wants to build it right where we're standing. So it would compete directly with Half Moon Bay."

He dropped his hands and stepped back, taking in the area. "Here? That would be a disaster! It would wreck the house reef."

Tears spilled down Sara's cheeks. "He had me so fooled. He told me it was time for me to step out of Hope's shadow and stand on my own. That any damage to the environment would be minimal. He sold me—hook, line, and sinker. I've been such an idiot."

Jack whipped his head to her. "No, you haven't. You got conned by an expert—don't blame yourself. Did you sign a contract?"

"No. I told him I needed more time to think about it. Deep down, I knew it was too good to be true, but he knew exactly which buttons to push." She squeezed his upper arms. "We've got to stop him."

Jack nodded. "Yeah, but how? I don't exactly have a fortune lying around to buy this land out from under him. Do you?"

Sara's worry turned into a small smile. *Not enough of a fortune.* "No. But I know someone who might. Who will want to help." She grabbed his hand and started walking down the beach. "Let's go find Hope and Alex."

As THEY WALKED down the pier, Sara's hand was soft inside his. Jack stroked his thumb over it, still shocked at the turn of events. He opened the door to the dive shop and Zach stood behind the counter.

"Did Hope go back to the office?" Sara asked.

Zach shook his head. "She said she was headed home." Then he turned his expectant face to Jack, whose heart sank. He knew what Zach was going to ask before he even opened his mouth. "You want to dive the nursery and see how our frag-ments are comin' along?"

"I've got something going on right now, but we'll do it soon, I promise." After leaving Zach somewhat mollified with his promise, Jack smiled as he led Sara up the pier. "That kid loves the coral project. He's out there any time he can get someone to go with him."

Sara hissed through her teeth as they marched down the beach toward the Monroes' house. "We can't let the house reef get ruined! We need to stop this spa."

Jack wasn't sure what Alex and Hope could do, but he didn't mind asking for help, especially since Sara was once again by his side. She knocked on the sliding glass door and Cruz appeared on the other side, tongue lolling in a smile. Hope entered the great room through a doorway, followed by Alex, who was pulling on a shirt. Both had wet hair, and Sara snorted. "Good thing we weren't here earlier. I think we would have been ignored."

Hope opened the slider, bouncing her gaze between Sara and Jack. "You two are a surprise."

"Can we come in?" Sara asked. "We need to talk to you."

"Of course." Hope ushered them in, indicating the two couches behind her. Jack had never been in their house before. The kitchen was large and modern, but the furniture in the great room was shabbier than he expected. They obviously prioritized the resort over their own furnishings. He sat next to Sara, their sides pressed together as Alex and Hope sat on the other couch.

Alex draped an arm casually around Hope's shoulders. "What's up?"

Sara sent Jack a nervous glance, and he took her hand, giving her support. "Jack and I just figured something out. Something you two need to know about."

Hope raised her brows, a small smile appearing. "You two look a lot closer than the last time I saw you. Which was just a few hours ago. Are you back together?"

The rest of the world faded away as Jack stared into Sara's rich brown eyes. At the same time, they answered, "Yes."

He brushed a soft kiss over her lips, and Alex let out a long sigh. "I couldn't be more overjoyed, but did you have something else to discuss? Or do you want us to leave so you can make out?"

Sara broke the kiss to smirk at Alex. "Like you should talk. Mr. and Mrs. Walking- freshly-showered-out-of-the-bedroom-in-the-middle-of-the-afternoon."

Alex stared at her, deadpan, and made a twirling motion with one hand in a *get on with it* gesture.

"Fine. I'll continue." Sara turned her attention to Hope. "It's about my mystery man, as you called him."

"The business mogul who turned out to be a douchebag?"

Jack laughed. "Couldn't have put it better myself."

Sara didn't join his laughter, instead sitting rigid as she said, "Hope, he's Creepy Guy. I had no idea. Jack saw us together and just told me."

The blood drained from Hope's face. "*What?* Are you sure? You've never seen him."

Jack nodded. "Positive. I have, and I recognized him."

Alex held up a hand. "Ok. As much fun as it is to play twenty questions, would one of you please tell me who the hell Creepy Guy is?"

Hope turned to him and something like fear entered her eyes. She spoke barely above a whisper. "He's Wayne Timmons."

Alex ripped his arm off Hope's shoulders and leaned forward, eyes burning. "You went out with Timmons?" Then he inhaled sharply. "Did he hurt you, Sara?"

Sara held out both hands. "No. I'm fine."

"I recognized him from when you confronted him in Frederiksted," Jack said, pulling Sara tightly against his side. "It's him, for sure."

"Let me explain from the beginning," Sara said. "We're going to need a drink for this."

After Hope returned with a six-pack of Leatherbacks, Sara told the whole story. She was crying by the end, and Jack drew her close, his heart twisting as he wrapped an arm around her shoulders.

"I'm so sorry, Hope. He had me so convinced I could do better than Half Moon Bay. He almost persuaded me to abandon you."

Hope's expression softened. "Believe me, I know what a smooth talker he can be."

"Have you signed any documents about this?" Alex asked. His words were clipped and even, but his jaw was set tight.

"Dammit, don't get mad at me, Alex! I feel bad enough already."

His expression didn't change. "I'm not mad at you, Sara. At all. But Timmons is using you to get at Hope and me. And he's going to regret it."

Jack's whole body had tensed, but he relaxed at Alex's explanation. The last thing he wanted was to get into it with the former SEAL, but he wasn't going to sit back and let Alex blame Sara for something that wasn't her fault. Fortunately, his anger was obviously directed at Wayne. Jack locked eyes with him, holding his gaze. "We need to prevent Wayne from getting that property."

"Or find a way to buy it outright?" Sara asked.

Hope took a drink of beer. "I'd love to buy it, and it must be for sale, if Wayne is speculating over it. But I don't know the owner. I've only met him once or twice when I was walking along the beach."

"I'm sure we can find the records online and make an offer on it," Alex said.

Jack sat back on the couch, numbness creeping over him. He stared at Hope and Alex, then slowly moved his gaze to Sara. "I might be able to help with that."

She opened her eyes wide. "Huh?"

A few minutes later, three pairs of amazed eyes stared at him. "You're *friends* with the owner of that land?" Sara squeaked.

"Yeah," Jack smiled slightly, no longer the outsider. "I have his phone number in my contacts."

"Well, that solves that problem," Hope said drily.

"But leaves the problem of money," Sara said. "Which brings us back to you two."

Hope and Alex both stiffened and moved their attention to Jack simultaneously as Sara continued. "I have no idea how much that land is, but maybe you two can swing it."

Jack was brought back to their double date, when Sara had made a drunken comment about Alex and Hope having a lot of money, and they had shut her down quick. Now, Hope and Alex stared at each other for a long moment, communicating without words, and Alex nodded at her. Hope set her empty bottle on the coffee table. "We've got some big expansion plans in the works. But we were concerned about the costs, so we've been planning another trip to Miami. If we do, we can probably swing both the land and the construction."

Miami? Jack was lost again.

Sara took his hand and held tightly. "Tell Jack. All of it."

Nodding, Hope smiled at him. "You're an integral part to all of this. We need Dexter, and you're the key to that. And you're part of the Half Moon Bay family now."

Even as soothing warmth spread through him at Hope's

words, Jack stared bewilderedly at Alex. "You had your turn with Creepy Guy. Now it's mine to be completely clueless."

"Not for much longer." Alex's gaze pierced into him, evaluating him. Jack stared evenly back. Then Alex shook his head and grinned, turning to Hope. "Baby, why don't you get another six-pack? We're gonna be here a while."

Chapter Thirty-Six

AFTER STOPPING at a sandwich shop for a meal they both wolfed down, Sara and Jack drove back to Serenity. It had been a long afternoon, full of lengthy explanations, and Jack had kept his bewildered look throughout dinner. After Sara opened her apartment, he headed for her deck while she retrieved two bottles of water from the refrigerator.

The air was salty as she stepped outside, and she inhaled its bracing scent. It was a calm, gentle night, and a nearly full moon was dropping toward the western horizon, bathing them in its pale light. Jack's features were clearly visible as she sat next to him on the couch and handed him the bottle. Unable to resist, she stroked her fingers over his chin and the soft hair that covered it. "What made you decide to grow a beard?"

He barked a quick laugh, as if he'd forgotten about it. "Just felt like something different. What do you think?"

She leaned back on the couch, facing him. "I like a beard. Nicely trimmed, that is."

"Duly noted. That's my preference, too."

She tilted her head, moving her gaze upwards. "Your hair, on the other hand..."

He ran a hand through it with a sheepish smile. "Yeah, it's been a while. Know anyone who can help me with that?"

"I just might. Come see me in the spa and I'll work you in when I've got some free time."

Jack stared absently at the horizon. "I'm still in shock. About all of it." After explaining about the treasure, Hope and Alex had suggested a meeting the following day to discuss a plan.

"They're being very closed-lipped about the treasure," Sara said.

"I can see why. Treasure hunters crawling everywhere wouldn't be a good thing." He turned a dazed smile to her. "But I'd love to see that rock pool and the cave."

"We'll hike out there sometime. It's really beautiful. Though the thought of diving that cave gives me major heebie-jeebies."

"Me too. I've never been interested in caves or caverns. I like to see the surface." He swiveled to her. "You think they have enough money to buy Dexter's land?"

Sara shrugged. "I don't know, but they hinted they have a lot." She met his gaze. "They insisted on giving me $100,000. It's sitting in the bank because I can't decide what to do with it."

He smiled and brushed her hair off her face. "That's smart. Better to let it sit there than blow it on something stupid."

She sighed and clenched her eyes shut. "Like investing in Wayne's spa. That's what I was planning on doing with it. Everything's so clear in hindsight—how selfish I've been. With Hope, and with you. You've always been there when I needed you, and I took you both for granted. Especially you." A tear spilled over, and he wiped it away, pressing a light kiss over her lips.

"I'm sorry too. I was so afraid of what you'd say, I never even gave you the chance. I just kept imagining the worst."

"You had valid reasons to be cautious, and I should have

been more understanding. Maybe both of us could stand to communicate a little better."

He twitched a corner of his mouth. "Yeah. You're pretty direct, but I need to speak up more. Even when I'm afraid of what I might get in response."

"Direct isn't necessarily a good thing either. I've got a tendency to make quick assumptions that end up being wrong. I'm very glad we're getting a second chance. I love you."

The pale moonlight allowed her to see every detail as his face lit up. "I love you, too."

Such a small sentence, those three words. And not one she had said very many times. But she meant it with all her heart now. She cupped his head, drawing him close as she kissed him, luxuriating in the sweet taste of his mouth, the new softness of his beard.

He grasped a handful of her hair, breaking their kiss to press it to his face and inhale. "I've missed you so much." Before she could respond, he pushed her back against the couch, kissing her deeply.

Sara circled her arms around him, rubbing her hands down the hard planes of his back. Gently pressing his tongue inside her mouth, Jack asked, not demanded. His kiss was perfect, and she tightened her hold on him as he slid a hand up her shirt and under her bra. She moaned softly as his thumb slowly circled, then yanked his shirt off.

They returned their mouths to each other, and Sara ran both hands over the warm, velvety skin of his chest and its smattering of hair. He moved back against the couch, and she went with him, gripping the bulge in his pants. He had her shirt and bra off in no time, stroking both breasts as their breath deepened in the balmy night.

Jack pulled back, resting his head on the couch with a sigh. "I'm going to have to go downstairs for a raincoat, aren't I?"

A giggle escaped Sara. "Not unless you want to. I've kept my patch on, in case you changed your mind."

A smile rose to his face, but it fell quickly, and he stared at her with an expression that went straight to her. "I never stopped wanting you. Ever."

"Neither did I."

They hurried out of the rest of their clothes, tossing them into a corner of the deck. The soft waves tumbled against the beach as they came together again. Sara pressed him down on the couch, folding over him as she kissed across his chest, then down his abdomen, moving her tongue in circles as he ran his hands through the strands of her hair.

Moving lower, she enveloped him, drawing him in and out as he lifted his knees up on each side of her. His deep breaths became pants, until he quickly withdrew, scuttling backward. "Oh, no. That's not how this is going to end. Not tonight."

Moving toward her again, Jack pushed her onto her back. He kissed one breast, then the other, slowly drawing his tongue in ever decreasing circles. Inexorably, he moved lower, and Sara threw an arm over her eyes, opening wider and relaxing, knowing she was completely loved and accepted.

When he finally climbed back up her body and settled between her legs, she pressed both hands against his chest. "No. I want to be on top."

A lazy smile spread across his face. "Your wish is my command." He moved onto his back, his trim body pale in the ghostly light and very ready for action.

Sara straddled him, guiding him inside her. She looked down, and her body was as fully visible as his. There was no trace of self-consciousness with Jack. There was no need for it. Not when he stared at her, his eyes half-lidded and ravenous. Not even when he slowly ran his broad hand over her stomach, her body clear in the moonlight. With a broad smile, Sara tipped her head back and closed her eyes, losing herself completely as they moved together.

THE NEXT MORNING, Sara awoke slowly. Slow, deep breathing came from the other side of the bed, and she broke into a satisfied smile. *Our clothes are still all over the deck.* Her chest shook with silent laughter as she turned her head. Jack lay on his back, his long eyelashes framing his face, and her heart filled. The situation with Wayne was far from resolved, but she couldn't remember the last time she had woken this contented.

Happy.

As if the earth was back on its axis. She studied him as he slept. The small scar on his neck was still visible just below the trimmed edge of his beard. She reached out and stroked it.

Jack opened his eyes and turned to her with a smile. "Good morning, darlin'. I love waking up next to you."

"That's what I like about you. You're easy to please." She gave him a quick kiss. "What's this scar from?"

He ran a finger over it absently. "Oh, I got it when I was ten. My brother pushed me out of a tree."

Sara bolted onto one elbow. "That's terrible!"

Jack laughed, a rich deep sound. "Nah, I deserved it. I tried to push him out first, but forgot he was bigger than me."

Sara joined his laughter and snuggled closer.

"I'll have to take you to Texas with me sometime."

She poked his chest. "The Powell clan sounds pretty daunting to someone with only one sister."

"Nah, we're pretty laid back. Most of us, anyway."

"Well, I was thinking about something else right at the moment." She shifted her hips against him, but he didn't need any encouragement in that direction. Yes, the world was definitely back on its axis.

THEY DROVE SEPARATELY TO WORK, and Sara headed straight for Hibiscus while Jack unlocked the gear room. She was waking up the computer when he popped his head in the door. "Ok, so when can I get that haircut, since apparently I look like a vagabond?"

Sara came around the counter, grabbed his hand, and led him toward her station. "No time like the present."

"Wait. I've got to get the boat ready."

"Please. I'm a professional. This won't even take ten minutes."

He shot her a dubious look as she wrapped the tissue around his neck. "If I'm late, you have to explain it to Alex."

She started her timer on her smartwatch, and eight minutes later, Jack stared at her in the mirror, his mouth agape. He shut it with an audible click of teeth. "Wow. Nice job."

Sara gave him a smug smile. "Told you. I know what I'm doing." She unwrapped the cape and he stood, drawing her in for a long kiss that got deeper by the second.

The bells above the door jingled as it opened, musical laughter filling the room. "Well, I wasn't expectin' that when I came up the steps." Selena moved to the glass counter. "I take it you two aren't fightin' anymore?"

"No, we're together again," Sara said. They kissed goodbye, and Jack left as Sara returned to the computer to check the schedule for the day.

Selena stared at her, scowling. "Don't you be all quiet on me. I need to know what happened. Details, girl!"

Sara sighed, but couldn't resist a light laugh. "It's a really long story. But the short version? Yesterday we found out we love each other."

"Oh. Well, that's really all that counts, isn't it?" With a wise nod, Selena headed toward the massage room.

———

At noon, Sara pushed through the double doors into the restaurant kitchen, which was a busy hive. The chief worker bee, Gerold, wore a spotless white coat as he whirled between a six-burner stove and the island behind him. Several raw hamburger patties sat on a tray, ready for the grill, and multiple pots bubbled away.

Sara stopped short. "Whoa. How do you manage all that at once?"

He grinned before turning back to the largest pot and stirring it with a wooden spoon. "Practice. Besides, I live for this." He lifted the spoon to his mouth and frowned before muttering, "Needs more salt."

"Hope sent me here on a mission."

"Oh yeah. Lunch for four." He pointed with the spoon to a neatly packed selection of paper bags. "I just boxed them up, so everythin' should be hot. Enjoy." With a graceful bend of his elbow, Gerold poured a clear liquid into a large sauté pan and it burst into multicolored flames. His face split into an enormous grin, the fire dancing in his dark-brown eyes.

Sara scuttled around to the other side of the island, rushing to pick up the bags. "You're terrifying me, Gerold. I'm out of here."

"Oh, come on! It's not even busy yet!"

As Sara walked across the warm sand, curiosity overcame her. Hope had texted her less than an hour previously, asking her to pick up lunch at noon and come to the house. As she let herself in through the slider, Hope stood in the kitchen, wiping down the island. "Thanks for picking up the food. I'll put it in the oven to stay warm. Alex texted that they're on their way back, so the guys should be along soon. I've had a bit of a crisis this morning. Clark's new son needs surgery, so he's going to need some time off. I'm putting together an ad for another bartender."

"Oh no! He's such a sweet baby."

"Apparently, he'll be fine, but Clark wants a couple of months off, and I'll make sure he gets it. We'll try to get everything settled on our lunch break, so I can get back to work."

"Everything?"

"Alex and I came up with a plan." She placed four cardboard boxes in the oven and several more in the refrigerator. "I got cheeseburgers for the guys and blackened fish sandwiches for us. I didn't know if you'd rather have salad or fries, so I ordered both."

Sara sighed, slumping against the granite island. The conversation about Clark only made it clearer how Hope always looked out for everyone. "After the last few days, make it fries."

Hope slammed the refrigerator door and whirled around. "I can't believe Wayne owns Serenity! I never would have rented your apartment there if I had known. That son of a bitch."

Sara just stared at her. Her bottom lip quivered as tears threatened.

"What?" Wrinkling her brow, Hope came around the island and embraced her.

That was all it took, and Sara started crying against her sister's shoulder. Hope patted her back, murmuring soothing nonsense, and she soon quieted.

"Sorry. I needed to get that out."

"You ok now?"

Sara nodded. "Your statement about the apartment brought it all back."

"That Wayne is a complete asshole?"

She choked out a laugh. "No, that you set up my apartment. And my job. And helped me with everything else I've ever had in my whole life. I feel so terrible. I was really thinking about opening my own facility."

Hope held her at arm's length, a small smile playing on her face. "It's ok to want your own success. I never want you to feel you're in my shadow. If you want to do something else, we'll talk about it and work it out."

"No, I want to stay right here. I've learned in no uncertain terms that the grass is *not* greener."

"That's where I want you too." Hope focused over Sara's shoulder and grabbed a box of tissues from an end table. "Here. Get it together. Alex and Jack are almost here."

Sara quickly wiped her eyes and blew her nose, and was back in control when Alex entered with Jack just behind. Alex made a beeline for his wife, kissing her before peering behind her at the mysterious boxes in the oven. "Lunch ready? I'm starved."

Hope snorted and smacked him in the chest. "Big surprise there. Sit down and I'll bring it over."

Jack kissed Sara before dancing his eyes over her face, concern narrowing them. "You ok?" he murmured.

"Yes, thanks. Hope and I just had a moment. Let's eat."

After they were done, Hope dabbed a napkin to her mouth and sat back. "Alex and I looked things over last night and I've checked our financials this morning. We've got two million dollars cash available to buy that piece of land."

Next to Sara, Jack jerked in his seat, and she tried to hide a smile.

Alex tented his fingers. "We weren't sure that would be

enough to cover the expansion we've been planning, and if we buy the land, it certainly won't be. We were already thinking about auctioning more of the treasure, so I'll start planning it."

"You mentioned Miami yesterday," Jack said.

Hope nodded. "That's where the auction house is where we sold the first lot. We'll put together a second one and deliver it to Miami. Piece of cake." A bright pink flush crept up her neck and she tossed a guilty glance at Alex. "I may be *slightly* headstrong, but I've learned a thing or two along the way." Sara guessed she was leaving something major out, but Alex just smiled and cupped the back of her neck, massaging softly.

Sara sat back with a grin. "Who would have thought? Both Collins sisters don't actually know it all?"

Alex and Jack reached for their water glasses at the same time, drinking with their eyes downcast. Both women laughed. "Maybe we can be a tad rash," Hope said.

Alex turned quickly to Hope, whisking his lips over hers. "I'd never change a thing. Ever."

Jack grasped Sara's hand under the table. "Me either, you know."

Tears pricked at her eyes again. *God, I'm turning into a sap.* "Thanks."

Hope and Alex managed to tear themselves apart and return to the conversation. Alex turned to Jack. "Can you get hold of Dexter and set up a meeting? Maybe here at the house? Doesn't matter where, as long as it's private. And fast."

"Sure, I'll call him after work and tell him it's about a business opportunity he might be interested in."

Hope leaned forward, looking at Sara. "You think Wayne is ready to buy that land?"

"Yes. It's a guess, but I really wonder if the other parcel was just a ruse to show me how much better the Half Moon Bay site is. I think his primary objective is to make competition for you two."

Jack put an arm over Sara's shoulders, focusing on her. "I'm sure of it. Dexter told me that someone was offering him a lot of money for it—that has to be Timmons. And if he could wreck you in the process, that only added to the allure, the son of a bitch."

Alex panned his gaze around the table. "Well, he doesn't know who he's up against, does he?"

Chapter Thirty-Seven

JACK GLANCED at the passenger seat as he drove around the
circle in front of the Half Moon Bay entrance and continued
along the sand road toward Alex and Hope's house. Dexter sat
alert, watching the vegetation move past the truck, and the four
southern bungalows that peeked from behind. He had tried to
be up front with the older man without going into specifics,
since that was the Monroes' end of things.

When Jack had called the previous evening, Dexter asked
him plenty of questions, but in the end, he was satisfied with the
explanation that Alex and Hope wanted to discuss a business
opportunity. Dexter's raspy, dry laugh had come over the phone
before he said, "I sure am popular all of a sudden. Got these
business opportunities all around. All right then, we'll see what
your friends have to say."

They stopped in an open area between the front of the
house and a large, detached garage/shop. A neat square of lawn
with two large trees lay before them. Jack's knock was answered
promptly by Hope, who was wearing a staff polo shirt and crisp
black slacks. She smiled warmly at Jack's introduction and

shook Dexter's hand. "It's good to finally know your name. We haven't talked in a while."

"You too, Mrs. Monroe."

Hope led them to the great room, tossing over her shoulder, "Please, call me Hope. This is my husband Alex, and my sister Sara." Hope and Alex sat together on the loveseat, while Sara took neutral territory in an armchair. Jack took a seat by Dexter on the couch, wanting him to feel as comfortable as possible.

Dexter declined Hope's offer of a beverage. "Well, I might not be one of those fancy psychics you see on the TV, but I reckon I know what this is about," Dexter said. "Folks seem real interested in my slip of land lately."

"You're right," Hope said. "We've recently learned of someone else interested in that parcel and wanted to talk to you about a competing offer."

"My son has wanted me to move for years, and I'm not gettin' any younger. I got an offer from another fellow—pretty eye openin', it was—but I'm interested in talkin' to you too."

"I imagine you can't divulge the name of the other interested party," Hope said.

Dexter shook his head. "He said it had to be confidential. Was real hush-hush about it."

I'll just bet. Jack and Sara exchanged a look, but remained silent.

"You don't need to worry about divulging anything," Hope continued. Jack had thought Alex would take the lead, but he remained quiet, letting Hope do the talking. "All four of us know Wayne Timmons rather well. Too well, unfortunately."

Dexter's eyes clouded. "How's that?"

Hope glanced at Sara before returning her attention to Dexter. "He told my sister about his plans. Did he detail his idea to you?"

The older man shrugged, rubbing one dark, gnarled hand over the other. "He just said he was buildin' a commercial facility. Goin' to put it at the tree line so it looked out over the beach."

Alex snorted at that but kept quiet.

"That's not exactly true," Sara said. "He was very forthright with me. He's planning on building a large spa facility at the edge of the spit, part of it right over the water."

Dexter frowned, shifting his position. "Not at the edge of the jungle? That can't be good for the shore there."

Alex finally spoke up. "It would be an environmental disaster. And Wayne has deep enough pockets to bribe any government officials to look the other way while he destroys everything around the building."

Hope glanced down before meeting Dexter's eyes. "It might also destroy us. And not just the competition a big spa like that would bring. We use the coral reef there nearly every day, and we're working hard to restore it and keep it healthy."

"I don't like the idea of him buyin' my land just to cause problems. That land has been in my family for generations, and the ocean's a part of me."

Hope pressed her lips together before speaking, rubbing a hand up her arm. "If you'll give us an idea of his offer, we can try to match it."

Dexter slumped. "Well, it was a very nice sum. I'm not tryin' to make out like a bandit here, but I don't want to give that land away, either."

"Of course not."

"Mr. Timmons said he'd take care of all the paperwork, and all I had to do is sign. He offered me one million dollars."

Jack's stomach dropped as he whirled toward Dexter. "*What?*"

"She asked, so I answered. I told you it was a lot of money."

"Have you discussed this with your son?"

"No! It's my business, not his."

Jack was stunned at the low figure. "Dexter, I know almost nothing about real estate, but that figure seems way too low to me."

Alex and Hope wore matching wide-eyed expressions, then Alex stiffened, his expression growing hard. Hope placed a restraining hand on his arm before turning back to Dexter. "I agree," Hope said. "We're prepared to offer you more. Fair market value."

"You said it yourself, Dexter," Alex said. "This is your birthright. Make sure you get what it's worth."

Dexter's face creased into a smile. "You people don't negotiate very well, you know that?"

They all laughed, and Jack rested a hand on his bony shoulder. "We may not be real estate barons, but we all like to sleep at night."

Hope's eyes sparkled. "Don't worry. We won't let you get too carried away. My attorney, Alistair, is commissioning a market analysis on the property. He should have it back any time now."

Dexter leaned forward, his bushy brows rising. "You know Al? We've been friends for years. Whatever price he comes up with is good enough for me."

Hope breathed a sigh and smiled. "It sounds like we have an agreement then. Based on the county property assessment, Alistair thought the fair market value would be around 1.5 to 1.8 million."

Dexter's face went blank. "That much? Now I'm really pissed at that other guy."

Get in line, Dexter.

"Why don't you leave me your phone number, and I'll let you know when Alistair has the report," Hope said. "I'll make sure you get a copy, and we can discuss a final offer then."

"That sounds fine." He smiled at Hope. "I like the idea of sellin' the last bit of Half Moon Bay to you."

She laughed. "So do we."

Dexter smiled but shook his head. "That's not what I mean. You won this resort in a lottery, right?"

Hope nodded.

"Well now, that's how my family got the land originally. Just seems like things are happenin' like they should. Half Moon Bay wasn't meant to be broken up."

LATER THAT EVENING, Jack pulled Sara tighter against his chest as they watched the ocean from his patio. The past two days had been a whirlwind, but there was nowhere he'd rather be.

Sara's phone buzzed again. "It's Wayne texting again, and I can't just ghost him. We don't want to give him any idea we know what's going on until everyone's signed, but he wants an answer on whether I'm in or out."

"Just text him back and say you're really busy right now, and you'll get back to him in a few days."

Her thumbs flew over the phone, and Wayne's response came back almost immediately. Sara smirked. "Asshole."

"What did he say?"

"He wants my answer in two days, or he's moving forward without me."

Jack was getting ready to make a choice comment when his phone rang. The caller ID said Alex, and he swiped to answer. "Hey. What's up?"

"Is Sara with you?"

"Yes, she is."

"Good. You can pass this on. Alistair just called with the market analysis, which came in at $1.7 million. He can meet

with us all tomorrow afternoon. There's only six divers scheduled due to a cancellation, but both Robert and April are busy. I
can work it with Tommy. Can you go to the meeting? I think
Dexter would be more at ease with you beside him."

"Sure, that's no problem. Don't you need to be there,
though?"

Alex laughed. "Hardly. Things like this tend to go better
when I keep my mouth shut. Hope is much more professional
and diplomatic than me. Apparently, Sara has several clients
tomorrow, so she and I can stay at Half Moon Bay. As long as
Hope and you are at the meeting, everything will go fine."

"I'll be there. Thanks, Alex. For trusting me with this."

"I do trust you."

Jack was smiling as he ended the call, wondering how he'd
ever felt like an outsider with these people, and summarized the
conversation for Sara. "By this time tomorrow, the papers could
be signed."

"Hope's right. I've got a busy afternoon until four."

Jack nodded, picking his phone back up. "I'll call Dexter
and make arrangements to take him to the meeting."

SARA CURLED a ringlet of the woman's hair, determined not to
check her watch. The afternoon had passed at a glacial pace, but
she was nearly done. Finished with the iron, she brushed out the
woman's black locks and they fell softly around her shoulders.

As her client signed the charge slip, Sara swept her gaze
across the room. Yes, Hibiscus was small, but nicely furnished
and decorated. Professional and yet homey. *You stuck your neck
out and nearly got it chopped off.*

The woman was their final client for the day and Selena
sighed. "I'm out of here. I need to check on the beach cottage.

Uncle's got a prospective tenant, so I need to make sure it's presentable. See you tomorrow."

Sara quickly locked up and descended the stairs. *Surface Interval* was tied up, and Alex was spraying down the deck, the water pouring over the stern platform. Her mind now free to imagine the meeting, the flutter in Sara's stomach returned as she joined him. Alex saw her and smirked as he shut off the water. "As tempting as it is, I'll refrain from blasting you with the hose."

"Good plan, unless you enjoy sharing Cruz's bed instead of Hope's." She peered into a bucket which contained a large branching length of coral. "What's this?"

"A damaged coral piece I came across and brought back. There's some empty space on one of the trees and this would be perfect. You want to help start it?"

She smiled at him. "Of course. Thanks." Shading her face with her hand, she gazed toward the house reef. "And by now, you and Hope might be new prospective owners. Have you heard anything?"

"Just that they're done and on their way back." He grabbed the bucket and moved it under the protective canopy as voices echoed down the pier. Both of them quickly stepped off the boat as Hope approached, with Jack and Dexter just behind. All three were smiling.

"Mission accomplished!" Hope held both arms up in a touchdown signal.

Alex shook Dexter's hand. "Congratulations."

"It does feel pretty good," Dexter said.

Sara gave Hope a hug, then moved to Jack's side, finally feeling like some good may have come from the whole Wayne disaster.

"Alistair said we should be able to close within a couple of weeks, since it's a cash offer," Hope said to Alex. "I have a copy of it. You can add your signature and we'll send it back to him tonight."

"What was the final price?" Alex asked.

"$1.7 million, exactly what the analysis determined was fair market value."

Jack scowled as he turned toward Dexter. "I'm really glad you didn't sign a contract with Wayne."

Dexter broke into a rough laugh. "Not as glad as I am!"

"Best of all, when he contacts you, he'll be too late," Sara said, a warm glow spreading through her.

Dexter's face fell. "Oh. I forgot about that."

"What?" Jack asked.

"He called me this mornin'. I told him I was havin' second thoughts and wanted some more time to mull it over. Before I knew it, he had talked me into meetin' him at the property first thing tomorrow mornin'. At eight o'clock."

"Just call him back and tell him you already signed a contract with someone else," Hope said.

Dexter shook his head. "Don't like the idea of that. Seems weaselly. I gave him my word that I'd be there."

"But there's no reason to meet him now," Sara said.

He straightened, jutting out his chin. "Doesn't matter. Better to meet in person and get it over with. Can't say I'm lookin' forward to it, though."

"I'm off tomorrow," Jack said. "So I'll go with you. I don't like the idea of you facing Wayne alone. Especially after he finds out he's been outwitted."

Dexter scoffed. "He wouldn't hurt an old man."

"Hopefully not, but I wouldn't put it past him," Alex said. "I think I'll join the party too. April's working tomorrow morning. I'll tell her an emergency came up and she's going to have to combine both groups."

Dexter was still frowning. "You don't have to go to all that trouble. Jack and I can talk to him."

A slow smile crept across Alex's face that sent a shiver down Sara's spine. "It's no trouble, I assure you," Alex said. "In fact, I'm looking forward to it."

"You expecting trouble?" Jack asked.

Hope smirked. "He's always expecting trouble."

Alex ignored her comment, intent on Jack. "Not necessarily. Let's just say I've learned it pays to be prepared."

With Alex there, nothing seriously bad could happen, and Sara was starting to feel left out. The meeting with the developer would be poetic justice in action. "We'll all go. I'd love to see the look on Wayne's face when he finds out."

Without moving his head, Alex shifted his gaze to her, eyes hardening. "No. You and Hope stay here."

Anger flickered, rising through Sara's abdomen. "What? We have every right to be there!"

"Sara, it could be dangerous," Jack said.

"So what? We're not some damsels—"

"Be quiet, Sara," Hope said, crossing her arms over her chest. "Alex is right. We'd only be a distraction."

Sara gaped at her sister, stunned she wasn't demanding to be there. Hope stared steadily back at her. "Alex knows more about security issues than you or I ever will. And I've learned that sometimes I need to listen, whether I like it or not. We stay here."

Sara turned her attention back to Alex. His eyes weren't cold anymore, but they held an iron glint she'd never seen before. Hope's words sunk in—Alex wasn't just a dive instructor. "Ok." She regarded Jack, who also looked at her seriously, then nodded. "We'll just have to save the celebration for tomorrow evening then." Sara started walking up the pier as the others turned to follow.

"Jack, can you hold back a second?" Alex asked, before sweeping his gaze over the remainder of the group. "You all go ahead. We'll catch up in a few minutes."

Sara and Hope ambled up the pier, with Dexter in between. Hope was in full tour-guide mode, pointing out the features of the resort, and Sara's irritation about the meeting fled as she watched the older man. Dexter wore a delighted and slightly dazed expression as he countered with reminiscences from his childhood.

This isn't about me or Hope, is it? Something big sister already realized. Maybe you need to listen more and barge in less, Sara.

Then she bit back a laugh at that last ridiculous thought.

Chapter Thirty-Eight

FLICKERING morning light danced through the green canopy as Jack gripped the wheel of his Ranger. He forced his hand to relax, trying not to worry about the upcoming encounter. Next to him, Dexter sat alert but not tense as they rumbled down the dirt track at the north end of Half Moon Bay. But Jack's mind kept returning to yesterday's conversation on the pier after the others had left. When Alex had pulled Jack aside, he'd been concerned about that morning's meeting.

"My Spidey-Sense is tingling. I don't like that Timmons wants to meet Dexter alone in an inconspicuous area. If it's only Wayne that shows up, everything will be fine. But I've thought about Beavis and Butthead a time or two. We've seen them twice—at our bar, and later with Wayne. I wonder now if Timmons sent them to cause trouble that night. I might be a little overcautious, but I don't want you two outnumbered."

Now Jack glanced at Dexter. "Alex told me he was going to get here early. We might not see him, but he assured me he'd be nearby."

The older man had been staring at trees outside the

window. At Jack's words, he turned and raised his brows. "I thought he couldn't wait to rub this fella's face in everythin'."

"I think it's more that he wants to assess the situation. So don't mention him, ok?"

Dexter shrugged one bony shoulder. "Doesn't matter to me, one way or the other. I reckon you and I can handle this man just fine."

They came to the end of the dirt road and Jack parked a good distance away from the same high-end Tesla he'd seen at Breakers. An old beat-up Ford Explorer was also there, and Jack frowned.

They walked over the hilly rise and sank into the sand, heading toward the spit. Jack casually glanced around, but there was no sign of Alex. The morning was very quiet, and the waves were nearly silent as they caressed the shore. Three men faced away from them on the rocky ground, and all three turned around at their approach. Wayne stood in the middle and narrowed his eyes at Jack. Pirate Dude and Earring flanked him, and Jack instantly went on high alert. Pirate Dude wore a black T-shirt emblazoned with the Jolly Roger, and his mullet was even longer.

Shit. So much for our friendly little meeting.

Wayne straightened, keeping both hands in his pockets. "Decided to bring company, Dexter?"

Dexter creaked a laugh. "Didn't realize you were so worried about an old man you needed two bodyguards."

Wayne smiled and ambled toward them. "Oh, they aren't anything that fancy. I'm just ensuring this process goes as smoothly as possible." He stopped in front of Jack, keeping the same cocky face, and the divemaster itched to punch him. "This really doesn't concern you," the developer continued, arching a brow at Jack. "There's a lovely restaurant at the resort down there if you want to get a cup of coffee."

Jack stared straight back, crossing his arms. "Not gonna happen, asshole."

Wayne's face hardened. "Watch it, or I might teach you some manners."

"I'd like to see you try."

The developer scoffed before turning his attention to Dexter. "I have a final offer to present to you. Unfortunately, my attorney uncovered a utility easement that runs right down the middle of the property, which lowers its value substantially. I have the offer in my car."

Dexter smiled. "Is that a fact? A utility easement, huh? Funny how this has been in my family for generations, and this is the first I've heard of it."

Wayne shrugged, looking bored. "That's island government for you. They probably never notified your family. I'm making you a very fair offer, Dexter. I'd suggest you sign now, before the value decreases further."

The old timer was openly laughing now. "You really are a piece of work, aren't you, son?" He shook his head. "No, Mr. Timmons. I don't think I'm goin' to accept your offer."

Wayne stiffened, the bored look gone now. "That would be a mistake."

Jack couldn't stay quiet any longer. "Oh, shut up, you prick. He's not as stupid as you think he is. Did you really think he'd just blindly accept your half-assed low-ball offer?"

Timmons clenched his jaw so hard his lips had nearly disappeared. Beavis and Butthead took two steps closer, while Jack placed both hands on his hips. "You're too late, anyway. The property has already been sold."

His spirit soared as Wayne's face went blank. But his surprise was quickly replaced by snarling fury. "You better be kidding. You're about to have your face rearranged, kid."

"Kid?" Jack laughed. "I bet I'm only a few years younger than you. Look, you lost. If you hadn't gotten greedy and tried so hard to recruit Sara, you might have been successful. She's also not as stupid as you thought."

"Sara? The hairdresser? What's she got to do with anything?"

White hot fury laced through Jack, and he stepped toe to toe with Wayne. Pirate Dude and Earring closed in tighter behind the developer. "She has everything to do with it, you son of a bitch."

Wayne burst into laughter. "Oh my God! This is hilarious. She's your girlfriend, isn't she?"

Jack remained silent, clenching his right hand as he glared at the developer.

Wayne's grin was replaced by a sneer. "Don't overestimate her importance. She was simply a means to an end. And maybe a piece of ass."

Without even thinking about it, Jack drew back his arm and smashed his fist into Wayne's jaw. Timmons's sunglasses flew off and skittered across the rock as he stumbled back into Earring's arms. Jack shook out his throbbing hand, and a grim smile rose as satisfaction washed over him. He stood lightly balanced on the balls of his feet, ready for anything now.

"Oh, you little piece of shit. You're going to pay for that." Wayne extricated himself, rubbing his jaw. Then he turned to Pirate Dude and Earring. "Beat the living hell out of him. Right now."

Both men focused on Jack. Dexter gasped, taking a large step back. Pirate Dude's face broke into a grin, and he moved forward, totally focused on Jack as he balled his right hand into a fist. Time slowed, and Jack's vision became crystal clear as he shifted his balance evenly, adrenaline coursing through his body. The atmosphere crackled with electricity, but no one spoke.

In the silence, a small, instantly recognizable sound filled the air—the *snick-snick* of a gun's slide being pulled to chamber a bullet. "I really wouldn't do that if I were you."

Jack whipped his head around. Alex stood at his side with a large pistol in his right hand.

Where the hell did he come from?

Aiming the gun at the ground, Alex held it casually, like it was an extension of his hand. The former SEAL stared with absolute authority at the three men before them. "I think it's time for this little party to end."

Wayne let his hand fall from his jaw, eying Alex warily. Wide-eyed, Pirate Dude and Earring both rushed their hands up in the air. Despite the tense situation, Jack found the action almost comical.

These clowns are the worst henchmen ever.

Wayne drew himself upright. "Not until Dexter and I finish our business."

"You're not listening, you idiot," Alex said, his voice tight and hard. He was dressed in an olive-green T-shirt and camo pants, which explained why Jack hadn't seen him. "It *is* over. Hope and I are buying the property. We signed the contract yesterday."

Earring placed a restraining hand on Wayne's arm, his eyes glued to the gun. "Come on, boss. Let's go."

"Alex is right," Dexter said with a slight waver in his voice. "We all signed at an attorney's yesterday."

Wayne jerked his arm away, glaring at Earring. "Piss off. Run away if you're so scared of him."

Alex slowly approached. He made nearly no sound, moving like a wraith as a cold, dangerous smile rose on his face. He stopped right in front of Wayne as Pirate Dude and Earring backed away. Wayne straightened his spine, like he was trying not to step backwards.

Alex spoke with a deadly quietness. "You should be scared, Timmons. You *really* don't want to test me."

Chapter Thirty-Nine

JACK STOOD FROZEN IN PLACE, ice crystals forming in his gut. His heart was nearly hammering out of his chest. Alex still pointed the gun at the ground, but shifted his grip, drawing attention to the weapon. The former SEAL stared at Wayne with no indication of nervousness. He looked like a man who could shoot Wayne in the head and sleep like a baby that night.

"Get out of here, Wayne," Jack said. "Now."

Wayne flicked his eyes to Jack before returning them to the gun. He slowly raised his gaze to meet Alex's. "Fine. I'm leaving."

Alex took another step forward. "I'd suggest leaving St. Croix altogether this time, Wayne. You have no future on this island—I'm going to see to that."

Wayne pressed his lips into a thin line, then without a word, spun and walked between his two guards.

They were turning to follow when Alex called out, "Hey, Joe Dirt." While Pirate Guy was turning around, he switched the gun to his left hand and fear flickered in the thug's eyes. Alex moved forward impossibly fast and punched him square in the mouth. Pirate Guy staggered backwards, mullet flying, windmilling his arms rapidly, and crashed into Earring, who caught him.

"That's for my wife's black eye, you son of a bitch. If I see you again, next time I won't pull my punch. Get out of here."

Alex glowered at the man, who was wrapped up in Earring's arms to keep from falling. Jack almost clapped a hand over his mouth to keep in the horrified laughter bubbling toward the surface. *Earring, you should try out for the local baseball team as a catcher.* Then he blinked rapidly. The stress was making him giddy.

Wayne hadn't even looked back, disappearing over the rise. Pirate Dude untangled himself from his friend and spat, his blood-tinged saliva bright against the white sand. He ran a finger over his teeth, but they were all there. "I told you that was an accident. We got no beef with you, man. We just work for that asshole. And not for long, either."

An engine started and the sound slowly faded as Wayne drove away.

"I seriously couldn't care less," Alex said. "If you're not out of here in the next thirty seconds, we're going to kick the ever-loving shit out of both of you."

Jack let a smile creep over his face and moved to Alex's side, gratified that he'd been included in the shit kicking.

Earring held out a hand. "Put the gun down. We're goin', ok?" The two men hunched off, Earring throwing one last glance over his shoulder. The old Explorer coughed and belched, but it started and soon Half Moon Bay was silent once again.

Alex turned his attention to his pistol, unchambering the bullet, then placed the gun in the small of his back before glancing at the two remaining men. "You two all right? Dexter?"

The old man raised a shaky hand to his forehead and

nodded. "Well, that was a bit more dramatic than I was hopin' for."

Jack opened and closed his sore right hand. His bloody knuckles were swollen, but nothing was broken. He placed a hand on Dexter's shoulder. "Let's get you back home. We've had enough excitement for one day."

"I'm not gonna argue with that."

Dexter clutched Jack's arm for support as the three men made their way back to his Ranger. Alex led, sweeping his head back and forth. He wore his T-shirt untucked, and the gun was invisible.

Frowning, Dexter stared at the tall man's back. "You always go around armed? I thought you were a dive guide."

Alex answered without looking back. "I am. Let's just say my previous occupation mixed diving and guns."

Dexter slowed for a few steps. Jack tightened his hold, but the older man waved him off. "Now I know why you look familiar. I read about you in the paper."

Alex's sigh was loud in the quiet jungle. "Yeah, I'm still waiting for that to die away."

They arrived at the deserted area around Jack's pickup. After it was unlocked, Alex climbed into the tight back seat as Dexter belted in. Jack turned to his boss. "You sure you want to ride along? You can just go home if you want."

Alex snapped his head up, eyes wide with mock horror. All traces of that cold, deadly man were gone. "Are you kidding? Hope and Sara are both back there. I'm not going up against them alone. We'll drop Dexter off, then come back to face the really formidable adversaries."

LATER THAT EVENING, Sara scooped a handful of ice into a zip-closed baggie. Elbowing the freezer door shut, she joined Jack on the couch in his great room. "Here, put this on your hand. I knew I should have taken this afternoon off. Did you even ice it?"

He shrugged, but obediently placed the ice on his swollen knuckles. "It's not that bad."

Sara sighed. *Men...*

Before leaving that morning, Jack had assured her he wasn't expecting any trouble. While the men were at the northern property, she and Hope had chit-chatted nervously as Hope made a mango coffee cake. Finally, Jack texted Sara, saying everything had gone well, and that Alex was riding along as he took Dexter home. Both women had breathed a relieved sigh.

Less than an hour later, Jack and Alex had walked in the front door. Jack was slightly subdued, but Alex was animated, a big smile cracking his face. "Done deal, ladies. Dexter is safely at home and Wayne has slithered back into his hole, outfoxed."

Sara had slumped against the kitchen island, euphoric relief washing over her. Until she looked at Hope, whose attention was focused on Alex's right hand. Sara followed with her gaze. A thin crust of blood covered her brother-in-law's knuckles. She whipped her head to Jack. His right hand was even worse, swollen and discolored.

Hope was now staring wide-eyed at Alex. "Is everyone all right?"

He placed both hands on her shoulders and spoke calmly. "Yes, everyone. A couple of punches got thrown, but it was no big deal."

Jack had agreed, and the two men presented a united front that the meeting was more of a tea party than a fist fight. Sara was sure Hope didn't believe it any more than she did, but the men wouldn't be moved from their position, only revealing that Jack decked Wayne while Alex hit someone else.

Now Sara lifted the ice from Jack's hand, inspecting his knuckles. "Do you need to have that looked at by a doctor?"

He scoffed as he opened and closed his fist several times. "It was one punch. I'm fine." Then he smiled. "But thanks for worrying about me."

She couldn't resist his smile and quickly kissed him. "You're welcome. I think it's adorable that you're friends with Dexter."

"Why? He's a cool guy."

"You're a pretty cool guy too. Is that why you punched Wayne? Did he threaten Dexter?"

Jack dropped his eyes before meeting her gaze again. "No... that was about you. He said something I didn't appreciate, and I let him know it."

Her heart squeezed. Being defended was a new experience for her. One she could get used to. "Thank you. I love you."

"Right back at you, darlin'." He readjusted the ice bag, flinching slightly. "I'm afraid I'm not much of a hero. I didn't land my punch well. Alex hardly scraped his knuckles."

"You're all the hero I need." She slid closer to him. "What really happened? Trust me, Hope will get the story out of Alex, so you don't need to worry about divulging your secret."

He sighed and took her hand in his left. "Wayne brought some muscle, and we weren't expecting that. I wasn't, anyway. Things were getting pretty tense until Alex appeared." He laughed, his face transforming. "Me throwing the first punch probably didn't help. Wayne might be a dick, but he's not stupid. He knew it was no use arguing and took off. The two henchmen followed pretty quickly, and we took Dexter home. End of story."

"Uh-huh." They stared at each other, but it was clear Jack and Alex had formed an agreement. She wouldn't get anything else out of him and checked the time instead. She had ordered takeout from the Serenity bar, and it should be ready. "I'll go get our dinner."

When Sara walked into the bar, several white paper bags sat on the counter. Heather stood at the other end, talking to someone she couldn't see. The bartender's body was rigid, and her face was tense. As Sara moved closer, the other person was revealed to be Wayne, and a bright red flame ignited in her gut. Forgetting about dinner, she marched around the bar toward him.

A grim, satisfied smile rose to her face at the livid bruise near Wayne's chin, and his jawline was swollen on the left side of his face. Heather stomped to the other side of the bar. Wayne sighed, then caught Sara's movement and looked up.

"Nice bruise there, Wayne. Exciting morning?"

He narrowed his eyes before taking a sip of his gin and tonic. "Oh, shut up. I'm not in the mood, so go away."

"No, I don't think I will. I want to make sure you understand that if you weren't such a greedy bastard, you might have gotten that land. You might have even run Half Moon Bay clear out of business." That was perhaps a slight exaggeration, but apt for the circumstances.

Timmons rolled his eyes. Sounding incredibly bored, he asked, "What are you talking about?"

"You and I started out flirty. But it wasn't until you found out I was Hope's sister that you really started pushing me to invest. And even harder on that particular land. You just couldn't resist the *pièce de résistance*—having me betray my own sister."

A faint smile crossed his mouth. "You have to admit, it was a nice touch. Very poetic."

"But Jack and I put the pieces together. I bet you were surprised this morning, weren't you?"

His smile was replaced by a growl, and he touched his puffy jaw for a moment. "Surprise isn't the word. And why am I talking to you, anyway? Piss off. You're nobody. Your precious sister is nobody. And your loser boyfriend is less than nobody. Get out of my sight."

Sara leaned down in front of his face, and a savage grin rose. "And that's what kills you, isn't it? A bunch of nobodies beat you at your own game. And judging from the bruise on your face, Jack isn't the loser here. You are. Go to hell, Wayne."

She straightened, picked up his drink, and tossed it in his face.

Whirling around, she marched back to the other end of the bar where Heather stood, mouth agape. "I'll pay later. I don't want that asshole coming after me."

The bartender held up both hands. "Oh, no. Your dinner is on the house. That prick just fired me for a really stupid reason. I couldn't hear what you were talking about, but after dumping his drink all over him, you're my hero." She pushed the bags toward Sara with a laugh that was only slightly unhinged. "Get out of here."

After promising to return later to hear Heather's story, Sara hurried out of the bar. A laugh tumbled out and echoed over the empty resort-style pool.

How about that? I got to have the last word. And dumping that drink in his face might have been a waste of good gin, but my God, was it worth it!

Sara picked up her pace. Jack was going to love hearing that his hand didn't look nearly as bad as Wayne's face did.

Chapter Forty

APRIL...

Sara carefully removed a coral fragment from the PVC tree and added it to the half-dozen others she held. Exhaling a long burst of bubbles, satisfaction filled her as she studied the coral nursery. There was no sign of damage—the repaired area was as good as new. Next to her, Jack squeezed her arm and flashed an ok signal. She returned it, tipping her head toward the house reef, and the pair moved in that direction. Two weeks had passed since the altercation with Wayne, and Sara had wanted to mark the occasion with a special dive, just the two of them.

And this was just the first celebration planned for the day.

She'd worked hard to earn this dive, improving her skills to make up for her previous blunder. Jack had dived with her several times to offer help and advice. And there was no one she'd rather be with. His tank was adorned with a large yellow and green Nitrox banner, but Sara just dove with a normal air cylinder. She, Hope, and Zach were arranging a group class with Alex to get Nitrox certified, but until then, it was air for her. Jack led her toward the end of the house reef and pointed to a bare section of rock. Then he removed a baggie of cement from the pocket of his BCD and demonstrated how to attach the coral piece to the reef.

Thirty minutes later, the stubby coral fragments were firmly attached to their new home. Sara had transplanted most of them herself and now watched the scene, filled with the pride of completing a long-held goal. The afternoon sun sent a spectrum of color over the thriving reef. A brown and white damsel fish investigated the new corals, flitting around them before rushing at Sara. She laughed, delighted the fish was guarding its new treasure.

She reached for Jack and traced her fingers around his, appreciating the texture of his strong hand as they returned to the pier. *Surface Interval* was out on the afternoon trip, crewed by Tommy and Robert, making for a quiet walk to the gear room. Kicking the door shut behind her, Sara grabbed Jack, kissing him fiercely as he made a deep thrum in his chest. "Thank you," she said. "I've wanted to transplant coral fragments since Alex first told me about the project."

"Hmmm. If that's how you're gonna react, let's do this again tomorrow."

She kissed him again, holding his bottom lip between her teeth, then let go and grinned. "Gratitude is highly underrated. And I'm very grateful—for you and this place."

"So am I. It's pretty cool, isn't it?"

"Yes, all of it. Especially knowing what could have happened to that reef."

He nodded. "Why don't you shower in the bathroom by the spa while I rinse our gear? I've got time to take one too before we head to Alex and Hope's."

"We can try not to collide with each other this time."

He answered her grin with a laugh. "Maybe we can collide another way later."

The boat had returned by the time they finished showering, and Robert joined them as they walked up the pier. He hooked an arm around Jack's shoulders and gave him a horse-collar hug, bursting into laughter. "Look at you two, back to bein' lovebirds. Love triumphs again."

Sara sent him a long side-eye. "Watch the sarcasm there, buddy."

Robert's trademark smile widened. "Who, me? You forget, I photograph weddings for a livin' now."

Sara let the comment go as they stepped off the pier onto the sand. Clark and Patti were walking toward them with Heather in between. Serenity's former bartender wore her long copper hair plated in a long side braid, and her light-blue blouse paired with white capris accented her trim figure. They stopped, and Sara noticed Heather's height for the first time—the bartender was at least six inches taller than she was. Patti started introductions with Robert. With a smile, Heather reached out her hand and they shook. As their eyes met, both froze mid-handshake.

"Heather and I already know each other," Sara said. "You're here to interview?"

But Heather didn't respond, standing motionless as she looked at Robert, who was staring straight back and wearing the same stunned, wide-eyed expression.

"Oh," Sara said. "Do you two already know each other?"

That broke the spell, and the two dropped hands and stepped back. A red flush crept up the bartender's neck. "No. It's nice to meet you, Robert." She turned her eyes to Sara and gave her a slightly bewildered smile. "Yes, I'm here interviewing for the bartender position. I met Hope earlier, and Clark and Patti are giving me a tour."

Patti stared at Robert with a frown. "Let's keep goin'. The restaurant is next." Robert was still staring wide-eyed at Heather as the trio turned away and moved toward the dining room.

When they were out of earshot, Jack turned to Robert and smirked. "What the hell's wrong? You didn't even say anything! Were you hypnotized or something?"

A broad smile crossed Sara's face, the wheels already spinning in her head. "I think that's exactly what he was. And it might have been mutual. Right, Robert?"

He shifted from foot to foot, blinking rapidly. "I don't know. My mind just went blank. That was kind of embarrassin'. Well, I'd better head home. See you guys later." Rubbing the back of his neck, Robert headed toward the parking lot, but not before tossing a final glance at the small group entering the restaurant.

Sara and Jack looked at each other and burst out laughing. "I've never seen Robert at a loss for words," Jack said.

"Well, if Heather gets the job, he'll have to figure out something to say." Sara took his hand and they strolled down the beach. "But we've got a party to attend."

THE CHAMPAGNE CORK arced across the great room, rebounding off the wall above Cruz's bed. The dog flinched and raised his head, sending the happy assemblage a grumpy look before rising to scratch at the sliding-glass door. Wearing a guilty look, Alex hurried to let him out. "Sorry, buddy. I didn't think that would fly so far."

Laughing, Sara accepted the filled flute from Hope and leaned closer to Jack. He pressed a hand against the small of her back before moving it lower and giving her a healthy squeeze. Without changing her expression, she bumped his hip with hers. Jack sent a sly glance her way, but returned his hand to her back, accepting his own champagne.

As Alex returned to the group clustered around their kitchen island, Hope pushed a glass toward Dexter before finishing with hers and Alex's. She raised it and a smile lit her face. "To Half Moon Bay, complete once again. And to the importance of family too." Her smile widened after she directed the last sentence at Dexter, and five champagne glasses clinked over the granite island.

"My son is gettin' my new cottage all ready," Dexter said with a laugh. "He's beside himself with excitement. My house in Frederiksted goes on the market next week, right after I move. And I don't mind tellin' you, all this extra money will come in handy too."

Jack clapped him on the shoulder. "We're all really happy for you, Dexter. This will be a great move for you. I can feel it."

Sara swallowed a lump in her throat, watching Jack. *He is such a good man. And I almost lost him because I was too afraid to admit how I felt. Too proud.*

"I think so too. It just took some time to come around to it." Dexter turned his lined face to Hope and Alex. "And havin' you two buy that property was fate. Don't try to convince me differently."

Alex planted a kiss on top of Hope's head as she smiled back at Dexter. "You don't need to convince us. Alex and I know something about fate."

"I've been driving into Frederiksted in the afternoons," Alex said. "Keeping an eye on Wayne's sailboat. It didn't take too much digging to find out where he was tied up. And I am extremely happy to announce he took off yesterday. Hopefully never to return." A round of cheers went up, and Alex opened another bottle, topping everyone off.

"You know," Hope said, "I have very mixed feelings about

Serenity. I never would have rented your apartment if I had known he owns it. Yet, if I hadn't done that, you and Jack might not have gotten together."

"Possibly," Sara said. "Or Jack might have just tried to kill me for several more months before we figured out we didn't actually hate each other. Being neighbors just sped up the process."

Jack grinned at her. "Who knows how much damage I might have done?" He shook his head. "I've always winced at rent time, but now I really do, knowing I'm lining that guy's pocket."

Dexter laughed. "Yeah, you guys might want to think about somewhere else to live."

Sara smiled to herself and took another sip. She and Jack had one more stop to make, but he didn't know that.

Dexter and Jack became engrossed in a discussion about Dexter's new adventure. Hope touched Sara's hand. "Thank you for sending Heather our way. I talked to her just before I came up here, and thought she was great. Plus, she's another Wayne Timmons refugee. What's not to love?"

Sara scowled. "She said Wayne fired her for 'excessive tardiness', but I believe her side of it."

"Oh, I don't have any doubt. When she indicated she wasn't interested in him personally, she was of no further use. I asked if she wanted to pursue a harassment claim, but she just wants to put it behind her."

Hope glanced toward the front of the house before turning back to Sara. "Come with me. I'd like to show you something." She led the way to her home office, unfurling a large architectural drawing on top of her wooden desk.

Sara joined her, peering over her shoulder. "Ooh, drawings for the new bungalow outdoor showers?"

"No, this is something else. But it's part of the same first phase, along with Half Moon Grotto. Alex and I will be going to Miami soon for another auction. But I want to show you this specifically. I just got the drawings yesterday."

Sara studied the schematic of a large rectangular structure, puzzled. "It looks like a big building."

"Yes, it is. The extra property on the bay finally gave me exactly the location I've been looking for. This building will be situated at the north end of the resort. One long side of the rectangle will face the ocean with the other facing the jungle, showcasing both aspects of the resort." She looked up and met Sara's eyes. "This is the plan for the new spa."

Goose bumps rose on Sara's arms. "That sounds incredible. The building looks huge."

"It will be. The idea is to make it a destination spa, so it will entice locals and even guests from other resorts. Is this more of your idea of what Hibiscus should be?"

"This is my dream," Sara whispered.

"I know. It's part of mine too. But I can't make it a success—this isn't my area of expertise. Only you can. Design it from the ground up, Sara."

Sara gasped, her heart thrumming as everything came together in her mind. "Now I know why I didn't want to spend the $100,000. I want to put it toward this. Can I buy an ownership stake?"

"Of course. That's the whole point, silly!"

They both laughed and turned back to the drawing. Sara wiped tears from her eyes, pointing to a vertical line dividing the structure. "What's this?"

"One of my other projects. Most of the building will be the new spa, but I'm also planning an art gallery for a smaller portion of it. The gallery will be part of the destination appeal. Everyone will be relaxed after their treatment and looking for some shopping." She waved an arm casually at the resort distantly visible through the window. "We have so many artists here—Robert, you, even Jack sketches. You could easily sell yours. So, I plan to open a gallery dedicated to local artists. The profit will be split three ways. One portion to cover the overhead of building and staff, and the rest will be split evenly between the artists and local charities. I'm going to start with the local domestic violence shelter and veteran's support chapter."

Sara gripped her upper arm. "Hope, that sounds incredible."

"It will be. Phase one includes the six new bungalows behind the current ones and this building. Phase two will be farther to the north, a showstopper of a restaurant. Gerold hasn't used a fraction of his talent. But that's for the distant future. You're looking at the near future."

Visions and possibilities collided in Sara's head as her heart sang. "Oh, big sister. We are going to do such amazing things together."

Chapter Forty-One

AFTER THE PARTY BROKE UP, everyone said their goodbyes and Dexter headed back to his house. Jack waved to him, a mixture of happiness and fulfillment rolling through him that everything had turned out so well for the old timer. He grabbed Sara's hand and they walked toward her RAV4.

He started toward the driver's side, but she placed a restraining hand on his arm. "I'll drive."

He grinned and swept his arm in an *after-you* gesture. "I'm kind of loving the new Sara. You want to be on top all the time, and now you want to drive. Next thing, you'll be trying to tie me to the bed."

Arching a brow, she broke into laughter. "Be careful what you ask for."

They got into the car and Sara started down the sand road. "I wanted to drive because I have a little surprise for you. But first I have to tell you why Hope pulled me into her office to talk. It's pretty amazing."

She explained about the new spa, practically exploding with enthusiasm, and he couldn't take his eyes off her. *Probably a good thing she's driving.* "That sounds made for you. I have no doubt you'll make an incredible success of it."

He faced frontward again as they turned off the highway. They bumped down a rough dirt track, but he wasn't watching, distracted by the changes in their lives. "Both of us are doing well. I've got all the work I could want at Half Moon Bay, and I get to spend every day getting paid to do what I love. That's pretty awesome."

"We're surrounded by a good group of people, aren't we?"

"It's rare. I'm really lucky." He reached out and squeezed her hand. "And not just in the job. Though I might look into becoming an instructor someday. That's the next logical step."

Sara laughed. "Well, you might want to check in with the other instructor first. I don't want any turf wars going on."

"I don't think Alex would mind. The other day, he was talking to Zach about getting Nitrox certified when the kid made a smartass comment about becoming the head divemaster there. Alex just looked at him and said, 'Maybe you will.'"

Sara scowled. "Not if it puts you out of a job."

"Don't think we need to worry about that for a while. Zach's got a long way to go." Jack said the words absently, leaning forward in the seat as the trees thinned out and a brilliant orange sky peeked through. Now he was curious about their surprise drive.

Sara pulled to a stop in front of a weathered cottage. Jack got out of the car, and the sound of ocean waves filled the late-afternoon stillness. "What are we doing here?"

"This is what I wanted to show you. Come on."

After they climbed the stairs onto the landing, she produced a key and opened the front door. Jack walked into a large, combination living room and kitchen. The furnishings were neat but plain, though colorful paintings adorned the walls. Sara pointed to their right. "Two bedrooms and baths are over there, but you have to see this first."

She grabbed his hand and pulled him across the white-tiled floor, opening a glass-panel door. The sound of ocean waves became much louder. Jack stepped through onto a large, covered porch. His experienced carpenter's eye picked out the old, worn wood, but it was solid enough under his feet. The condition of the small house didn't hold his attention long. In front of him was a short flight of stairs leading to a small beach. The vista called to him, and he moved without conscious thought.

The sand was a fine mixture of dark and white, and the cottage sat at the head of a small cove, completely private. It was similar to the hidden cove near Serenity, except the ocean was much calmer here. Even in the flat light of near-sunset, dark areas of coral reef were visible throughout the bay. "Wow. This is incredible. But why did you want to show me?"

"Selena's uncle owns it and rents it out. This would solve the paying-Wayne-every-month problem. Pretty cool, huh?"

"Beyond cool. How much does it rent for?"

When she told him, he raised a brow. "Can you afford that?" He didn't want to make any assumptions about her finances, especially since she told him she was investing in an ownership share of the new spa.

A curious expression came over her face, a mixture of hope and uncertainty. It was the look that always clutched at his heart —the rare times she showed her vulnerable side. "No, I can't... but the two of us together could."

It took a moment for what she had said to sink in. Then his heart started hammering. "You want us to move in together?"

"Can you think of any place better?"

He tore his eyes from hers and once again studied the placid sea within the cove. The orange ball of the sun was setting just behind, and he couldn't help the bark of laughter that tumbled out. "No, I can't. Not in a million years." He turned back to her, regarding her closely. "But are you sure about this? Living with me would tie you down."

Sara lifted her chin, a gleam in her eye. "I'm very sure. I mean to make a life in St. Croix. I'm not just here on some Half Moon whim, you know. And I want that life to be with you. This could be our start."

Didn't I want a gesture that she was serious?

Jack stroked a finger down her velvety cheek. "Nothing would make me happier."

A wide smile rose on his face, and she answered it with her own. In unison, they moved toward each other, softly pressing their lips together as they embraced tightly. Behind them, the sun continued its slow descent, leaving a broad swath of crimson and orange streaks as the first stars lit up the night's sky.

THANK you for reading *Half Moon Whim*! I hope you fell in love with Sara and Jack (and if you want more, keep reading!). They were a fun couple to write about, and I may return to them...

But for now, the Half Moon Bay series is moving on to another couple. Get ready for Heather and Robert in:

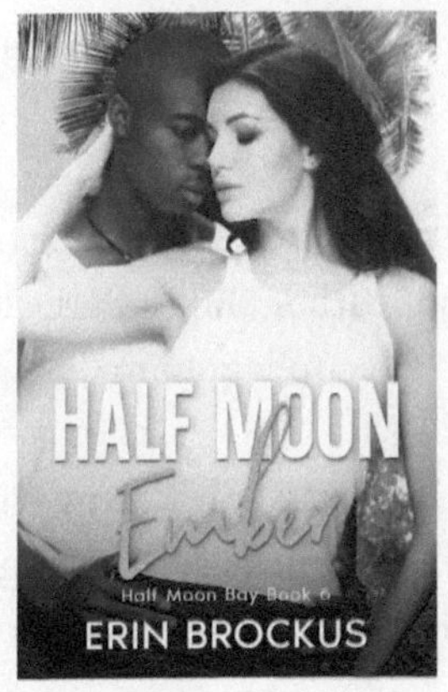

HALF MOON EMBER: HALF MOON BAY BOOK 6

She's fleeing her past. He's deeply rooted in his. When different worlds collide, can their love survive?

Heather Galen, an alluring redhead with a secret, came to St. Croix to start over as Half Moon Bay Resort's newest bartender. Her life starts turning around when her bruised heart is lifted by a charming, handsome divemaster.

Robert Davis is walking a tightrope, caught between honoring his Cruzan heritage and following his dreams. When Heather roars into his life like a forest fire, he is swept away by their passion. When he learns about Heather's family, he questions whether they can overcome their differences.

His traditional parents already worry about him forgetting his roots. With Heather in his life, they are sure of it. Heather finds her greatest wish inextricably linked to Robert. When a crisis threatens to tear his family apart, their relationship only adds fuel to the fire.

Can cutting words be forgiven? Can catastrophic decisions be overcome? Can Heather and Robert's love survive the conflagration?

Escape to the islands with this sexy interracial standalone beach read, featuring a captivating couple from different worlds.

Order Half Moon Ember: Half Moon Bay Book 6 now!

WANT to keep up with all the goings-on at Half Moon Bay? **Want more Sara and Jack?**

Sign up now for my Beach Read Update (www.erin-brockus.com/Whim), and I'll send you a **free bonus scene** featuring Sara and Jack that takes place shortly after they move into their new beach cottage. It's both touching and funny!

My Beach Read Update subscribers hear about all my free content, plus exclusive offers and sales. I'd love to have you along!

Sign up to download this exclusive bonus today
(www.erinbrockus.com/Whim).

If you're already on my list, I've got you covered! At the
bottom of each newsletter is a link to all my free content for
subscribers. Just find your last email from me to read this bonus,
as well as any others you might have missed. Or you can simply
sign up again—you'll have your bonus in a flash.

Keep reading for a my Author's note and a sneak peek at *Half
Moon Ember*, Book 6 of the Half Moon Bay series...

Author's Note

I hope you enjoyed Sara and Jack's story. When I finished *Forever Hope* and it was time to move the Half Moon Bay series in a new direction, Sara was the first character I thought of. I've always enjoyed her gleefully nosy personality, and I loved getting to know this softer, more hidden side to her.

Jack is a salt-of-the-earth guy and loyal to the end. He's exactly what Sara needs. I think they complement each other wonderfully. And I couldn't resist bringing Wayne Timmons back for an encore performance. He's so wonderfully slimy!

I loved writing the scenes between Sara and Alex as she was learning to dive, as well as the chapter where she kicks over his coral trees. These coral-restoration projects are popping up all over the world, and most islands in the Caribbean are trying to preserve and restore this delicate habitat, which is under a variety of assaults.

What's next for the series? Book 6 is also a standalone. Robert Davis has been a part of the Half Moon bay family since Book 1, and I'm excited for you to read more about him. I also think you'll enjoy getting to know Heather. Clark's new counterpart didn't get off to a good start on St. Croix. Maybe her luck is about to change...

Keep reading for an excerpt from *Half Moon Ember*.

Erin Brockus
September, 2022

# Half Moon Ember Excerpt

THE CAR COUGHED, then lurched disconcertingly, causing Heather Galen to return both hands to the steering wheel. She had been driving with her knees while hastily twirling her long, copper-colored hair into a bun. But the Chevy Malibu returned to its normal purr, and she relaxed, speeding up just a little more as she drove north toward Half Moon Bay in St. Croix.

Heather glanced at her watch and winced, stomping more on the gas pedal. It was 11:45 and the burning sun was nearly overhead. She'd gotten out the door later than she'd hoped because of her less than ideal living situation. "I need to set my alarm a few minutes ear—" The Malibu gave another wheezing, chugging cough and she gasped. She gripped the wheel, knuckles white, as she stared in stunned disbelief at the gas gauge, pointed at *Empty* with its ominous amber light flashing. The faltering cough became continuous as she murmured, "No, no, no..."

Then... silence.

The sound of birds singing in the bush around her amplified as the car slowly decelerated. The wheel, now heavy and sluggish, Heather eased the Malibu to the side of the narrow highway. With her heart hammering, she slammed a fist into the wheel. "I can't be late! I just can't! How could I be so stupid?"

Pressing her lips into a grim line, she studied her watch before glancing at her surroundings. "Ok, I'm less than a mile from the resort. If I hurry, I can still make it on time. Get a move on, girl."

Heather grabbed her purse from the passenger seat and exited. Shimmering waves of air rose from the black asphalt as she locked the car and crossed the highway, hurrying along the left shoulder. She wore her work uniform of a light blue polo shirt with Half Moon Bay Resort's logo on the left breast and black capris, which didn't make her any cooler.

She turned left off the highway and rushed down a paved access road as tendrils of sweat raced down her back. The jungle vegetation arched overhead, making a tunnel over the road and holding in the stifling humidity.

Can't be late, can't be late.

She still carried the sense of stunned disbelief that she'd been fired from *two* jobs in the last three months. She'd moved to the island from California to make a new start, yet failure trailed behind her like a black, sulfurous cloud.

Before long, the road ended in a circle in front of a cheery, yellow one-story cottage—the lobby. But Heather trotted around this, following the brick path to her destination. Soft calypso music filled the air as she breathed a relieved sigh and swiped a hand over her sweaty forehead. A long, rectangular infinity pool opened before her, with a bar attached at one end. One side held a row of bar stools, and the opposite side was next to the pool, where patrons could sit on submerged stools.

A tall, thin man of about thirty with ebony skin stood

behind the bar, polishing wine glasses as Heather rushed behind the warm, polished-wood structure. She glanced at her watch and smiled triumphantly—it was exactly noon. "I'm here, Clark! And on time, too." Her shirt was stuck to her torso, and sweat dripped down her face and arms.

His brows rose to the sky as he looked her up and down. "What happened to you? Did you run here?"

"Almost. My car ran out of gas, and I had to hurry." She plucked her shirt away, waving it to dry off.

Clark laughed, his silver tooth glimmering. "You could have called, you know. I wouldn't have minded."

"Nope. I refuse to be late."

Heat rose into her face, and no doubt her face was even redder now. And she was pretty sure everyone at the resort knew why she'd been fired from her previous position as bartender at the upscale apartment complex Serenity. The official version anyway, which was euphemistically listed as *Excessive Tardiness* on her termination paperwork. But *Refusing to Sleep with the Boss* would hardly do, would it?

Clark stopped polishing and gave her a long look, tilting his head to one side as he spoke with a lilting Caribbean accent. "You can be late once in a while. We understand, and none of us believe Wayne Timmons's side of things, anyway. We all met him, remember?" He laughed again, then hung the glass upside-down from a rack in the ceiling.

She had only worked at Half Moon Bay for a week and was determined to make a good impression. Despite her life being turned upside down yet again. "Thanks, but I'm usually very dependable. I can't believe I let my car run out of gas."

He waved absently at her. "Don't worry about it. We're pretty laid back. Well, here at the resort, anyway. You don't want to show up late down at the dive shop. Alex is a different story." Clark broke into musical laughter again, and she couldn't help joining in. Heather had met the undisputed alpha male of the resort her first day. Tall, excessively handsome, and with a natural authoritative air, Heather had expected to hate Alex Monroe at first sight. But he'd pleasantly surprised her by not exhibiting the typical alpha male personality, being friendly and affable. As they had been talking, his wife—resort owner Hope Monroe—had joined them, and Heather had further warmed after seeing how obviously devoted to her he was.

She turned to Clark with a laugh. "Alex has been pretty nice every time I've met him."

"He is nice. As long as you don't make him mad. Then it's a whole different story."

"Duly noted. I'll try not to do that. Which shouldn't be too hard, since our paths don't cross that often."

She could believe he had a darker side. An article displayed in the lobby described his history as a Navy SEAL and an altercation he'd been involved in. Friendly or not, Alex wasn't someone to be trifled with. The dive staff worked from the long wooden pier that jutted into the Caribbean Sea, using the resort dive boat *Surface Interval* for scheduled dive trips several times each day. But Heather wouldn't have minded if her path crossed with one particular member of the dive staff a little more often.

When she had interviewed for the job, she'd run into a couple who had lived at Serenity, Hope's sister Sara Collins and divemaster Jack Powell. With them had been another divemaster, Robert Davis. Heather had never met him, but when the resort manager had introduced them, she'd been captivated, hardly able to believe her reaction.

Robert was a local and looked in his early thirties, slightly older than her twenty-eight. His shaved head emphasized his rich brown skin, but his eyes were what had positively entranced her. A much lighter brown than expected from his dark complexion, they held a warm expression, and his dazzling smile had made her heart pound. But, a casual question to Clark had revealed that Robert was only an occasional worker at the resort, and he made his living as a photographer.

Now, Heather bent down and rummaged under the counter, finally locating a spare staff shirt she kept handy. Being a bartender ensured that wardrobe changes were not infrequent. She held it up. "I should probably go change."

Clark grinned. "Good idea. You look like you just ran a marathon."

Behind him, Clark had pinned a family photo of himself and his wife Kamila with their two children into the wall. The main reason she'd been hired was to give Clark some much-needed backup and time off. "How's Eli?" she asked.

"He's hangin' in there, poor little guy." Clark's wife had delivered Elijah a few months previously, but he had suffered a succession of stomach maladies, finally needing surgery. "We've got the operation scheduled in St. Thomas next week. We were hopin' to get it done here, but they decided he needed a more complicated procedure, which isn't available on St. Croix."

"Oh! I'm sorry. Poor baby."

"Thanks. But the doctor said this should cure his problems, so it'll be worth it. Kamila has family there, so we'll probably stay there for a month or so. I'm thinkin' about takin' off two months total. Hope said it should be fine. And you're pickin' it all up fast, so the resort will survive. Probably."

Grinning, Heather grabbed a rag and bottle of disinfectant and started wiping down the counters. "Thanks. I really like it here." Clark was a dream to work with, funny and self-deprecating despite winning an island-wide bartending contest the previous year.

Hope appeared and sat down on a stool, accompanied by her dog Cruz, who circled and lay down at her feet. A beautiful woman, her rich chestnut hair fell to her shoulders, and she wore a colorful yellow sundress. She gave them a sunny smile, which faded when she took in Heather's sweaty, disheveled appearance. "Are you ok?"

Heather laughed and held up the polo shirt. "Yeah. My car ran out of gas, and I had to rush here on foot. I keep a spare shirt under the bar, so I'll head to the restroom to clean up." She quickly changed out of her sodden shirt, and a quick wipe-down with wet paper towels washed the worst of the sweat away. She wet her hair to tame the flyaways, and returned, looking—and feeling—more professional.

When she moved behind the bar again, Hope pointed at her. "Clark just told me about you not wanting to be late. Don't worry about it. I have extensive experience with what a jerk Wayne Timmons is, and you're doing a great job here."

"Thanks, but I do my best to be on time. I hope you have enough work for me after Clark gets back from his leave." Heather was under no delusions who the primary bartender was, which she worried about.

Hope opened her eyes wide. "That's why I came down here, to check if Clark has any last-minute instructions for either of us, since I help out too. And we're getting busier by the day, with six new bungalows being built. I'm planning on adding a permanent bar to the restaurant, so the waitstaff won't have to trudge back and forth from here. So, we'll need both of them staffed."

"That's music to my ears," Heather said with a big smile.

Clark hung up the final wine glass and stood somberly with his hands clasped in front of him. "Well, I guess it's official then. Since I only have a couple of days left, it's time to pass on my secrets."

Hope drummed her feet on the ring at the base of her stool, a wide grin forming. "Oh! You're finally going to spill the beans?"

Clark lifted his chin, his serious expression remaining as he turned to Heather, though his cheek was twitching a bit. "Heather, this is a great responsibility. I'm goin' to teach you how to make my secret drinks, Half Moon Hope and Half Moon Dream. Especially the second one." This was the drink that had won the competition. Heather had tasted both and they were spectacular, especially Half Moon Dream.

Hope was still grinning broadly, but Heather stilled her face, trying to match the mock seriousness of the occasion. "I'm honored that you're passing on your knowledge, Clark."

"You should be," Hope said. "He only gave me the recipe because I've been filling in for him. Otherwise, I'd still be in the dark."

Finally, Clark's serious expression morphed back into his typical smile. "Ah, it's not too complicated. But there's a special ingredient in Dream that's unusual." The drink was based on a mudslide, and he'd added orange liqueur to it. There was a subtle flavor underneath that anchored the whole drink, and she hadn't been able to figure it out.

"I can't wait to learn your secret ingredient."

Order Half Moon Ember!

Also by Erin Brockus

HALF MOON BAY SERIES:

MAIN NOVELS:

Finding Hope: Half Moon Bay Book 1

Defending Hope: Half Moon Bay Book 2

Rising Hope: Half Moon Bay Book 3

Forever Hope: Half Moon Bay Book 4

Half Moon Whim: Half Moon Bay Book 5 (Standalone)

Half Moon Ember: Half Moon Bay Book 6 (Standalone)

Half Moon Aqua: Half Moon Bay Book 7

Crowning Hope: Half Moon Bay Book 8

ASSOCIATED SHORT STORIES AND NOVELLAS:

Tropical Dawn: A Half Moon Bay Prequel Novella

*Tropical Chance**: A Second Chance Half Moon Bay Novella

*Tropical Hope**: A Half Moon Bay Prequel Short Story

* Subscriber exclusives

CALYPSO KEY SERIES:

Main Novels:

Visions of You: A Small Town Single Dad Romance

Because of You: A Small Town Fake Relationship Romance

Memories of You: A Small Town Second Chance Romance

Shades of You: A Small Town Forbidden Romance (Coming Oct, 2024)

Associated Short Stories and Novellas:

Traces of You: A Small Town Rivals to Lovers Romance*

* Subscriber exclusive

Standalone Books:

In Too Deep: A Second Chance Romance

Beached in Bali: A Friends to Lovers Romance

Dive into steamy small-town romance, where passion meets paradise!

Erin Brockus writes steamy small town romances that transport readers to exotic, tropical destinations, and provide a perfect beachy getaway from everyday life. Her mature, relatable characters are impossible not to root for, and she weaves breezy romantic adventure into her stories, emphasizing scuba diving and the ocean.

Drawing on her twin passions for diving and travel, Erin infuses her characters and narratives with a sense of excitement and passion. Her idea of the perfect day involves sipping a cocktail on the beach after exploring the ocean depths.

Erin lives in Washington wine country with her husband, who is also a scuba instructor. She is currently hard at work on her next island adventure. When she's not writing, you might find her out for a run or cycling through the countryside on the next quest for adventure.

www.ingramcontent.com/pod-product-compliance
Lightning Source LLC
Chambersburg PA
CBHW051239210726

48287CB00002B/316